A Psalm for Falconer

A Psalm for Falconer

Ian Morson

VICTOR GOLLANCZ

LONDON

First published in Great Britain 1997
by Victor Gollancz
An imprint of the Cassell Group
Wellington House, 125 Strand, London WC2R 0BB

© Ian Morson 1997

The right of Ian Morson to be identified as author of
this work has been asserted by him in accordance with
the Copyright, Designs and Patents Act, 1988.

A catalogue record for this book is
available from the British Library.

ISBN 0 575 06046 8

Typeset by CentraCet, Cambridge
Printed by St Edmundsbury Press Ltd,
Bury St Edmunds

97 98 99   5 4 3 2 1

Acknowledgements

My thanks to the staff of Morecambe Library
for supplying me with such interesting
information about that part of Cumbria which
was Lancashire. Thanks also to Brian Innes
for some sound advice on the state of a body
long dead. Any errors made in using that
information are entirely my own.

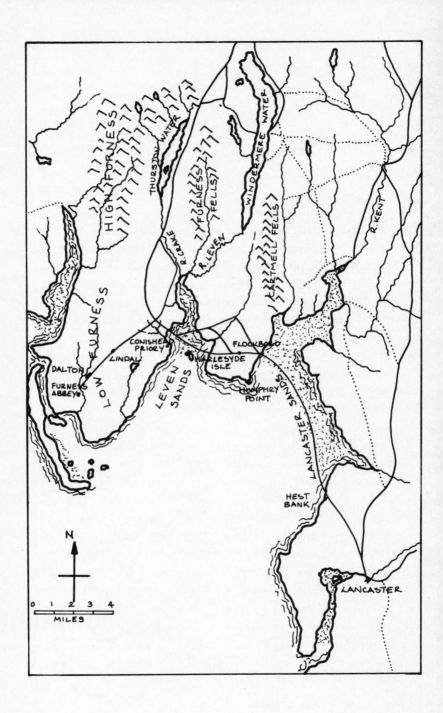

Prologue

The sun was dipping redly behind Humphrey Head, and John de Langetoft felt the chill of the stream called the Kent nipping at his bare legs. He settled the heavy bundle more comfortably on his back, shifting it with a shrug of his shoulders, and stepped out of the tug of the stream's flow on to the soft sandy bank. His sandals, slung round his neck by their leather thongs, bounced awkwardly on his chest. The screams of the seabirds lent an uncanny air to the broad vistas of the bay that he had never come to terms with. It was as though the souls of lost travellers darted and wheeled above his head in a perpetual limbo. This awful image was strengthened by the heavy, lowering clouds that boiled over his head, presaging the arrival of a storm. He shivered, and not just because of the physical cold of the desolate place.

'Best not stand still too long, you may find you'll sink into the quicksand.'

Heeding his travelling companion's warning, de Langetoft pulled his feet from the suck of the sand. Still he cast a sad glance over his shoulder at the darkling hump of the Head behind him, wondering when next he might see it, and the priory that lay out of sight beyond the moody promontory. The sun was nearly gone and out to sea a flash of lightning illuminated the bay. If they were to avoid the storm, they had to press on. Just ahead, the rocky shelves of Priest's Skear stuck out of the mud like the back of some beached sea-leviathan. This meant they only had the Keer to ford, and they would be on terra firma at Hest Bank.

De Langetoft had set himself two tasks that day — tasks he

must complete before he could assume his rightful place at the priory. The first was to purge his own weakness from his soul, and he had already carried that out — more easily than he had expected. He hoped that his purpose in Lancaster could be as swiftly concluded. That was his second task, and related to others' weakness. And the business he intended to transact there should allow his triumphant return to the priory. Indeed, he could imagine no other conclusion that he could live with; especially as he was so close to being elected prior. He hoped his fellow traveller did not know what he had planned in Lancaster, and, settling the bundle on his back once again, he strode out across the mudflats to the grassy shoreline. His pace soon took him ahead of the smaller figure with whom he was crossing Lancaster Bay. At the bank of the treacherous Keer, he hitched up the skirt of his habit and turned to ask if this was the correct spot to cross.

His last vision was that of a water-demon that leapt straight out of the dying sun, its claws glittering in the strange half-light. The lightning flashed again, and it felt as though the jagged bolt cut through him to the heart. The pain as his soul escaped his chest was excruciating, and as he tumbled into the icy waters his final thought was for the safety of his travelling companion.

MATINS

Know that the Lord is God,
He has made us and we are His own.
Psalm 100

Chapter One

Regent Master William Falconer glumly surveyed the sad bundle of his worldly possessions. Besides what he stood up in, he had managed to accumulate a heavy black robe turning green with mould at the edges, a woollen cloak loaned him by Peter Bullock, a cracked pair of leather boots, a sugar-loaf hat in red given him by a widow in Mantua who had feared for his health, and a spare pair of underdrawers of indeterminate age. Peter Bullock laughed at the sorry sight.

'At least you will not need the wagon train that the King drags round with him on *your* travels.'

Falconer determinedly set aside the shabby robe, sure it would not be necessary on such a short journey. He would only be away for a month or so, and the one he stood up in would suffice. Then he stuffed his clothes, still damp from their sojourn in the chest that lay at the foot of his bed, into the capacious leather saddlebags the constable of Oxford had brought round for him. There was room for as much clothing again in the bags, but Falconer was satisfied to fill the empty space with his favourite books. He tucked his copy of *Ars Rhetorica* down next to Peter de Maharncuria's *Treatise on the Magnet*, then balanced their weight with Bishop Grosseteste's own translation into Latin of the *Epistles of Ignatius*.

It was Grosseteste who was the cause of these preparations — he and Falconer's great friend Friar Roger Bacon. Though it was odd that they should have such an influence on the regent master's current actions: the bishop had been dead for over fifteen years, and the friar incarcerated by his Franciscan Order since 1257. At that time Bacon had been whisked away from Oxford because of his dangerous ideas, and banished to a cell in Paris. Falconer had not heard from him for ten years thereafter. That silence had but recently been broken.

Watching his friend distractedly stuff yet more texts into the saddlebags, Bullock scratched his head and began to review his opinion that Falconer wouldn't require a wagon train. The old soldier had long ago learned the merits of travelling with as small a load as possible. An army might rely on the baggage train to carry its needs across enemy lands. But each foot soldier knew that in battle he could be separated from his comrades, and have to forage for himself. A light load and a sharp eye were essential. And, for Bullock, Falconer's journey to the wildest part of Cumberland was no less daunting than a war expedition to Burgundy.

'What do you need all those books for? Aren't there enough where you're heading?'

Bullock knew that Falconer's goal was Conishead Priory on the shores of Leven Water, and that he was going in search of a particular book. Though why any book should take someone to the edge of the world was beyond the ancient soldier.

'These books are my travelling companions. And more valued because they don't answer back,' retorted Falconer tartly.

He instantly regretted chiding his friend, and realized how the prospect of the long journey had served to agitate him. That and the letter from Friar Bacon. After that silence of ten years, to send a summons to immediate action, coded for safety's sake, had been typical of the mercurial friar. The cryptic message had taken some time to decipher and, in the meantime, the man whom Falconer was asked to seek had become embroiled in a murder. The consequence of delivering the message to its recipient had resulted in this further quest.

That the thought of such a journey now seemed daunting to the regent master was an indication of how the Oxford life had seeped into his bones. Half his years had been spent traversing the known world, and it had only been with reluctance that he had settled to the academic life, truly believing at the time it would merely be an interlude between wanderings. Now he fretted about travelling a few miles across England.

Shamefaced, he hefted the saddlebags to his shoulder and felt the weight of them. He grunted in concession to Bullock's good sense.

'You are right – the nag I have hired will probably expire under me before it reaches Woodstock with this weight to carry.' He opened the saddlebags again. 'I shall be a little more discerning about whom I travel with.'

Reviewing his collection of books, he discarded some lesser mortals, and redistributed the remaining tomes between the two panniers. Now there was space in plenty, and Bullock passed him his second robe to pack. Wordlessly he added it to the burden. He was ready, but still he hesitated. He cast his eyes around the room – this little universe so familiar to him. The jars that held decoctions of the quintessence, local herbs and dried preparations from the East, the stack of books, and the jumble of cloth and poles in the corner that represented his as yet unsuccessful attempts to understand the means of flight. Presiding over all, his eyes baleful and staring, sat the ghostly white form of Balthazar, the barn owl who shared this universe in a room with the regent master. A constant and silent companion, he lived his life as independently as Falconer aspired to do. There was no fear that he would starve while Falconer was away – he fended for himself anyway, quartering the open fields beyond Oxford's city walls at night. Falconer often unravelled the furry balls Balthazar coughed up like little presents for his friend, and marvelled at the assemblage of tiny bones he found therein.

Even so, Falconer asked the constable to visit Balthazar regularly, for even the most reclusive creature desired company now and then. Bullock promised to pay daily court to the bird, and hustled the master out of the room before he could become maudlin about leaving his cellmate. Downstairs in the lane, a young lad stood at the head of a sturdy rouncy, whose well-filled flanks gave the lie to Falconer's deprecating remarks about his hired mount's stamina. Having settled the precious saddlebags on the horse, Falconer swung up into the saddle and took the reins from the stable lad. He leaned down to the stocky figure of the constable.

'It is now, what, early January? Tell Thomas Symon that I shall have returned before the end of February, and in the meantime I trust him to teach well in my stead.'

Bullock knew well enough that Falconer had spent several evenings already with the unfortunate Thomas, one of his pupils now become a master himself. He had gone over what Thomas was to teach in the minutest of detail – the truth being he trusted no one, even his most respectful and able of students, to follow his precepts fully. It was a failing and he knew it. Nevertheless Bullock patiently promised to pass his message on. Reluctantly Falconer turned the head of the rouncy, and headed towards North Gate. But not without casting a glance over his shoulder at the bent-backed constable, who waved him off with impatient and dismissive gestures. At last, Falconer was gone and Bullock turned towards his own quarters in the west of the city. Hardly had he gone ten paces, though, when he heard a high-pitched voice calling his name.

'Master Bullock. Master Bullock.'

It was a nun who pursued him, her long grey robes spattered with mud at the hem and her wimple askew. There was a look of sheer terror in her eyes. He stopped, and the dishevelled sister nearly ran into him. He held her gently at arm's length as she tried to gasp out a message between heaving gulps for air.

'There . . . Godstow . . . the abbess . . .'

'Calm down. What on earth is the matter?'

If the nun was from Godstow, it was strange for her to be in Oxford. The new abbess deemed it a den of iniquity: a sentiment with which the constable had to agree. It was some moments before the nun could recover her breath. Then the words tumbled out.

'At the nunnery . . . there's been a murder at the nunnery.'

Chapter Two

After a journey of twelve backside-aching days in the saddle, William Falconer was glad to be on foot again. He had stabled his rouncy in Lancaster, where he would pick it up on his return, and had made for the foreshore of Lancaster Bay to seek out a guide to take him across the treacherous sands. If the tides were right and the weather improved, he could cut three days from his journey by resorting to this ancient route instead of going round the coastline. The previous evening he had found the nearest inn and sheltered while a great thunderstorm raged over his head. There were several travellers trapped like him by the weather, and even one or two faces he had encountered before on his journey from Oxford. Of course it was common to find you were sharing your route with others. But on this occasion, Falconer had had the uncanny sense he was being observed — all the way from Oxford, through Lichfield and Stone, and up to Wigan and Preston. At every stop he was sure that a pair of eyes bored into the back of his head. But whenever he had turned to look, there had been none but innocent travellers. In the market at Lichfield, a heavy oak barrel had crashed at his feet, sparing him by a hair's breadth. The apologetic cooper had not been able to understand how it could have tipped over. They agreed it must have been an accident, but Falconer had been more alert since that day.

With no further incidents to trouble him, he had tried to shrug off his foolishness at Lancaster. And over some ale, he had fallen into the company of two lay brothers from the great abbey at Furness, which lay across the bay. The brothers fished for salmon nearby and, though it was out of season, they still travelled regularly to and fro between the fishery and the abbey. Consequently they knew the tides along this coast at all times of the year. It was the brothers' advice that had got Falconer out of bed before dawn the following day. Luckily the storm had cleared and he was optimistic of getting across Lancaster Bay and achieving his goal that very night.

Leaving the town, he looked back, and was relieved to see no one following him. He fell into a speedy, loping stride, and soon he was topping the rise above Hest Bank, where an unreal scene opened up before him. He had once seen a map drawn up by a monk at St Albans that showed the world laid out on the surface of a disc. England was at the furthest point from the centre of the world, which was naturally Jerusalem, and this part of England stood on the very edge of the disc. The traveller in Falconer did not accept this picture of the world, but surveying the view before him now he could almost have convinced himself otherwise.

A wide expanse of water extended to the farthest horizon, where a lowering bank of cloud obscured the edge of the world. Falconer fumbled in the pouch at his waist, and extracted the eye-lenses that corrected his short sight. As he held the two circles of cleverly ground glass to his eyes, the clouds resolved themselves into a low range of black hills. Beyond them, as though floating in the sky, towered a ragged pile of snow-flecked mountains. The pinkness of the reflected dawn shone behind them, as though supporting the belief that the end of the world lay beyond, immersed in a fiery glow. Even as Falconer watched, the distant mountains took on more solid form with the rising of the sun. He could almost imagine them reforming themselves from some primeval mass every dawn.

The sheet of pale blue water between himself and the farthest shore slipped away to the west, shimmering as it retreated. It left behind brown banks of sand that were quickly populated by wheeling flocks of little sea-edge birds that scudded back and forth in their search for food. As he revelled in the glory of God's creation Falconer was not sure when he had first become aware of the dark shape that moved in the middle of the bay. At first indistinct, it gradually resolved itself into a person crossing the sands. The figure must have started from the farthest shore, but in the magic of that dawn Falconer was quite prepared to believe it was a water-demon that had sprung from the retreating sea. He was almost disappointed when it became clear through his eye-lenses that the figure was a youth of fairly plain appearance. This was probably his guide across the bay.

Peter Bullock wished that Falconer were still in Oxford. He had come to rely on the man to solve the mysterious deaths that inevitably occurred in this turbulent community, and he was lost now without him. At first he had relished the idea of uncovering the murderer of Godstow Nunnery by himself, but patience had never been one of the constable's traits. And it seemed that patience was needed here. At first glance, nothing should have been simpler to resolve than the slaying of a young nun in a building closed to the outside world. However, simple it had not been – almost two weeks had gone by and he was no nearer the truth than he had been when he stood outside the gates of the nunnery that first morning.

Indeed, that was the main problem – he had got no further than the gates. The abbess, the Lady Gwladys, had forbidden him from setting foot inside the buildings that made up the core of Godstow Nunnery. So far he had only succeeded in talking to each of the inmates through an impenetrable grille that afforded him no glimpse of the nuns' faces. How could even Master Falconer be expected to distinguish truth from lies, when the speaker's expression was thus rendered invisible? He had to find a way to interrogate the nuns face to face, or at least provide a substitute who could do this for him. Of course, it would have to be a woman in order to satisfy the harridan who ruled over the nuns' little world. But whom could he trust to serve his need? And what would Falconer have done?

The minute he thought of Falconer, a solution sprang into his head, and he smiled a wicked smile.

'Take care as you cross the rocks – the weed is slippery. But the footing gets better as we reach the sand.'

The youth, who said his name was Jack Shokburn, led the way over the rocky foreshore and down on to the flat reaches of the dark brown sand. His long, blond hair hung low over his forehead, framing a face already dark-tanned by his outdoor occupation. Falconer imagined that the sun, reflecting off the sheets of water that formed the bay, soon turned every rosy-cheeked child into a leathery-faced denizen of this region. The youth was tall for his age – Falconer judged him to be no more than twenty – and well muscled, though slim. Sinewy was the word that sprang to the master's mind. His cheap robe of brown fustian was extensively patched and his legs and feet were bare.

'Let me take your saddlebag,' he offered as Falconer gingerly picked his way across the slippery seaweed clinging to the rocks they were crossing.

Falconer gripped the bag tightly. 'Thank you, but I will hang on to it myself. I regret it's full of books, and not the lightest of burdens.'

Jack shrugged his shoulders, and strode off across the muddy margin to the open bay. At first his direction puzzled Falconer, for he seemed to be walking out to sea, not towards the hump of promontory across the bay which he presumed to be their goal. But the youth turned and clearly signalled Falconer to follow him with a wave of his arm. The master set off in the same direction, his boots sinking into the slimy mud that coated the foreshore. Dampness penetrated the cracks and fissures in his boots and he was glad eventually to reach firmer sand. Ahead of him, Jack Shokburn had stopped beside a bush growing incongruously in the featureless ridges of the sand, and was waiting for Falconer to catch him up.

'There's the next brobb,' he said as Falconer approached, and he pointed off at an angle. Without his eye-lenses, Falconer could see nothing and questioned the strange word.

'Brobb?'

'It's a marker, so I know where to go avoiding the quicksands.'

He gestured at the bush near his bare feet. Falconer realized it was not growing from the sand as he had imagined, but was a mature laurel branch thrust into the sand by the youth.

'First we must cross the Keer and then the Kent. So I suggest you take your boots off. Unless you want them ruined.'

Falconer could not imagine them being worse than they were already. He looked down. A line of salt was already forming around the wet, mud-spattered toe-end of each. But he leaned on the youth's shoulder and, hopping ungracefully, yanked his boots off and pushed them under the flap of his saddlebag. When he was ready, Jack Shokburn stepped into the swift-flowing stream, whose waters eventually reached his knees. Now Falconer knew why the youth habitually went bare-legged. He hoisted his own shabby robe up around his thighs and, making sure his precious load of books was safely slung across his shoulders, stepped into the icy waters.

The pull of the river on his legs was strong, and he hesitated in the middle feeling the grainy, shifting sand beneath his toes. He heard an involuntary cry that at first he took for a seagull, but when it came again he recognized it for a human voice. Looking upstream he saw some indistinct dark shapes huddled by the far bank of the river he was fording. He thought of calling his guide, but Jack was already clear of the stream, and plodding off to his next laurel brobb. Falconer fumbled in the pouch at his waist for his eye-lenses, dropping the hem of his robe in the process. His fingers closed on the metal of the device, and he raised it to his face, careful not to drop it in the water where he might never recover it. The shapes he had spotted upstream were indeed human, and they seemed to be digging feverishly in the riverbank. One stood up for a moment, and the sun glinted off something he lifted from the mud.

Falconer was suddenly aware that Jack was calling him, and pointing to his feet. He remembered the youth's mention of quicksands, and pulled his legs from the clinging silt. Lifting his now thoroughly soaked robe out of the water, he climbed up on to the bank of the river and hurried towards his guide. As he approached, he gesticulated with the lenses that he still held in his right hand.

'What might they be doing?'

The youth squinted towards the little group of people clustered at the edge of the Keer, but they were too far away. It was impossible to make out clearly what their actions represented. He shrugged indifferently – it seemed to be his main means of expression – and turned on the final leg of his winding course across the Lancaster sands to the shoreline of Humphrey Head. With one more look over his shoulder, and his lenses safely stowed back in his pouch, Falconer too walked on.

The knock that came at Peter Bullock's spartan quarters at the base of St George's Tower woke him from his doze. He was surprised that he had been asleep, remembering that he had eaten a small repast consisting of bread, cheese and ale. Not enough ale to send him to sleep, surely. Perhaps the years were creeping up on him, and he was turning into a mewling infant again. The tentative knocking became more insistent, and he shook his head to clear his senses.

'I'm coming. I'm coming. Don't batter the door down.'

Not that anyone could possibly effect such a deed. The door, his quarters, and the dungeon below had all been constructed to withstand the mightiest of onslaughts on this end of the city of Oxford. The new city walls were sturdy enough – the old castle at the city's western end was impregnable. A suitable residence for the town constable, charged by the burghers of Oxford with keeping the unruly hotchpotch of students, merchants, sturdy clerics, and passing travellers in some sort of order. An old soldier, Peter Bullock used every artifice he had learned in battle, and in the gaming between battles, in order to keep the peace. He preferred the art of gentle persuasion. But if force were needed, he was still capable of swinging his trusty sword – even if all he did was bring the flat of the blade down on someone's crown, giving the malefactor a sore head rather than splitting it open. His reputation, and the sight of his bent back and leathery face, was often enough to subdue all but the rowdiest drunk.

But perhaps age was getting the better of him at last. He yawned cavernously as he swung the heavy door open, only stifling the gape with his calloused fist when he realized it was a lady who stood before him. Her figure was a little fuller than when last he had seen her, but none the worse for that. Her golden hair was half hidden beneath the net she habitually wore, but its lustre was as great as he remembered. What pleased him most, and had done when he first saw her, was that she stood tall and fearless. Now a gentle smile played over her clear, even features, and her voice chimed on his ears.

'Do you cultivate the mien of an ogre to frighten your citizens, or does it come naturally?'

Bullock ruefully scrubbed his whiskery chin, and a grin split his wrinkled face. 'You always knew how to compliment a man, my lady Segrim.'

'Well, am I to be allowed in? Or are we to conduct this conversation on your threshold?'

Bullock laughed – Ann Segrim had not changed, and he was glad of it. She would need all her wits about her for what he was going to request of her.

Ralph Westerdale scurried along two sides of the cloister, his sandals slapping on the cold stone slabs. That the precentor and librarian of Conishead Priory should have his office on the opposite side of the cloister to the main book presses spoke eloquently of the triumph of comfort over convenience. The cupboards housing most of the five hundred books at Conishead were positioned in recesses on either side of the entrance to the chapter house. Ornate semicircular arches defined all three doorways. In contrast, the office of the precentor was a small partitioned area of the undercroft below the lay brothers' dormitory. More important, it stood next to the kitchens. But at times such as these the human comfort of daily warmth compensated little for the inconvenience of having to shuttle back and forth between office, book presses and library carrels.

The sound of his sandals forewarned three of his brethren, who were solemnly pacing the cloister, of his approach. They stepped aside and smiled indulgently as the short, rotund monk puffed past them. He disappeared into the first book press like an oversize mouse into a hole. As the other monks passed the cupboard at a more leisurely pace they heard Brother Ralph clicking his tongue in exasperation.

The precentor's problem was that he had neglected to check the catalogue against the library itself. Ten years he had carried out his responsibilities, and he had not thought to make a complete check of all the books there were supposed to be in the collection. Now this regent master was coming from Oxford, and he couldn't find several of the texts that were in his care. He could only hope that they were merely misplaced – that a brother had borrowed them without permission, or that they had been erroneously shelved in the small vestry collection, or the dorter cupboard. He would simply have to check everything.

He wondered if he should tell Henry Ussher, the prior, who would be very concerned about the specific texts that were missing. But he decided it was too soon to admit to such a dereliction of his duties. He should first be certain whether the texts were missing or not – time enough to admit failure when he was sure they were. His stomach rumbled in protest, already guessing that the urgency of his task would mean a delayed repast this afternoon. Ralph Westerdale stepped back into the cloister and carefully locked the book press door behind him. No other texts had better go astray.

As Ralph traversed the two sides of the cloister on his return journey to his office, he noticed the cellarer emerging from the passage that divided his office from the kitchens. Brother Thady Lamport was a cadaverous man whose habit hung on his spare frame like an oversized sack enclosing old bones. His skeletal face was dominated by the sunken pits of his eyes, and many a novice at Conishead was fearful of his devilish stare. He had a manner to go with his unprepossessing mien, and most of his brothers avoided him.

Ralph presumed he had come from the kitchens or the outer courtyard, and had not been seeking him. However, the cellarer started up the bottom of the cloister, putting him on a course to meet Ralph near the intersection of the west and south ranges. Just in case he was wanted, the precentor prepared for the encounter, and for his part was ready with a friendly benediction. But as he turned the corner, all he was presented with was the back of Brother Thady disappearing rapidly in the opposite direction. The monk had abruptly turned round and retreated from him. Ralph puffed out his cheeks in annoyance – the community at Conishead was too small to permit of any long-held grudges. Life would be intolerable otherwise. The fact that Ralph now held the very post formerly occupied by Brother Thady was no reason to snub him.

'You want me to enter a nunnery!' Ann Segrim couldn't believe what she had heard from the lips of the constable.

'Not permanently.'

'I'm glad to hear it.'

'Just for a while. What's it called? On . . .?'

'Retreat. An old warrior like you should know the word.'

Ann could not resist the jibe. Peter Bullock's face tightened, then he exploded with a rasping sound that Ann interpreted hopefully as laughter. She joined in with her own more melodious peal. When they had both regained their composure, it was Bullock who spoke first.

'You're right. An old warrior is one who knows when a battle is lost. Leave honour to those who want to die young and virginal.'

There was a moment's silence, and in response to the unspoken question Bullock told her that Falconer was not in Oxford, and unlikely to be back for several weeks. Lady Ann was silent, and Bullock wondered when she and Falconer had last seen each other. That she was married, and he was supposed to remain unmarried while a regent master at the university of Oxford, made for an interesting relationship: more curious in that it had sprung up while Falconer was investigating a murder that Ann's husband, Humphrey Segrim, might well have committed. That he was not guilty, and in the process of the investigation Falconer had returned him from the dead, made the thought of their trysts even more exotic. Still, it was not for the constable to wonder on the antics of his friend – he had a murder to solve, and he believed Ann Segrim was the only one who could help him.

'There's been a death at Godstow.'

A solemn cast fell across Ann's handsome features. 'And you think it's murder?'

'I wish I knew. The abbess won't even let me on the premises to see the body. I have to question the nuns through an impenetrable grille that tells me nothing of their state of mind. All I know is the Lady Gwladys must think it's murder, or why should she have called for my services? She could have simply buried the unfortunate, and there would have been an end of it.'

'So you want me to enter the nunnery and ask your questions for you?'

Bullock's response was almost too eager. 'Yes. You are the right sex, after all. And—'

He broke off before he said too much, but Ann finished his

statement for him. 'And my, er, proximity to Regent Master Falconer may have allowed some of his technique to brush off on me.'

Bullock examined the toe-ends of his scuffed boots. 'Well, I wouldn't have put it like that, exactly. But if anyone can penetrate the veil of secrecy in the nunnery, you can.'

Ann was not sure whether the punning allusion to veils was consciously coined, but she thought it fitting nevertheless. And the thought of outdoing Regent Master Falconer at his own game appealed to her.

'My husband is away on business at the moment. I will speak to the abbess this very day.'

The constable's relief at her acquiescence was palpable, for he too relished the idea of solving a murder without recourse to his old comrade. Successful, he would constantly remind Falconer of his prowess. If he personally had to retreat in deference to a more suitable candidate for the chase, then so be it. Defeat could not be countenanced.

Falconer's first sight of Conishead Priory was from the opposite bank of the Leven estuary. Having completed the crossing of Lancaster Bay in the taciturn company of his youthful guide, his trek up and over the hump of the Cartmel headland had been conducted in solitude. For the normally loquacious Oxford master, this had been almost unbearable, and he had longed to encounter a fellow traveller. At the place called Sandgate, on the shores of the Leven, his wish had been fully granted. Guiding wayfarers across the Leven Sands from this point was the responsibility of the monks of the priory, ably carried out on this occasion by two garrulous characters – Brother Peter and Brother Paul. Their faces were bland, rounded and well scrubbed and, though each introduced himself, Falconer soon could not tell one from the other, referring his questions to a composite "Peter-Paul".

They had been forewarned of his possible arrival, and hurried him straight on to the flat expanse of mud. They explained that the tide would soon sweep in and make the crossing impossible. In order to reach the priory without waiting for the falling tide would then require a lengthy and tiring detour inland to the bottom of Furness Fell. "Peter-Paul" could not contemplate such a delay and sped on ahead, their voices ringing out with inane chatter. This part of the journey was nothing compared to the crossing of the great sweep of Lancaster Bay, and the river to be crossed no more than a stream.

The sun was already beginning to sink lower in the sky, and the cleft of the river valley was rather gloomy. Falconer thought he heard a hollow, thumping sound, and peered round to gauge where it came from. It seemed to echo from the wooded slopes on both shores, so he looked out to sea. Sitting at the neck of the river estuary, like a cork in a wine bottle, was the dark and dismal outline of a tree-covered rocky outcrop. The position of the sun behind it and his poor eyesight afforded him no detail of the island. But as he stared, he was convinced he saw a movement in the trees – a flash of something white.

'Peter, Paul, what is that island?'

Peter, or possibly Paul, turned to face him. 'What, Harlesyde Island?'

'Does anyone live there?'

Peter-Paul grimaced, and rubbed his stomach. 'If you can call it living. There is a chapel on the island, and it is occupied by a Hospitaller. His name is Fridaye de Schipedham.'

He scurried off to catch up with his comrade, his sandals making loud squelching noises as they slapped on the mud. Suddenly both brothers seemed at a loss for words, and an involuntary shudder ran down Falconer's backbone. He looked back at the island, but there was now no sign of life. What was evident was that the tide had turned. Water lapped at the base of the island, and would soon cut it off from the outside world.

Falconer hurried on in silence to escape the oncoming waters, but as he scrambled up the bank to the shore he once again heard the eerie regular thudding sound. It seemed inhuman, almost unworldly.

Chapter Three

Falconer awoke with a start, not knowing at first what had roused him. Was it the inhuman thump again, or had he simply dreamed that? Something had intruded on his weary repose. Then he heard it – the solemn tolling of the priory bell. He sat up and thrust the coarse woollen blanket off his body. The long, communal sleeping room that was the priory guest house was cold and not a glimmer of light came in through the open window arch. His breath came out in icy plumes from his lips, and he shivered, pulling the blanket back round him. He had only been asleep for a few hours, and felt bone-wearily tired.

Suddenly the bell ceased its tolling, and a strange silence fell. Not true silence, because by straining his ears Falconer could discern the lapping noise of water carrying up from the shore. Then something else intermingled with this sound of nature – a rustling and flapping like some wild animal escaping through undergrowth. He rose from his bed and, clasping his arms around him for warmth, scuttled to the window. Looking down, he realized that the guest house lay on the quire monks' route between dormitory and chapel. It was a few hours after midnight and the monks had risen for matins and lauds. In silence they processed along the pathway, their robes swishing on the ground and sandalled feet slapping stone. Their frosted breath spoke wordlessly of the coldness of the hour, and Falconer hurried back to the warmth of his bed. Unfortunately, since he had thrown the blanket off, the straw-filled pallet had already given up his body heat to the night. He sighed, dressed quickly in his robe, and joined the monks in their devotions.

The monks' entrance to the church was a small door leading into the top of the nave just below the south transept. When Falconer followed the procession in, he had to duck to avoid hitting his head on the low, old-fashioned arch of the doorway. With his head bowed he was unprepared for the beauty of the interior. It was vast — almost too large for the community of monks who lived there — and the arches of the nave soared into the darkness which still prevailed above his head. A faint glimmering of dawn illuminated the multicoloured glass of the east window, still only a shadow of the beauty that full daylight would bring to it. The chancel would during the day be lighted by the row of windows down either side. For now, the only light was afforded by burning torches suspended over the quire that occupied the centre of the church, and even the light cast by these brands was swallowed by the lofty darkness above. What by day must be an inspiring house of God was to Falconer in this pre-dawn moment an oppressive and dismal place. The fifty or so monks assembled for their devotions sat on benches that ran the length of each side of the quire, and Falconer quickly found himself a place where he could observe at least half of this group of monks — those that faced him across the central void. Further away in the darkness that was the body of the great church, the eerie slapping noise was repeated. There, the lay monks were assembling.

The quire monks were the elite of the community, living a life of contemplation and devotions broken only by a short period of manual labour each day. The bigger community of lay brothers had given up their worldly lives outside the walls, to labour on behalf of their senior brothers. They slept apart and ate apart, but in return for their work gained a more secure life than those outside the priory walls. On the surface this was a placid and well-ordered society, but Falconer guessed it would still reflect the greater society outside the walls. There would be cliques and alliances, resentment and abuses of power. He hoped he could avoid all these and complete his work in peace.

In the front row of the lay brothers' assembly, the only monks he could identify by name – Peter and Paul – sat side by side with identical smiles on their beatific faces. They seemed oblivious of all those around them. Falconer scanned the quire seats, trying to put faces to the names the loquacious brothers had fed him yesterday. They had spoken in awe of Henry Ussher the prior, and warmly of Brother Ralph, whom Falconer knew already as the keeper of books. Their description of Brother Adam, the holder of the priory's funds, was as unflattering as the look of distaste they had shared with each other. Falconer wondered what was behind that look. Apart from some fearful advice to steer clear of Brother Thady, the only other senior brother they had spoken of was Brother John, the sacrist. His name had occasioned a shared snigger and comparisons with a tame rabbit.

As Falconer scanned the quire brothers for these exemplars of religiosity, he spotted a minor commotion. Lower down the bench opposite there was a shuffling as a large, imposing brother motioned abruptly for a young novice to move up. The overbearing Brother Adam, wondered Falconer? The monk then plonked himself down beside another older brother, who cast his pale face to the ground at the intrusion. The big monk flicked his fingers in some strange way, then touched his tongue, causing the other's face to turn even whiter. The second brother then fumbled in the folds of his voluminous sleeve. Falconer silently cursed the fact that he had left his eye-lenses in the guest house in his hurry to join the monks. He squinted hard as something seemed to change hands between the two quire brothers. Then both of them stared fixedly in front of them.

Falconer was suddenly uncomfortably aware of being observed himself. Straight across from him sat a tall, cadaverous individual whose eyes were buried deep in his skull. From their dark pits, those eyes bored into Falconer's very soul, as though seeing through to all his past sins. He returned the stare, and for an eternity their eyes were locked together across the width of the quire. Then the spell was broken as the pale-faced monk (Brother John, the tame rabbit?) scuttled forward to meet an imposing figure, obviously the prior of Conishead, entering the quire.

Falconer had been advised that Henry Ussher was an ambitious man, whose desire for power extended beyond the backwater of this small priory at the outermost edge of the kingdom. His features matched his reputation, for his head was large and powerful, split by a great sweep of a nose that gave him the look of an unstoppable force. His hair, though tonsured, fell in silver waves about his face. With his pale-visaged sacrist at his feet like a loyal dog, he began to intone the psalms.

After the service, the lay brothers disappeared out of the west door of the church to begin their daily tasks. The quire monks, however, filed into the chapter house for the period of quiet contemplation until dawn. Falconer observed that for some monks the contemplation turned into something more soporific. As for himself, the regent master was aware that his stomach was audibly protesting at the lack of attention it had been paid. He felt a tug at his sleeve, and turned to his left to confront a rotund little man with a wide grin on his face. The monk indicated that Falconer should bring his ear down to the level of the other's mouth. He did so, and the brother provided some whispered solace.

'We eat after prime.'

Falconer wondered if he could last that long before his stomach involuntarily broke the monks' vow of silence again. In the meantime, he perused the room in which he sat. The glimmering of dawn lighted the chapter house through the six circular windows deliberately set in the eastern wall. This was a place intended for morning meetings. The ornate stucco on the walls was shaped in panels that enclosed geometrical figures, deftly decorated with gold. Some earlier prior had had ideas of outdoing the great abbey of Furness, no doubt. The effect unfortunately was of a provincial knight inappropriately over-dressed in cloth of gold on a visit to London. Pleased with having dreamed up such an appropriate image, Falconer felt he had summed up the room and soon became bored. He let his mind wander on to the books he was seeking at the priory.

When Robert Grosseteste, Bishop of Lincoln and one-time chancellor of the university of Oxford, had died, he had bequeathed his library to the Oxford Franciscans. Unfortunately, the friars had proceeded to scatter the books throughout England. In the dispersed collection there had been many rare and valuable texts. It was said Grosseteste had had a fair copy of Aristotle's fabled advice to Alexander — the *Secretum Secretorum*, which encompassed physic, astrology and the philosopher's stone. He had also possessed some books on magic like the rare *Sapientiae nigromanciae*. Both these were amongst the texts that Falconer was seeking for his friend, the exiled Franciscan friar, Roger Bacon. Roger claimed to have glimpsed them when the collection had been donated to his Order, and wanted to see them again. At the command of Pope Clement IV, Bacon was compiling a great treatise on the sciences from his exile in France. He had not been released from close confinement by his Order, but had at last been allowed to communicate with the outside world, hence the recent letter to Falconer.

But what Falconer sought most avidly for himself was a late version of Grosseteste's *De finitate motus et temporis*, in which Bacon insisted the bishop resolved basic matters about the eternity of the world. Before Falconer's eyes danced images of the celestial spheres lit by the light of God, streaming from the beginning of time to the present day, and shortly beyond it to the Final Judgement that so many thought imminent. Falconer imagined he could feel on either side of him the pressure of all the souls that had ever existed crushing against him, as they were raised from the dead.

With a start he woke from the doze that had overcome him in the quiet of the chapter house, to realize that the monks were getting up to return to their devotions. He was glad that it was the motion of the living, and not the resurrected dead, he had felt pressing against him. He was not yet prepared for Judgement.

When the monks processed into the chapel again for prime, Falconer detoured into his room and retrieved his eye-lenses. He would not be caught without them again. Catching up with the portly little monk who had spoken to him, he began to ask him about the other members of priory. But the monk silenced him with a finger to his lips, and no more words were forthcoming. Falconer did avoid disrupting the rendition of the psalms with another embarrassing rumble, but only by coughing loudly to cover the noise of his empty gut. Finally the monks moved to the frater, where a frugal meal was made available.

The quire frater, where all the contemplative brothers' meals were taken, was a lofty hall whose roof was supported by a line of pillars along the centre of the room. The monks ate at two tables running either side of the pillars down the length of the room. The simple fast-breaking bread and beer felt like a banquet to Falconer, and he consumed every crumb. As he ate in silence, he kept seeing the brothers wave their hands or wiggle their fingers at each other. Suddenly he realized that they were communicating with hand signals. By a process of inference he was soon able to recognize the pulling of one's little finger as the sign for passing the flagon of milk. Symbolic of pulling on a cow's udder, no doubt. He thought how useful this might be in other circumstances – silently and secretly communicating at Mass, for instance.

As he rose to leave the communal table, his arm was taken by the little monk who had reassured him after matins. He guided Falconer to one side as the rest of the monks made their way back to the chapter house for a reading of the Rule, and to hear any business that the prior wished to pass on to the community for that day. Apart from their chanted devotions and this monk's handful of words earlier, no one had spoken since he had risen.

Falconer did not realize at first that the monk at his side had asked him a question: already, he had become unused to hearing human intercourse.

'I'm sorry, what did you say?'

The little monk smiled. 'It is a little perturbing at first, isn't it? Our regime of silence.'

He spoke in a whisper still, but to Falconer's ears it seemed as if the monk's voice boomed out like a mummer in a marketplace.

'I was saying my name is Brother Ralph – Ralph Westerdale. I am the precentor and keeper of the books. I've been expecting you, and have been given permission to break silence to speak to you.'

'I am glad to have met you at last, Brother Ralph,' Falconer replied. 'I am very anxious to look through your collection, in particular for certain texts that belonged to Bishop Grosseteste.'

A frown creased Ralph's face, and he looked away for a moment. 'Yes. I want to talk to you about the library. But first we must attend the reading and find out what the prior has to say today.'

He took the impatient Falconer by the arm and led him back to the chapter house, where the assembled monks sat reverently with heads bowed as one of their number read from the heavy tome that contained the Rule of St Augustine. Words tumbled eagerly out of the mouth of the lector.

'The Rule calls for strict claustration. The ideal monk should be without father, mother or kinfolk.'

Falconer surreptitiously pulled out his eye-lenses and concentrated his gaze on this zealot. He was the tall, cadaverous monk who had looked into Falconer's soul in church. Now, his eyes sparkled like stars from the deep pits of their sockets. A stream of spittle flew from his lips as he advocated the necessity and moral value of manual labour. At this, some of the more soft-skinned and well-proportioned monks, who clearly did not observe this rule to the letter, sank lower in their seats. But the lector continued on his inexorable route.

'Above all you should obey the three great rules of the Counsels of Perfection. And these are Obedience, Poverty and Celibacy.'

He endowed each of the three with a capital letter, around which he conjured up an image of the most ornate of illumination in red, blue and gold. He especially dwelt on the last, as though he attributed a greater significance to celibacy in the context of this particular establishment.

He let his words hang in the air for a long moment, then slammed the tome shut. In the ensuing silence, the prior rose from the ornate chair he occupied at the head of the congregation. Standing as he was on a raised dais that ran across the end of the chapter house, he towered over the congregation. He wore a solemn mask on his lordly features.

'I regret I have some bad news for you all.'

He paused, and swept the assembled throng with his gaze.

'A body has been recovered from the bay. I have agreed that it should be brought here for burial, and Brother Martin is coming over from Furness Abbey to examine it.'

Ann Segrim stood in the reception hall at Godstow Nunnery, and wondered again why she had been persuaded into this escapade by Peter Bullock. Until recently, the separation of the nuns from the outside world was but laxly observed. Sisters from wealthier families were known to entertain relatives and friends, including men, within the convent walls. But a few years ago Ottobon, the Papal Legate to England, had tightened up on the Benedictine rules. Now no nun could converse with a man except there be another sister present; the lesser nuns were not allowed to leave the cloister at all; and on no account was a nun to speak with an Oxford scholar for fear of exciting 'unclean thoughts'. All this Ann had learned from the gatekeeper, who stood at the only entrance through the four-foot-thick walls that enclosed the nunnery. The gatekeeper, Hal Coke by name, was a sullen old man, who had grumbled about the new rules, and

the new abbess who enforced them. His main complaint concerned his loss of earnings from conveying gifts, letters and
tokens from convent inmates to scholars and back again. The
abbess had put a stop to all frivolous communication. All that
was left for him to do was to conduct visitors to the abbess's
hall, and there to leave them to the tender mercies of Sister
Gwladys. This he had done for Ann, suggesting all the while that
she was a fool to contemplate entering the nunnery, and that he
might be able to provide her with 'better entertainment'. He
was such an objectionable fellow that Ann would have been glad
to be delivered to Hell's ferryman in order to escape his foul
tongue.

After she met Sister Gwladys, she was sure that it would be
easier crossing the Styx into Hell than gaining access to the
nunnery. The abbess had been apprised of the constable's plan,
and Ann Segrim's part in it. But she was still far from convinced.
They began a stiff and formal conversation under the watchful
eye of an old crone by the name of Sister Hildegard. Ottobon's
rules had also demanded that any exchange between nun and
outsider should be observed by an 'ancient and discreet nun',
and even the abbess was not exempt from this injunction. On
this occasion, Sister Hildegard carried out that function, and her
wrinkled, puggish face put Ann in mind of Hell's guardian,
Cerberus. It was Sister Gwladys who first broached the subject
of Ann's real purpose.

'I do not like the idea of you prying into the activities of my
nunnery, but this . . . death . . . leaves me with no option.' The
word 'murder' was clearly one that the abbess had not yet come
to terms with. Ann was surprised at her openness in Hildegard's
presence, and leaned forward to whisper her response.

'I thought we planned to keep my role a secret. That I was to
be seen as a corrodian – merely a temporary boarder.'

A puzzled look crossed Sister Gwladys's patrician features.
She was a handsome woman, whose face was lined with the cares
that her severity of purpose impressed on her. The hair that

poked out from under her headdress was silver even though she could only have been in her middle years. The edges of her mouth were turned down in a perpetual grimace of disapproval, whether at others' or her own failings Ann could not surmise. Probably at both. She suddenly realized what Ann meant, and something that Ann guessed was intended to be a smile contorted her features. She achieved it by merely turning down the corners of her mouth even further.

'Don't worry about Sister Hildegard. I chose her because she is deaf, but will not admit it. She will pretend she can hear us, but you may speak openly all the same.'

As if in confirmation, the ancient nun nodded her wrinkled face in agreement with what she imagined her abbess might be saying. Gwladys continued.

'As a corrodian, you will be free to speak to all the sisters. There are only twenty of us at present. On each of three sides of the cloister you will see a house; in each lives six or seven nuns. St Thomas's Chapel is next to the gatehouse – though you may prefer to use the smaller domestic chapel – and the frater where we eat is beyond that.'

'Which household did the nun who . . . died . . . live in?'

'Sister Eleanor lived in the middle of the three – to the north of the cloister. I have arranged for you to stay there.'

Ann hoped that didn't mean in the murdered nun's very room. 'And can you show me where she died?'

The abbess's face froze, but eventually she rose and flicked a finger at Ann. 'Follow me.'

She led Ann from the hall and into the inner courtyard of the nunnery. The cloister was a pleasant sanctuary with religious scenes painted on the white plaster of the inner walls. Across the middle of the cloister ran an open stone conduit conveying water to the three households ranged around its perimeter. The abbess's voice was as cold as the stone flags on which Ann stood.

'She was found there, face down in the water conduit. She had drowned.'

LAUDS

Praise the Lord from the Earth,
You water-spouts and ocean depths,
Fire and hale, snow and ice,
Gales of winds obeying His voice.

                                    Psalm 148

Chapter Four

A solemn procession of monks preceded the body into the church of Conishead Priory, led by the imposing figure Falconer had guessed to be Brother Adam. He had a pompous look of self-importance on his jowly, red face. The monks' demeanour was more dignified than the body, and those that bore it. The corpse was wrapped in nothing more than a coarse grey blanket, and this was held at each corner by four sturdy men in short drab tunics that finished well above their knees. The tunics were all well patched and salt-encrusted around their lower hems.. The men's legs and feet were bare. Their weather-beaten faces, from which their eyes squinted through half-closed lids, spoke of their trade as fishermen. Falconer had heard of these men who spent their days out in the bay laying traps for the flat fish the locals called flukes. Their hours were dictated by the comings and goings of the tide, their lives shortened by the harshness of the conditions. Clearly to them the proximity of death was a constant factor in their lives. The contents of the cheap shroud they carried could have been their father, or their son.

They followed the line of monks into one of the side chapels, and at Brother Adam's imperious gesture hefted the bundle on to a bench. To Falconer it seemed curiously light, and rather small for a body. God forbid it be that of a child. The monks, including the prior, stood in a hesitant circle, as though afraid to uncover the doleful shape enclosed by the tattered blanket. With a sigh Falconer stepped forward and lifted a corner gently. What he saw was totally unexpected, and he suddenly understood

41

exactly what the men had been digging out of the sandy river bank he had passed the day before.

Pulling the covering back carefully, he revealed not an identifiable body, but a skeleton. The assembled monks gasped in surprise, and retreated into a huddle near the altar. They had all been expecting a form fully clothed in flesh and were shocked to be confronted by nothing more than a bag of bones. It would not be so easy to solve the mystery of this person's identity. The skull sat atop the ribcage, and the eye cavities stared darkly out at Falconer. The interior of the skull was packed with dark brown sand, and as he examined it a thin trickle of mud ran out of the nose cavity and down the yellowish expanse of cheekbone. Arm and leg bones had simply been thrown into the blanket with no regard for their place in life, but the head, ribcage and hipbone somehow still hung together. They appeared to be held in place by a white, suety mass that mimicked the body shape of whoever this had been in life. A gritty covering of sand was plastered haphazardly to all the bony surfaces.

As Falconer looked more closely at the jumble, he could see shreds of cloth stuck to the soggy white pulp. Unfamiliar with what burial in wet sand might do to flesh, Falconer assumed the pulp was all that remained of the person's fleshly body. Across the skull the remnants of black hair ran in a fringe around the sides of the head. As he looked more closely, a lugworm poked out of one eye socket, waving its head blindly in the air. He watched entranced as it slithered across the cheekbone and fell to the stone-flagged floor, where it curled up into a tight ring. Returning to his examination of the remains, he saw a dark line tangled in the ribcage, and eased his fingers under it. It was a chain with something on its end that now lay tucked up in the sand inside the skull. Falconer put his hand inside the gaping mouth, and drew the chain out. On its end a cross, blackened by its time in the sands of the bay. It was only when he rubbed it that he realized it was a very fine silver cross that no ordinary fisherman would have possessed. Its surface glistened in the weak sun that filtered through the chapel's window in a way it could not have done for many years. Falconer felt a restraining hand on his arm. Henry Ussher spoke quietly into his ear.

'This poor soul has long been dead. We should leave his remains for Brother Martin, who is appointed by the King to examine those drowned in the bay. He will not be long in coming from Furness.'

Falconer was impatient to continue his own examination, but as a guest of the priory he deferred to its principal. He allowed Henry Ussher to take the silver cross from him, certain it would be useful in identifying the body later. He only wondered at the medical skills of this Brother Martin of Furness Abbey, and whether they were equal to those he could call upon at Oxford University. In the meantime, he supposed he still had his original quest for Grosseteste's books to begin. As he left the chapel, he passed Brother Adam, and noticed the intense interest on his heavyset face. The monk had seen his prior secreting the cross in his robes.

Ralph Westerdale had no wish to see the body that had been brought in from the bay. Besides, he had other problems. With Grosseteste's collection securely locked away, and for good reason, how was he to tell the regent master from Oxford that he could not look at the books he was seeking? How was he to keep the priory from being involved in a scandal, which must certainly follow if the truth became known? And then there were the missing books. He knew the first thing he had to do was confront Brother Thady, and that was something he was not looking forward to.

The cellarer frightened him, with his staring eyes and wild manner, and not for the first time he wondered why Prior Henry did not do anything about him. The monk needed disciplining — preferably in a solitary cell out on Coniston Fells. Instead, as his behaviour became more erratic, Ussher had merely transferred him from the post of precentor to that of cellarer, where Thady had begun to wreak havoc with the priory's supply of food and beer.

Now he was proving elusive, at the very time that Ralph urgently needed him. Thinking the cellarer might be with the others in the chapel where the recently discovered body had been taken, Ralph scurried round the cloisters to make his way to the priory church. The pale winter sunlight cut in shafts across the arched avenue, which was curiously empty for the time of day. It was the period set aside for manual labour, but the arrival of the body had obviously been sufficient cause for most quire brothers to seek to avoid their obligations. The quietness worked in Ralph's favour, however.

In the normal bustle of activity, Ralph might not have seen Thady Lamport slip out of the side door of the church, and thus might have missed him. Without the distraction of other activity, he did spot him, and called out for Lamport to wait. The tall monk cast a glance over his shoulder, then strode purposefully in the opposite direction. The portly little monk gave a cry of exasperation, and set off in pursuit. Lamport was not going to escape again.

Reaching the side door of the church where the cellarer had appeared, Ralph was just in time to see his quarry's thin form disappearing under the archway beneath the main dormitory. His route could only be taking him upstairs to the dormitory or beyond to the brewhouse. Ralph called out again, and scurried after the elusive monk. Entering the dormitory archway, he peered up the stairs, but there was no sign of Lamport. Thinking even the cellarer's long legs could not have carried him out of sight already, he went on under the arch and stopped dumbfounded. Lamport was nowhere to be seen.

In the time he was out of Ralph's sight he could not have reached the brewhouse door that stood at the far end of the range running below the dormitory – it was too far away. The man had disappeared like some unearthly being. Ralph turned back and climbed the stairs to the communal dormitory. The long and airy hall was still and empty, each narrow bed as tidy and regimented as its occupant's life. The sun shone through dust motes that drifted lazily in the air. It was obvious no one had come this way recently. Puzzled, Ralph descended the stairs and stood in the archway looking at the door to the brewhouse. If he had run full tilt, Lamport could perhaps have hidden there, but to what purpose? The first place one might look for a cellarer would be in the brewhouse. Then Ralph realized there was another door leading off the range, and a shiver ran through him that was not the result of the icy draught that blew down the tunnel of the archway. The door to the guest house.

Falconer was reluctant to leave the bones, but Henry Ussher had been firm in his resolve that Brother Martin should be the first to examine what was left of the corpse. He therefore decided to find Brother Ralph and ask to see the books in his library. Having enquired about the location of the precentor's office, Falconer left the church by the main doors. He had been told that Ralph Westerdale kept his records in the undercroft at the opposite corner of the cloister, next to the kitchens.

The proximity of food was an attraction to the hungry master in itself. He thought he might be able to beg something to tide him over until the main meal of the day, which was still hours away. But having found the precentor's door, and guessed it was the kitchen door opposite, he was disappointed to encounter no more promising aroma than that of rotting winter cabbage. His appetite thoroughly ruined, he knocked on Ralph Westerdale's door. There was no reply. He knocked again, and when the ensuing silence confirmed the precentor's absence he turned to leave, feeling frustrated that he could make no progress as yet. Only a few paces from the door, however, he stopped, aware of the complete silence that hung over the cloister.

'Who's to know?' he mumbled to himself, in justification of his next action. 'I'm sure Brother Ralph would not mind.'

He sneaked another look round the cloister, then turned back to the precentor's door. He grasped the handle and turned it — as he had hoped, the door was unlocked. He stepped quickly inside and closed the door behind him. The room was neat, and depressingly bare, with an arched ceiling that was not symmetrical. It was obvious that the far wall was a partition that had cut off one corner of the much larger undercroft storage area below the lay brothers' dorter. All the walls were limewashed and devoid of any decoration. Nowhere was there any place for books, except on the table that stood in the centre of the small room. On it lay a heavy tome with ornate leather binding. It was closed, and Falconer noticed that one of the pages seemed to be sticking out at a peculiar angle. He needed no further invitation to investigate. He quickly rounded the table to stand before the book which lay with its back cover uppermost as though someone had just completed a task and closed it. He looked round for a chair but there was none in the room, so it was clear no one was intended to linger here. He lifted up the heavy cover, and leafed through the sheaf of pages at the back of the book.

On several pages was a list in two columns, written in the neatest of hands. The first column was of people's names, and against each name in the second column were what Falconer immediately saw were titles of books. He scanned the last three lines.

Henry Ussher, prior	Historia scholastica
Peter Lewthet, monk	Testamentum Ciceronis
John Whitehed, sacrist	Topographica Hibernica

The list was periodically broken up by dates. Brother Ralph obviously kept a meticulous record of the books borrowed from his collection. Most of the loans were noted as returned, but occasionally a work was marked with the accusatory word 'perditur'. Falconer wondered what penance the monk who lost a book had to undergo at the hands of Brother Ralph. However, all this was not of immediate interest to Falconer and he turned back some more pages. This looked more promising – the list changed to a different format.

Here each entry began with a number, followed by a book title, then a name which Falconer guessed was the donor of the book, and a list of contents. This was followed by a location somewhere in the priory, which varied from the regularly used *'communis libraria'* to the rarer *'in archa cantoris'*. Occasionally the words *'libraria interior'* occurred. Books were obviously scattered around the priory, wherever Brother Ralph and his predecessors had been able to find space. In the circumstances, Falconer was glad that generations of precentor had kept such an accurate catalogue of the priory's holdings. It should make his work much easier. It looked as though the catalogue listed books chronologically as they were added: the last recorded work, entitled *De viris illustribus*, was numbered 453 and had been added in the previous year. The books belonging to Bishop Grosseteste would have come to Conishead some fifteen years earlier. If they were here at all, Falconer would find them catalogued further back.

Ralph Westerdale tiptoed up to the guest house door and pressed his ear to the studded oak surface. There was not a sound from within, and he pondered what to do. If both Thady Lamport and Master Falconer were within, then Ralph imagined his brother monk might be blaming the precentor for the disappearance of the books Falconer sought. His own appearance hard on Thady's heels would only seem to support the accusation. If Thady were on his own, then this was Ralph's opportunity to trap him and confront him. He took a deep breath and opened the door. The guest hall was empty, with even the darkest corners devoid of life. At first Ralph thought the house was deserted, and turned to leave before he was discovered. Then he heard a rustling noise like the sound of mice foraging through the rubbish scattered in the corners of the priory kitchen. He stood still and held his breath. There it was again; but this time it was followed by a low uncanny moan. It came from upstairs. Slowly Ralph climbed each step, hardly daring to make a sound. He feared that whatever was present would overwhelm him. Again the rustling sound was accompanied by a low moan, to his ears more human this time. Was Falconer ill? Or was Thady Lamport harming him in some way? He reached the top of the stairs and, summoning the last of his courage, he opened the small dormitory door. Inside was a snowstorm, and at its centre on the floor sat Thady Lamport, moaning in despair. Ralph was confused, until he realized the snow was shredded paper, and he suddenly felt sick with horror at the thought of such destruction. Lamport was tearing a book to pieces, and one written on paper at that, not even cheap parchment. Words laboriously reproduced by a fellow scribe floated in front of his eyes, and he could hardly encompass the scale of Thady's destruction. He snatched the book out of the cellarer's hands, but too late – it was no more than two empty covers. The mad monk's lips still formed the word he had been moaning.

'Evil. Evil. Evil,' he repeated. Ralph bent down and shook him by the shoulders.

'Why have you done this?'

The monk's penetrating eyes bored into Ralph. 'Because it is evil. Like the other ones.'

Ralph glared back at Lamport, his anger at the desecration overcoming his previous fear. 'The other ones – do you mean the missing books? Did you take them and destroy them?'

'Evil.' The cellarer's eyes sparkled with cunning. Then he spat the words out in Ralph's face. 'He took them.'

'What do you mean, he took them? Who is he?'

But he was to get no more out of Thady Lamport, who unwound his legs from under him and rose above the little precentor. He shrugged off Ralph's grip and strode out of the room, leaving Westerdale surrounded by devastation.

*

It was fast approaching terce and time for Mass, and Henry Ussher had still not resolved what to do about their visitor. Harm enough that he should poke his nose into the matter of Bishop Grosseteste's books. There was a bad odour around those, which he would no doubt sniff out given half a chance. And the stench still clung to the prior's clothes. Almost in unconscious reaction to his thoughts, Ussher drifted to the open window of his office as though the breeze there might cleanse him, though he knew it was only by constant prayer and deed that he might effect such a cleansing. The passage of time had led him into a false sense of safety. Worse still that all those years had now been bridged in a single moment, and the memory of them flooded back.

It had begun innocently enough, with his curiosity piqued by the arrival of Grosseteste's collection. The bishop had a fearsome reputation that lived on after his demise, not least for asserting the friars were heretical for not denouncing the sins of the rich. Not a statement likely to endear him to those rich and powerful who ruled England. The first book of Grosseteste's he could lay his hands on was entitled De finitate motus et temporis, *and it fired his imagination from the start. It averred that the pagan philosophers fell into the error of believing the world had no beginning. The bishop stated that before time and motion there was the eternity of the creator. And as the world was created by God it must have a beginning and thus be finite. There was nothing there to challenge belief, and he shared the concept with his friend and rival John de Langetoft. He was shocked when John sneered and asserted that anything the old Bishop of Lincoln wrote must be an error. As he stood there fiddling with the silver cross that hung suspended by a chain round his neck, he gave Henry the first intimations of his narrow-mindedness.*

As soon as Falconer had lifted the cross from the body, Henry Ussher had known who the bones belonged to. Fifteen years, and the past was back to haunt him. He ran his long fingers through his thick mass of silver hair and stared blankly out of the window arch, seeing nothing. His gaze was turned inwards towards his own soul, and he feared for its safety. In the other hand he loosely held the tarnished silver cross. There was no doubt about it — the last time he had seen it was fifteen years ago, about the neck of his greatest friend and rival. What had happened then must never come to light, or his very future would be imperilled. Ussher sighed and crossed to his desk. One way or another this Master Falconer must be got rid of.

Chapter Five

Working slowly back through the library catalogue, Falconer was fascinated by the contents. He had been diverted from his main task by the sight of old familiar friends, and works he had heard of but never seen. The lists encompassed Horace, Sallust, Statius, Macrobius, Claudian, Boethius and Apollonius of Tyre. There were histories by Jordanes, Bede, Josephus, a *Hystoria Britonum*, a *Mappa mundi*, and a *Cronica Francorum*. He noticed that most of the rarer works were located in the '*libraria interior*', and supposed it to be a safe repository for irreplaceable texts. He imagined that that was where Grosseteste's books might be located. But so far he had not come across them in the catalogue.

He came to a point in his backwards search through the tome where the writing changed. One scribe's hand was very much like another, as the skill of writing was handed down within each monastery's walls. The more recent text was clearly that of Brother Ralph – neat and precise. But at the point Falconer had reached, the hand was much more free and carelessly illustrated along the margin -- an indulgence that Ralph had not allowed himself. Falconer found himself wondering who Ralph's predecessor had been and whether he was still at the priory. Could he guess who it was just from his hand? An interesting exercise that might prove useful in the future.

He looked more closely at the shape and form of the letters rather than the meanings they conveyed. The tails of some letters became more wild as Falconer scanned the page from top to bottom. But what caught his eye were the illustrations at the side of the page. Earlier entries were simple designs of flowers entwining random letters – a yellow rose that grew up a letter R, comfrey sprouting from the centre of a C. Towards the bottom of the page murky demons with long tails twined the letters, their eyes staring from the parchment in rage and madness. At the very bottom was a different image still. Squashed in beneath the claws of an ugly behemoth was the tiny image of a monk. Falconer drew his eye-lenses out and peered more closely. The monk was dressed in Augustinian robes, as those of Conishead were, and next to him stood an indistinct figure, only completed in outline. All that was fully drawn was its arm, and that was plunging a knife into the chest of the monk.

'Ah, Master Falconer.'

The quiet voice startled Falconer, who was so engrossed in the detail before him that he had not heard anyone enter the room. Now he was embarrassed to have been discovered, and straightened up with an apology on his lips. But it was Brother Ralph who apologized first, hardly able to get his words out clearly. Falconer was only aware of '. . . I regret . . .' and '. . . that it should happen here . . .' and '. . . there will be full restitution, of course.' Gradually it became apparent that Ralph was saying one of the monks had destroyed a book belonging to him. He blanched at the thought it might be the *Treatise on the Magnet*, for he would have great difficulty in replacing that. Then he sighed with relief when Ralph shamefacedly held out the empty cover of *Ars Rhetorica*. That, at least, was a familiar text he could replace, though the cost would beggar him.

An embarrassed silence hung between the two men as they both counted the cost of the monk's mad rage. It was broken by Ralph, who saw the opened library catalogue on the table. Turning it towards him, he sighed.

'I see you have come across some more of Brother Thady's ravages.'

In response to Falconer's puzzled look, he pointed to the clutter of images down the margin of the page.

'Thady Lamport, who has just ripped your book to shreds, was my precursor as keeper of the library. These . . . scribbles . . . are his doing. I intend to scrape the pages clean when I get the chance.'

'Have you seen what's there?'

Westerdale was abrupt and dismissive 'The ramblings and outpourings of a disturbed soul, and I'm afraid they sully the purpose of the catalogue.'

It was apparent to Falconer that the little monk had not looked closely at the detail of these 'outpourings', and he resolved to keep the result of his scrutiny to himself for the moment. What was interesting was that the recorder of the miniature murder scene should also be the destroyer of his book. Was the murder he depicted real? Was it in the past or in the future? Or was the man merely deranged, as Ralph Westerdale suggested? Time enough to resolve that when he had had a chance to examine the bones lying in the chapel. For now he must concentrate on the original purpose for his visit. He indicated the catalogue, which now lay face up on the table.

'I am impressed by the breadth of your collection.'

The precentor's whole body puffed up with pride. But Falconer's next words were enough to deflate him.

'But I have not yet found reference to the texts I am seeking. The books the Franciscans gave you that belonged to Bishop Grosseteste.'

'I . . . er . . .'

Falconer gave him no time to respond, and opened the catalogue close to where he had got to in his chronological search. 'They must be recorded hereabouts.' He flipped another page over and gasped.

'What's wrong?' asked the worried Westerdale.

'Look at this.'

The monk peered down to where Falconer was pointing. The page that Falconer had previously noted was misaligned when the catalogue was closed was now uppermost, and a long cut ran halfway down it close to the binding. There was a crease from the bottom of the cut across the whole page, causing it to stick out. But that was not the worst of it. The cut had obviously been caused by the wholesale removal of the page above it. All that was left of that was a long stub of parchment.

The church gradually grew silent as the brothers filed out at the end of midday Mass. They now had three hours for their own devotional tasks until they reassembled at sext for the fifth service of the day. John Whitehed, the sacrist, found comfort in this inexorable cycle that came and went each day like the tide on Leven Sands. Before and after each service he was fully occupied in preparing the vessels, and the bread and wine for Holy Eucharist. In between this tidal flow of devotion were the low points where stretched the endless mudbanks of time, during which he thought only of the perdition that faced him on his death. He tried to busy himself with other matters, but his office relieved him of the necessity to carry out any manual labour, other than to supervise the burial of the dead. It was also his duty to respond to the letters that arrived at the priory.

One such letter had come from Regent Master Falconer some months previously. Unfortunately, Ralph Westerdale had been present when he had opened it, or he would have firmly denied Falconer the opportunity to visit Conishead. The precentor, however, had insisted that they invite the man, especially as he had been a student of Bishop Grosseteste. To have a scholar with such illustrious antecedents visit the priory and its library could only enhance its reputation. Whitehed was sure that Brother Ralph was thinking about enhancing his own reputation in the process also. So the die was cast, and the sacrist began to fear the day that would bring the man from Oxford. Then the inevitable would happen. Now he was here, Brother John could only wait in fear of imminent discovery, and pray that it might not take place. That his terrible secret was known to Brother Adam already had been enough to make his life a misery these past few years. But that was almost tolerable – still allowing him to continue in his office at the priory – compared to the possibility of having what he had done becoming public knowledge.

Nervously he washed out the vessels, storing them in the cupboard ready for the next Mass. His hands trembled, causing the silver cups to strike one against the other, and the sound, like cymbals, echoed through the stillness. Try as he might he could not still the tremor in his hands, and he grasped the altar rail hard until his knuckles turned white. He was a weak man, he knew, but he also knew that only drastic action would resolve his situation.

Brother Martin Albon's head was bowed over the nameless remains in the side chapel when Falconer returned, accompanied by a whey-faced Ralph Westerdale. The back of his habit was an immaculate white, as was the custom with Cistercians, but when he turned round to see who was disturbing his work, Falconer saw that the front was already stained with mud and grains of sand. The sleeves were rolled up, and exposed a pair of stringy but muscular forearms. Bits of the suety remnants of the body stuck to his fingers, and Falconer knew he was not afraid to delve into the innards of the bodies that confronted him. To complete the picture of a man of science, a wispy halo of white hair floated around his pink scalp.

'Ah, you must be the celebrated scholar from Oxford, come to look at Brother Ralph's library. I am Martin Albon, appointed coroner by the King to investigate the many deaths the sands throw up for us.'

His voice was firm, but half an octave higher than it would have been in his prime. And as he droned on, Falconer wondered for a moment if his mind also betrayed his advancing years.

'And many deaths there have been over the years. There are always those foolish souls who underestimate the dangers of Lancaster Bay. Most of them end up in the same position as this poor soul.' He flicked a piece of soft pulp from the body off the end of his index finger. 'Why, I remember once being called to verify the demise of a cartload of people, who had tried to cross the bay without the guide. The whole cart and its contents were swallowed up at Black Scars Hole, and no one knew what was happening as the wind drowned out their cries for help. They must have stopped the cart, or slowed down – you see, if you do so the sand washes from under your wheels, and the cart tips up.'

'Can you tell us anything about the body?' asked Falconer bluntly, not expecting much. If the old monk rambled on so, the master wasn't certain he would get any useful information from him at all. He was probably just a cipher, there to confirm the obvious.

Albon looked across at Henry Ussher, who was standing in the shadow of a pillar as though not wishing to be associated with the unpleasant task in hand. In response to Albon's quizzical look, the prior waved his hand in resignation. Falconer was here, and might as well hear what the Cistercian had to say. Albon pointed to the pile of bones, which he had now arranged as they would have been in life.

'It is the body of a man. It's sometimes difficult to tell when you lay the bones out on the ground, but I would say this was a tall man. As tall as you, Master Falconer.'

Falconer grunted in agreement, and Albon continued.

'And his hair was black – you can see some remains of it on the skull. Now I cannot be sure, because most of the flesh is gone, but there is no hair on the top of the scalp. So he was either naturally bald, or he had a tonsure. Here . . . ' between his forefinger and thumb, he picked up a shred of material . . . 'we have a piece of cloth I found stuck to the ribs. No doubt I would have found more in the sand that formed his grave, had I been present. It is finer linen than a fisherman would wear. All things considered, I would say he was a wealthy merchant or a brother monk.'

Falconer was pleasantly surprised, and had to rapidly revise his earlier opinion of this man. He clearly had an eye for detail as Falconer did. He was going to mention the silver cross that Henry Ussher had taken from him, but a quick glance at the prior told him there was something wrong here. Ussher was looking away, not wishing to assist in the identification. Maybe he was distracted by more important matters, or maybe he had something to hide. For the moment, Falconer decided to keep quiet.

'Of course, I am used to having more recent remains in order to assist in my examination,' Albon continued. 'Lungs full of water clearly speak of a drowning, and there are other signs, if the quicksand was their downfall. Here I have nothing but the bones and this soft mass that is all that remains of his outer form.'

Henry Ussher spoke for the first time. 'Then there is nothing here to tell us it was more than an unfortunate accident.'

It was a flat statement, not a question, but Albon ignored the clear suggestion. 'Oh no. It was no accident. It was undoubtedly murder.'

The prior's eyes were cold and blank – Falconer was reminded of the stare of a dead fish on a fishmonger's slab. But his own eyes lit up at the word the old monk had spoken.

'Murder, eh?'

'Oh, without a doubt. Look here.' Albon knelt, drawing Falconer down with him to examine the ribcage. 'What do you see? Here, and here.'

He pointed with a work-coarsened finger at the ribcage where he had rubbed away a layer of grit. Falconer could immediately see what had not been obvious to him at his previous cursory glance at the bones. He took out his eye-lenses and looked closely, ignoring the ripe odour now coming from the soft pulp inside the ribs.

'There's a chip on the bottom of this rib, and on the top of the one below it. A single, deep cut that could only have been made by something sharp.'

'Exactly.' Albon stabbed his finger dramatically in between the ribs. 'Someone plunged a knife straight into our mystery man's heart.'

A vision suddenly swam before Falconer's eyes. It was of the tiny picture in the margin of the library catalogue, drawn by Brother Thady Lamport.

The little domestic chapel at Godstow Nunnery was more to Ann Segrim's liking than St Thomas's Chapel — especially as the central aisle was dominated by a large stone coffin. When she had first discovered it, she thought its size incongruous in so small a place. But then she realized who was interred within. She leaned against the cool stone and traced her fingers along the letters carved in the surface, repeating them under her breath.

'*Tumba Rosamundae.*'

She felt some affinity with the fair Rosamund, who had been mistress to Henry II until he had forsaken her to marry Eleanor. She had taken the veil at Godstow, and some said she was forced to take poison by Henry's vengeful new wife. But a hundred years was long enough for facts to be forgotten, and for legends to thrive. Who knew where the truth lay, other than in the long-dead heart of Rosamund, focus of continuing pilgrimages? And here she was, interred beneath the stone Ann now touched.

Ann had a passing thought to render her own stay at Godstow permanent. At least it would resolve her unsatisfactory life: married to a man she despised on the one hand, and on the other attracted to a certain regent master of Oxford University who seemed unable to make up his mind about her, restless and prodigious though that mind might be. William Falconer was frustrating.

'No more than a harlot.'

Abbess Gwladys's words cut cruelly through the quiet of the chapel. At first Ann thought the nun had looked into the depths of her soul, then blushed when she realized Gwladys was talking about the fair Rosamund.

'Oh, the nunnery derives some funds from the few pilgrims who still come to pray at her tomb. But the bishop was right seventy years ago when he called her a harlot, and demanded that her bones be removed. If I had been abbess then, I would have complied and scattered them on the nearest dunghill.'

Ann believed her. After a number of years of scandal, Godstow Nunnery was run strictly according to the Benedictine Rule recently expanded by the Papal Legate. The abbess had gone through the rules at length with Ann, when she arrived, impressing them on her soul. It seemed there should be no drinking after compline, when the nuns should retire to bed. The sisters should not talk with secular folk except in the hearing of a nun of sound character. (Ann hoped for the sake of her investigations she was not deemed to be secular, at least for the time being.) All the doors of the nuns' lodgings that led to the outer court were to be stopped up, and no sister was to travel to another town except by licence of the abbess. Not least was an injunction never to talk to Oxford scholars, who could be guilty of exciting 'unclean thoughts'. Ann smiled wryly – that indictment at least was true.

'You wished to speak to me.' Gwladys's tone was uniformly cold, and increasingly impatient. It reminded Ann why she was here, and she nodded hesitantly. She had been putting off this question, but knew she had to ask it. The abbess's severity did not make it easy.

'Was Sister Eleanor liked?'

The abbess's forehead knitted in a frown as she wrestled with this foreign concept. 'Liked? She was a sister in God, and carried out her devotions adequately. We are all here by God's will, and whether one is liked or not is of little consequence.'

Ann knew that God's will often had little to do with why girls found themselves in a nunnery. For wealthy families it was a convenient means of discarding a feeble-minded, ugly or other-wise unmarriageable daughter. Peter Bullock had assured her Eleanor was none of these. Eleanor had indeed been quite beautiful, according to the constable. Undaunted, Ann pressed on with her enquiry.

'I need to know if any of the sisters were particularly close to Eleanor.'

'I am not sure what you mean.' The red flush that started around Gwladys's neck and crept over her cheeks suggested that she knew exactly what Ann meant. However, she was not going to admit to any improper activity in her establishment. Ann tried a different tack, though with little hope of success now.

'Then, was she disliked for any reason?'

The abbess's whole face was now a mottled red, and it was obvious to Ann that Gwladys was already regretting being persuaded by Peter Bullock into this unorthodox enquiry.

'The sisters' time is devoted to worship. There is no time for idle tittle-tattle, enmities or the establishment of . . . personal relationships.'

The last two words were spat out as though they were likely to sully the virginal and holy lips of the speaker. Her opinion clearly demonstrated, the abbess spun on her heels and stalked out of the chapel, leaving Ann to think she could have got more useful information from cold Rosamund in her stone coffin.

The view from Henry Ussher's private solar was normally a consolation to him when he was troubled. That he could see down into the cloister was of little consequence, though he sometimes found it useful to see who was talking to whom. Especially when they thought themselves unobserved. He had cowed many a brother with his apparent omniscience, and secretly delighted in the effect. That he could see the fishponds and fields beyond was usually of some satisfaction to him. They furnished the priory's everyday needs and were a symbol of its stability. But that he could see over the priory walls, to the banks of the Leven and beyond, was what afforded him most joy in his position. He dreamed of stepping outside those walls, and having power over those little people who dwelled in the wider world.

Indeed, he clutched in his hand a sealed message he needed delivered to Lancaster to await the arrival of the Papal Legate. The joint epistle from King and Legate had been a burdensome worry, with its demands for money. But it offered an opportunity for the prior to meet the Legate and impress him with his abilities. Now all his aspirations could be shattered by a heap of old bones.

Deep in thought, he left his residence and hurried over to the gateway, where the message-carrier already awaited him. As he walked, he twirled the mud-covered silver cross in his fingers, trying to piece together a plan that would preserve his secret. He had recognized the cross immediately, and had managed to pluck it from Falconer's hand before any of the other monks could see it. He knew whom it had belonged to, and didn't want the man to come back to haunt him as his own memories did.

He was being sucked deeper into the complexities of Bishop Grosseteste's ideas. He now began to understand the concept of the eternity of light. God as light, the prime form carrying with it the whole matter of the universe. Grosseteste explained that the 'primum mobile' generated the form of the celestial heavens by diffusing its light downwards. The light from the stars generated the first of the planetary spheres, and so on down until all seven spheres had been created. Then came the four spheres of elementary bodies that were under the moon. Thus in descending order each sphere affected the lower sphere by casting light, and so on down to men. What was beginning to excite Henry were the descriptions of experiments in the science described by the bishop as optics. By this means Brother Henry could see a means of capturing eternal light. He would try to set up an experiment, but he would not involve Brother John, who had mocked his previous attempts at explaining Grosseteste's concepts. He would have to think of someone else, someone who could understand the true glory of his searching. Perhaps the precentor, Brother Thady, would help. He was responsible for the books, after all.

*

All this trouble over a striving for the truth. Now he didn't know whether he could prevent the truth from emerging, but he would have to try. The insistent calling of his name brought him back to the mundane. He realized it would shortly be time for the nones service, so he expected to see the fussy little sacrist dancing attendance on him. Instead it was the altogether bulkier frame of the camerarius, Adam Lutt, which waddled in his direction.

Much as he hated the ministrations of John Whitehed, the sacrist was a harmless little man. Adam Lutt was another matter. Along with his responsibility for the accounts of the priory, he seemed to have adopted an attitude of self-importance that irritated most of those with whom he came into direct contact. And as he was in charge of the dormitory also, he was in an excellent position to make any monk's life a misery if he were crossed. But for now the man was more concerned with imitating the fawning sacrist.

'Forgive me for interrupting you, prior, but Brother John has had to attend to other business. I am here to ensure you are ready for the service, and wondered if we might speak of a discreet matter on the way.'

Ussher was too distracted to wonder at Whitehed's desertion of the routine he so loved. He simply sighed, and, slipping the silver cross surreptitiously into the pouch at his waist, motioned for Lutt to follow him. 'I must ensure this message is sent first.'

The camerarius fell into step with him, prattling on about inconsequential things until they reached the gate, where the messenger stood waiting. Once his letter was out of his hands, the prior's thoughts returned again to the man discovered in the sands. The bones themselves could have been passed off as those of any erring traveller caught in the quicksands or the tides that sweep up Lancaster Bay at the speed of a racing horse. Damn Albon for being so clever, and spotting the marks on the ribs, and for suggesting he was a monk. Even so, there was nothing to link the remains with Conishead. Except the cross. As Falconer was a stranger in the priory, he would not know the significance of the cross. On the other hand, Ussher could not rely on him to keep his mouth shut. No, the sooner he could be got rid of the better. Engrossed in his own thoughts, he suddenly realized he was ignoring what the camerarius was saying.

'Now, what's this discreet matter you must raise with me?'

A sly grin played across Lutt's lips. 'It's to do with John de Langetoft.'

PRIME

Like men who watch for the morning,
O Israel, look for the Lord.

                                    Psalm 130

Chapter Six

Darkness had fallen, but the northern side of the cloister was lit by the scraps of light that shone through the lattice-work doors of the reading carrels ranged along the edge. In each carrel there was a central table shaped like an inverted V to provide a sloping support for books. Over the table was a candle-holder for the winter evenings – in the summer the pierced carving of the carrel door afforded some light to read by. On each side of the table was a narrow bench, so arranged that the two occupants of the carrel faced each other. The ten carrels thus allowed up to twenty monks to read books borrowed from the library, whose presses were close at hand. The more senior members of the order were allowed to take their books to their own quarters, and read in seclusion there.

Not every carrel was occupied that evening. There were monks in the two or three together at the furthest point of the range, but the carrels nearest the book presses were empty and dark save for the third one along. There, a candle indicated occupants, but inside there was precious little reading taking place. Immediately after nones, Falconer had grabbed Ralph Westerdale's arm and dragged the precentor into the vacant carrel to question him about the priory. After about an hour of interrogation by Falconer, Ralph had stopped to light the single, fat candle that was fixed above the reading table. Its flickering light now cast long shadows that danced over the master's features as he picked the precentor's brains.

'A tall man with dark hair. A monk who must have died at

least ten years ago, judging from the bones. If you were to guess who the dead monk was, what would be the name you came up with?'

Ralph could see the candle flame reflected in Falconer's piercing blue eyes. He lowered his gaze to the scarred surface of the table, and picked at the marks with his fingernail. The silence pressed heavily on him until he eventually was moved to speak.

'Someone who disappeared fifteen years ago, not ten, in mysterious circumstances. Someone whose absence our present prior didn't exactly regret. Indeed, the man who was camerarius and his rival for the office of prior at the time. John de Langetoft was his name. There was a suspicion that the sands guide, Shokburn, had robbed and killed him, but it could not be proved. He always wore a rather ornate silver cross, and I suppose it could have been a temptation to someone with no money or scruples. Anyway, it's too late to reopen that debate – Shokburn died several years ago. It's his grandson who now acts as guide.'

'The youth who brought me over.'

'The very one – the Shokburns keep the trade in the family, and pass on the secrets of the sands like something magical. The old man looked as if he was going to take the knowledge to his grave, because he only had a daughter, and women aren't admitted to the secrets. But she obliged with a boy child before the elder Shokburn expired. You could often see the old man in the middle of the bay showing the toddler how to read the sands almost before the child could walk. It used to scare Ellen – his mother – seeing her son perched on the old man's shoulders and the tide roaring in.'

'Ellen?' Falconer wondered why the precentor used her first name in such a familiar way.

'Ellen Shokburn. She works here at the priory.' In response to Falconer's querying look, he expanded. 'Only outside the walls, of course. Though sixty years ago the priory did admit lay sisters into the house. But that was all stopped when Furness Abbey was placed in a position of superiority over us.'

Falconer detected a note of resentment even after so much time in Ralph's reference to the abbot of Furness's power over Conishead. He thought to pursue this line, but Ralph continued with his explanation.

'We are still responsible for the crossing of Leven Sands, and Ellen sometimes takes people over the bay, and carries letters for us. Employing her was one of Ussher's first acts when he was elected prior. Some say the first and last generous act of our good prior. You see, the father of the boy ran off soon after he was born, and she was in need of some means to support him. Ussher gave her work here. If you see her, though, take care. Some say she has the evil eye and bewitched the prior into employing her.'

Falconer looked hard at Ralph, but could not detect whether the monk was being jocular or not. He knew some took the ancient occult power of the evil eye seriously. He had even heard of a man who had run a woman through with a pitchfork, claiming she had cast a spell on him. He had successfully evaded hanging by claiming *quasi se defendendo contra diabolum* – self-defence against the devil. For himself, he scoffed at such superstition.

He shifted uncomfortably on the narrow seat, and eased his long legs under the table. He longed for the space of his own solar back at Aristotle's Hall – never again would he complain it was cramped. Then, in the silence, he heard a creaking sound that appeared to come from the carrel next to the one he and Westerdale were occupying. But when he leaned out to peer through the grillework of the door, he could see no illumination on either side of them. They were still alone.

'If it is de Langetoft that lies in the chapel, who would have had reason to kill him?'

Westerdale continued his nervous picking at the splinters in the table. 'Hmm. If you think that attaining the highest office here is sufficient cause to kill, then our present prior must be suspected. Though I do not believe he did kill de Langetoft –

they were rivals but still close friends. Adam Lutt and John Whitehed were also hoping to be considered. Lutt is the keeper of accounts, and you have seen Whitehed at each of the services. He's the sacrist, the skinny one who tries to anticipate the prior's every move.'

'Did he behave thus with the previous prior? I would have thought it wasn't a very successful way of achieving high office.'

Ralph smiled grimly. 'The brothers didn't think so either.' He paused. 'And then there's Brother Thady, of course. He hates us all as sinners, but he despised John de Langetoft most of all.'

'That's interesting. Why do you think that was?'

Ralph's brows creased in a deep frown, whether trying to recall long-past enmities, or worrying about revealing secrets best kept, Falconer could not tell.

'Who knows what goes on in Thady's mind? The poor soul is demented and should be shut away in some solitary cell for his own good.'

Falconer clearly understood the last words to mean for the good of the other monks at Conishead, but didn't comment.

'It seems that there are several with good reason to have killed de Langetoft.'

'And little chance after fifteen years of discovering just who it might have been,' said Ralph gloomily.

'A difficult task, I grant you. But not an insuperable one. I could spare some time to talk to each of those concerned.'

The precentor leaned over the rim of the bookstand that separated the two men, and hissed at Falconer in surprise. 'You don't mean you are going to try and discover who the murderer was yourself?'

Falconer permitted himself a wry smile. 'I have a certain reputation in Oxford. Indeed, some say I can't resist meddling in matters that do not concern me.'

He was thinking of the former chancellor of the university, Thomas de Cantilupe, who had more than once been exasperated by Falconer's insatiable curiosity when it came to puzzling deaths.

Falconer had proved time and again that the simple application of Aristotelian logic could resolve such practical problems.

'I suppose I should start with the prior.'

'You will have to rise early. He leaves tomorrow before matins to supervise the ironworks on the opposite bank of the Leven, then he'll be going to the fishery at Craik-water.'

Falconer groaned at the thought of another day started before dawn. Noticing this, Ralph made a suggestion.

'The prior will be travelling on horseback, and taking the long route overland. You might catch him up on foot by crossing Leven Sands – and could therefore lie abed until after lauds.'

The final point clinched it for Falconer, and he decided that it would perhaps be interesting to intercept the prior at the ironworks. He would like to see it in operation anyway. He was about to ask Ralph if he could find a guide to take him across the Leven tomorrow when he heard another creaking sound, quickly followed by the snick of a carrel door being closed. It was very close, but by the time he had slid along the bench, disentangling his long legs from under the table, and opened their door, there was no one to be seen. He looked to left and right, but the only movement was that of the light from the farthest carrel drifting across the cloister's slab floor as the candle inside flickered and guttered in the wind. Then behind him there was a soft thud.

Turning sharply round, he saw that the door of the first carrel was swinging to and fro in the same wind that disturbed the candle flame. As he watched, it thudded shut again. He was sure the door had been firmly closed when he and Westerdale had entered the third carrel. Had someone overheard their private conversation, deliberately hiding himself in the darkness?

As darkness fell, Ann Segrim strove to read the last few sentences of her book. Her husband would have been surprised to find that she read anything other than the Bible, let alone this translation of Aristotle's *Metaphysics*. It was a copy loaned her by Falconer, the latest of many works she had consumed voraciously after becoming horrified at her own ignorance: an ignorance revealed at her first encounter with the regent master, and measured in its truly awesome size at their many other meetings. At first she thought that his lending her a book had been to ensure her return. Indeed that may have been the case, the first time. But when she expressed a desire to learn at the second visit, he didn't treat her request with disdain as she had been afraid he would, and had prepared a plan of study equal to that of one of his students. A backward student, perhaps, but one soon showing promise, she liked to think.

'You're the mistress Ann.'

Once again she had been surprised by the quiet arrival of one of the nuns. She blushed and slipped the heavy Aristotle on to the bench beside her, where it was hidden by the table. It would not do for Sister Gwladys to be aware of such profane texts within the walls of Godstow. Before her stood a frail young woman whose Benedictine robes seemed to pin her insubstantial body to the ground. But her thin and angular face bore the glow of someone halfway to heaven, and Ann could imagine her praying every night for release from her earthly confinement. Now, however, there was a cloud across her features that spoiled the otherwise certain nature of her calling. She glanced nervously over her shoulder at the doorway of the library where she had found Ann Segrim sitting. Ann felt a shiver of excitement run through her, sure that at last something was going to be revealed about the death of Sister Eleanor.

Another frustrating day had passed since her conversation with the abbess, and she was none the wiser about the murder. She longed for Falconer's presence, sure that he would know what action to take. But now it would seem that the next step had come to her. Though the abbess had virtually forbidden her to question the nuns, that didn't prevent the nuns from speaking to her. And here was one who, with a little gentling, looked ready to talk. Fortunately Ann could bring her name to mind from the brief introductions that the abbess had conducted on her arrival at Godstow.

'Sister Gilda. Please sit down.'

The nun ignored the offer made by Ann's outstretched hand, as though something stopped her from settling. And Ann's invitation had increased her agitation, as though the conflict of disobeying an older woman added to the disquiet of her already tortured mind. She continued to flit around the silent library like a butterfly in high summer, afraid of being squashed by a heavy hand. She gave another glance at the ominously open door, as though in two minds whether to escape or risk staying. Ann strode purposefully to the door and closed it, leaning against the studded oak. The act of trapping her resolved Gilda's crisis.

'You want to know why Eleanor was . . . why she died?'

The question required no answer. Ann was a little surprised that her purpose had become so obvious, and wondered if Sister Hildegard, the ancient nun present at her interview with the abbess, was as deaf as Gwladys imagined. She had certainly not spoken to anyone else about the murder in such a way as to give the impression she was anything other than a normal corrodian, seeking temporary shelter from a wicked world.

'Why should I concern myself with whatever happened here before I came?'

As soon as she had said it, she could have cut her tongue out. In wishing to play down her involvement, she could risk permanently closing the door to her only avenue of information so far.

'But I thought, when Sister Hildegard told us not to—' Gilda stopped in horror.

'Not to speak to me?'

Gilda's pale face had turned even whiter at her mistake, and her eyes quartered the room in a horror-stricken search for a way out other than the one Ann blocked with her body. If she could arrange to die on the spot and ascend to heaven, Ann felt sure she would. She tried to retrieve the situation.

'You know, I had a younger sister once who broke one of our mother's favourite cooking pots. A poor servant was blamed for my sister's error and whipped. My sister suffered two days of agony before she sought my advice. I told her to confess – that she would feel better for it.'

Something lit up in the child-like nun's eyes. The thought of confession and martyrdom clearly appealed to her. Ann didn't tell her that her spoiled brat of a sister had never admitted the broken pot was her fault. Indeed, it had been her sister who had blamed the poor servant in the first place. It would not do for Gilda to know that some people could lie and cheat with a clear conscience. And get away with it.

'Is there something you want to confess?'

Gilda's eyes now positively glowed in the dark of the chamber. Ann took her arm and led her to the solitary table, sitting her down on the bench. Ann sat next to her and the words tumbled out of her thin lips.

'Eleanor was not observant of the rules. Before Sister Gwladys came she used to deck her robe with ribbons bought by the gatekeeper's son in Oxford. And her family stayed here often before the bishop forbade it. She . . . entertained in her cell.' Her eyes were as round as platters as she listed the horrors of Eleanor's unruly life. 'She didn't like it when Sister Gwladys changed everything, and applied the rules strictly. And there were one or two others who took her side at first. Sister Gwladys punished them.' She spoke the last words with relish, and perhaps a little regret that she could never be so evil as to merit righteous punishment. 'But Eleanor still defied the abbess.'

Ann was shocked. 'Wait. Are you suggesting that . . .?'

Gilda's eyes were now enormous. 'I am afraid that the abbess might have got a little carried away with her punishment.'

Henry Ussher was beginning to think that matters were getting out of hand. He was so perturbed that he had barely been able to get through vespers. He hoped that the others had not noticed the tremor in his voice. But everyone must have heard when the prayer book slipped from his fingers and crashed to the ground. The echoes of the noise still rang around his skull. It was that damned regent master's stare that had unnerved him. After completion of the service, he had hurried off to his rooms, ignoring even Lutt's call asking after his health.

In fact, Lutt presented another problem. He could barely cope with the matter the camerarius had presented him with this very afternoon. Had it really been within the compass of one day that so many disasters had occurred? It had begun with the announcement of the discovery of a body in the bay. Nothing unusual in that — many fools were caught in the tide or by the quicksands. To discover it was the body of de Langetoft had been a blow. He had hoped that fifteen years had wiped away all possibility of his rival's returning to trouble his advancement. Now his bones lay in the chapel in mute accusation. Even that misfortune could have been overcome if the meddling Falconer had not spotted the cross. The prior did not doubt that his actions in taking the cross from the Oxford master would only delay discovery, not prevent it. But he was adept at weaving tales to obscure the truth.

His next step must be to spirit Thady Lamport away, something he should have done long ago. Fifteen years ago, when all this started.

The thin monk's skull-like face creased in perplexity. He could understand the bishop's thesis, expounded by Brother Henry, that 'lux' begat 'lumen' by multiplying a likeness, or 'imago', of itself in all directions without reference to time or space. Much as God created man in his own image. And he knew enough of astronomy to know that the light from the stars affected men differently, just as each celestial sphere affected the lower spheres with its light. What he could not understand, no matter how he tried, was the conflict between Grosseteste's assertion that light was 'inextensa' — unextended in itself — yet propagated itself in straight lines, or extensions.

The tension in his head was building intolerably, and the pain interfered with his visions. He wished that Brother Henry had not drawn him into his affairs. It was the talk of the other brothers that the long friendship between Henry and John had ceased with some acrimony. Now Brother John skulked around the priory muttering that he was going to reveal to superior authority certain ungodly acts of his former friend. Thady had no wish to be caught in the midst of this conflict, but if there were a side to choose, he had good reason to avoid Brother John's.

He groaned as another lightning bolt of pain crackled inside his skull. Brother Henry droned on about how he would set up the experiment, but all Thady could think about was those above, whom he had neglected so of late. The pressure of their insistent thoughts lay like an oppressive stone on the top of his head. He was fearful it would burst.

Fifteen years past, thought Henry. He had been puffed up with pride then, and imagined he could control even a madman like Brother Thady. It had been a sort of bravado not to get rid of him, a show of strength to have him around still. But now there were too many threads to the deceit, and he was a more cautious practical man these days. With Thady out of the way, there would be one less worry. He would deal with it before he left for the ironworks and Craik-water tomorrow.

Since Lutt had entered the picture, the web of lies was becoming ever more tangled. He could do as Lutt asked, but knew that would not be the end of it. No, if he were to advance his career in the church, he would have to make hard decisions sooner or later. Why not start now? If Lutt thought he could manipulate the prior, he was in for a nasty surprise. Outside his window, the darkness of the priory bore down like an unbearable weight as he planned for the morrow. If he had seen what was being enacted below, he would have wished he had acted sooner; but darkness hid the encounter.

It was late and Falconer knew that, if he were to rise early tomorrow, he would need to be abed soon. The archway under the dormitory turned the grey dusk of the cloister into an impenetrable blackness. If he had been strolling the lanes of a gloomy Oxford, he would have been on the alert for the night-walkers' attack, but he little thought to be accosted in the sanctuary of this remote religious establishment. So when he stepped into the dark, and found himself pinned in a vice-like grip, he was too surprised to struggle.

His attacker spun him round, and he was confronted with the staring eyes of Brother Thady Lamport. The monk pressed his face close up to Falconer's and the master smelled the fishy breath that emanated from his mouth.

'There's evil here. You can smell it.'

Falconer refrained from confirming that he could, and that it was Lamport's own fetid exhalations. Close up, the monk's eyes positively sparkled in their deep pits. Falconer could imagine Lamport cowing other souls with his look, but he had encountered too many fanatics himself to be afraid of any of them.

'And destroying my book is going to root it out?'

'All knowledge that is not God's must therefore be the devil's. I have tried to winkle out the evil, but it is too firmly rooted in these walls. The three Counsels of Perfection have been broken, and he who indulged his own pleasures is now placed above us.' He stared meaningfully at the window of the prior's quarters. 'He keeps his secret locked away.'

Falconer did not know what this riddle meant, and before he could ask the cellarer to be more clear Lamport's ravings had moved on.

'We have brought it on ourselves, of course. Because we have failed in our task.'

'And what task is that?'

'To provide the fruits of the earth to those above.'

Falconer was completely lost, not knowing what the monk was saying. He tried to brush Lamport's hands from his shoulders, but the cadaverous man surprised him with the strength of his scrawny arms. His fingers dug into Falconer's flesh through his heavy robe, and Falconer found himself pushed back against the wall, deeper into the darkness. Lamport shook his head in exasperation at the Oxford man's stupidity, and spittle flew from his lips.

'Those from the magic land, who come to us in ships. They sail in the clouds collecting grain and fruits in return for wisdom. Then they return to God, to fill in the book of our lives. We have ignored them – you have ignored them, with your petty little pursuits. Your games of logic and rhetoric.'

Falconer saw that Thady was quite mad. In his head lay cluttered a jumble of ancient lore mixed with Lamport's own version of the Christian faith. Falconer recalled cloud-ships from his youth. He remembered his own grandfather swearing that he had seen an anchor let down from one, and grappled to a fence. The rope attached to the anchor had pulled taut, as though the invisible ship was attempting to pull free. But the anchor was caught fast. Eventually a sailor had descended the rope going up into the sky, and tried to release the anchor. But before he could do so, the man died, suffocating in the lower earth's thick air. His grandfather swore he knew where the cloud-sailor's grave was, though he had never taken the young Falconer to see it. He even recalled the name his grandfather had given to the magic land the ships sailed in. Magonia.

Falconer's thoughts suddenly returned to the little drawing in the library catalogue. Was Lamport's drawing of a monk being stabbed connected to the death of de Langetoft? Perhaps by humouring Lamport now, he would be able to discover if it was there more than just by coincidence. Perhaps Lamport had actually seen something.

'Was John de Langetoft taken by the cloud-ships?'

The mention of that name stopped Brother Thady in his tracks. His sparkling eyes narrowed, and retracted deeper into his skull. For a moment he held his breath, then he exhaled his fish-breath all over Falconer in a rictus of laughter. He positively brayed, and his hands fell off Falconer's shoulders.

'Taken? De Langetoft got what he deserved. I was there. He was killed by a demon.'

Chapter Seven

For most of the monks at Conishead Priory, the following morning was like the one before and the one before that. Latest in a long and comforting procession of days that would lead inevitably to the Final Judgement. Matins was followed by lauds which preceded prime in a succession of devotions that obviated any need for dangerous and original thought. For a few, deviation from the routines of the priory heralded danger as threatening as an unexpected change in the sands of Lancaster Bay. One incautious step and all would be lost.

Adam Lutt sat impatiently through prime, aware that the prior had sent for Thady Lamport as soon as everyone had risen. Now the cellarer was nowhere to be seen – and it was odd for him to miss the services. His madness drove him to greater devotion, not lesser. Back in the corner of the dorter he used as his office, Adam fiddled with a copy of the recent circular letter to all clergy from the King and Papal Legate. It reminded clerics that the King's tithes to cover the next three years were now owed. Moreover it demanded the sum of 30,000 marks for the restoration of the King's dignity, owing to the fact that the Legate would claim the aforementioned tithes to pay Prince Edward's debts in Sicily, Apulia and Calabria. The figure was outrageous, and though there were other demands in the letter it was the money that Adam had to concern himself with. But he could not concentrate, not while John Whitehed, the sacrist, had still not returned from whatever mission had taken him away from the priory the previous day. The prior himself was absent, but then he had long ago arranged to visit the ironworks on the far side of the Leven, and the priory's fisheries at Craik-water. The circular journey would take him all day, and required an early start.

Still Lutt felt uncomfortable that the prior, the sacrist, and the cellarer were all out of his sight, even for a day. Most of all he worried about the cellarer, who had no reason to be absent. Lutt hated not knowing everything that was happening in Conishead. Knowing everything was how he had survived in a position of power for so long. There had been too much uncertainty of late – he had even had to change the location of his little treasures for fear of discovery. Now, at the very last minute, Brother Paul had delivered the message that he was to attend to the monies being spent at the ironworks immediately. Paul said it was a summons from the prior, but, if so, why had the latter not arranged for the camerarius to travel with him today? It all seemed so irregular, and Adam Lutt disliked irregularity. As he was unsure of the route across the bay on foot, he decided to take a horse and go round the long way. Even if he missed the prior, he supposed that the ironmaster would know what it was all about. At least he was sure that that interfering, but slothful, Regent Master Falconer was still safely abed.

In fact, Falconer was already up and, much to his own surprise, reasonably alert. He had adopted the routine of the priory quite quickly, and though he didn't attend matins and lauds he had woken at dawn. The icy cold water in the water-butt outside the guest house had contributed much to his state of alertness. His face still tingled from its vigorous immersion in the butt. He had slipped out of the postern gate while the inmates of the priory were in the chapter house, and now made his way to the banks of the Leven. There he had agreed to meet the guide Ralph Westerdale had said he would arrange for him.

For once, the sky was clear and birds sang from the trees that surrounded the priory. It was cold, but, wrapped in a monk's woollen travelling cloak that Westerdale had obtained for him, Falconer was glad to be abroad. He felt that he had thrown off a shroud of oppression that hung over him within the priory walls. Inside there was no privacy, and it seemed to him that everyone's very thoughts were known to everyone else. And to a man who thrived on original thinking that was very unsafe. He wondered if the murderer of John de Langetoft was known already to the monks. Had been known from the first day. He could not imagine that anyone could keep a secret inside the walls of Conishead. Perhaps he was the only one not in the secret.

Standing at the bank of the Leven, seeing the sun reflected in sparkling points of light from the receding waters of the bay, he laughed at his own sick imaginings. The gloom of the priory was having an effect on him, and he was determined to throw it off. He thought of Oxford and the perpetually optimistic procession of students that had passed through his hands. Then inevitably he imagined Ann Segrim, sitting comfortably in her manor house at Botley, with the walls of Oxford visible from the upper room she used so much. In his mind he heard her tinkling laughter, especially the peal which had come when he told her he was entering a monastery. He laughed himself now, envying her comfort.

'It's not often I hear laughter in these parts.'

It was a woman's voice, and for a moment Falconer imagined that his thoughts of Ann had created her in the flesh. But the woman who stood at the end of the narrow track that led down to the water's edge was smaller, and dark-haired. Her face was tanned brown, like so many in these parts, and the creases of a hard working life spread from the corners of her eyes and mouth. Yet her looks were well formed, and Falconer could imagine her turning a few heads when she was younger. Still only of middle years, she would have been more attractive now if it weren't for the veil of coldness that hung over her eyes. The eyes, thought Falconer, that were claimed to cast spells. Looking at her, he felt sure it had not been occult powers that attracted men to her in years past. The words she had uttered were spoken softly, but Falconer knew there would be a hard edge to her conversation. This woman had struggled to survive.

He realized he had been gazing rather long at her. But she had returned his gaze unflinchingly and he knew his assessment of her was true.

'You are to be my guide across the Leven, I would guess.'

'You guess rightly.'

She offered nothing more about herself, and when Falconer showed no signs of moving she turned and made off the way she had come, throwing a comment over her shoulder. 'You'd better stir yourself before the tide returns.'

Falconer grunted in acknowledgement and set off in her footsteps. He was slowly realizing that the inhabitants of these parts had an imposed routine as tyrannical as that of the monastery. Only this one was imposed by nature and the ebb and flow of the tide: in its own way as inexorable as the demands of worship for the monks. They stepped on to the oozing mud of the estuary and Falconer put his guess at his guide's identity to the test.

'You must be Ellen Shokburn. Your son Jack guided me over Lancaster Bay recently.'

Once again he got no response other than a grunt. He assumed it was one of acknowledgement, and they both trudged on in silence until Falconer attempted to begin the failed conversation again.

'Have you guided many across these sands?'

The woman snorted. 'Don't be afraid. I know what I'm doing – I've done this since I was a child. Just because I'm a woman it doesn't mean I'm useless.'

Falconer was sure this sharp, hard-working woman was anything but useless. 'A pity then that your father didn't teach you the secrets of Lancaster Bay. You might have been able to save the poor soul whose bones have just been brought to the priory.'

Ellen walked on a few paces before she replied. 'If he tried to cross without my father's help, he has only got himself to blame.'

Remembering that her father had been suspected of the death of John de Langetoft, Falconer wondered how she might respond if he said the bones had been identified. It was worth trying.

'A monk went missing some years back – it could be him.'

The woman stopped in her tracks, and stared coldly at Falconer. He tried the name on her.

'His name was John . . .'

'John de Langetoft.' Ellen spoke the name, but there was nothing but coolness in her eyes. If her father had murdered the monk, she either didn't know the truth or was well able to hide her fears. 'Looks as if the weather could break up soon.' She pointed to the mouth of the river, startling Falconer by the sudden change in subject.

He peered short-sightedly past the blur of Harlesyde Island that shimmered in the haze rising from the retreating waters around it. He could see nothing.

'There – out to sea. There's bad weather brewing.'

Falconer was not sure, but he thought he could discern the faintest wisp of darkness low down over the furthest edge of the sea. Her eyes must have been truly sharp to spot it.

'It should not bother us, should it?'

The woman hissed at his lack of understanding of the world he occupied.

'It will be on us with the returning tide.'

Another man of book-learning who did not know how to read nature, she thought. Mid-winter Mass-day had fallen on a Monday, and Ellen knew as surely as the next incoming tide that it betokened a tempestuous spring, and death amongst women and kings. She felt borne down by the weight of her fatalism, and sighed. One could only live from day to day, and accept the will of God.

At the shoreline, she stopped and pointed out the way to the ironworks to Falconer. 'When did you intend to make your return?'

'I'm not sure. I have to speak to the prior at the ironworks. How far is that from here?'

'With the time it takes to get there and back, you will not have long at the ironworks or you will miss the tide. I will wait until the last moment to cross and no longer. If the weather worsens, we should not try to cross at all.'

Falconer peered back across the estuary, and tried to figure out where they had crossed. If the woman was not here on his return, could he make the crossing on his own? He wondered what he should do, if he were trapped on this bank for the night. Turning to ask her if there were shelter near, he realized Ellen Shokburn had gone without making a sound.

At the moment Falconer found himself alone on the shores of Leven Sands, John Whitehed, the sacrist, was making his return across the larger and infinitely more treacherous Lancaster Bay. His guide was Ellen Shokburn's son, Jack. The youth was only a stripling, still to fill out into manhood. But he knew the secrets of the sands, taught him by his grandfather, and he strode confidently from one leafy twig of a marker to another. Whitehed trudged behind him, damp soaking into the habit that he carelessly let trail on the wet sands. He was downcast, and his trip to Hest Bank had not raised his spirits. Usually, when he saw Isobel, he returned happy that she was still safe and sound, and anxious for his next opportunity to see her. That it all came at a cost disturbed his conscience, but it was worth it.

Or had been until that fat weasel Lutt had poked his nose into his affairs. Now the price had risen, and Whitehed wondered if it were too high. He had seen off one attempt to use his secret against him many years ago; perhaps now the time had come to do the same again.

'Take care, sacrist.'

The youth's voice came like a knell to Whitehed, and at first he thought he had been thinking out loud. The very idea sent shivers coursing through him. But then he realized Shokburn was warning him about a sandy gully in the long, spiky grass they were traversing. In his reverie, Whitehed had virtually reached the shores of Humphrey Head without realizing it. And his inattention had led him off the path that his guide had been making. It was only when Jack looked back that he had seen the sacrist heading for a slimy pit hidden by the high grasses. His warning cry was just in time and Whitehed, waving his arm in acknowledgement, turned back on to the right track. He was also now sure which track he had to take for his own safety.

The way along the shoreline was easy for Falconer to follow. It was a well-trodden path that afforded glimpses through the trees of the secluded inlet of the River Leven. Falconer would have expected to see and hear abundant wildfowl in such a spot, but the whole stretch of silty mud either side of the stream was devoid of life as if abandoned by God. The water itself appeared dull brown and turbid. Then, as he rounded a bend in the river, he heard it. The same heavy thud-thud-thud that he had heard near Harlesyde Island on his arrival. It drove the air before it in regular gusts, oppressive and deadening. As on the first occasion, Falconer was put in mind of the heartbeat of some monstrous beast that roamed the estuary. He was walking towards the sound, and his own heart matched rhythm with the beat. Thud, thud, thud, thud.

Suddenly he was out of the trees, and into an unnatural glade made hideous by the hand of man. Everywhere he looked stumps of trees thrust out of the churned-up soil. It was as if the monster, whose heartbeat was now louder still and pressing on his ears, had torn up the woods in a frenzy. Advancing across the wasteland, he realized the picture in his mind was not far from the truth.

The river bank took an abrupt right turn at this point and

above him, on the edge of the glade, was a hive of human activity. Long tables piled high with stones stretched down the side of the river, which at this point flowed narrow and swift. A series of waterwheels drove massive hammers down on to the stones shattering them into chips. These were the nodding heads of his monster, served by scurrying human forms dressed in rags. The dust-covered men hurried to supply coarse stones to the altars of the trip-hammers, and then sweep away the crushed ore. Youths with baskets carried the ore to pits lower down where they tipped it into the maw of the roasting ovens. Sweat-soaked men, as red in the face as their comrades on the trip-hammers were pale with dust, served the fiery blaze that burned below the bowl-furnaces. It was a scene from hell – the ironworks of Conishead Priory.

A harassed-looking man, his face red and his rough tunic spotted with burn holes, scurried over to him.

'What do you want?'

He gave the impression that whatever Falconer wanted, he would see that he did not get it. Falconer dealt with him as he would anyone full of their own importance. He ignored him, and strolled across to the wooden shelters lining the edge of the site. Their interiors were lit by the red glow of two forges, and at each a beefy-armed smith plied his trade, shaping the iron bloom that had come from the last firing of the bowl-furnaces. Their hammers pealed in counterpoint – a living sound which contrasted sharply with the thud of the ore-breakers that still pounded away. In the corner of the shelter lay a pile of nails, chains and the makings of hinges and heavy locks.

'Can you tell me where the prior is?' he asked of one of the smiths as the man returned the half-shaped lump of iron he was working on to the forge. The man didn't bother looking at him to see who was asking. He simply pointed with his hammer to a path running down the side of the shelter. It was guarded by the red-faced man, who was even redder at Falconer's disdain. This time the regent master could not ignore him, but a penetrating stare was all that was necessary to establish who was in control. Grumbling under his breath, the man stood aside, and Falconer followed the path upstream.

Eventually he came to a second clearing in the woods, where trees had been felled. In this smaller glade stood a well-groomed horse that obviously belonged to someone of power. The prior must be hereabouts. There was a huddle of figures on the far side of the glade, standing around another bowl-furnace. It was smaller than the ones lined up at the main ironworks, but halfway across the glade Falconer could already feel the heat of the fire that stoked it. There was a curious hissing sound followed at intervals by a roar, and Falconer was put in mind again of a tethered monster. Suddenly excited voices broke out over the noise, and the group was suffused with an unearthly glow. It took all of Falconer's scientific resolve to approach and observe for himself before succumbing to panic.

At his approaching footsteps the men turned, a look of annoyance on their faces. It was Henry Ussher who recovered first, and spoke.

'Regent Master, you arrive at a fortuitous moment. Llewellyn the Welshman here has wrought a small miracle.'

The short, dark-complexioned man at the prior's side cast his eyes to the ground in embarrassment, muttering something in his own tongue.

'Come and look.' The invitation was from Ussher, and he motioned for Falconer to look in the top of the bowl-furnace. Llewellyn lifted the heavy lid invitingly. He walked over to it and peered in, expecting to see a glowing lump of iron bloom sitting among base clinker, for that was what a furnace normally produced. In its stead was a white-hot, spitting liquid. Ussher leaned over his side for another look as the liquid rapidly cooled, leaving a black scum on the top.

'The red haematite hereabouts is particularly good. The means of making charcoal is plentiful. And Llewellyn has contrived to melt the ore to a liquid.'

Falconer could immediately see the benefit of this process over the normal one which produced a lump of iron that needed re-smelting and re-heating to work it. His question as to how this miracle was achieved was answered by the prior's dragging him round the back of the furnace to see a huge set of bellows linked by cogs and axles to a waterwheel, which was driven by the same river that fed power into the trip-hammers lower down.

'Water-powered bellows,' explained the prior. 'They drive the heat of the furnace up to the correct temperature for liquefaction. Llewellyn had seen it done, and swore to me he could reproduce it here. He has been proved right. But take care – the molten ore is extremely dangerous.'

Both he and Falconer stepped back to allow the ironsmith to continue the process. With long tongs the Welshman pulled a plug in the side of the furnace and the glowing iron poured into a channel below it. The iron, already thickening as it cooled, filled a long, narrow mould of wet sand. There it crackled and subsided.

'Now you have seen enough of our little secret. What brings you to the ironworks?'

He led Falconer out of the glade, and back down the track to the main part of the works. His groom followed with the prior's horse at a respectful distance. With a glance of regret over his shoulder at the mechanical marvel, hidden in woods at the edge of the world, Falconer dissembled at first. 'I am afraid I found being cooped up within the walls of the priory a little . . . constricting. I decided to stretch my legs.'

The prior was not fooled. 'Across Leven Sands, which would have required a guide, and out to here where I happened to be? When there are plenty of safe paths leading in the opposite direction not requiring planning ahead?'

Falconer smiled and Ussher answered for him. 'You wanted to speak to me informally outside the priory, where we might not be overheard.'

Falconer nodded, and the prior continued. 'And I know what you wanted to talk about. John de Langetoft.'

Was the prior about to be open with him? Or was this approach merely the ruse of a devious man? Falconer could not decide, but let Ussher speak anyway. He would make up his mind later as to whether he was being given the truth.

'As soon as I saw the cross I knew the bones were those of de Langetoft.'

'Then why try to hide the identity from everyone else by taking the cross, and not admitting its existence when Martin Albon was examining the remains?'

A wry smile crossed the prior's features. 'Fear, I suppose. De Langetoft was a rival for the post of prior fifteen years ago, and I was immediately afraid that the community would revive the rumours that circulated then about my doing away with him.'

Falconer was sure that simple fear was something this man never felt, but let him go on.

'Of course, when there was no body in evidence, the rumours soon died and my appointment was confirmed. It was assumed that de Langetoft had fled for reasons of his own. Now a body has, quite literally, surfaced, I suppose my first reaction was to try and cover up its identity to prevent those rumours arising again. Now is the wrong time for me to be under any suspicion.'

He didn't expand on his last statement, leaving Falconer to assume that preferment was in the wind for Henry Ussher.

'I now realize what I did was foolish, and, if anything, likely to throw more suspicion on me. Have you told anyone yet about the cross?'

Falconer said he hadn't and the prior nodded. 'Good. As soon as we return, I will confirm the identity of the remains myself. It will be better coming from me than you, I think.'

He went to mount his horse, and wrapped the cloak offered him by his groom round his long frame. A chill wind blew across the open site and dark clouds scudded over the face of the sun. Suddenly Falconer felt cold. The prior looked down at him and suggested he return quickly by the estuary route.

'The weather looks as though it is worsening, and you will find it swifter on foot across the Leven. I and my entourage are moving on to the fishery, and will have to return the long way round to get the horses back. It would not be proper for the prior of Conishead to be seen to be inspecting his lands on foot.'

He laughed and wheeled his horse away from where Falconer stood. With another glance up at the darkening sky, the regent master hurried off along the path he had come. His last view of the ironworks was of Henry Ussher leaning down out of his saddle to talk to the red-faced man, who had taken a dislike to Falconer. They were both looking in his direction.

Adam Lutt knew he was too late to speak to the prior when he arrived in the churned-up clearing that was the ironworks. There were no horses, except the one he had ridden in on. And the air of frenzied activity that would have prevailed when the prior was inspecting the work was lacking. In fact there was hardly any work in progress. The ore-dressers sat on their upturned baskets, casting incurious eyes in his direction. His presence clearly did not warrant their putting in a semblance of work. The only sounds were the ringing tones of the smiths in their shelter. Even the heavy trip-hammers, which could sometimes be heard from the priory, were stilled. From the path that ran up the side of the shelter emerged the ironmaster and that damned Welshman the prior was so fond of. They were deep in conversation, until the ironmaster, known only by his title and not by any name, spotted Lutt. Breaking off, he strolled across the clearing as though the camerarius was of no importance. This made Lutt angry, and he hoped the money matter that the prior wanted him to examine would embarrass the red-faced man.

Lutt remained astride his horse, to have the advantage of

height over the ironmaster. 'Ironmaster, why aren't these men working? We pay them enough.'

The ironmaster's full lips curled in contempt at the uninformed comment. 'Can't you see there's a storm brewing?'

Lutt's retort was sharp. 'They can work in a blizzard for all I care. Set them to work immediately.'

The ironmaster insolently stood his ground. 'I would make them work, if it were worth it. But when it rains the furnaces go out. And when the furnaces go out there's no need to feed the bowls with ore. No ore needed, no crushing needed — simple as that.'

Having given Lutt this basic lesson in ironmaking, he turned his back on the camerarius and walked over to the idle workers. Lutt swung down from his horse, swiftly closed the gap between himself and the ironmaster, and grabbed the man's arm. He stuck his face in the other's and hissed a warning. 'I am here on the prior's business. To see how you spend our money.'

The ironmaster looked truly puzzled. 'He said nothing of that when he was here. What's it all about?'

As Lutt did not know, he was nonplussed for a moment. The silence between the two men was broken by the hiss of rain, and suddenly everyone was making for shelter. The workers melted into the forest and back to their ramshackle hovels. It was as if they were made of clay and had been washed away by the downpour. Even the ironmaster followed them, ignoring Lutt, who stood for a moment in the rain before making for the cover of the smithy. Underneath the sloping roof, he moved close to the fires that had been abandoned by the smiths. They still retained their warmth, and Lutt, pulling his cloak about him, glumly resigned himself to a long wait. The prior's instructions would have to be carried out another time.

The hiss of the rain on the shelter's roof must have caused him to doze off, because he suddenly woke up in the dark. The coals in the forge had long turned ashy and grey, and he was stiff with cold. Suddenly, he was alert to a sound outside the hut.

Thinking the ironmaster had perhaps returned, he put a stern look on his face and turned to face the low opening. When he saw who it was, he was surprised.

'What are you doing here?'

The rain also delayed Falconer. He had to shelter under the imperfect cover of a blighted oak, and had endured an eternity of cold water dripping down the back of his neck. By the time the rain had stopped, and he had reached the bank of the Leven where he was to be met by Ellen Shokburn, he was cold and miserable. Moreover it was later than he had hoped. He thought he heard a rustle in the undergrowth near to him, but when he called out there was no reply. Even the birds seemed stilled, as they had been higher up the river by the noxious presence of the ironworks. There was no sign of his guide.

Peering cautiously at the expanse of glistening sands, he was sure he could make out the opposite bank, even though there was a mist crawling upriver from the sea. The incoming tide was nowhere in sight, and he considered the options available to him. He could take the chance of crossing on his own, or stay here overnight and die of the chills. In his wet condition, he reckoned there was no choice but to cross. After all, he thought he could remember the route, which was a straight crossing, unlike the zigzag journey across Lancaster Bay. Keeping his short-sighted gaze on a prominent ash on the opposite bank, he stepped out on to the mud.

It seemed simple until he realized that the mist was thickening. His marker on the opposite bank kept disappearing and reappearing. Then it was gone altogether. The mist that lapped around him was chill and dank, and he shivered. He told himself not to panic, and stood still for a moment, peering at where he thought his goal lay. For a moment he was sure he saw the ash tree looming out of the mist. He tried to fix the position in his mind's eye, and strode purposefully towards it.

It was almost with relief that he found himself stumbling into knee-high water. This was surely the River Leven — he had only to cross it and keep straight on and he would be home safe. He lifted the skirts of his robe and stepped further into the icy waters. He was immediately confused for he could not tell which way the water was flowing. At first it seemed to tug at his legs from right to left, like the river flowing out to sea. But then it appeared to drag the other way. Was this the incoming tide trapping him in mid-crossing? He must make a decision about what to do.

Suddenly the air above him was rent with the tolling of a ship's bell. Were Thady Lamport's mad ravings about Magonia true after all? He heard a splash behind him and imagined a cloud-ship had dropped its anchor. Then he laughed. He was a scientist, and cloud-ships were nonsense dreamed up centuries ago by the superstitious. He was just disorientated by the mist. Even so, he was still in grave danger, if not from the cloud-sailors, then from the very real threat of the incoming tide. He hitched his robes up and waded through the water that had now risen to his thighs. There was another splash behind him, and, as he turned, the cloud-ship's anchor hit him squarely on the skull and he fell into a pit of darkness.

TERCE

Thou hast rescued me from death,
To walk in thy presence, in the light of life.

Psalm 56

Chapter Eight

They met on the river bank on the Port Meadow side, making it seem like a chance encounter. The attractive, mature woman with hair the colour of straw, and the bent-backed old ruffian – it was an unlikely tryst. Ann Segrim had gained the permission of Sister Gwladys to leave the nunnery at Godstow, but had not told her she was meeting the constable of Oxford. He had been summoned by her surreptitious message sent through the agency of the gatekeeper at Godstow. They walked together in silence until they were out of sight of the nunnery. As they strolled along the crumbling bank, the soft earth of the water meadow squelched under their feet, and Ann lifted the hem of her gown clear of it. She was wondering how to pass on what the nervous little sister had spoken of the previous day, when Peter Bullock broke the silence.

'I got your message.' It seemed a foolish thing to say, for here he was on Port Meadow. But he was unsure how to coax Ann into talking about what it was that perturbed her. 'The gatekeeper's son brought it – I wonder how many secret liaisons he has been instrumental in arranging. No doubt a lucrative little sideline for him.'

Ann snorted. 'No longer. The abbess has the nunnery guarded and sealed as tightly as the convocation that elects the Pope.'

She cast a worried glance at Bullock, still not sure of her course. But the honest, open face she saw convinced her that the constable would be able to separate gossip and truth.

'There is a rumour that the abbess was . . . too severe with

Sister Eleanor. That she was punishing her for her errant ways, and went too far.'

Bullock frowned, and looked unconvinced. Ann almost regretted speaking out.

'You think I'm foolish to believe it,' she said flatly.

'What I think is that it is possible. But if I learned anything at all in the interrogations I was allowed to carry out, it was that there was resentment of the abbess's strictness on the part of some of the nuns. Some had enjoyed a comfortable life before she arrived, entertaining their families . . . and men who claimed to be their cousins, but bore no family resemblance. If you know what I mean.'

He stared hard at Ann to emphasize his point. With unwanted daughters sent to a nunnery often against their will, a genuine vocation to serve God was not always present. So a lack of desire to observe the rules, especially celibacy, was not uncommon. Ann knew what the constable meant.

They stopped at a bend in the river, now that the nunnery on the opposite bank was hidden behind a belt of trees. Momentarily free of the stifling atmosphere of the place, Ann wanted just to give it all up, and return to her home. With her husband Humphrey somewhere in the north about his own business, it was even more appealing than usual. His appetite for becoming involved in conspiracies had grown again, despite almost costing him his life the last time. But if it kept him out of her hair, she cared but little.

She watched as a youth poled a flat-bottomed barge up the shallow reach of the river. The water plopped monotonously against the barge's flat prow as it was forced upstream. Each time the youth slipped the pole into the water, it grounded with a crunch on the gravel bed of the river. Then he had to strain every sinew to push against the pole, moving the barge a little further upstream each time. Watching its progress, she understood that her search for the truth was a little like pushing against the river's flow. If this youth could stick at his task, and deliver whatever he had loaded in the barge, so could she. And she had promised to help Bullock. Anyway, she could not bear the thought of Falconer returning to be told she had failed to solve a simple murder in an enclosed nunnery.

Bullock almost read her mind. 'Think how Falconer would approach it. Collect all the truths you can, and compare them to uncover the greater truth. Don't turn a deaf ear to anything.'

Ann thought of Falconer safely ensconced in his remote priory at the edge of the world, and had a sudden inspiration. She kissed the startled Bullock on his leathery cheek. 'Peter, you're a genius.'

The world spun him round in circles, and he could not tell which way was up. The greyness of the water mingled indistinguishably with the greyness of the mist as he tumbled along. He was too weak to regain his feet, and didn't even know if there was solid ground on which to put them. Through the mist he thought he heard the sound of a slowly tolling bell. Was there truly a cloud-ship somewhere, and was he bobbing in the sky-waters of Thady Lamport's Magonia? He was struck in the middle of the back by something hard and sharp. It almost knocked the breath out of him, and he cried out. But he was so numbed with cold that he hardly felt any pain. He cried out again, not really believing that anyone could hear him in this unreal land. The bell stopped, or had he just imagined the ringing in the first place? The cold of both water and air sucked the life out of him, and his mind was drifting into oblivion when suddenly something grabbed hold of him. His relentless tumbling was arrested, and he was being lifted upwards effortlessly, as though he was no weight at all. Were the cloud-sailors hauling him into their ship, or was his dying mind playing tricks on him? He blacked out again.

Ralph Westerdale wished now that he had not provided the Oxford master with such an unreliable guide as Ellen Shokburn.

He knew she frequently crossed the Leven Sands to carry out her tasks at the priory. But could a woman truly be relied on? The secrets of crossing Lancaster Bay were passed on to the Shokburn men in each generation, excluding the women. Perhaps she had led Falconer into some gully even on the less dangerous Leven Sands. He certainly was not in his room in the guest house, and it was now night.

All the other monks had retired to their dormitory, but Ralph was still awake. He sat in his office, checking the catalogue to keep his mind off the missing master. He turned the pages of the loan records, the thick parchment crackling in his fingers. He came again to the missing page, and drew his finger down the sharp edge of what remained. What had there been of significance on that page? The entries went back a number of years – back to Brother Thady's time, if the records either side were to be believed. Maybe something else had been written there? He racked his brain to try to recall anything unusual in the records he had taken over from his predecessor. There was nothing that he could remember.

It was the sound of sandals slapping on stone that woke him up, and made him realize he had once again dozed off over his precious catalogue. He crossed the room and poked his head out of the door, expecting to see his brother monks processing to the church for matins. But it was still dark, and there was no sound. Not morning, then – he could not have been asleep for very long. He tiptoed into the cloisters to see who was the owner of the footsteps that had woken him. Who, besides himself, had not retired for the night. There was no one. He was about to turn back to his office, assuring himself that he had imagined the noise, when he heard a creak. That sound was familiar to him – it was the door of the west book press. He had asked Brother Paul several times to deal with the faulty hinge, but it had never been done. Now someone was opening the press in the middle of the night. Which was impossible, as Ralph had the only key.

Then suddenly he saw the flicker of a candle in the opposite corner of the cloister from where he stood. Someone was indeed near the presses. Casting caution to the wind, he scuttled round the cloister only to see that his noisy arrival had disturbed the mystery man. The candle lay snuffed out at his feet, and the door to the west press was ajar. He peered cautiously round the jamb, but there was no one inside. The books were stacked on their shelves as they should be, and there was nowhere to hide within the little room. A sound off to his right caused him to spin round, and he thought he saw a shape disappearing under the dormitory arch. He hitched his robes up, called out and ran as fast as his short legs could carry him. But when he got to the arch, it was the same as when he had chased the elusive Brother Thady. There was no one in sight, and whoever had fled could have gone a number of different ways.

Disconsolate, he trudged back to the open door of the west book press, and looked inside. In the gloom he could make out little — the stacks of books seemed to be as tidy as he had left them. Perhaps he had disturbed the thief before he could take anything. But to be certain he would have to check all the records tomorrow, comparing the numbered books with the catalogue, and the list of those works that were loaned to the brothers. It would be a massive task, but one he was resigned to. Knowing that certain books were already missing, he must be sure if anything else had gone. The presence of the Oxford master made his task all the more pressing. If he knew what was lost, he could at least fake some loan records for the relevant books, and hope Falconer did not pursue the matter. He shuddered at the thought of lying to the man, but that was infinitely less worrisome than the thought that the book thief had to be one of his fellow brothers.

He closed the heavy door to the book press, and locked it — though that seemed a pointless gesture now. If someone else held a key, he no longer had control over the very valuable books that lay within. The only recourse was to pretend that this lock was broken, and ask the prior if the ironworks could supply a new one. As he began to retrace his steps, something crunched under his sandal. Bending down, he rubbed his hand over the normally smooth surface of the cloister flagstones. He felt something coarse under his palm, and on closer inspection realized that it was grains of sand. Whoever his thief was had been down to the shore recently.

Falconer came to in a gloomy chamber lit by the fitful flickering of a single tallow lamp. He sat up, throwing aside the bearskin under which he lay, and, as he could feel no motion, assumed he was not on board a cloud-ship after all. The stone-flagged floor and solid walls confirmed that he was very much in the real world and on terra firma. What dragged him back into his previous nightmare, however, was the continued tolling of that bell. It came from somewhere above his head. He got to his feet, still groggy from the blow he had taken on the back of his skull. He felt it gingerly — there was an egg-sized lump there already. Looking down at himself he saw that he was dressed in an ornate robe with elaborate patterns picked out in golden thread, only slightly dulled with age. Definitely nothing from his own wardrobe. His feet were clad in the softest of leather slippers. Perhaps this was heaven and he was dead after all.

He crossed to the narrow window arch opposite the bed were he had been lying. Looking out, he could detect the last roiling threads of mist drifting away from the smooth surface of the water that sparkled in the moonlight. He was in a tower, and the water surrounded it as far as he could tell. Then, drifting over the still surface of the water, he heard a thudding sound. Was it the steady beat of the trip-hammers up at the ironworks, or his own heart pounding? For a while it ebbed and flowed, and then was gone. He was not really sure if he had heard it at all. Looking round the room again, he saw through an arch the bottom steps of a staircase. He went over, and peered upwards. The stairs spiralled away above his head, and the sound of the bell was closer though a little muffled. He climbed the steps, feeling his way along the rough wall with his left hand.

Higher up, a yellowish light spilled down the spiral, getting brighter as he proceeded. As his eyes came level with the top step, he was confronted with one of the strangest sights he had ever encountered. At first he thought he saw a legless, eyeless apparition with one long arm that pulled incessantly on a rope. Then he realized it was a man like himself, sitting cross-legged in Eastern fashion on the cold floor of the tiny room. He also had two arms — the one not pulling on the bell-rope was hidden underneath the longest beard Falconer had ever seen. It flowed from the apparition's bowed head, down over his chest, and into his lap. All Falconer could see was the top of his head, which was covered in a mass of white hair that blended in with the white of the splendid whiskers.

The tolling stopped, and slowly the man raised his head. Buried deep in the thatch of hair was a pair of red, rheumy eyes that spoke of unspeakable horror endured. What was visible of the face was pale, the skin hanging in folds. The toothless mouth opened, and the words seemed to creak as they came out. It was as if the man was unused to employing the human attribute of speech.

'You are well?'

'Glad to be alive, and to be able to feel pain. I presume it is to you I owe my salvation.'

'Your salvation is something I have not yet striven for. However, it was I who pulled you out of the Leven.'

Despite his obvious years, the man rose effortlessly to his feet, uncurling his legs in one fluid motion. He was dressed in a coarse grey tunic, his legs bare and sinewy. Falconer wondered if the sumptuous robe he wore was the old man's only other item of clothing. He was tall, taller than Falconer even, and his presence filled the little bell-tower.

'My name is Fridaye de Schipedham. Welcome to Harlesyde Island.'

*

As Falconer was stranded on the island until the tide retreated, he and de Schipedham sat together in the lowest chamber of the tower in front of a fire that Falconer suspected the hermit had laid especially for his visitor. He did not seem the sort of man who resorted to the self-indulgence of warmth and comfort, even on a winter's night. The glow of the flames temporarily gave a natural pinkness to de Schipedham's pallid face. He stared into the fire with dull eyes as he explained how he had heard Falconer's cries from the bell-tower. Temporarily abandoning his task of tolling the bell that warned it was unsafe to cross the sands, he had quartered the rocks below until he had come across Falconer, more dead than alive. He made little of the task of dragging Falconer up from the rocks to this tower, but the Oxford master knew it must have been no mean feat, especially for a man of advanced years. He described how he had stripped off Falconer's soaking black gown, and wrapped him in the only other warm robe available – his own – and buried him under the thick bearskin for warmth.

'It was then up to you whether you lived or died,' was the hermit's lugubrious prognosis. Fortunately for Falconer his constitution was strong, and although he still felt chilled to the bone he was sure he would recover from his immersion. Curious about de Schipedham, he asked where the robe that warmed his frame had come from. Fridaye focused those pain-filled eyes on Falconer.

'From a Saracen.'

'You killed him?'

'No. Nasir-Daoud, Prince of Kerak, was my friend.'

The strange statement hung in the air for what seemed an age, until de Schipedham exhaled a great breath, and continued. 'In my youth I joyously went on Crusade under the banner of my Order, the Hospital of St John of Jerusalem.'

A Hospitaller. And a Crusader.

'It was the Sixth Crusade, and the Emperor Frederick and the Pope were squabbling between themselves. In Outremer, however, the Hospitallers still knew who their enemies were supposed to be, and I revelled in the killing. But then at a little skirmish at Napoulous, I was captured and held hostage. The problem was, no one came to ransom me. Of the twenty years I spent in the Holy Land, fifteen were in captivity.'

Falconer marvelled as the old man told his story. The Sixth Crusade had been instigated forty years earlier, yet here was someone who spoke of it as if it were yesterday. He spoke of Pope Gregory and Emperor Frederick – the direst of enemies, yet on the same side – as if they lived. To Falconer they were only half-remembered shades.

As dawn broke, and poked a fitful shaft of light into the chamber, de Schipedham spoke of his captivity. He talked of being seduced by the Saracen ways, and by one of their women in particular. He broke his vow of celibacy, and revelled in the pleasures of the flesh that he discovered. As the pool of light progressed across the floor towards them, the words tumbled out of de Schipedham's mouth. It was as if he was making up for years of isolation on this little hump of land, when he had had no chance to speak to anyone.

'Then they came for me. The leader of the Hospitaller commanderie in Outremer appeared one day, negotiated my release, and took me home. Except it was no longer my home, and the other Hospitallers were not my comrades. Not the comrades I had left, anyway. They were all long dead, or returned to England. I had been forgotten about till this time. They soon realized I was an embarrassment. Perhaps because I was too understanding of the enemy, or because I reminded them of their own failing in not gaining my release sooner. You see, they only came to know of me by chance as they negotiated the release of the captive Hospitallers after the battle of Arsuf. A battle I only learned of later. Either way, the commander resolved to return me to England. Once there, I was shipped off to the remotest commanderie they could find, at Berdsey.'

But not even that had been far enough for his Order. His

strange moods and preoccupations had ensured his banishment to this solitary rock, where he was responsible for warning travellers of impending doom. He laughed hollowly.

'Fitting that I should spend at least as long here in penance as I spent in Outremer itself.'

Had he truly been squatting on this rock for twenty years? Falconer wondered if he knew anything of the death of John de Langetoft, and the events that led up to it. He thought he would ask while the old man appeared eager to talk.

'What do you know of your neighbours at Conishead Priory?'

'I know it was a leper hospital before it was a priory. But that is not the reason why it stinks. There is evil-doing in its walls, and too many secrets. Secrets pile up and rot, if they are not cleared out. And I can smell the rot from here.'

Chapter Nine

The tides had permitted Falconer to leave Harlesyde Island just as the prime bell was ringing over at Conishead. The white-bearded Hospitaller had taken him partway across the sands, then pointed out the way to Spina Alba, the crossing point on the western side of the bay. Falconer had thanked him for his assistance, and the information he had gleaned in the long hours before dawn. The old man gazed briefly at Falconer with his world-weary eyes, made the sign of the cross, and said he would pray for him. Then he turned and made his way back to his solitary existence. Falconer did not dare take his eyes off the point on the river bank he had been directed to, so only looked back after he had reached it. By then Fridaye de Schipedham was nothing more than a white wraith shimmering in the glare that rose from the slick surface of the bay. His form wavered like smoke in the wind, and disappeared amongst the trees that fringed the rocky shoreline. Like everything in this remote spot, the Hospitaller seemed insubstantial, and more than a little unreal.

Back at the priory, Falconer hung his still damp robe over the sill of his window, and donned his only other robe: a shabby garment, with frayed cuffs. However, he was glad that Peter Bullock had persuaded him to add it to his saddlebags instead of Ali ibn-el-Abbas's *Liber regalis*, and the magical work *De pentagono Salomonis*. It was a good trade in the present circumstances. He tried to smooth his grizzled hair into place, and winced when he accidentally knocked the large lump on the back of his head. It reminded him that he needed to work out who had attacked him.

If he assumed that cloud-ships existed only in his imagination (which was their rightful place), he knew he would have to look to the priory for the perpetrator of the murderous assault. It had hardly been planned much in advance, but it had been opportunist, and could only have been carried out by someone who knew where he had gone yesterday. That included the prior, the ironmaster, Ellen Shokburn, he supposed, and whoever had been the spy in the adjacent carrel the night before last. Unfortunately, this last could have been anyone.

He presumed the reason for the attack had been because he had uncovered, or was close to uncovering, something that was best kept quiet. He mentally retraced his conversations of the last two days. The prior had seemed quite at ease about the silver cross, but did that hide his true anxiety? He had asked Falconer to keep quiet about it – perhaps he had decided to seal his lips permanently. As he may have done with John de Langetoft fifteen years ago. The mysterious occupant of the carrel had heard him discussing the death of de Langetoft with Ralph. Was he the murderer, and did he decide to kill Falconer before he found out too much? And then it occurred to him there was Ralph himself.

Almost as though prompted, the door of his room burst open, and a harried Westerdale stumbled in. His face was red, he was out of breath, and he looked startled at Falconer's presence. At first he was unable to frame his words, then they flooded forth.

'Forgive my precipitate entrance, but I am so relieved to see that you have returned to the priory. I would not have forgiven myself if something had happened to you.'

Falconer feigned puzzlement.

'What could have happened to me?'

'Well . . . when you didn't return last night, I feared that something might have been amiss. The tides are treacherous and visitors unfamiliar with the area are inclined to underestimate its dangers.'

Falconer's temples were beginning to throb, and he winced as a dagger of pain stabbed into his head at the site of the swelling. Maybe his judgement was clouded, but he found Ralph's protestations unconvincing. Had Westerdale not expected to see him alive? He closed his eyes to organize his thoughts, then realized the monk was still talking.

'Whoever it was left sandy footprints and the *Psalterium Hebraicum* is missing.'

'Forgive my inattention. Are you saying there is a thief in the priory?' Falconer was reminded of de Schipedham's opinion of the odour of Conishead. Wide-eyed with disbelief, the monk nodded. 'How many other books are missing?'

'It's difficult to tell. In order to know that, I would have to check the presses, the catalogue and the loan records.'

'And even then, you could not be certain that those which had been borrowed were still in the priory.' Falconer knew from experience that some students at Oxford supplemented their meagre income by selling books, arranging for them not to be missed by the master who owned them by ensuring they were permanently 'on loan'. Brother Ralph paled at this thought, and made to suggest that the monastic community was an honest one when it came to what it had borrowed.

'No.' Falconer was insistent. 'If there is a thief in our midst, you can make no such assumptions. You must arrange to have all the books returned. Then we will check the catalogue.' A thought occurred to him. 'If these thefts go back long enough, it may even be that John de Langetoft's death and the missing books are somehow linked.' He mentally added the attack on himself to the chain of events, but said nothing to Ralph.

The announcement was made at Rules in the chapter house, and soon the monks were returning to the cloister with the books they had borrowed. Because there was no separate room used as a library, the books were returned to Brother Ralph's office. A procession of monks made their way to the passage shared by his room and the kitchens, and queued up to enter. Inside, Falconer stood behind Ralph as he received each of the works, and marked them off in the ledger. The precentor had relieved the austerity of his cell by bringing in two chairs – it would be a long day.

There were some amused remarks about the early arrival of Lent this year, when Ralph normally carried out this task. And one young monk entered on the verge of tears to announce that he could not find the book he had borrowed. Falconer leaned over Ralph's shoulder to see what rare text it was that was missing, and smiled when he saw the monk's finger pointing at the record. The young monk had borrowed a copy of Priscian's *Grammar* – a common text that every student at Oxford possessed. Hardly the target of a discerning thief. Still Ralph made the unfortunate young man stand trembling, as he sternly penned out '*perditur*' against the record. Then the return of books continued, piling up on the table at which Ralph sat, until no more monks came and nothing but a shaft of sunlight filtering through the empty doorway.

'Has everything been returned?' Falconer's anxious enquiry was met by silence. Ralph was still scanning the list of books that had been loaned out the previous Lent. At last he spoke.

'There are the two works the prior has. But I did not imagine that he would stand in line with the other brothers. I will go and collect them myself. So the only other person not to return his book is the camerarius.'

'Adam Lutt?'

'Yes. In fact I don't think I've seen him today at all.' He smiled. 'Now I remember – Brother Adam is on some errand for the prior, at the ironworks, and missed Rules. He will be unaware that I have asked for the return of all the books.'

The prior's voice came from the doorway. 'Adam is on no errand for me. And I shall want to know why he failed to attend the chapter house meeting this morning. In the meantime, here are my books.'

He stood in the doorway with two leather-bound works held

out in front of him. He clearly expected Ralph to come and take them from him, as though his humility in returning the books himself only brought him as far as the threshold. Before the precentor could rise from his seat, Falconer stepped forward and took the books from the prior's hands, eager to see what the man read. He was disappointed. They were two religious works – the Lives of St Dunstan and St Milburga. It was as though the prior was deliberately displaying his piety to Falconer, and the master wondered if the books had truly been in his possession since the previous Lent. Or had he obtained them recently to impress his visitor? The mocking smile on Henry Ussher's lips as he left suggested to Falconer he had guessed correctly. He turned back to Ralph as he noted the books' return in the ledger. The record was at the bottom of the list, and could have been placed there at any time. Perhaps this knowledge would be meaningful later – for now he would just store it away.

Falconer was now anxious to begin comparing all the records to see if there were discrepancies and lost items. Would there even be someone who consistently lost his borrowed book? But then the terce bell rang out, calling the monks to Mass, and Ralph slammed the ledger shut. He pushed the protesting Falconer out of the room, insisting that he was responsible for the safety of the books contained therein, and that he was not even going to allow the Oxford master to remain inside while he was at Mass. Thereupon, he locked the door and scuttled off to the church, leaving Falconer fuming, but impotent. He could do nothing but pace up and down the cloister as the strains of the Mass came steadily from behind the massive church doors.

Ellen Shokburn trudged down the open slopes of Cartmel Head from Headless Cross, her shoulders hunched against the grey drizzle. The day had started dull and had got worse as the morning progressed. Jack, her son, had told her not to go to the priory, that he could support them both. His youthful face and pleading eyes had almost swayed her. She knew he was mutely begging her to allow him to become the provider. To be the man his missing father had never been. Whenever Jack had asked his mother about his father — why he wasn't with them, and never had been — she told him the man was a wastrel. She had been duped into his bed, and he had fled soon after. He didn't even know he had a son, who, she assured Jack, was worth ten of his father. But she knew the time had now come to tell him the truth, and that was going to be very difficult for her. Still, she was proud of Jack — what he had become. But he did not yet earn enough from guiding people across the bay to put sufficient food on their table. She needed the work at the priory, and so she had wearily wrapped some old sacking around her shoulders, and set off for Conishead.

The drizzle turned into a pounding rain as she reached the shores of the Leven. The island at the head of the river, with its wraith of a hermit, was barely visible in the greyness. She trudged across the cloying mud, and gathered her skirts about her slim brown legs as she prepared to wade into the stream. The water in the Leven was running fast with all the rainwater from the fells. She had to step carefully to prevent the insistent tug from sweeping her feet away from under her. She dug her toes into the muddy bottom and pressed on. Something swept out of the greyness and bumped against her thigh. She put a hand down to push whatever it was away from her, and her arm became entangled in a clinging mass. Not sure if it was the branch of a tree with a shred of sodden cloth attached, she pulled hard to free herself from its grip. The trunk rolled over and a bare, bluish arm emerged from the cloth. She opened her mouth wide in a silent scream as the fingers at the end of the arm slid down the quivering skin of her uncovered leg.

It took four monks to carry the waterlogged body into the church, where it was placed in the same side chapel as the bones brought in only a few days earlier. This person had died altogether more recently, however. The skin was puffed out due to its immersion in water, but there was no sign of the telltale stomach bloat showing rot of the internal organs. No, Adam Lutt had always been a large man, and the distended stomach was rather from self-indulgence in life.

Falconer made sure he and Brother Ralph were left alone with the body before he conducted any further examination of the remains. It was lucky he did so, because when he peeled the monkish robes away from the head they had enfolded Ralph recoiled in horror. Not so much on seeing that it really was the camerarius, but more from the ghastly distortion of his features. His eyes had both popped out of their sockets and hung on his cheeks. His tongue also protruded from between his lips, half severed by his own teeth. The face, so rounded in life, was crushed flat, side to side, and the grey mass of his brains oozed from the broken shell that was his skull. The impression given was that someone of enormous strength had taken Lutt's cheeks in either hand and simply squashed them together.

'What happened to him?' Brother Ralph gazed in disbelief first at the corpse, and then at Falconer.

'Can't you see?' Falconer bent over the grisly sight and poked at the shattered side of Lutt's head. The skin was broken and bloody, and shards of stone were embedded in what was left of his ear. He shuddered as he recalled the ominous thudding he had heard the previous night. 'Someone put his head under a trip-hammer at the ironworks and let slip the mechanism. I dare say if you examine the ore bench underneath each hammer, you might be able to specify the very device which crushed his skull.'

A shiver ran down Ralph's spine at the gruesome thought of what he might find on the bench, and the face of the hammer concerned. 'I don't think I wish to take my curiosity that far. But who would have done it, then?'

'Ah. That's a more difficult question to answer.' Falconer's eyes lit up at the thought of the hunt. 'I would first have to know something about the dead man's life. Tell me — what does this signify?' He rubbed his fingers and thumb together in a certain way, and touched his tongue with his forefinger. At first Ralph looked confused, not sure what this had to do with Adam Lutt's life – or his death. He did recognize the sign the regent master was reproducing, however.

'Oh, that. As we cannot talk while we eat, but merely listen to the readings at table, we have some practical signals. You know, silent signals for requesting more bread and so on.'

'And this one?' Falconer repeated the movement with his fingers as best he remembered it.

'That means pass the salt.'

'Hmm.' Falconer's face clouded over as he pondered on this. Ralph opened his mouth to speak, but the master suddenly brightened up. 'As camerarius, Lutt must have kept his records somewhere.'

'Of course – he has . . . had a room at the end of the quire dorter above the warming house.'

'May I see it?'

Ralph looked a little worried at this bold action. 'I think we should consult the prior before doing so, don't you?'

Falconer thought not – he would rather conduct his investigation without the constrictions of the prior's wishes. But he didn't want to lose the cooperation of the little precentor. After all, they still had the books to check, and Ralph had the only keys to his room and the book presses. He put on a solemn visage. 'Of course. It would be best if you see the prior on your own, though. I wish to examine the body further.'

The squeamish Ralph shuddered at the idea of being present as Falconer worked on the flaccid corpse. He hurried off, just as Falconer had hoped he would. Once he was sure Ralph was out of the cloister, the master hurriedly covered the grotesque head that lay before him and exited the church by the side-chapel door. With everyone else at their labours, there was no one to see him dash down the west side of the cloister; and climb the day stairs to the quire dorter. The long room was silent, its orderly rows of beds defining the structured regimen the monks lived under. In one corner was an area screened by two walls of plain panelling with a small door set in one of them. Falconer guessed this must be Lutt's office. He quickly crossed the dormitory, dust rising with each step, and stood before the door. He tried the handle – the door was unlocked.

'Let him see Lutt's office. What could he find amiss?'

Westerdale was surprised at Henry Ussher's response. He had expected the prior to resent Falconer's nosiness. Had he not tried to divert him from prying into the dark nooks and crannies of John de Langetoft's death? Now he seemed to care not a bit that the Oxford master wished to turn over any stones surrounding Adam Lutt's. Ralph himself worried that the search might not stop with Lutt. There was still the matter of some missing books. He voiced his hidden fears to Henry Ussher, fears he had hoarded for so long now that he saw them as pale worms growing bloated in the darkness.

'He will soon find out that the very books he has come to read are not there. I cannot delay him much longer.'

'That was your fault for encouraging him to come.' If the prior was angry, he hid it well under a mien of urbane calmness.

'I didn't know then that he would want to see Grosseteste's books specifically. And yes, I was flattered that a scholar from Oxford should wish to see our collection. I should not have been – I know pride could be my downfall now. But you must tell me what we can do about it.'

'We?' Ussher's calm slipped a little as he snapped out the word. Then he recovered, and smiled coldly at Ralph. 'You are the one who appears to have something to hide. Your salvation is in your own hands. I have nothing to fear at all.'

Especially now that Lutt was dead and Lamport was safely rid of.

Falconer closed the door and looked about him. It was dark – the window was covered by shutters – so he had to stand a while before he could make out what was in the room. As his eyes adjusted he could see it was larger than the one occupied by Ralph Westerdale, but at the same time appeared more cramped. It was cluttered with possessions. A long bench fully took up one side, and its surface was scattered with ledgers and papers. Where Ralph's room had originally been devoid of chairs, this one offered the luxury of an upright stool at the bench, and two high-backed chairs pulled together in one corner.

Falconer guessed that Brother Adam had not been in the room since yesterday. The closed shutters confirmed that — shut at dusk the previous day, and not reopened this morning. The times all fitted with Falconer's half-heard sound of the trip-hammers last evening. Nearly drowned he might have been, but he was more convinced than ever that he had heard them thumping. And therefore had heard the means of Lutt's death at a moment that had almost brought his own.

He pulled open the shutters at the window arch above the bench to give himself some light. The view was of the open fields where the lay brothers no doubt toiled in the summer. Now the earth looked sodden and uncooperative. Falconer imagined it was a perfect spot to keep an eye on much that happened around the priory. A lone figure worked at the sluice that controlled the water levels in the fishponds which stretched off to one side of the vista. Rainwater dripped off the ragged edges of the sacking that covered the person's shoulders. The figure was slight, and when the brown face turned up to look towards the priory even Falconer's weak eyes saw that it was Ellen Shokburn. Her discovery of the gruesome remains of Adam Lutt had clearly not exempted her from her daily routine. He did not think she could see him, and he stood idly watching. As he did so, the wiry figure of her son came into view from under the priory wall. The youth stopped to speak to her, and the conversation became animated. Jack turned his back on his mother at one point, and she put a tentative hand on his arm. Falconer was a little embarrassed when they suddenly hugged each other, and he cast his eyes down. When he looked again, the youth had gone and Ellen had returned to her labours.

Falconer too returned to the task that had brought him to this room. At first he leafed through the strew of papers that cluttered the desk, not knowing what he might be looking for. They were all documents relating to the financial administration of the priory – records of tithes received, and debts owed. Most conspicuous was a letter in the name of the King demanding money. All quite normal in the office of a camerarius.

But Falconer was looking for something that would not be obvious or on display. The idea had come to him when he had recalled what he had seen the first morning he had been at the priory. In church Lutt had pushed his way to one particular monk's side and made a strange hand signal, which had brought fear to the other's eyes. That the signal was more appropriate to the frater and mealtimes, as he now knew, made it all the more significant to Falconer. Especially as something had changed hands. A request to pass the salt could have been a blackmailer's way of demanding his offering. If Lutt had been blackmailing the sacrist, John Whitehed, what hold did he have over him? Knowledge of a fifteen-year-old murder perhaps? If he could solve the first murder, then he felt sure he would have the solution to the second. Was Whitehed guilty, or did the finger of suspicion point at Henry Ussher? Falconer recalled that Ralph had thought the prior had called Lutt to the ironworks. But then Ussher had immediately denied doing so. As he might have done if he also was a victim of Lutt's coercion. Had Lutt been blackmailing others at the priory? And if so, was there a record of it in this room? Where did the theft of the library books fit in all this? There were so many questions, and so little time to come up with solutions. Falconer scanned the room, trying to imagine where he might hide incriminating documents himself.

Suddenly the room appeared bare and incapable of providing a hiding place. His eyes finally lit upon the cluttered table — perhaps the safest place was in full sight. With a sigh he began to leaf carefully through the heaps of documents.

Chapter Ten

When Ralph Westerdale returned to the chapel, he was a little surprised to find the Oxford master still there. He had imagined that his insatiable curiosity would have driven him to sneak a look at Brother Adam's room. But here he was, sitting quietly by the side of the body as though maintaining a vigil. Fortunately a cloth had been drawn over the battered head, or Ralph would not have been able to approach. When he told Falconer that the prior had given permission for him to enter the camerarius's room, he was once again surprised by the master's response.

'What? Oh, never mind that now. We have a much older mystery to solve, and I am convinced it has to do with the losses from your library.' He took Ralph Westerdale by the shoulder, and propelled him out of the church. 'Come, let's see what's missing from your catalogue.'

The monk, who had thought Falconer distracted from this task, reluctantly allowed himself to be guided round the perimeter of the cloister to his room. Falconer did not even give Lutt's chamber a glance as they passed the dorter stairs. Ralph fumbled with the key to his room, and dropped it on the floor. Falconer merely furnished him with an amused look, stooped and, inserting the key in the lock himself, turned it. The room still stood as it had done when they left it to attend Mass. So much had happened in the short interval that the monk could almost have convinced himself that the return of all the books had never taken place. But the piles of musty leather-bound texts on his table were all too real. It now remained to tally the books here and in the book presses with the catalogue to see what was missing.

Falconer sat at the table and pulled the big ledger towards him. He motioned the monk, who still hovered in the doorway, to go to the books. 'If you read off the title and its catalogue number, I will find it and mark it down as not missing. Is that all right?'

Ralph nodded dumbly and watched as Falconer drew a fresh quill from the pot on the desk. Then, with trepidation, he picked up the first book and read out its title. 'The Life of St Milburga. Item number seventy-three.'

Ann Segrim was finding it extremely difficult to talk to the rest of the nuns who made up Sister Eleanor's small household on the north range of the cloister. Besides the fearful Gilda, there were five others. But whenever Ann tried to talk to them as they went about their daily tasks, her footsteps were dogged by the persistent and ancient Sister Hildegard. Her sour, wrinkled face silently reprimanded each sister as she opened her mouth to speak to Ann. With Sister Mary, it was near the fishponds. Ann had just asked the young nun if she knew Eleanor's family when Hildegard popped up out of nowhere and shook her head in censure. Mary scowled, but lowered her eyes, and tightened her lips. She turned her back on Ann and continued feeding the fishes. Sister Joan had been on her knees scrubbing the tiled entrance to Rosamund's chapel. Hardly had Ann spoken when Hildegard poked her sour face round the heavy oak door, and complained that Sister Joan had not got the red and blue patterned floor sufficiently clean. She must do it again. Joan flushed as red as the tiles she was scrubbing and averted her eyes from the exasperated Ann Segrim. Hildegard's look was of pure triumph. And so it was all day. Every time Ann broached the subject of their dead sister with the residents of the north house, Hildegard was close by to put a stop to Ann's questions.

In the end, Ann decided to approach the problem head on. She knew that after vespers the ancient sister stayed on her knees in the church, while the others repaired to the frater for a simple supper. An old woman, no more than parchment skin stretched over bone, she seemed to need less sustenance than her fellow nuns. Perhaps she fed on her interference in others' lives. This evening was no different. As the plumes of incense drifted into the gloom of the rafters above them, and the other nuns shuffled out, Hildegard stayed on her knees before her God. A few rows back, Ann too buried her face in her hands, and prayed. She, though, was asking for some success in her encounter with the old crone. Peter Bullock's words had given her the idea – now it was time to try it out.

After a few moments, Ann rose, walked up the aisle of the church, and slid her worldly, well-rounded form on to the bench behind the spot where Hildegard still knelt. She knew by the slight stiffening of the old woman's shoulders that Hildegard had heard her quiet arrival. As she suspected, the woman wasn't deaf at all.

She leaned forward and breathed her words into Hildegard's ear. 'Don't pretend to be startled. I know you can hear me.'

Reluctant to give up the subterfuge that had served her well, Hildegard swung sharply round, and cupped a claw of a hand around her ear. 'What did you say?'

Her eyes were bright with animal cunning, and her disdain for the younger woman clearly showed. Ann smiled coolly.

'If you want me to shout out loud for all the world to hear, I will. But when you hear what I have to say, I think you might wish we had kept our conversation confidential.'

Hildegard's toothless mouth crumpled into a sneer, but the hand fell away from her ear. For Ann it was a minor triumph – she wondered if she would win the battle of wits entirely.

'The abbess said you washed and prepared Eleanor's body for burial?'

Hildegard looked puzzled by the question, and a curt nod was all Ann got. She realized this was going to be as painful as a tooth-puller at a fair, but pressed on.

'Were there any marks on the body?'

'Marks?' If Hildegard was going to answer her every question with a query of her own, this was going to be a long interview. But Ann could be patient, and persistent when she wished.

'Were there any bruises or cuts on her body?'

Again the old woman sneered, and Ann was reminded of the gargoyles that squatted open-mouthed at the corners of the new tower of St Mary's Church in Oxford. She only wished the words might flow from Hildegard as swiftly as rainwater through the gargoyles' lips during a downpour.

'Of course there were bruises, her head was held under the water until she drowned. There were fresh bruises on her neck, here and here.' Her knobbly claw of a finger pointed at the spot either side of Ann's neck where a murderer might grasp someone if they sought to hold them face down. Ann shivered at the old woman's touch, and framed her next question. But Hildegard continued without prompting. There were also bruises on her back, as though whoever murdered her had knelt on her as she committed the deed in order to hold her down.'

Ann noted that the old woman did not share the abbess's dislike of the idea of murder, nor her refusal to accept that a sister nun might be involved.

'Of course, the old marks you will not need to know about.'

'Old marks?'

Hildegard's lined face broke into a malicious grin. 'The marks left by the discipline meted out to Eleanor in times past by Sister Gwladys.'

It took Ralph Westerdale and Master Falconer until vespers, but finally they had marked off in the catalogue all those books which were physically present. Ralph was shocked – there were fourteen missing. Falconer went through them to see if there were any connections.

'The *Treatise on the Magnet*, a *Topographica Hibernica*, Aristotle's *De Anima*, *Ad inclusionem spiritus in speculo* — that's a book on magic — Cicero's *De senectute*. The Hebrew Psalter, of course. No less than seven medical texts. And a copy of Vacarius's Commentary on Justinian.'

Despite himself Ralph was gripped by the mystery. 'That last one is very rare.'

'I know. Vacarius lectured on Roman law at Oxford over a hundred years ago. The story is that King Stephen himself forced him to desist, and all his works that they could lay hands on were destroyed.'

'What about the others? I know the text on the magnet is difficult to obtain, and the *Topographica*, but what about the medical texts? They are not particularly rare.'

Falconer smiled at the monk's lack of knowledge of the world outside the priory. 'They may not be rare of themselves, but they fetch a ready price from the right scholar. Many people are interested in medical science at present.'

The monk shuddered at the thought of looking too closely at how the human body worked. It was enough for him that it was God's own creation. Too much curiosity verged on blasphemy and only served to create difficulties, as he well knew. Besides, the mess that lay inside the bag that is the body was best left there — he did not relish the sight of the bag once it was burst open. This morbid line of thought brought the image of Brother Adam's squashed visage back to him, and he shivered.

Falconer's brows were still furrowed. 'There is the difficulty of the missing page, of course. We don't know what was recorded there beyond the four books in the west press that do not now appear in the catalogue. We know from their numbers — 343, and 354 to 356 — that they must have been on the missing page. And as we cannot find any of the books that formerly belonged to Bishop Grosseteste in the presses, we can assume that they were catalogued as works 344 to 353. But what they were, and whether they are truly missing, is impossible to tell.'

'It is a shame indeed. Especially as this part of our library was what you particularly sought, I understand.'

Falconer thought the monk's expression of sympathy sounded hollow, but agreed. 'Yes. There were a couple of titles that I was hoping were in your collection. Now I will never know. Unless . . .' A smile crossed the master's lips, and he shot up from the table, almost knocking the chair over in his excitement. He crossed to the door, and wrenched at its latch. 'I must speak to the prior.'

With that he was gone. Ralph was left to rush after the disappearing figure, whose worn, black robe flapped at his heels. 'Why?'

The answer was flung over Falconer's shoulder as he sped round the cloister. 'I need to know where Brother Thady is.'

The prior was adamant.

'I cannot tell you the whereabouts of Brother Thady. He is on retreat for the good of his soul – solitary retreat.'

Falconer didn't doubt that Thady Lamport's banishment had more to do with the good of the prior's position than with the deranged cellarer's own salvation. But the triumphant face of Henry Ussher told him that it was useless pursuing the location of Lamport's lonely cell with him. He would have to discover it another way. And speak to the monk he would, for he was sure that the former precentor would recall what texts from Grosseteste's collection had found their way to the priory. They would have been catalogued by him, after all. At the same time he could ask about the interesting little decoration he had found in the ledger. It may have been pure coincidence that Lamport had drawn the stabbing of a monk. But it had been done just at the time John de Langetoft disappeared, and no one had known until recently how he had met his death. No one, that is, except the killer, and anyone who had observed the killing.

Much had happened around the time of de Langetoft's disappearance. The old prior had died, and Henry Ussher had become his successor — his passage eased by the disappearance of his rival de Langetoft. Thady Lamport had become deranged and been removed from the office of precentor. Oddly, the new prior had merely appointed him cellarer, as though he owed Brother Thady a debt. Adam Lutt too had benefited from de Langetoft's departure, succeeding him as camerarius in his continued absence. Ralph Westerdale had been favoured by Henry Ussher, and appointed precentor in Lamport's stead. Only John Whitehed, the sacrist, had not prospered, probably because he had failed to ally himself with Henry Ussher at the proper time. An error he was making every effort to rectify now. It all spoke eloquently of rival factions and cliques as convoluted as any Roman intrigue around the appointment of a Pope. Just who killed de Langetoft and now Lutt, and had made an attempt on his own life, eluded Falconer for the moment. But he was certain that the lost books also fitted in the tapestry somewhere, and Brother Thady could be the key to it all.

'Forgive me, prior, for being so insensitive.' Falconer's tone was as obsequious as he could make it, which was not much. 'I had thought Brother Thady could enlighten me over some missing books. You must be more concerned with the sad demise of Brother Adam than my petty problems. Will Brother Martin Albon be back to carry out a post-mortem?'

Ussher's brow furrowed. 'He will. And I am sure this time there will be no nonsense about murder spoken. Everyone else believes his death was an accident, so I would be grateful if you kept your own counsel also.'

Henry Ussher sat in his high-backed chair, relaxed and confident that he had the better of this Oxford academic. He was a master of intrigue, and was sure his powers could block Falconer wherever he poked his nose. How could someone who had his head in a book all day, and taught an unruly rabble of children, outwit the prior of Conishead, who was soon to move on to greater things? Henry Ussher nodded his satisfaction as Falconer bowed in apparent defeat and left the room.

The following morning dawned dull and grey, much like the previous one. The leafless trees poked their twisted branches into the mist that swirled around their trunks, making Falconer feel as though he truly was a drowned man trapped at the bottom of the sea. It was as if the evil lurking inside the priory's walls was beginning to infect the outside world. He looked up and gulped for breath as the doleful bell on Harlesyde Island clanged in the ancient grip of Fridaye de Schipedham. But it was air after all, not seawater that he sucked into his lungs. Living on the edge of the world played tricks with the mind, even the rational one of an Aristotelian Oxford master. He laughed nervously.

'You're always laughing when we meet. I cannot understand why.'

She had done it again, creeping up on him without his noticing. Falconer was annoyed that his normally sharp senses had now twice let him down, but he did not show it. He needed Ellen Shokburn's help today. He turned and smiled. She wore the same threadbare dress she had had on the day before, when he saw her at the fishponds, and the same frayed sack over her shoulders to protect her from the damp that hung in the air. She seemed to be able to read his mind.

'There are many days like this, when the rain can't decide to fall and just hangs there. You'll get used to it, if you stay much longer. Now if you'll excuse me.'

The top of her head barely came to the level of Falconer's chest, but she surveyed him coolly. Thrusting her hard, but not unpleasing, face up to his, she stared into his eyes. He noticed hers were as blue as his own, and once again imagined her, younger and softer, turning the heads of the local youths. As for himself, he liked a woman who could hold her own — he would have to be careful not to be attracted to her.

'I need your help.'

'I have work to do.' She made as if to push Falconer's bulk out of her way, not caring that he was twice her size. He stepped back, but still blocked the narrow path through the trees.

'I need you as a guide – I will pay.'

'Where do you want to go?' Her eyes narrowed at the thought of a few extra coins, but she wondered how much this threadbare scholar could afford.

Falconer smiled. 'Only you can tell me that.'

Ellen was annoyed – she was not in the mood for riddles, now or ever. She pulled the sacking tighter over her shoulders, and took a step away from him.

Falconer hastened to explain before she decided the money wasn't worth the trouble.

'Where would the prior send a monk who had incurred his wrath? A solitary cell somewhere where the culprit is out of harm's way, but not so far away that he cannot be controlled.'

'That's simple. There's a cave above Thurston Water on Bethecar Moor. Whoever you are seeking will be there.'

'How far is it?'

Ellen cocked her head to one side as she estimated the journey. 'It will take us all day to get there and back.'

Falconer produced a coin from his pouch. 'Will you take me?'

As they climbed higher the weather improved, and they emerged from the mist that had hung in the river valley. At first Ellen had taken Falconer along the bank of the River Craik, travelling due north. The grey mist, hardly distinguishable from the turbid stream that ran at their side, still reminded Falconer of his near-drowning. Images of struggling to walk at the bottom of the ocean flitted through his mind, especially when they passed the location of the ironworks on the opposite bank. The murderous thump of the trip-hammers echoed dully through the mist, like some dying man's heartbeat. The thought of one of them descending on poor Lutt's head made Falconer shudder. He saw the sound had had the same effect on the woman, whose shoulders tightened until they were out of earshot of the unnatural noise. He literally breathed a sigh of relief as they came out of the mist, like a lost sailor pushing his head above the waves and gasping for air.

Now the sun began to break through the heavy clouds, and Falconer almost skipped across the stones where they forded the river. The higher they got the more the land opened up before them, until finally a magnificent vista of snow-topped mountains was visible rising beyond the sparkling sheet that was Thurston Water. Even Ellen Shokburn appeared moved by the sight. Her normally cold features melted into a fleeting smile, as though she were presenting something she owned for admiration. The thought seemed perfectly appropriate to Falconer, for the land might belong to the priory, but not the view and the sense of place. Only those who truly lived in it, and with it, could be said to possess that.

He looked at the woman to share his joy, but the transitory pleasure she had revealed was gone. The permanent veil of hard purpose was drawn over her eyes again.

'You didn't tell me whom you were seeking here.'

'Brother Thady. I fear his rantings finally became too much for the prior.'

Falconer thought there was a flicker of fear in Ellen's eyes when he mentioned Lamport's name, but he could not be sure. The woman remained in strict control of her feelings. Still, he could understand it if she did not relish the company of someone as odd as Thady Lamport. His peculiar behaviour might seem on the verge of violence to some, though Falconer doubted that it would ever turn in that direction.

'Where should I go, then?'

She raised her arm and pointed ahead of them. 'The cell you want is at the top of this rise, just beyond that rock there – the one that sticks out like a finger. I will wait here for you.' She sat down on a flat spur of rock, and stared off over the lake.

Falconer nodded, and continued along the narrow path leading round the crag. Scrambling over the rocky outcrop that Ellen had pointed out, he was suddenly struck hard on the chest. He gasped and looked around, rubbing the sore spot where the blow had landed. No one was in sight, but looking down he saw a stone the size of a fist lying at his feet. From the corner of his eye he was aware of a movement in the jumble of rocks to his right, and he instinctively ducked. Another large stone whistled over his head. This time it was accompanied by a hoarse cry.

'Get away, demon.'

Falconer ducked behind a large rock as a third stone flew past him. He called out. 'Brother Thady, it's me, William Falconer – the visitor at the priory. I want to talk to you.'

'You're the devil's spawn. Go away.' This imprecation was hurled at Falconer along with another stone.

'Please. I want to talk to you about John de Langetoft. I need your help.'

There was a pause in the rain of rocks, and cautiously Falconer raised his head. He could see Thady Lamport standing in the mouth of a dark and gloomy cave. He had stripped down to a simple loincloth, and his pale, stringy body was outlined by the blackness behind it. Falconer was reminded of Fridaye de Schipedham, and wondered if this remote land called people back to their elemental nature, and away from civilization. Travellers were said to have encountered giants and people with a single eye in the middle of their chest at the edges of the world. The tales did not surprise Falconer now.

The monk dropped the stone he was holding in his hand, and stepped into the darkness of the cave. Falconer clambered over the rocks and, hesitating for a moment at the cave mouth, followed Lamport in. Once his eyes had adjusted to the gloom, he saw that the cell was truly spartan. Beyond the narrow arch of the entrance, the cave opened out into a large vaulted space. Damp stains dribbled down the face of the rock in several places.

In one corner was a natural hearth below the funnel of a fissure in the rock that ran upwards like a chimney. There was no fire lit.

Opposite the hearth a flat slab of rock projected from the side of the cave. It served Thady as a bed, but the coldness of its surface was alleviated only by a thin mattress. In the rear of the cave stood a pile of jars and greasy cloths that no doubt contained Lamport's supply of food. The monk himself sat cross-legged on the rocky slab, illuminated by a single candle at his side that had been burning for a long time, judging by the spikes of wax that hung down from the edge of the slab. Thady Lamport's eyes burned feverishly, and his face was even more skull-like than when Falconer had last seen him in the priory. He was mumbling something under his breath that Falconer could not catch — a phrase repeated time and again in time to the rocking of his body.

The cell felt chill and Falconer wondered if Lamport ever lit the fire to ease his discomfort. He leaned over the ashes, and felt them. They were cold and damp. He enquired if he should gather some sticks together, and the reaction was immediate.

'Leave it. If Adam Lutt can endure without a fire, then I shall too.'

Falconer refrained from saying that Adam Lutt no longer had need of earthly fires to warm him. He stared as Lamport continued to rock his scrawny frame in silence. Then suddenly the monk stopped, and the words poured out of his mouth.

'You wanted to know about John de Langetoft. I will tell you. John de Langetoft broke his vows. Broke them, yes. He is a sinner, only interested in himself. A sinner — yes, a sinner. He must not become prior. He must be stopped.'

Falconer put his hand on the monk's bare arm, and felt the taut tendons stretched almost to breaking point. He whispered gently in his ear. 'Brother Thady, John de Langetoft is long dead. He cannot become prior.'

'Dead?' The conundrum puzzled Lamport.

'Yes, dead. He died fifteen years ago – I think you know that, don't you? I saw the drawing in the book catalogue that you made. Brother, did you "stop" him – did you kill him?'

Deep pain registered in the monk's eyes, and he thundered a warning. 'Thou shalt not kill. Thou shalt not kill.'

Falconer lurched back at the verbal onslaught. He would have to be careful, or he could tip the dangerously deranged monk into a state in which no information would be forthcoming at all. He tried a different approach

'What sort of man was de Langetoft?'

Before the monk could reply, Falconer thought he heard a rustling at the entrance to the cave. Maybe Ellen had decided to follow him after all. Thady Lamport must have heard something too, because he turned at the same time. They both peered at the narrow crack that formed the doorway, where a beam of weak light filtered into the cell. But there was nothing there, and no more sounds came.

'Who would have had a reason to kill him?'

At Falconer's question, a cunning look came over Lamport's face. He grabbed the front of the master's robe, pulling him down until their faces were pressed close together. 'He knew things, and used them like currency to buy what he wanted.'

Falconer endured the stale breath that emanated from the monk's broken-toothed mouth. 'What things did he know?'

'Let us just say that Henry Ussher would never have been prior, if Brother John had had his way.' Grotesquely, Lamport winked at Falconer. 'You see, he took the books.'

Falconer's interest was fanned into hot flames by this statement from the madman. He was convinced the books were part of the key to the old murder. Yet how could John de Langetoft be the thief of all the books? Many had been taken after his death. Perhaps Thady was referring just to the missing books from Bishop Grosseteste's collection.

'The books? Grosseteste's books? Can you remember what they were called?'

'Called?'

'Their titles. There is a page missing in the catalogue.'

Lamport hesitated, then closed his eyes and recited, as though turning the pages of the catalogue in his mind and reading the listings on the back of his eyelids.

'Item 344 – Bishop Robert Grosseteste – *De Luce*. Item 345 – Bishop Robert Grosseteste – *De Sphera*. Item 346 – Aristotle – *Secretum Secretorum*. Item 347 – unknown author – *Sapientiae nigromanciae* . . .' Lamport hesitated and his eyelids flickered. Beads of sweat formed on his brow, though the cell was icy cold. He continued uncertainly. 'Item 348 . . . Bishop Robert Grosseteste . . . *De finitate motus et temporis*. Item 349 . . . Bishop Rob . . . *De infini* . . . *lucis* . . . *nitate* . . . *lucis*.'

Suddenly, Lamport shook Falconer's grip from his arm, dropped from the shelf and scuttled across the cell like a pallid spider. He crouched in a corner and folded his arms over his head for protection from some unseen assailant.

'The light – we killed the light. So now there is no light to shine on us.'

Falconer took a step towards the bundle of misery that was Thady Lamport, but was stopped in his tracks.

'Get thee behind me, Satan,' the crouching figure wailed, the light in his eyes finally dulled.

Falconer knew the thread was broken, and sat back on the cold slab that was the monk's bed. As Thady sobbed, he pondered on what he had learned. The trouble was, he was not sure how much of the information he could trust. But if at least some of the facts were accurate, they were invaluable truths to which logic could be profitably applied. He was now anxious to return to the priory, and Lamport looked as though he was oblivious of the presence of his guest anyway. The monk was rocking backwards and forwards, muttering the same prayer he had intoned at the beginning. As it got louder, Falconer realized what he was saying. Over and over again, Lamport was reciting the three vows of monastic life – Obedience, Poverty, and Celibacy.

SEXT

Deep in his heart, sin whispers to the wicked man,
Who cherishes no fear of God.

Psalm 36

Chapter Eleven

'Where have you been all day?' Ralph Westerdale looked flustered. It was evening, and vespers had passed before he had been able to locate the Oxford master. Falconer smiled enigmatically, and indicated that he had sought a solitary place where he could marshal his thoughts about the deaths of both John de Langetoft and Adam Lutt. There was no untruth there, of course. Just a lack of information about whom he had shared the solitary place with. The precentor was still uncertain, but had to satisfy himself with a disapproving grunt, as though Falconer was some errant novice who had not followed the rules of the order.

'The prior wished you to see Brother Adam's office. He's there now himself as a matter of fact. Trying to make sense of the accounts.'

Falconer allowed himself to be led to the camerarius's room, though he wished simply to repair to his bed at the end of a tiring day. He regretted having allowed his body to soften under the undemanding regime of a university teacher, and realized how unused he was now to long journeys on foot across uncertain terrain – unlike his earlier years spent traversing parts of the world little known to man. Merchant and mercenary seemed unlikely preparations for a Regent Master of Arts at Oxford University. But then to the younger, keener-eyed Falconer a scholar's life would have seemed an unlikely pursuit. Until he had met Friar Roger Bacon. Then the power of science and logic had literally changed the course of his wanderings. Now here he was, footsore and tired, obeying the command of some self-centred cleric running a remote priory on the edge of the world.

'Ah, Master Falconer. I am glad you are here. I want to show you something.'

Henry Ussher stood in the doorway of the camerarius's office, his halo of silver hair lit up by the candles that burned inside the room. He took Falconer's arm without questioning where he had been, and guided him inside. At first glance the room was as Falconer had left it on his surreptitious visit the previous day – except the desk had been tidied. No longer were there papers scattered all over it, as Falconer had seen it – it was now orderly with records and ledgers neatly arranged. He assumed that the prior had sorted out the papers, and was curious to know what Ussher wanted to show him. The prior pointed at one of the ledgers.

'I wanted to show you this as you were curious about poor Adam's demise. I have not moved anything, so you can be sure it is as Adam left it.'

Falconer's eyes did not flicker at the prior's words, which did not fit with his previous assumption. He casually clarified his doubts. 'And you have not allowed anyone else access to the room?'

'No. I asked Ralph to lock it last night.'

Westerdale nodded to indicate that he had done so. But his eyes were downcast, leaving Falconer to wonder who had interfered with the papers. Who had something to hide, that Adam Lutt, the blackmailer, had possessed? And what was it that Henry Ussher was keen for him, and only him, to see? At least the last question would be answered.

'Take a look at that ledger, which records all the income and expenditure of the priory.'

Falconer opened the cover of the ledger, and scanned the first page, puzzled as to what he was supposed to be looking for. The prior leaned over his shoulder and flicked through the stiff pages to the latest entries. He pointed an accusatory finger at one line in particular. 'There, the entry for the monies paid to the ironworks for the last quarter-year.'

Falconer took note of the figure, which showed a sizeable income from the manufacture of locks and hinges. More than he earned in a year as a regent master.

'Now look at these papers I took from the ironworks on my last visit – individual records of payments from the sale of goods.' He thrust a sheaf of battered papers at Falconer, stained with the sweat and metal residues that tainted the hands of the ironmaster. 'Add them up.'

Impatient at the prior's peremptory tones, Falconer neverthe-less added up the figures recorded on each sheet. There was a discrepancy. Lutt had recorded less income than the papers represented. Before Falconer could comment, Henry Ussher drew his own conclusions.

'Adam Lutt was clearly abusing his position as camerarius, and stealing from the priory funds. He must have been over-come by remorse, and took his own life fittingly at the site of his iniquity – the ironworks. It is a terrible sin that he did so, but in deference to his previous efforts for the community here I propose not to make it known. And I would be glad if you dropped your . . . investigations here and now, Master Falconer.'

Henry Ussher looked down his patrician nose at the seated Falconer, and swept from the office. Ralph was obviously under instructions to lock the room up again, and looked expectantly at Falconer, the key in his hand. To his consternation, Falconer remained seated at the table, poring over the pile of papers the prior had given him. While the embarrassed monk hopped impatiently from sandal-clad foot to sandal-clad foot, he carefully read the text on each, and even turned them over to examine the blank reverse. After a while, he grunted in satisfaction, and rose from the table.

'I can see you are anxious to get to your bed, Brother Ralph. I too am tired – I must let you lock the room.'

He stood over the precentor as he once again drew the heavy key from the sleeve of his habit, locked the door, and returned the key to his sleeve. They walked in silence to the dormitory stairs where Falconer surprised the monk by grasping his arm with one hand, and shaking his hand with the other. He thanked him profusely for all his assistance over the books, and promised to limit his attentions to his academic work tomorrow. The bewildered monk did not notice the wry smile on Falconer's lips as he trudged off to the guest quarters.

Try as he might, Falconer could not stay awake. He had sat in the only upright chair in his chamber, but the exertions of the day still overwhelmed him. The first he knew that he had fallen asleep was when his nodding head roused him with a start. He cursed under his breath and peered out of the window, breathing a sigh of relief when he saw it was still pitch-dark. There still might be time to carry out his investigations before the monks stirred for matins. He began to put on the boots he had pulled from his sore feet the previous evening, then decided that they might make too much noise. He slipped down the wooden stairs of his quarters, and gasped as his bare feet touched the icy cold of the flagstones at the bottom. Almost wishing he had risked the heavy boots, he tiptoed softly round the cloister, the soles of his feet aching from the cold.

He mounted the day stairs that took him up to the sleeping quarters of the quire brothers. Gently opening the door, he prayed that the hinges were well oiled. His prayers were answered, and he slipped unheard into the lofty room that housed the sleeping monks. A mixture of snores, sighs and the threads of regular breathing muffled any noise he made crossing the floor to Lutt's enclosed space. He stopped in front of the door locked by Brother Ralph, and took the key from his pouch.

It had been surprisingly easy to steal it from the precentor, using a technique taught him by one of the more rascally of his students. Thomas Foxton had been incarcerated by Peter Bullock for two weeks for stealing a kerchief from the purse of the vicar of St Aldate's Church. That he had convinced the normally sceptical constable of the childish nature of the action meant he had avoided greater punishment. But Falconer wondered how many more items had found their way into Thomas's hands without their owners knowing. Still, he had been amused himself to learn the trick, and now it had stood him in good stead. Lack of practice had made him rusty, and he had almost dropped the key as his fingers had closed around it. But Brother Ralph had been unaware of his blundering effort.

He put the key in the lock and turned it. In a moment he was inside the office, with the door closed behind him. He groped in the pocket of his robe for the stub of a candle he had brought, and fumbled in the dark to light it with his flint striker and tinder. Shading the small flame with the palm of his hand, he crossed the room to the desk. His hopes of finding any documents relating to Lutt's blackmailing activities were low. His clandestine and hurried visit yesterday had uncovered nothing, and since then the prior had had a chance to conceal anything incriminating. But he had to try. An age spent poring over the papers on the desk revealed nothing, and he slumped into one of the high-backed chairs set against the exterior wall of the chamber. He smelled something odd, and rose out of the chair, sniffing the air. As he moved away from the wall, the smell receded. He turned back to the chair and lifted it away from the wall, taking care not to make a noise. There was a blackened crack in the plasterwork that had been hidden by the chair. He put his nose to it, and smelled soot. Suddenly a stray piece of information came unannounced into his mind, and he almost cried out with joy. He still had a chance.

Hurriedly locking the chamber door and tiptoeing past the sleeping monks, he scuttled down the exterior stairs. In his excitement, he was now oblivious of the stinging cold on the soles of his feet. He stopped at the bottom of the steps, and stood in the cloister getting his bearings. Up to his left was the end of the quire dorter where stood Lutt's office, and next to it, in the corner of the cloister, was the warming room. A massive chimney rose up the side of the undercroft and dorter, exactly where Lutt's office lay. Falconer knew that the warming room was the one concession to communal comfort in this and other monasteries. It was the sole place where monks had access to the warmth of a fire in the freezing depths of winter. Moreover, the flue backed on to the wall of Lutt's office, and would have inevitably warmed it without his having recourse to the warming room itself. So why would he have stopped the lighting of fires recently? Falconer thought he knew.

He didn't know how much time he had left before the monks rose for matins, so he raced across the cloister to test his theory. The warming room was gloomy and, in contradiction to its name, cold. On one side of it stood a massive opening spanned by a huge oak beam. It would have been possible for several men to stand in the fireplace itself, and Falconer could imagine the blaze that would have been stoked there. Now the hearth was black and depressing. Crouching down in the cold ashes, he thrust his free hand up the chimney and groped around in the soot and dust. At first he could feel nothing save the crumbling stonework. Perhaps he had been wrong to read too much into Thady Lamport's passing comment. He had been sure that the solitary monk's reference to Lutt's refusing a fire had been significant. It had not struck him that Adam Lutt was an ascetic. Refusing others the chance of warmth, perhaps, but not at his own expense. There had to be a reason for his not wishing a fire to be lit in this hearth. Falconer stood the stub of his candle in the hearth and pushed his arm further into the opening above his head. Suddenly his fingers felt the edge of a box. He gripped it and pulled it out. Sitting triumphantly amidst the ashes and fallen soot, he dusted the lid of the box, and opened it. His eyes widened. Within lay a set of papers, and a stack of coins.

*

The day had been dull and grey, the clouds hanging heavily over Port Meadow like unwashed blankets. Even the river had lost its sparkle, running turbidly between its banks. Ann Segrim had had plenty of time to ponder her dilemma. She had been placed in Godstow Nunnery by Peter Bullock with the agreement of the abbess, Gwladys, to discover who had killed Sister Eleanor. Now all the evidence that Ann had gathered pointed at Sister Gwladys as the murderer. She had come to the nunnery to bring some semblance of order to it. Discipline had been lax, and Eleanor had enjoyed a life barely different from that of any woman living outside the walls of a convent. The young nun had suffered more than anyone at the hands of the new abbess, who enforced discipline with a strong right arm. Could Gwladys have killed Eleanor in a fit of excessive zeal? And still have allowed Ann Segrim into the nunnery to carry out the constable's investigations for him? Perhaps she had thought she had no choice — she certainly had not been totally cooperative.

All these conflicting thoughts crowded in on Ann as she walked a lonely path along the river bank. With her mind so occupied, she did not notice the worsening of the weather until the downpour hit her. Within moments she was soaked, and the plain woollen dress she was wearing in deference to the new-found severity of her companions hung heavily on her shoulders. The bank was barren of shelter, and there was nothing to do but turn back, and dream of the dry clothes awaiting her in the convent. A pity the simple cell was so cold. She hoped this soaking wasn't going to bring on a fever.

Hal Coke, the gatekeeper, let her into the nunnery, complaining at having been called from his own warm, dry lair to do so. He appeared blind to the state of her clothing. She entered the cloister, leaving a trail of wet footprints behind her. By now it was early evening and the nuns should all have retreated to their solitary cells, so Ann was surprised when she heard a muffled squeal carry across the cloister yard. She had almost convinced herself it was a night bird when it came again: clearly human this time. Peering into the gloom from where it came, she realized there was a bar of light spilling out from the edge of a half-closed door. It was the door to the Rosamund chapel.

She tiptoed round the cloister, dripping water from the hem of her dress as she went. Another wail came from behind the door, but this one was cut off and ended in a throaty gurgle. Ignoring the wet, chafing dress that clung to her uncomfortably, she put her eye to the crack in the doorway. What she saw drew a gasp of shock from her. For a moment the tableau before Ann's disbelieving eyes was suspended in time. Sister Gwladys stood like an avenging angel over the cowering figure of another nun. They were both sideways on to Ann, so she could clearly see the abbess's face. It was an implacable mask, pale and rigid. The other's face was invisible, because the abbess held the nun's head pressed down to the cold stone floor. She held it there with one hand encircling her victim's neck in a vice-like grip. Just as Eleanor had been held. With her other hand she pushed down on the back of the head, grinding the other's face into the ground at the foot of Rosamund's tomb. Then, in response to Ann's gasp, the tableau changed.

Gwladys looked sharply at the door, her face red with exertion, and she released her hold on her victim's neck. As the other nun raised her head, gasping for air, Ann saw it was poor little Gilda. She pushed the door open and stepped into the chill air of the chapel, which, as well as being the house for a tomb, now felt like a tomb itself. Gilda's face was raw on one side where it had been ground against the rough surface of Rosamund's last resting place. Her eyes were round orbs that filled the inverted triangle of her face, her thin chin quivering in fear at its bottom point. She looked up in supplication at the bedraggled form of her saviour, struggled to her feet, and flew soundlessly out of the chapel.

Falconer wished he had his trusted friend, Peter Bullock, with him now. It was so useful to discuss his ideas with the constable, even though he understood little of the logic that lay behind them. Simply to have someone to talk to was helpful. He would have liked to confide in Ralph Westerdale, but was not sure how far the precentor was involved in the web of secrets that had caused both the death of John de Langetoft and, fifteen years later, that of Adam Lutt. The papers had told him a great deal. and he had to share some of his knowledge with Westerdale because he knew the writing on some documents was not Adam Lutt's. He had been able to compare it with the ledger he knew was in Lutt's hand. And though the common script of the monks was very similar, being learned from the same source, he knew that the oldest documents from the box hidden in the chimney were not written by the late camerarius. He simply had to trust Westerdale.

So it was that he drew the rotund little man into an empty carrel as soon as Brother Ralph was free of his morning devotions. He passed one of the papers over the top of the bookrest. It was folded, and when Ralph opened it he gasped in surprise.

'This is the missing page from the catalogue. Where did you find it?'

'Never mind where it came from. It is sufficient to know that it lists, amongst other items, the books from Grosseteste's library that I have been seeking. Thady Lamport's recollections were correct.'

'Brother Thady?' Westerdale was dumbstruck. 'When did you speak to him? He is supposed to be—'

'In solitary confinement. If living in a cell with the whole of Thurston Water to roam can be said to be confined. I spoke to him yesterday, and he recited the titles of several works passed on to here from the bishop's collection. Including one I had not heard of, entitled *De infinitate lucis* – the infiniteness of light. You can see it listed there.'

Ralph kept his head bowed, as though closely perusing the text. Falconer wondered if he had been wise in confiding in him after all. But he had to continue. He passed an older document over to Ralph and asked him whose writing it was. Westerdale peered at it closely, not really paying attention to the content. He hummed and hawed, hesitating, then held it to the light that filtered through the door's grillework.

'I don't recognize it as that of anyone who holds office at present.'

'Could it belong to . . . someone now dead?'

'What are you asking?'

'Could it be the hand of John de Langetoft?'

Ralph's face fell. 'You are asking me to identify the hand of someone who died fifteen years ago? Where did you get this document, anyway?'

As before, Falconer refused to answer. He simply asked Ralph another question. 'What sort of man was de Langetoft?'

The precentor dug back in his memory. He recalled Brother John as unsociable, and disinclined to share confidences with his fellow monks when they were all young novices. There were few occasions for sharing problems, and those who were uncertain about their future life whispered fleetingly in the darkness of the dormitory for common reassurance. Ralph had indulged in this comradeship along with the others. But John de Langetoft had been a man apart even then. He had been sure of himself, and of his inevitable progression to the highest rank — that of prior of Conishead.

Falconer recalled Thady Lamport's opinion of de Langetoft as someone who had broken his vows. This was not the man Ralph was describing.

'Could you see him as a sinner?'

Westerdale snorted. 'John de Langetoft considered himself a saint, and all those around him as composed of weak flesh. I regret his piety was somewhat insufferable.'

'Then, if you can't identify his hand, could he have written what you see in the document you are holding?'

Ralph looked down at it, and began to read. '"Brother Thady is destroying books. His clouded thinking is becoming intolerable.

Lay Brother Paul has twice failed to attend matins on pretext of stomach pains, yet he is well able to eat his food after sext. Brother Peter . . ."'

Falconer waved his hand impatiently. 'No, no. At the bottom of the page. Read that.'

'"Brother John the sacrist . . ."' Ralph looked interrogatively at Falconer in case this was still not what he was supposed to read. Falconer nodded vigorously, so Ralph read on silently. When the words before him began to sink in, Ralph could not believe what he was reading.

'In answer to your question, yes, I believe Brother John could have kept records of his brothers' . . . foibles. They could be currency spent in obtaining his goal – the office of prior. But this says that . . .'

Falconer nodded. 'That John de Langetoft, if that is his hand, knew some dark secrets about this community. Chiefly that fifteen years ago your little sacrist was sneaking off to visit a woman named Isobel, whom he was maintaining with the proceeds of books stolen from your library.'

'But the books are still going missing now. There was the one I told you of only the other day.'

'The psalter, yes. Then perhaps your sacrist is peculiarly faithful to this woman. I am fairly certain also that, on the strength of this document, Adam Lutt was blackmailing him. Remember the finger sign I asked you about?'

'The sign for passing the salt? Yes?'

'It was having seen Adam Lutt making that sign to John Whitehed in church that convinced me of what Brother Adam was intent on. And John paid him off. Now, I think it's more likely he would do that for a current misdeed than for one error of fifteen years ago. I do know we should keep our eyes closely on Brother John from now on.'

The light of comprehension began to dawn in Ralph's eyes. He leaned forward to whisper conspiratorially to Falconer. 'But if John de Langetoft knew of his sins, and Brother Adam found this document after he replaced de Langetoft, then that provides good reason for suspecting John Whitehed of killing both of them. Should we not report this to the prior, and have him imprisoned and interrogated?'

Falconer grimaced at such a crude approach, yet suddenly felt at home with this naive man. His proposed actions were no better than what Peter Bullock would have recommended.

'I prefer to have proof in the shape of evidence – truths that the murderer cannot deny – rather than force a confession from him. One that may turn out to be false, and based on fear of torture. We should monitor his movements, and catch him in the act. If he has stolen a book recently, we may not have to wait too long for him to betray himself.'

Chapter Twelve

The monks had a double and sombre ceremony to perform the following morning. Henry Ussher had decreed that the funeral rites of both John de Langetoft and Adam Lutt would take place after matins. And the prior went out of his way to ensure that the recent death caused no undue ripples in the normally placid surface of the pond that was Conishead. As far as the rest of the religious community was concerned, the truth of Brother Adam's death was that he had drowned in an unfortunate accident. Falconer joined the assembled community in prayers for the souls of the dead. Incense hung heavily in the air, like the perpetual mist that hung over the whole Leven valley. Below the altar lay two shrouded figures. That of Adam Lutt's body was large and bloated, the other – John de Langetoft's bones – scarcely disturbed the smooth surface of the dull, white cloth.

Unused as he was to ceremonial, Falconer found his eyelids drooping, until he received a sharp dig in the side from Ralph Westerdale, who sat next to him. Questioning the monk with an impatient look, Falconer was directed to the sight of John Whitehed scurrying round the legs of the prior like some faithful hound. He groaned, hoping that Ralph wasn't expecting him to follow the sacrist's every move. After all, he could safely assume that Whitehed would not disappear halfway through his devotions. Nevertheless, he nodded, then placed his hands over his face, as though in prayer, and tried to catch up on the sleep he had missed over the last few nights.

Not for the first time, he thought of Peter Bullock safe in his bed in Oxford with nothing more than the excesses of some young students to disturb his daily routine. He also thought of Ann Segrim, and could almost smell the sweetness of her yellow hair; could imagine it tumbling from the net that habitually kept it in check when she came to Oxford market. He imagined his guilty thoughts being censured by some composite image of a cleric, whose face wavered between that of the elderly prior of St Frideswide and Thomas de Cantilupe, former chancellor of Oxford University. Then the admonishing tones became real, and he awoke from his doze to hear Henry Ussher berating his community at large. But, listening carefully, Falconer was sure the words he spoke were directed at him personally. He even recognized the message as from the words of St Augustine.

'Whatever knowledge man has acquired outside Holy Writ, if it be harmful is there condemned, if it be wholesome it is there contained.'

Falconer could not square this stultifying religiosity with the excitement in the eyes of the prior when he had explained the new means of producing molten iron at the ironworks a few days ago. It was becoming clear that Henry Ussher was publicly distancing himself from the taint of any form of scientific enquiry, but Falconer was not sure why. Still, the more pressing matter was to observe John Whitehed's actions, which could lead to much more promising conclusions. The sacrist looked pale and unhappy.

Ann Segrim was wishing she could talk to William right now. Sitting facing the terrified Sister Gilda, whose face was still raw and oozing, Ann did not know what more to ask her. Their exchange to date could not be graced with the description of conversation. Ann had questioned Gilda, and the waif had responded with nothing more than a whispered yes or no, forced out through her tears. Now Ann had run out of questions. And it had all seemed such a good idea last night when she had found

Sister Gwladys grinding poor Gilda's head against Rosamund's tomb in a murderous rage.

When the weasel-faced girl had fled, Ann was left facing Gwladys, whom she now firmly believed to be Eleanor's killer. She wondered if she should flee herself, slamming the door on her adversary. However, Gwladys didn't look like a crazed murderer who had just been thwarted of her second victim. She merely looked embarrassed at being discovered by the younger woman. She looked like what she was — an awkward disciplinarian of an abbess, with her greying hair awry. They stared at each other, both uncertain of what to do. Suddenly Gwladys sniffed haughtily, and quickly took Ann by the arm. Ann flinched, and wondered if her chance of escape had passed.

'You're soaked, and should get out of those clothes immediately.'

The abbess's words were stiff, but obviously meant as an invitation to talk. They could also have been intended to divert Ann from the unusual circumstances of their meeting, and the abbess's role in it.

'Come with me.'

Ann decided it was best to follow.

In the solitude of the abbess's own room, which predictably was at least as severe as those of her flock, Ann peeled off her soaking dress. Though she would have liked to remove her shift as well, she left it on. The abbess no doubt would have been scandalized by the sight of her nakedness. Fortunately it was only slightly damp, and she used it to dry herself, rubbing some warmth back into her body. Unprompted, Gwladys began to speak, in an attempt to justify her actions to her guest.

'Gilda needed discipline — she had allowed Eleanor's death to affect her as the sister affected her in life.'

Ann frowned as she donned the coarse grey robe that the abbess offered her. 'And you needed to terrify her, and to skin her alive, to get the message over to her?'

Gwladys's whole posture stiffened. 'You don't understand these girls.' Ann wondered if she included Hildegard amongst the 'girls'. 'They were licentious when I arrived, allowing family members into the nunnery. And men into their cells. They decked their habits with ribbons and even kept pets. I was charged with rectifying the situation by the Papal Legate himself.

'As you know, the tomb in our chapel holds the remains of Rosamund, the old king's whore. And that is the fate of the licentious – to end up as a bag of bones, unloved and ignored by God. Gilda needed reminding of the rewards of licentiousness, and I was showing them to her. And I shall continue to do what is necessary to ensure good discipline.'

'Even to the extent of killing someone?'

Gwladys paled, and her hands went to her throat, plucking at the wrinkled flesh that Ann noticed for the first time. That, and her beak-like nose, suddenly made her look like some farmyard chicken about to have its neck wrung. She almost choked over her words.

'You cannot believe that I killed Sister Eleanor? I am here to save souls, not despatch them.'

'And did you think Eleanor's worth the effort?'

'She was a sister in this house for which I am responsible. I would think the value of her soul goes without saying.'

'Was Eleanor here by choice?'

The abbess sneered, and explained the dead nun's background.

It emerged that Eleanor had been placed in Godstow Nunnery by her family to hide her away from a boy whom they thought an undesirable companion for their precious child. Though a clean-faced youth, Thomas Thubbs had been no more than a farmer's son with fanciful ideas about his future. When Eleanor had been removed to Godstow, he had fled also. The abbess cackled harshly.

'His father insisted his son had gone to study at the university of Bologna. But he probably got no farther than the next village. But to answer your question – no, Eleanor de Hardyng had no vocation. That is why I was harsh with her. But I did not kill her. And I will continue to be as harsh with our little Gilda, until everything improper is beaten from her.'

'Will you let me speak to her?'

Gwladys frowned, and Ann thought she had pressed too far. But the abbess sniffed and agreed. 'If you think it worth it.'

'Alone?'

Gwladys nodded curtly, and dismissed the other woman.

Now Ann was faced with a Gilda who seemed able to provide very little information, and her ideas for solving this cloistral murder were running out. She tried one final question. 'Why did the abbess think you had acted improperly?'

Fresh tears welled in Gilda's eyes, and they coursed stingingly down her ravaged face. She shrugged her thin shoulders. 'Because I was Eleanor's friend, I suppose.'

'And Eleanor had behaved improperly?'

Again the non-committal shrug. But Ann was not to be deterred this time.

'Even after the abbess's arrival? Even recently?'

Gilda's soulful round eyes oozed pain and sorrow. 'She entertained a secret visitor. At night. But it was only her sister.' The last part came out as a wail, and Gilda clutched Ann's sleeve.

'Her sister? And was she here the night Eleanor was killed?'

The sorrowful Gilda looked deep into Ann's eyes, and nodded vigorously.

The day had proved a complete waste of time. After the solemn obsequies for the two dead, the prior and the sacrist had led their brother monks to the priory cemetery. There, on a suitably grey morning with more than a hint of drizzle in the air, the final words were said over the remains as they were lowered into their respective graves. The other monks hurried away to shelter from the rain, but John Whitehed stayed behind to supervise the two lay brothers filling in the holes they had dug the previous day. He stood under a tree to keep dry, but similar shelter was denied Ralph and Falconer. In ensuring they stayed out of sight of John Whitehed, but did not lose sight of him themselves, they stood beside the outer wall of the priory. It afforded them little shelter, and as the downpour got worse they got wetter. Watching the earth thudding down on Adam Lutt, Whitehed sighed as if finally believing that the man was dead, and could not return. Eventually, all that remained of both monks were wet mounds in the gloomy cemetery. The sacrist scurried back to the priory church, followed by his shadows.

There he prepared for prime, then obediently sat through Rules in the chapter house. Falconer did not understand how anyone could endure the life of routine that was John Whitehed's. His duties consisted of endlessly tidying the vessels and vestments used in the church. And he carried those duties out with loving care and meticulous attention to detail. While Ralph knelt in prayer in the church to keep an eye on their quarry, Falconer returned to his room to contemplate the other documents in the hidden box. He was excited by recovering the missing catalogue page and reading of an unknown work by Bishop Grosseteste – *De infinitate lucis*. He knew the bishop's obsession with light and optics, and longed to study this text to see if there were anything new revealed in it. It was a stray ray of sunlight piercing the gloom of the day that showed him something about the catalogue entries he had not spotted before. He held the page up closer to the window, and saw that the shiny surface of the parchment had been dulled in places. After each of the entries relating to Grosseteste's books, there was an oblong patch where someone had scratched out information. No matter. He knew of a simple way of revealing what was lost.

Ralph Westerdale was rather annoyed that the Oxford master did not appear again until after sext, when it was time to eat. Not that the work of keeping an eye on Brother John had been onerous. In fact, he had given no indication of his supposed misdeeds, sticking strictly and devoutly to his routine. Ralph was beginning to wonder if his theft of library books and furtive visits to the Isobel woman were all in John de Langetoft's imagination. But he could not escape the fact of Brother Adam's demanding money from the sacrist, nor his own opinion of Adam Lutt as someone who poked his nose into matters that were not his concern.

'Thank goodness he didn't know about me,' he muttered as he sat down on the hard bench that ran the length of the refectory table.

'Who didn't know about you?' The tall Oxford master slid easily in beside him, and began to ladle fish stew on to his trencher. The precentor was startled.

'Oh, I was just thinking that it was lucky Brother John didn't know I was observing him.'

The other monks around him hissed their disapproval at his speaking in the frater, and Ralph pursed his lips. He was surprised at his own facility in lying to Falconer, and felt rather sorry that the deeds of fifteen years ago should have reared up and so sullied his quiet life. He studiously avoided Falconer's eyes and concentrated on the Bible reading that accompanied the repast. He prayed for inner strength.

As they rose from the table, Ralph made to follow John Whitehed, but Falconer indicated that they should go to Ralph's austere office by way of the kitchens. There, Falconer stopped to speak to the cook, who explained that his excellent stew was the result of taking raw fish, putting it in a pot with parsley, minced onions, raisins, pepper, cinnamon, cloves, saunders and salt, and boiling it with wine and vinegar 'soakingly, till it be done'. Ralph could not believe that Falconer could be so relaxed, when they had a murderer loose in the priory. And one he had insisted until now that they keep an eye on. Having dragged the master away from the cook and his reminiscences of former repasts, he taxed Falconer on this very point. Falconer's reply was a reassurance.

'Don't worry, Ralph. I don't think John Whitehed is going anywhere in this weather. He will be in the church even now, preparing for the nones service. What I am more interested in is where the *"libraria interior"* is located.'

Ralph blanched at Falconer's words. How did he know of the secure location where the rarest of the books were kept? And did he know that Grosseteste's books were there? He had taken care to expunge the location from the catalogue before the page had disappeared, scratching out each entry. Was the man a magician?

Falconer must have read his mind, for he explained how it was possible to dampen the surface of a parchment, and, by holding it up to the light, read what had been erased.

'I could barely make out the words, but I recalled seeing them elsewhere in the catalogue against a few particularly rare texts. So I could assume that Grosseteste's books were equally rare, and deserving of this secure location. Am I right?'

Ralph nodded glumly.

'So, where is it?'

'It's a cupboard in the prior's lodgings. You will need his permission to gain access to it, though.'

'Keep an eye on John Whitehed. I'll talk to the prior.'

For such a large man, Falconer could move swiftly when he wished. Before Ralph could protest, he was out of the door, leaving the precentor to wonder what he would find. This Oxford master had the apparent ability to deduce past events from the dust left behind by deeds best forgotten. If that was what the teachings of Oxford resulted in, Ralph was glad he lived far away from it. The past should remain undisturbed. He sat at his desk for a moment longer, then wearily rose to his feet. He had better continue his surveillance of the sacrist. If the man disappeared while he was brooding in his room, no doubt Master Falconer would see collusion there, and suspect him of complicity in the two deaths. Ralph shivered at the thought, and, hunched against the persistent rain, scuttled off to the church.

The main door was open, and an eerie silence hung over the

interior. He should at least have been able to hear some sounds — the clink of vessels on the altar stone, the thump of books. Ralph's heart gave a lurch. Where was Brother John? He hurried up the aisle, the slap of his sandals breaking the stillness. Bowing briefly to the altar, he looked quickly in each of the side chapels. No sign of the sacrist. He rushed into the little room where the prior robed himself for the services. The vestments were neatly laid out, but the room was empty. Offering up a small prayer for help, Ralph hurried out of the side door of the church. Perhaps John was in the dormitory, where he had made a retreat for himself in one corner of the large, draughty hall.

Just as he turned the corner of the dormitory building, something landed with a thump at his feet. He looked down in amazement and saw it was a book. Had it fallen from the heavens, or from one of those cloud-ships that Brother Thady was so fond of talking about? He peered up at the sky, but in the encroaching dusk all he could see was the glimmer of a yellowish moon. The sound of someone descending the stairs brought him to his senses, and he scooped the book up, hiding it in his sleeve. Suddenly the missing sacrist burst out of the gloom of the archway, his eyes on the ground. It was a moment before he realized that Ralph stood in front of him. And with a startled expression on his reddening face, he mumbled something about preparing for the service, and made off towards the church.

Once he had closed the side door, Ralph pulled the book from his sleeve. It was the missing *Psalterium Hebraicum*.

Falconer could not believe it. To come so far, to be so close, and find the cupboard bare. For that was literally what had happened. He had expected to have to persuade the prior into revealing the secrets of the '*libraria interior*' on the grounds of scholarship. And if that had failed, to argue with him about Grosseteste's own wish that his library should be open to all. He had been dumbfounded when the prior readily agreed to open the

cupboard. He led Falconer into a side room where a pair of
sturdy doors were set into a recess in the wall. He took a key
from his purse, and put it in the lock.

'I think you'll be disappointed.'

The comment was thrown over his shoulder as he turned the
key. He opened the doors and stepped aside. There was nothing
in the cupboard but empty shelves. Falconer gasped with shock,
hardly registering the words the prior spoke.

'The books have been missing for a number of years. Did not
Brother Ralph tell you?'

Falconer mumbled thanks as empty as the bookshelves, and
left the prior to smirk at his retreating back. In a daze he retraced
his steps towards Ralph's office, wondering if all the losses could
be attributed to John Whitehed. How had he managed to steal
and sell all Grosseteste's books without being noticed? Immersed
in these thoughts, he bumped into a figure lurking in the archway
under the dormitory. An apology on his lips, he realized the
figure was that of Ralph Westerdale. But before Falconer could
question him, the monk came out with some fanciful tale about
a missing book's miraculous return. Falconer slowed him down,
and tried to concentrate.

'You say it fell from the skies just here?'

Ralph nodded. 'Do you believe that Brother Thady's cloud-
ships exist? That they stole the book, not Brother John?'

Falconer was about to scoff at Ralph's suggestion when he
recalled his own vivid imaginings as he was drowning, and merely
smiled. 'Before we assume the fanciful is true, let us eliminate
all the possibilities of this earthly existence.' He peered up at the
grey face of the dormitory building. It was blank. But when he
produced his eye-lenses, and held them up to his face, he noticed
a narrow slit directly above their heads. 'What's that?'

Ralph looked up to where Falconer was pointing. 'It lets air
into the rere-dorter.'

'Show me.'

They climbed the stairs to the long, open dormitory, and

Ralph led Falconer into the dank chamber where the monks emptied their bowels. From below the circular holes cut in the stone bench that ran along one side of the room, Falconer could hear the splash of the water that carried the waste into the river. A thin chink of light shone down from the slit in the wall that was the rere-dorter's sole access to fresh air. Falconer was able to reach it only by standing on the stone seat, taking care not to put a foot down one of the holes. He could put his hand into the slit easily from that position.

'Give me the book.'

Westerdale passed him the stolen book, and Falconer slid it into place.

'Can you see it from down there?'

The precentor said that he couldn't, and Falconer grunted in satisfaction. He looked down at the astonished Westerdale.

'I think this would make an excellent hiding-place, until you were in a position to retrieve whatever it was you had secreted here. I dare say your thief was used to using it, but in his haste to retrieve it today pushed the book out. And nearly hit you on the head with it.'

He stepped down from the toilet bench, and handed the book to Ralph. He leaned back on the well-worn stone and felt something rough under his palm. Curious, he looked more closely. There was a patch of yellowy grains of sand on the smooth, grey surface. His own boots were bereft of sand, so this was the end of the thief's trail from the book press. A thief who had been out on the bay prior to these activities, and who could have attacked him and Adam Lutt. He realized John Whitehed had been conspicuously absent from the priory at the time.

'And Brother John appeared shortly after the psalter fell at your feet?'

Ralph nodded.

'Now he has lost this book, I think you are due for another clandestine visit to your library tonight. But this time we will be ready.'

Chapter Thirteen

The owl hoot that echoed softly round the confines of the cloister reminded Falconer of Balthazar, and the comforts of his own solar back in Oxford. His envy of the barn owl's silent flight had spurred him to experiment with different means of replicating its aerial skill. He had rapidly come to the conclusion that he could not emulate the flapping motion that lifted a bird from the ground, but had tried to master the skill of gliding. He had spent much of the time that should have been devoted to his students studying the birds that populated the river and marshes around his home town. The soaring, still-winged gliding of the herons; the careering stoop of the kestrel; the effortless wheel of the buzzard. The closest replica he could make had been a crude affair of parchment, twig and cord. Launched from the battlements of Oxford's city walls, it had flown for a few glorious moments, then plummeted to the earth, shattering on a rock. Falconer was far from trusting his own frail flesh to a similar device. If only he could speak with Roger Bacon, he was sure he could resolve the problems. Dr Admirabilis, as his friend had been dubbed, had an infuriating way of seeing through the thicket that obscured most scientific problems. He wished the friar were here now.

'He's here.'

For a moment, the daydreaming Falconer thought Ralph Westerdale was referring to Bacon. Then he realized that he was pointing to a dark shape hovering at the door to the west press. The shape had its back to them, and was outlined by the light of the candle the man held in front of him. He was rubbing his fingers along the upper hinge of the massive door.

From inside the kitchen, Westerdale peered through the crack of the jamb. They had chosen this as their vantage point as they were unlikely to be disturbed, and it afforded a view of both the book press doors. However, the aroma of numerous meals had done nothing for the Oxford master's stomach, which rumbled in protest at the frugal fare it had endured recently. Falconer raised his eye-lenses, and looked over the monk's shoulder. He smiled.

'He's carrying out a bit of work you've been waiting to have done for some while. You told me you were disturbed last time by the noise of the door hinge. Brother John is oiling it for you. He doesn't want to be disturbed as he was before.'

They watched as John Whitehed completed his task with the tallow from the lamp he held in his hand. He then took a key from his sleeve and inserted it in the lock.

'I should like to know where he got that key from.' Ralph was annoyed. 'I am supposed to have the only one.'

'Keys can be copied, and you have an ironworks up the valley. Can you honestly say that your key has never been out of your sight in ten years?'

Ralph made as if to speak, then flushed when he saw how easy it might have been to 'borrow' his precious key for a day. He turned back to observing Whitehed's actions to cover his own embarrassment. The little sacrist had opened the press door and, with a quick glance around to confirm that he had disturbed no one, he slid through the opening.

'I've seen enough.' Ralph pulled on the door latch, but Falconer was too quick for him. His massive fist closed over the door frame and stopped it going any further. He pushed it closed, and flattened Westerdale against it.

'Don't do that -- you'll disturb him. I thought we agreed to follow him so that we knew exactly what he was up to?'

Ralph held his hands up in apology. 'I'm sorry — yes, we

agreed. It was just the thought of him taking yet another book from my library. I am charged with their safety, and with enlarging the collection. Not allowing it to wither away. I just lost my nerve.'

He swallowed hard, and tried to still his thumping heart. Falconer nodded and let go of Ralph's shoulders. The monk almost slumped to his knees, and Falconer took hold of him again, gently this time. He motioned for Ralph to move aside, and carefully opened the door again until there was a sufficiently large crack to observe the book thief. Luckily John Whitehed must still have been at his work, for the book press door was slightly ajar, and a flickering light played around the opening. Ralph's voice hissed in Falconer's ear.

'Do you think he'll make a move tonight?'

Falconer lowered his eye-lenses. 'Oh yes, I'm sure of it. The tide is right to cross the Leven at midnight, and the moon is full. Besides, if he had made arrangements to sell the book yesterday, he will not want to keep his contact waiting.' He stopped and lifted the lenses up again. 'Here he comes.'

John Whitehed eased past the half-open door, the light from his lamp spilling on his face. He looked fearful, and cast anxious glances around him. He closed the door silently and locked it behind him. Falconer watched as he crossed the upper range of the cloister, and breathed a sigh of relief as the monk walked past the archway that led up to the dormitory. Whitehed was not returning to bed. He stepped into the moonlight that shone palely on to the herb garden next to the prior's quarters. He was making for the side gate that led out on to the home fields, and north to Dalton. Convinced by the evidence of the sand that the sacrist was going to cross the Leven, this route puzzled Falconer. Perhaps he was simply going to double back round the priory walls. But there was no one to see him leaving by the main gate anyway. He must be going in another direction.

Though Westerdale pressed nervously at his back, Falconer waited patiently until the sacrist was out of sight, and only then did he step into the cloisters. Ralph fumbled with the key to the kitchen, dropping it on the stone floor with a clatter. He grimaced at Falconer, picked the key up, and with trembling fingers locked the door. Falconer was beginning to wish the precentor had not wanted to accompany him. But Ralph had insisted that if he were to allow the sacrist to steal yet another book, he was not going to let the man out of his sight. Falconer had reluctantly agreed, and would now have to ensure that the fat little man did not give the game away. There would not be a second chance. If John Whitehed had truly murdered de Lange-toft because the would-be prior had discovered the secret of his thefts and the reason for them, and then killed Adam Lutt for the same reason fifteen years on, this was the moment to uncover that secret for good. At least Ralph would prove a reliable witness when the case was laid before the prior.

Grasping the precentor firmly by the arm, Falconer followed the route Whitehed had taken to the side gate, and once again waited. The sacrist had shown how scared he was, and like a skittish horse would shy at the slightest sound. Falconer wanted him to be well away from the gate before he opened it. He nodded his head as he mentally counted the time. Then, sure that Whitehed would be clear away, but hopefully not out of sight, he eased the gate open and stepped through. For a moment his heart sank – he couldn't see the monk on the path that led round to the Leven. Then Ralph pulled at his sleeve and pointed in the opposite direction. An indistinct figure was crossing the field to Falconer's left – Whitehed was going north to Dalton after all. At least this would make it easier to follow him. Falconer had always been worried that the sands crossing would afford Ralph and himself no cover. Going north there was an abundance of trees to hide their pursuit, even though they were bare at this time of year.

The track was rutted and icy underfoot, and at one point Ralph almost cried out as his ankle turned beneath him. Falconer just managed to stop his cry with a hefty palm, which he held in place until Ralph nodded to show he was in control. He still winced when he put his foot back down, and limped behind the Oxford master, slowing their progress considerably.

The strange procession, lit by fitful rays of moonlight as clouds scudded across the sky, continued through the silent hamlet of Lindal. It seemed everyone there slept a drug-like slumber – not even the dogs were roused to disturb the quiet of the night. First the edgy John Whitehed scurried past the low, grey buildings, followed a while later by the measured tread of William Falconer, who himself was dogged by the limping and tired Ralph Westerdale. Falconer gauged it to be around the middle of the night now – if Whitehed did not meet whoever was going to buy his book soon, he would not have time to visit the Isobel mentioned in de Langetoft's notes before the start of the monastic day a few hours hence. Would they then be able to prove John Whitehed was anything more than a common thief?

It was not long, however, before Falconer could see the dark shapes of buildings rising out of the gloom. This had to be the outskirts of Dalton, where local people gathered weekly for the sort of market that identified the town, like Oxford, as a crossroads for the area. Though Dalton was on a much smaller scale than Falconer's own city, the opportunity for pleasure taken in good company was similar. Despite the hour, it was clear that one tavern on this side of the town had still not rid itself of its more persistent customers. The flickering light of tallow lamps played across the frozen ridges of the roadway, and illuminated the lower half of John Whitehed's body. He hesitated before the doorway of the tavern, his feet shuffling in the pool of light.

Falconer, who had stopped as soon as his quarry had, was suddenly pushed from behind. There was a muffled cry, and Falconer felt Ralph's hands grasp his shoulders. He heard a whispered apology. 'Sorry. I didn't see you.'

Falconer sighed, and sat the exhausted monk on a convenient

rock at the roadside. Seeing that the sacrist had entered the tavern, he told Ralph to stay where he was, and hurried down the road. The door to the tavern was half open – indeed the state of its hinges suggested that this was its permanent state. Hidden by the darkness, he peered cautiously through the gap in the doorway into the tavern. It was a low-ceilinged, gloomy establishment catering, at this hour, for a handful of dubious characters. Three were hunched over the rickety table at which they sat, snoring into the dregs of ale that lay in pools across the surface. Two others were still awake, slouched bleary-eyed over a game of nine-men's morris on which there was a considerable wager to judge by the coins that were scattered in front of them. One man groaned as the other's fingers flew over the pegs in the board. From the picture framed by the door's arch, Falconer could imagine many a shady deal hatched on these premises, which clearly made it suitable for the sacrist's purpose. No one would poke his nose into anyone else's business here for fear of ending up in the middle of the roadway spilling his life's blood into the mud. But where was John Whitehed?

Falconer felt for his eye-lenses, and squinted through the crack on the hinge side of the door. In one corner he could just make out a pair of well-shod feet stretched out underneath a table marginally more steady than the ones used by the sleepers and the gamers. They were not the feet of the sandal-clad sacrist, but were they the feet of the man he had come to sell the book to? As he turned his head to get the fullest view the narrow crack would allow, his question was answered. John Whitehed leaned forward, his face coming into sight. He looked pale, but there was a determined line to his pursed lips. Then his face disappeared again, and into the narrow range of Falconer's vision appeared a pair of hands, tremulously clutching a book. A gloved fist came from the opposite side and made as if to take the book. But Whitehed wasn't letting go, and for a moment a strange tug-of-war took place. Finally a silent agreement was reached and Whitehed laid the book on the table between the two men.

Falconer could only hear the low murmur of their voices, but their hands spoke volumes. First, the dealer's leather-clad palm opened the bidding, to be followed by the monk's soft fingers jabbing a refusal. The dealer's hand offered more, but Whitehed's waved it away. Several rounds were conducted in similar fashion, until Whitehed leaned into view again. Whatever he was being offered still seemed unsatisfactory, for he shook his head. But by now the buyer's gloved hand lay on the book as though he already owned it. There was a pause, and Whitehed's features disappeared again as he rocked back. The dealer's fingers drummed gently on the surface of the book. Then suddenly the sacrist's face reappeared, his eyes empty and downcast. He nodded, and the buyer's other hand came into view with a leather purse hanging from the fingers. The sacrist abruptly rose, and turned towards the door. Falconer backed away, intending to slip into the darkness.

At first he didn't realize that the figure approaching him from behind was Ralph Westerdale, or he would have pulled him into the shadows also. When he did see him, he hissed a warning, but the precentor was too slow. Ralph merely stood in the middle of the road, his eyes staring uncomprehendingly at Falconer. At that moment John Whitehed came round the door of the tavern, tucking the money bag into his sleeve. Confronted by his fellow monk, he too stood stock still not comprehending what might have happened.

The first to come to his senses was John Whitehed, and he emitted a despairing wail at realizing he had been discovered. Falconer, seeing the game was up, stepped forward to grasp the sacrist's arm. As fate would have it, Ralph too saw that action was required, and made a grab for his quarry. He only succeeded in grabbing Falconer, almost knocking him to the ground. Once Falconer had disentangled himself from the clutches of the apologetic Brother Ralph, the other monk was nowhere to be seen. The stricken Whitehed had fled into the night.

*

There was only one way into the inner cloister of Godstow Nunnery and that was through the great gatehouse that stood in line with the rickety river bridge. There were two other doors between the cloister, where the nuns lived their now secluded lives, and the outer court. But these had been locked and firmly bolted under Sister Gwladys's regime. Ann Segrim walked round the cloister perimeter, and tried both of the doors. The bolt on each had had time to rust into place – there was no evidence that anyone had recently sneaked in from the outside. It was still most likely that the murderer of Eleanor de Hardyng had lived with her inside the nunnery. But Ann now knew that Eleanor had had a visitor the night she died. Her sister, Gilda had said. Would her own sister really have killed her? For what reason?

Grimly determined to gather all the facts and solve the mystery, Ann made her way finally to the main gate, hitching up the ill-fitting habit she had borrowed. The material was coarse, and chafed her skin painfully – she would be glad to escape this purgatory, and don some more comfortable, worldly garments. Before her loomed the tower of the gatehouse, casting its gloomy shadow over the cloister. Beyond it, the sun shone on an altogether more pleasant world – inside its portals it felt chill and grey. The outer court, beyond the gate, was occupied by the convent's steward, bailiff and rent-collector. And the gate itself was guarded like the gates of hell by the ever-scowling Hal Coke, the Cerberus of Godstow Nunnery.

Having encountered him on her arrival, Ann Segrim knew him for what he was: a woman-hater, who probably took as much pleasure in keeping the nuns inside as in preventing the outside world from getting in. It had not always been thus. A year ago the Papal Legate, Ottobon, had deemed it necessary to lay an injunction on the gate-keeper not to pass 'gifts, rewards, tokens or letters' between the outside world and the nuns. Such trade must have been quite lucrative for Hal Coke, and its cessation provided added reason for his present sour demeanour. To have been able to recommence it must have proved irresistible to him.

As Ann approached the gate, Coke appeared under the arch and stood four-square in the opening. His lumpy, scarred face was set above a pair of broad shoulders that almost filled the gateway. Hands on hips, he thrust his head forward, peering at Ann with screwed-up eyes. His stare reminded Ann of Falconer's own myopic gaze.

'Going walking on your own again?'

His voice was rough and carried an undertone of disbelief, as if he could not imagine any woman not wanting to be in the company of a man. Ann wondered briefly if he had seen her talking to the constable, Peter Bullock. She decided he hadn't, and was merely being his usual churlish self. She shook her fist, rattling the coins she held in it.

'Tell me about Sister Eleanor's visitor.'

Falconer sat disconsolately in the precentor's office idly leafing through the library catalogue, awaiting the return of Ralph Westerdale from the monks' morning meeting in the chapter house. He had persuaded the prior that nothing definite should be said about John Whitehed's absence until they could locate him. Or until he became another missing person, as John de Langetoft had been for fifteen years.

Everything had gone wrong. Not only had his chief suspect for two murders disappeared off the edge of the world; the very books he had come to find had disappeared too, presumably spirited away by the missing murderer. Only the last book to be stolen – the one from last night – had been recovered. Falconer had been in time to stop the dealer sneaking away with his prize. Though he claimed to have bought the book fair and square, a threat from Falconer to hand him over to the nearest constable had made it clear he knew the item had been stolen, and resulted in the prompt return of the book. The dealer had been left with a loss on the night, but it had been a small price to pay for his freedom. It also appeared that the sale had been effected in Dalton because the dealer was there for the market. He normally dealt with the sacrist in Lancaster, but had agreed to vary that routine as Brother John had seemed anxious to conclude the sale. Falconer could only assume that John Whitehed had needed the money urgently because of Ralph's recovery of the previously stolen book. If the sacrist did cross the bay to sell the books, and the sand found at the site of the thefts and in the rere-dorter would suggest that, then it was possible the mysterious Isobel was to be found over there as well. It also meant Brother John could have been the perpetrator of the attack on Falconer. Logic said the murderer had been identified, if not apprehended.

There seemed little to keep Falconer at Conishead now, for John Whitehed could hide himself away in the remoteness of the hills beyond Thurston Water for ever if need be. To the Oxford master it felt like an unsatisfying end to his investigations. Truly the sacrist had had reason to kill both John de Langetoft, who had uncovered his thefts and his breach of the vows of celibacy, and Adam Lutt, who had discovered the same secrets, only to use them for the purpose of blackmail. He had cause to attempt the slaying of Falconer himself, knowing that he was investigating de Langetoft's death. He could have brought sand into the priory on his sandals the very night of the attempt on Falconer's life. Sand from the estuary where Falconer had been walking.

Thady Lamport, moreover, had said that all three monastic vows had been broken at Conishead. Obviously, the vow of celibacy had been broken by John Whitehed, and the vow of poverty broken by Adam Lutt, with his greed for accumulating money. But to whom did Lamport attribute the breaching of the vow of obedience? Perhaps he laid that at Henry Ussher's door, in his prideful search for power. Whatever his meaning, it mattered little now.

But still the unfinished nature of his deductions nagged at William. The catalogue of Conishead's library lay before him, and it was open at the loans records. He realized that they were complete back to well before Ralph was responsible for the library — much was in the familiar hand of Thady Lamport.

Leafing through he came across an old record of a borrowing by John Whitehed.

John Whitehed, sacrist   Ad inclusionem spiritus in speculo

One of the books he had stolen and sold. A year later, there was another record.

John Whitehed, sacrist   De Anima

Another lost book. The sacrist clearly borrowed a book to check its worth before stealing it. For the sake of completeness, though it mattered little, Falconer began to cross-check the stolen books against Whitehed's borrowings. It might at least tell him when Grosseteste's works got into the hands of the book-dealer. As he worked through the catalogue, he saw how Lamport's orderliness gradually turned to chaos. His writing became more illegible, and his records more brief, until he was just recording borrowers' initials and the book's catalogue number.

JW–135
PM–27
HU–349

In order to check out the continuing story of the thefts, Falconer had to refer back to the main catalogue records. It became a laborious task, but he was determined to stick to it, though his eyelids felt heavy. At one point he jerked his head up from his chest, not knowing if he had just dozed off, or if he had slept for an age. The careful, hand-drawn letters on the page melted one into the other, and he knuckled his eyes back into focus. He felt sure there was something of great import staring him in the face, but he was too tired to see it.

He tried once again to assemble all the facts at his disposal, and to arrange them into a semblance of good order. Try as he might, they just kept turning into fantastic visions. John White-hed scurried across his eyes, pleading his innocence despite all the evidence to the contrary. He was followed by a solemn procession of monks led by the prior, Henry Ussher, who was trying to hide a pile of books under his habit. Thady Lamport was next in line, whipping the back of the prior with a huge knout and screaming 'I know, I know.' Ralph Westerdale clawed ineffectually at the inexorable rise and fall of Lamport's whip arm. Adam Lutt followed them all, gathering coins that fell from his fellow monks' robes. A skeleton dressed in a monk's habit, who Falconer somehow knew was John de Langetoft, hovered over them all in a ship. He was throwing down books with large numbers on their covers. In embarrassment, Falconer realized that the skirts of all the monks' habits were concealing but poorly the rising of their manhood.

A sudden draught lifted the corner of the page he was staring at uncomprehendingly. He looked up at the door, and saw a hazy, white shape hovering before him. He rubbed his tired eyes again and the shape resolved itself into the ancient form of Fridaye de Schipedham. The white, wispy hairs of his long beard stirred in the breeze from the open door, and his eyes were bottomless pools of sorrow.

Falconer tried to speak but his mouth was impossibly dry and no sound came forth. The Hospitaller seemed to drift rather than walk across the room to Falconer's side. With a start the Oxford master realized the candle that stood on the table had been extinguished by the gust of wind that had stirred the pages of the catalogue. A thin, twisting column of smoke rose from the blackened wick. Yet there was light in the room to see by. Falconer looked more closely at his silent companion. Clad only in a loincloth, the pale skin of his exposed torso had a glow of its own that illuminated the room. His face appeared more skeletal than when Falconer had last seen it. He expected the apparition to speak, but though its mouth hung slackly open no sound came forth. It was the eyes that drew Falconer, drew him down into the very soul of the troubled Hospitaller. On their surface, Falconer thought he saw some shapes that were not the reflection of the room as they should have been. Instead, he clearly saw a young knight, shrouded in a white surcoat on which was blazoned a large red cross. He instantly knew this was the youthful de

Schipedham. As he stared, the Crusader's garb melted into the very robe Falconer had worn after being saved by the hermit. He stood stiffly to attention, and at the youth's feet knelt a woman, whose face was cast down to the ground. His lips moved, though Falconer could hear no sound, and the woman looked up. Her hair was raven, her eyes the shape of almonds, and her lips a voluptuous bow of red. She was undoubtedly the hermit's nameless princess, and Falconer knew why he could not have resisted her. As he watched, the young de Schipedham's stiff posture collapsed, and he drew the woman up towards him.

The apparition blinked and suddenly, though there were still two people reflected in his eyes, their faces were different. Falconer recognized immediately who they were, and he smiled. A long sigh escaped the lips of the ancient hermit, as though a tiring penance had at last been completed. He turned towards the door, hesitated, and pointed a long finger at the catalogue in front of Falconer. The Oxford master peered at the page in puzzlement, his eyelids now heavy with sleep. He did not know if he had fallen asleep, but suddenly he jerked his head off his chest and looked up. The door was closed, and de Schipedham was gone.

Having been plunged into darkness, Falconer fetched a lamp from the corridor outside Westerdale's room, and looked at the page again. He saw a fresh ink mark against a particular entry, then another, and another down the page. It was not the page he last remembered looking at, though. Had the wind blown the pages over? Had he marked the entries himself virtually in his sleep? Or had the hermit really come to the priory, and pointed him to the right track in some uncanny way? Truly he cared not, because he now had all the pieces of the riddle in his grasp.

When Ralph Westerdale returned he was surprised to find Falconer poring over the catalogue, a scrap of paper at his elbow filled with numbers, and a broad smile on his face.

NONES

If I take my flight to the frontiers of the morning,
Or dwell at the limit of the western sea,
Even there Thy hand will meet me,
And Thy right hand will hold me fast.

Psalm 139

Chapter Fourteen

'Brother Paul . . .'
        'Peter.'
'Brother Peter. You travelled with the prior when he visited the fishery and the ironworks recently?'

The monk hesitated at Falconer's question. He did not want to be drawn into anything that may reflect badly on the prior. And this tutor from Oxford seemed a slippery customer, able to turn anything he might say the wrong way. Falconer knew what was in Peter's mind, and draped a friendly arm over his shoulder. As they walked along the edge of the fishponds, he cast a glance back up to the window arch he knew overlooked them. As far as his poor eyes could tell, there was no one in the camerarius's office. The only other person within sight was Ellen Shokburn, wading up to her thighs in the farthest pond. She was dragging out weed with a long-handled rake. Too far away to hear what was being said.

Brother Peter got the message – even if he said something untoward, no one would know it had come from him. His shoulders relaxed under Falconer's arm.

'Yes. The prior taxed the lay brother at the fishery severely for not supplying enough fish to restock the ponds.' He waved a pudgy hand at the pools around them. 'He thought the brother was being lazy. The prior is a very . . . active man, and expects us all to share in the communal effort.'

Falconer was amused by Brother Peter's obvious desire to express his admiration of Henry Ussher, emphasized by the earnest look on his face. But he kept a straight face and let the monk ramble on as he described the prior's visit to ironworks and fishery. Eventually Peter came to the storm and the difficulties the little group had experienced in returning to the priory. He recounted how a peasant had gladly volunteered his hovel to the monastic party, leaving with his family to shelter in the woods. Falconer could imagine how 'glad' the peasant had been to give up a dry roof for the damp and chilly forest. And how he had been ordered to 'volunteer' his accommodation.

'So you all sheltered there overnight?'

Peter nodded happily, sure that he had not unconsciously betrayed the prior in any way.

'And you were with the prior at all times?'

Peter nodded so vigorously, Falconer feared for the safety of the head on his shoulders. 'I had the pleasure to serve the prior through the whole trip. Only when he returned to the ironworks to retrieve his missing gloves was I not at his side.'

Falconer held his breath. Dare he ask the monk to clarify what he had said, or would he just clam up and deny everything? He need not have worried — the guileless fellow simply carried on explaining.

'I thought it odd at the time. For we had settled in for the night in the dry, and the prior realized he had left his gloves at the ironworks. I offered to get them myself, but he insisted that as it was his fault he should retrieve them. But to do so while it was still raining was penance indeed.'

'Was he gone long?'

'Oh, some time — as long as between nones and vespers.'

Long enough to return to the ironworks and murder Adam Lutt, for example.

'Have I been of help?'

Falconer roused himself from his mental calculations, and thanked the artless monk for his assistance. He had indeed been of help, and this put a new light on the matter of John Whitehed's guilt. The prior too was in the vicinity of the ironworks at the right time, but did he have a motive? Falconer thought he knew of one. He hurried off, hardly giving a second glance to the bare, brown limbs, dripping water, that Ellen Shokburn revealed as she clambered out of the pond.

Henry Ussher paced his office impatiently as he listened to Ralph Westerdale's report on the failure to find the missing sacrist. Several of the lay brothers had been despatched northward with instructions to comb the fells for any trace of John Whitehed. As far as they knew, he had wandered off in some unreasoned distress and needed their help. The prior was not yet ready to reveal the suspicions about the sacrist's involvement in the deaths at the priory. Ralph thought more could and should be done, but Henry Ussher had taken charge of the situation. His instructions were to be obeyed, even though Ralph privately thought they had little chance of success. If he had known that success was the last thing the prior wanted, he would have been shocked.

Ussher was in fact more concerned about the impending arrival in the region of Ottobon, the Papal Legate. Though the relationship between the papal hierarchy and the monastic orders in England were strained – usually by the persistent demands for money that the one made on the other – the prior knew how to make use of connections in that hierarchy. Indeed, money could be put to good effect in smoothing the path of personal preferment. The last thing Henry Ussher needed in the circumstances was rumour and scandal attached to the priory, or himself. No – much better to keep the whole matter quiet, and deal with John Whitehed when Ottobon had gone. The handful of lay brothers sent to scour the fells was more for show than to provide results. Though he did still need to pin the blame of the double murder on the sacrist, before any more awkward questions were asked. Thinking of awkward questions, he asked Westerdale where that nuisance of an Oxford master was. The response was worrying.

'He's gone to the ironworks. He said he wanted to look again at what you showed him before. Said he had a scientific interest. Does that make sense?'

The prior paled, and hurriedly dismissed the puzzled precentor.

At the ironworks, the sullen ironmaster had been suddenly won over when Falconer said he had come expressly to see the new furnace. He had guessed it was the man's pride and joy, and that any interest shown in it would raise the esteem of the enquirer in his eyes. Falconer wondered if the prior yet knew of his destination, for he certainly would not be able to keep it secret. Secrets were impossible in the claustrophobic atmosphere of Conishead, as John Whitehed had discovered to his cost. The wonder was that the sacrist had kept his from all but one person for so long. No, the prior would know soon enough where Falconer was. Indeed, how he reacted to Falconer's visit to the foundry could provide yet more clues for the master to weave into the tapestry of his investigations. Let all the others rush hither and thither in search of John Whitehed; he was on a more purposeful track.

When he crossed the estuary below the priory, he had wished he had an excuse to see the old hermit on Harlesyde Island. He was sure that Fridaye de Schipedham knew more than he was telling. And he still was not sure if the visitation last night had been a physical manifestation of the hermit or not. But in the early morning light there was no sign of him on the island, and Falconer felt sure he would be unwelcome unless invited. The hermit's twenty-year penance for his conduct in Outremer was saddening. Did he truly regret so much the time he had spent with his Arab princess? The vows made to his Order were harsh and cruel in Falconer's eyes. He would leave the man alone for now, but he still might have to breach Fridaye's self-imposed exile one day.

His solitary journey across the sands, disturbed only by the call of the wading birds, gave Falconer time to mull over what he knew for sure, and what he could deduce. Though it was still possible that John Whitehed had killed on two occasions, separated by fifteen years, Falconer nevertheless had some questions about other monks at the priory: chiefly the prior's possible presence at the ironworks when Adam Lutt was killed, and the supposed embezzlement of funds by the camerarius. And he would not be content until they were answered.

The ironmaster was uncharacteristically loquacious as he led Falconer down the track to the site of the furnace where iron could be melted.

'Iron is the tool that makes us what we are, you know. Without dread of iron the common good is not preserved. Without iron innocent men cannot be defended. No field can be tilled without it, nor building built. Now I have the means to shape it as I wish.'

Falconer felt sure he had borrowed those words from someone more learned than he. But there was still truth in them. When they reached the new furnace, the ore had already been loaded in the top of the bowl, which was now sealed. The heat from the furnace was building up as the water-powered bellows rhythmically pumped air over the coals. The Welsh ironsmith presided over the proceedings and a group of grimy workers stood ready to deal with the resulting hot liquid. One of the group — a short man with a pock-marked face — stared fearfully at Falconer. He appeared shifty, and to be sweating more than even the heat from the furnace would warrant. On another occasion Falconer might have taken more notice. But he was distracted by the ironmaster's explanation that the process had some while to run before the ore liquefied. He decided it was time to tax the man with a question about Lutt's presence at the ironworks that fateful night.

The ironmaster looked suspiciously at Falconer before he replied. His piggy eyes, pressed deep into the bulging flesh of his reddened face, registered none of the calculation that was going on behind them. He shrugged, coming to the conclusion he had nothing to lose.

'He said he had come to investigate the finances of the ironworks, though there was no reason for him to do so. Everything I undertake is carried out with scrupulous honesty.'

Falconer could have said that he would be unique in his profession if that were the case, but he needed more from the man. He nodded and let him go on.

'Mind you, he didn't have time to do what he came for. The storm interrupted all that. And I must say he was more than a little confused in the first place. He said the prior had sent for him. But you know that the prior had just spoken to me – you were here – and he gave no indication then that he had any concerns.'

Falconer rolled around his brain the idea that the prior had secretly arranged for Adam Lutt to come here. This was more and more interesting. He pressed the ironmaster on his last point. 'No concerns at all? About your paperwork?'

The ironmaster's red face paled a little at the last word, but he still shook his head. Falconer pulled a piece of parchment from his pouch. It was one of the documents from Adam Lutt's desk – the one that did not tally with Lutt's accounts, and mutely accused the camerarius of embezzling the money from the sale.

'Do you recognize this document?' Falconer did not allow the ironmaster to take the parchment, but held it before his face. 'That is your mark at the bottom, is it not?'

The ironmaster had to grudgingly agree.

'Strange that the surface looks so clean, when all the other documents that come from here are marked and stained with the honest sweat of your hands. As soon as I saw it on Lutt's desk, I thought there was something wrong.'

The ironmaster began to deny the accusation, but the look in Falconer's eyes told him it was useless. He looked at the ground in embarrassment.

'He told me to mark it. He said there was something wrong in the accounts, and this would put it right. And he said that if I didn't agree he would make sure Lutt found something wrong — at my end.'

'He?' Falconer needed to be sure.

'The prior — you saw us talking about it. It was just as you were leaving the clearing that day.'

It was clear the prior had faked Lutt's embezzlement of funds to cover something more serious. Falconer had hardly begun to think about the implications when there was a cry from behind them. The rhythmic roar of the fire as the bellows blew air across the white-hot coals was overlaid by a crackling and spitting. Suddenly the plug that held the contents of the bowl-furnace in place burst free and liquid fire poured forth. Falconer and the ironmaster had been standing nearby, Falconer with his hand resting on the sandy hollow that the molten ore was to flow into. If it had been left to the Oxford master, they would have been standing in the path of the hellish liquid still. But the ironmaster was wise to the dangers of his foundry.

He flung himself at the not inconsiderable bulk of Falconer, and they both tumbled over on the muddy ground. As the liquid hissed into the hollow, some of it splashed over the side. The ironmaster's face, pressed close to Falconer's own, suddenly turned ashen, and a grimace contorted his face. Suddenly his body was a dead weight in Falconer's arms. The Oxford master scrambled to his feet, and dragged the now unconscious ironmaster away from the devilish liquid that dribbled sluggishly in the mud. Too late — the man's left foot was covered with a slimy grey deposit, and his boot was blackened and cracked.

The eerie silence that reigned for a moment but lasted for an age suddenly ceased, and pandemonium broke loose. The iron-workers plunged on their master and hoisted him up in their arms. They were led by Llewellyn, whose spitting monster had bitten back at last. The ironmaster was carried away down the woodland track towards the main encampment. All Falconer saw of him was a limp arm that dragged in the mud. He was left alone in the desolate glade where a filthy slurry steamed odiously at his feet, giving off an unnatural stench, overlaid with the smell of burning flesh, that tore at the lining of his nose. He retched, but stood his ground, and examined the site. Holding the sleeve of his robe over his face, he approached the furnace. The plug that should have held back the flow of molten iron was gone. Either it had been poorly fitted, or someone had deliberately knocked it out. There was a chance it had been a tragic accident. But the fact that the weasel-faced worker had been nowhere to be seen when the others crowded round their master made Falconer think otherwise. This had surely been another attempt on his life, and he had only been saved by the quick thinking of the unfortunate ironmaster. A man whose name he didn't even know.

Ralph was bewildered. First the prior had dismissed him from his presence, then shortly before terce had sent for him urgently. Ussher appeared agitated, and was in the process of packing a large saddlebag with the most sumptuous of his clothes.

'I must leave at once. The Papal Legate is due in Lancaster the day after tomorrow, and I must be there to meet him.'

Ralph wondered why the prior had decided to act so late in travelling to meet Ottobon. He must have already long known the Legate's itinerary, for no one had arrived at the priory today who might have brought new information. And the way he was treating his best robes, stuffing them unceremoniously in saddlebags, was entirely uncharacteristic of the meticulous Henry Ussher. Ralph stood in the middle of the whirlwind, wondering what the prior wanted of him. He was soon told.

'Bring the young bay guide here. I must speak with him about the tides, and when I might cross Lancaster Bay.'

Ralph Westerdale nodded. 'I will send his mother to fetch young Jack – she is working at the fishponds still.'

Though given his orders, Ralph was still perturbed by the prior's mad activity, and only stirred himself to action when

Ussher's impatient glare fell full on him. He scuttled off to find Ellen Shokburn.

Having learned that his saviour was still alive, though grievously hurt, Falconer began the return journey to Conishead. The ironmaster would live to battle with ore again, whether it be the solid bloom that came from the old furnaces, or molten flux from the new. He would not walk very easily, but he could still bully his underlings into sweating shape into the iron. Falconer cursed under his breath when he realized he still had not asked the man his name. At the time he had been too glad to retreat from the confines of the mean and odorous lean-to where the man lay, his face still strangely grey and clammy. Falconer was never at ease with illness – his own or others'.

Now the quiet of the track leading down the river bank restored his humour, and he once again went through the facts he had gathered about the monks at Conishead Priory. It was as Fridaye de Schipedham said, a house of secrets. And John Whitehed seemed to have the most. He had been stealing and selling books for years, in order to pay for his alliance with the mysterious Isobel. Odd, though, that Falconer just did not see him as a breaker of the monastic vow of celibacy. Such an obsequious, frightened little man. Falconer reserved judgement on who had been uncelibate. Who else harboured secrets? Thady Lamport was undoubtedly mad, and he had drawn an accurate picture of John de Langetoft's death by stabbing. Only if he had been there could he have known what happened – seen it or perpetrated it. Brother Ralph had no possible links with the deaths, so far as Falconer could tell. Which left the prior, Henry Ussher. He was in the vicinity of the ironworks when Adam Lutt was killed, and had falsified papers to accuse Lutt of embezzling priory funds. Had he done this in order to counter a blackmail threat by Lutt, and had Lutt known something that John de Langetoft had also known, to his cost? Death had been the price for the camerarius's breaking the vow of poverty.

De Langetoft and Ussher had been intense rivals for the post of prior. Breaking the vow of obedience could certainly be laid at both their doors. And de Langetoft could well have known something about Ussher that he would have preferred to keep secret. But had it been reason enough for Ussher to kill de Langetoft?

And then there was the matter of Grosseteste's missing books. None of them had been borrowed by the sacrist, so they did not fit into the pattern of the books stolen by him. Not taken by John Whitehed, then, but missing nevertheless. Falconer felt sure the books had something to do with whatever was Ussher's secret, and his examination of the library catalogue had furnished him with some intriguing facts. Yes, the prior had some answers to provide. The Oxford master began to stride more determinedly along the muddy track, as the questions to ask formed themselves in his mind.

Chapter Fifteen

If Henry Ussher was travelling to Lancaster, he would normally take the longer land route round the head of both the Leven and the Kent. This would allow him to ride on horseback, and transport the several trunks of clothing that he usually deemed his dignity to require. But today's journey was precipitate, and the need to be in Lancaster on the morrow demanded he travel on foot across the sands of both Leven and Lancaster Bay. The boy, Jack Shokburn, had been spoken to, and had agreed reluctantly to take the prior across the vast expanse of Lancaster Bay in the gathering gloom that the tide time demanded. It was either that or wait for dawn. And Henry Ussher wanted none of that – he needed to make the journey now. The final preparations were in the making, and the youth was to go ahead to prepare lamps for the crossing.

But first Ralph escorted him to the camerarius's empty office, to get the coins that the prior insisted Jack be paid for his inconvenience. The sullen youth stood rubbing his chapped hands together as Ralph opened the chest, which till now had been Adam Lutt's responsibility, and extracted a small leather bag. The coins were counted into the youth's hand where they lay sparkling in the candlelight. The door flew open at that moment and Falconer rushed in.

'Ah, Brother Ralph, I've found you at last. I have news of John de Langetoft's murderer.'

He stopped abruptly as Shokburn turned round. He had not recognized the youth's back, and now wished he had not spoken up so openly. It would not do for him to hear Falconer's theories. Realizing that the master was embarrassed by his outburst, Ralph Westerdale dismissed the youth, and hustled Falconer out of the dormitory and round to his own simple room. When they were settled either side of the bare table, Ralph spoke.

'Let's not tell everyone about our little . . . difficulty.'

He was angry, knowing that unpleasant rumours were already circulating about John Whitehed, and that young Shokburn could easily have confirmed them, if Falconer had said any more. It would not do for the local people to lose their respect for the priory and its residents. He asked Falconer for the news about the missing sacrist. A frown crossed Falconer's features.

'Why should I know about John Whitehed?'

'But you said you had news of him.' Ralph was getting exasperated with this obtuse academic.

'News of Whitehed? No, I said I had news of John de Langetoft's murderer, and I believe him not to be Whitehed.'

'Who could it be, then?'

Falconer leaned forward, and smiled knowingly. 'I must see the prior first.'

Westerdale gasped, and threw up his hands in horror. 'You cannot suspect the prior of the deed, surely?'

Before Falconer could reply there was a scraping sound from the other side of the door. The Oxford master rose swiftly to his feet, and flung the door open. There was no one on the other side. He peered across the cloister, his lenses held up to his eyes. All he could see was the retreating back of Jack Shokburn. Why was he still around? Had he gone to the kitchens to beg some food, or had he been listening outside Westerdale's room? He shrugged his shoulders, and stepped back inside. A white-faced Westerdale still awaited his reply. Instead, Falconer asked another question.

'Did you know that Henry Ussher borrowed the Grosseteste books before they were lost?'

Brother Ralph's face betrayed the fact he did, but still he

blustered. 'How could you possibly know that? We are talking about something that happened more than fifteen years ago.'

Falconer laid his hands on the massive catalogue that lay between them, swivelling it round to face Westerdale. 'Thady Lamport's records were sketchy at the end, but he still wrote down who took which book from the library. Look here.'

He flipped the tome open where he had inserted a scrap of parchment, and poked an accusing finger at the page. 'Here. It reads "HU – 349". And here.' He turned a page and stabbed down with his finger again.

'It reads "HU – 345". And there are other entries, too. Item 344, and so on. HU – Henry Ussher. Now look up the entries in the catalogue for items 344 and 345 and 349. Or should I say look them up on the stolen page. For that is where they are recorded.'

He flattened the crumpled page on the table top.

'Item 344 – *De luce*, originally property of Bishop Grosseteste. Item 345 – *De sphera*, originally property of Bishop Grosseteste. Item 349 – *De infinitate lucis* – Grosseteste.'

Ralph sighed and hung his head in silence, so Falconer pressed on.

'What was a man who professes to uphold Augustine's doctrine that anything not in the Bible is wrong doing with such . . . startling works? I mean, I know that the bishop asserts in *De sphera* that *per certa experimenta* the stars are not fixed in the heavens. And demonstrates that the world is round by showing that the Pole Star, high in our sky, is low to the horizon in the Indic lands. Did Ussher think that by hiding the books he could hide the knowledge also?'

Ralph became agitated, rising from the table and pacing the room. 'No, no. You have it all wrong. The prior has always been a man of infinite curiosity.'

'What was he doing with the books, then?'

Ralph gulped, his mind racing. At last he spoke. 'Copying the experiments written down by the bishop.'

*

As Brother Henry fiddled with the lens, he asked Brother Thady to read him the section from the book again. The cadaverous monk lifted the heavy tome in his hands and held it to the weak dawn light that filtered through the shutter on the window arch.

'He says that in optics light — he uses the word "lux" here — symbolizes the highest form of perfection. Lux produces lumen, his other word for light, from nothing, much as God produces creatures out of nothing. Light is the "prima forma corporalis" of Creation spreading to the limits of the universe in the first moment of time.'

'The "prima forma corporalis",' muttered Brother Henry reverently. He set the prism, a piece of glass he had obtained with great difficulty, in proximity to the lens, and arranged it so the first beams of sunlight would shine on the wall of the room. Thady set the book down and frowned at the arrangement of metal armatures and glass. He was getting more and more perturbed about Brother Henry's efforts. What did he call this? Oh yes, finding out from his own experience — "per experientiam propriam". He called it an experiment.

'Why should we need to repeat what Grosseteste has already shown?'

Henry tutted in exasperation. 'I have already told you. The bishop says there is a world of difference between knowing a truth solely from a book, and knowing it from personal experience. To know that something is so is a lower knowledge than to know why it is so. I seek that higher knowledge of why.'

'And what will this . . . arrangement do?' Thady waved his hands once again at the lens and prism. Henry stepped forward and shielded his set-up.

'Careful. It has taken me an age to align them, and you nearly ruined it all with one wave of your clumsy fingers.'

Thady clenched his bony fists together and thrust them out of harm's way up the sleeves of his habit. Henry recovered his temper and tried to explain.

'Grosseteste avers God is light — "Deus lux est". This experiment should draw perfect light through the celestial spheres on to this wall.'

Thady was getting frightened. 'The bishop also said before he died

that the Pope was Anti-Christ, and the Church would not be freed from
servitude except by the edge of a bloody sword.'

Henry snorted. 'That was mere politics. This is science.'

He strode over to the window and flung open the shutter, letting the
early rays of the sun fall on the crude lens. This lens in its turn focused
light on the block of glass that was the prism. Both monks turned their
gaze to the wall, one eagerly, the other with apprehension. What they
saw filled them with horror.

'And he really thought he had dissipated the very matter of the universe?'

'It's what drove Brother Thady finally mad. He thought they had shattered the very essence of God, and he ran off. The prior — Brother Henry as he still was then — came to me that same morning. It was the first time I had seen him not in control of himself. He told me to find Thady and care for him. He had the prism in his hand and he threw it to the floor — ground it under his foot. As for the books, I was later told he had locked them away in the cupboard in the prior's quarters. For all I knew they were still there when you came. I did not discover until yesterday that they too were missing.'

Ralph shuddered at the recollection of the incident, and could not understand why Falconer was smiling at such an horrific event. Falconer, for his part, saw in Ralph's eyes what effect such a simple happening as the splitting of light through a prism into its constituent parts had had on the monk. His superstitious fear of a natural and scientifically predictable event was as harmful as Thady Lamport's fear of cloud-ships and their inhabitants. Perhaps it was something in the remoteness of the spot that created demons in the minds of those who lived here. Falconer thought it best to keep his counsel, and asked him what happened next.

'And did you find Thady?'

Ralph shook his head. 'It was days before he returned, and by then his mind was gone. The experiment had been too much for him.'

Falconer smiled grimly. 'I think it was more than the experiment that night that turned his head. I believe he saw the murder of John de Langetoft also.'

Ralph's jaw dropped. 'And never spoke all these years?'

Falconer's response was cryptic. 'Perhaps he thought the death was divine retribution. But tell me, if John de Langetoft knew about these experiments, do you think him capable of using the knowledge against Henry Ussher?'

'If he knew about them, he would feel duty-bound to inform his superiors in our Order, whether it benefited him or not. His sense of righteousness knew no limits. That it should also benefit him would no doubt add a certain pleasure to the revelations, though.' He paused. 'Do you think that was reason enough for the prior to kill him? And Adam Lutt, who may have "inherited" that secret also?'

Falconer pondered on this thought. Once again, Thady Lamport's voice echoed inside his skull, conjuring up three words – Obedience, Poverty, Celibacy – the three substantials of monastic life. He knew now that of those the third, celibacy, was the key, and was about to respond to Ralph's surmise when the door to the precentor's room burst open. It was Brother Paul, his face flushed from having rushed straight from the gatehouse. He could hardly gasp his message out.

'The lay brothers – they've found him.'

'Who – John Whitehed?'

Paul nodded vigorously, his eyes wide open. Falconer sat him down in a chair and made him take deep breaths, until he was able to get out the rest of the story. John Whitehed had been seen on the outskirts of Hest Bank, right across Lancaster Bay. The lay brothers who had spotted him had not had the common sense to keep quiet and follow him. Instead, one of them had called out, then had all but lost the fleeing monk again amidst the narrow wynds. Fortunately, his pursuers had seen him ducking into a hovel in the meanest part of the village, and had cornered him.

'They broke down the door, though that took little effort. And found the sacrist in the arms of a woman. Or rather she was in his. They've brought them both back with them.'

'Where are they now?'

'In the church. Brother John expressed a desire to pray.'

Falconer rushed round the cloister to the church door, with Ralph in pursuit as fast as his short legs could carry him. Inside the church, the last rays of a weak afternoon sun filtered down on the bowed head of the little sacrist before the altar. Seated on the bench at his side was the notorious Isobel, for whom he had risked all. Her face was in shadow, and Falconer walked slowly over to her. She was rocking gently backwards and forwards, no doubt fearful of the predicament that she had suddenly found herself in. Falconer stood before her, and spoke quietly.

'My lady.'

Isobel leaned forward at the sound of a friendly voice, and her face came into the shaft of light. Falconer grimaced, and knew his suspicion that Whitehed was not the breaker of the vow of celibacy was correct. Her features were plain, almost coarse, and her hair lank and grey. Her tongue played languidly at the corner of her thin lips. Most obvious were her eyes. Deep and brown, they showed no evidence of intelligence whatsoever. She was an idiot.

'Please leave her alone.'

The voice of the sacrist spoke at his shoulder, and Falconer looked at the anguish in those eyes. So different from poor Isobel's.

'She doesn't understand any of this. Or what is happening to her.' Whitehed swept his gaze across the whole congregation who had gathered in the gloom of the church to witness his discomfiture. 'You don't understand. I have been taking care of her since she was born. No one else would.'

189

His eyes bored into Falconer's.

'She's my sister.'

Ann once again stood waiting for Peter Bullock on the flat plain of Port Meadow. She was sure she felt the same excitement she had seen in William's eyes when he knew he had solved a particularly tortuous mystery. All that was left were a few brush strokes to complete the entire picture. She prayed that Peter would be able to provide them. She had sent him to Woodstock, where the de Hardyng family still lived, with questions to ask about Eleanor's sister. He had also been commissioned to enquire for the existence of a particular student amongst the hundreds that thronged Oxford. A chill breeze blew along the valley, whipping up little wavelets on the normally placid river. Ann's own emotions were equally turbulent – had she solved the mystery? Just as the sun was sinking redly behind the scudding clouds, and Ann had almost given the constable up, she saw a plodding figure crossing the meadow towards her. It had the unmistakable lurching gait of Peter Bullock. She was scarcely able to control the thudding of her heart. What if she was wrong? But she couldn't be – she was so sure. She hurried towards him, but could read nothing in his lined, impassive face as they approached each other. Finally they stood face to face.

'Well?'

Bullock sighed. 'The first part was easy. Yes, he is a student in Oxford. But as for the other part . . . it was a wasted journey.'

Ann's face fell, and Bullock felt impelled to explain. 'All the way to Woodstock to find there is no sister. I don't know who told you there was.'

Ann grabbed the astonished Bullock by the arms and danced an impromptu jig, twirling him around. 'Thank you, Peter. Now I know the truth.'

*

At Conishead, the whole truth was not long in coming. John Whitehed had hidden it for so long, it was like opening the floodgates to the priory fishponds after a drought. His sister's was a difficult birth during which their mother had died. Something had gone wrong, and it was soon obvious to the wet nurse that little Isobel was not normal. Talk of disposing of the scrap of life shocked the young boy who was John Whitehed, and he vowed to look after his sister while she lived. That had proved a bigger burden than he had at first imagined. Once grown, she had been sent to a nunnery by their father. But when he had died, and the nunnery no longer received donations from the family, John was left to cope with her on his own. He was by then making his way in Conishead Priory, and had arranged for someone to care for her in Hest Bank. But money was still required to pay the woman who looked after her. And poverty was one of Whitehed's sacred vows. That was when the sacrist had started stealing books to sell.

'But I did not kill Adam Lutt, though at times I might have wished to. Nor John de Langetoft fifteen years ago – I did not even know he had uncovered my secret until Brother Adam came to me for money.'

They were now seated more comfortably in the guest quarters occupied by William Falconer. Isobel sat on his bed, still rocking and humming tunelessly, oblivious of the disaster that had come to her brother. John Whitehed stared fixedly at his feet, his fingers twining round themselves like a box of worms awaiting the fisherman. He looked up in hope.

'Though I cannot prove where I was when de Langetoft was killed, I am sure the old woman who looks after Isobel will confirm that I was with her and my sister when Brother Adam was killed.'

Falconer patted him on his slumped shoulders. 'I am sure you were. I know you killed neither man.'

The look was now that of some faithful hound. 'You do?'

'Indeed I do. Ralph, it's time I spoke to the prior.'

'You can't. He's gone.'

Falconer roared in anger, and leaped from his chair, toppling it backwards. 'Gone? Gone where? Why didn't you tell me?'

Ralph's indignant reply came out wrong, sounding more like a squeak. This academic was so unpredictable, and a little frightening. 'I didn't know it mattered any more, when we were told that Brother John had been taken. I thought the affair was closed.'

Falconer snorted. 'Gone where?'

'To Lancaster. Young Jack Shokburn is guiding him over this evening, before the tide comes in.'

Falconer became quite agitated, hopping from one foot to the other in the process of pulling his boots on. If he could have run and put them on at the same time, he would have.

'We must catch them up. He's in mortal danger.'

'Who is?'

But Falconer was gone before he could reply.

Chapter Sixteen

Having left Ralph Westerdale to take care of the unfortunate John Whitehed and his sister, Falconer got one of the Brothers Peter and Paul to take him across Leven Sands. Though he had crossed on his own before, it was beginning to get dark and he could not risk losing his way. A red haze shone from the far rim of the sea beyond Harlesyde Island. Falconer was once more put in mind of the edge of the world. If he stayed in this part of England much longer, even he might begin to believe in a flat earth. He squinted at the island as they passed, but it was no more than a black outline set in a sea of red. Perhaps the hermit had exhausted his spirit coming to Falconer last night, for Harlesyde seemed truly dead tonight.

A chill wind suddenly gusted in from the sea, and a dull rumble forewarned of a storm. A blackness fell over the ruddy glow out to sea, squeezing the last rays of the sun out of existence. Falconer prayed that the onrushing bad weather would delay Henry Ussher. But he doubted it would and hurried on — there was no time to lose.

The mud on the river bank now looked grey in the poor light, and it sucked at the two men's feet as if working for the prior, delaying their progress. On the shoreline at Sand Gate, the monk passed Falconer a tallow lamp, and wished him luck. Once lit, the lamp did no more than flicker fitfully in the darting wind that scudded in from every direction. Falconer hid the yellowish flame in his fist and plunged on up the steep bank of the headland he had to cross before reaching Kent's Bank and the Shokburns' cottage. Then the whole of Lancaster Bay would lie before him. He doubted he would be there in time.

His legs began to burn as he stumbled up the grassy bank, the tallow flame hardly lighting more than his own fist in front of him. He forced one foot in front of the other, matching his breath to the movement. But soon his breathing was as ragged as his strides. He had spent too long sitting on his backside in the comfort of Oxford. Twenty years earlier, he would have surmounted this little hill easily, and in the heat of battle at that. His life had not always been that of an academic, and he had seen sights across the world that some of those at Oxford only dreamed of. Falconer had been present when the monstrous plague of Tartars, devastating the world, was repulsed on the banks of the Danube by the King's brother, Conrad. Now his legs trembled climbing a gentle grassy knoll.

At last he reached the top, and took a moment to regain his breath at the point the brothers called Headless Cross. Ahead was the sweep of Lancaster Bay, the sands and shallow pools sparkling in the moonlight that broke suddenly through a gap in the massive banks of heavy cloud. Then the moon was gone again as the clouds rolled together, thunder rumbling on their fringes. Still Falconer could see light reflecting from the smooth surface of the bay, and he fumbled in his pouch for his lenses. Bringing them up to his face he realized the reflection was moving. It could only be Henry Ussher and Jack Shokburn out on the sands, with one of them carrying a lamp or a burning brand. Falconer gritted his teeth. The weather had not stopped them, but they were still this side of the Kent river. He could catch them up.

As if in cruel response to his optimistic assessment of the situation, the skies opened, and Falconer's view of the bay was obscured by driving rain. The tallow lamp died in his hand and he flung it aside, plunging down the hillside in the pitch dark. He had gone halfway in a trice, when he stepped on a loose rock that slid from under his foot. His ankle went over, and he rolled head over heels down the hillside until the unyielding trunk of a tree stopped his fall abruptly. He felt a sharp pain in his side, his head hit the ground and he blacked out.

Peter Bullock had tracked down the youth, Thomas Thubbs, to Colcill Hall. It was curious that after all her deductive work, Ann Segrim should end her quest in the student hall that stood right next to William's own Aristotle's Hall. The route she took to the front door of the hall was thus well trodden by her, and she knocked on it with some authority. As she waited to be admitted, she threw a glance over her shoulder at the nervous Sister Gilda. The pinch-faced little nun had scurried at her heels through the bustle of the busy market streets of Oxford like a nervous puppy. Now she hid behind the ample curves of her guide, as though afraid for her safety.

It had taken all Ann's persuasiveness to convince the abbess that she needed to take Sister Gilda to Oxford on her quest for the errant student. Gwladys had only agreed when Ann threatened to bring Thomas Thubbs back to the nunnery. The temporary release of a sister nun into the turbulent and sinful world of Oxford had been deemed the lesser of the two evils. Still, the abbess had made clear to Ann that Gilda's immortal soul, no less, was in her hands.

She had raised her hand to knock once more upon the unopened door, when it was pulled ajar with an ominous creak. In the doorway stood a yawning and dishevelled youth who had clearly been enjoying the pleasures of the myriad inns in Oxford the previous evening. Judging by the darkness of the stubble that peppered his chin, Ann judged this was not the peach-faced youth she was seeking. When she enquired if Thomas Thubbs was present, she was invited into the hall with a vague wave of the youth's hand. He then abandoned the open portal, and returned to the mattress from which he had been dragged so rudely. This nest of straw and tattered blankets lay in a corner of the dark and odorous room at the centre of which stood a much-abused refectory table. Another youth lay stretched out on its greasy surface, his snores echoing in the mean and low-hung rafters of the blackened ceiling. Colcill Hall may have been located cheek by jowl with Aristotle's, but they were worlds apart in mood and comforts.

'Does milady seek her son?'

The thin and quavering voice came from the shadows of a doorway at the back of the ill-kept room. It belonged to a slim and pale-faced youth who was obviously nursing his own headache after what must have been communal excesses the night before. At first Ann was annoyed that she should be thought old enough to be the mother of a student at the university – then changed her mind when she thought of the alternative possibility that might have sprung to the youth's fuddled brain. He might have mistaken her for a woman of the night come from the stews of Beaumont to collect her unpaid fee. Before she could reply, the youth went on in wheedling tones, as though used to framing lies to placate those adults who called in unannounced on this unruly hall.

'You see before you the unfortunate result of seeking solace in cups of ale. The only excuse I can offer is that when death has stalked one who lodges here, he can but seek comfort in the living. You see around you good comrades who rallied round when someone was in need.'

Ann guessed that behind the pallor of the youth, beneath the dark rings that surrounded his dulled eyes, was the face of Thomas Thubbs. The boy who could pass himself off as a girl to the weakened eyes of Hal Coke, gatekeeper of Godstow Nunnery. To be certain, she turned to Sister Gilda, revealing her to the youth for the first time. His face fell at the sight of her religious garb, and he dropped to his knees, vomiting up a foul-smelling brew from the depths of his stomach. The effect on Gilda was equally startling. She darted across the floor and fell upon her prey, her hands outstretched like talons. She grasped him by the neck and shook him, her inhuman screeches outdoing the snores from the soporific youth on the table.

'That's him. That's him. He was the one who defiled her. Stole her.'

Ann grabbed her arms from behind, and tore her off the cowering Thubbs. He rubbed his violated neck, and wiped the smears of vomit from his cheeks. As the nun struggled vainly in her arms, she looked coldly from one to the other.

'Now I want the truth.'

Ellen Shokburn pushed the shutter aside, and peered out of the window across the bay. She could no longer see the lamplight that before the storm had marked Jack's crossing. The rain poured down in a solid sheet, obscuring even the shoreline only a short distance away. It hissed on the thatch above her head, and a steady drip fell in the corner of the dark, box-like room. The water that came in ran across the sloping floor and out of the door; the cottage had been built with a canted floor because it was so close to the shoreline. Some very high tides actually swilled into the cottage, and Ellen was used to such ravages of nature. Everything she and Jack possessed was virtually within arm's reach. In one corner of the room hung a ragged cloth that gave her some privacy at night, and in the opposite corner was the mean shelf that was her son's bed. A sturdy, well-scarred table filled the space in the centre of the room, and Ellen sat down at it, toying with the hard crust of yellowed cheese that had been her supper. Despite the meanness of her home, she knew she would do anything to keep it for herself and her son. Anything.

A buffet of wind hit the cottage wall, and the opened shutter slapped against the daub. She prayed for her son's safe return, not understanding why he had been so amenable to the prior's demand to make the journey despite the weather. It had been obvious that a bad storm was brewing, and in any other circumstances Jack would have refused to cross the bay in the surly tones he had learned from his grandfather. But the prior of

Conishead had hardly to press him, and Jack had agreed. It had been left to Ellen to try to dissuade them from setting out at dusk in a storm. But Jack had been adamant that they could accomplish the journey safely. They had barely got on to the sands before the storm had broken.

Ellen was resigned to staying up all night waiting for Jack's safe return. So when she heard a shuffling noise outside the cottage, all her senses were alert. She leapt up from the table, a sigh of relief on her lips. She imagined that Jack had abandoned the crossing, and he and the prior, soaked to the skin, were even now returning to the sanctuary of the cottage. She was moving towards the door when a flash of lightning lit up an apparition in the open window. She gasped at the sight of a grey face, smeared with dark streaks, staring in at her. The apparition's eyes were wild, and its hair was plastered to its skull. An eerie moan escaped its lips, and Ellen wondered if the pelting rain had called some water-demon from the deep.

A second flash of lightning lit the darkness again, and the face was gone. It had disappeared so quickly, she wondered if she had imagined it. But then through the constant hiss of the rain she heard the low moan again. This time it sounded more like a human being in pain than a demon. She cautiously slid the bolt on the door, and pulled it open a crack. Under the window sat a bundled figure, clutching its side, water streaming down its face. As the eyes turned towards her, she recognized the Oxford master who was staying over at Conishead. The one who was poking his nose into the murders. What was he doing out on such a night? And what on earth had happened to him?

She helped him to his feet, and supported him as he staggered inside the cottage. She dropped him down on Jack's bed, and got a cloth to wipe away the blood that ran down one side of his face. His soaking wet robe was covered with grass stains and mud, and torn in places. She realized he must have fallen somewhere on the headland. Not surprising on such a night.

After a while, he appeared to be recovering his senses, and she helped him sit up. He winced and clutched his side.

'Thank you. I thought I had got lost out there, and then I saw the cottage. I hoped it would be you.'

Her hands had felt soft to him as she sponged away the blood on his face. He was seeing the other side of this cold and solitary woman, and could imagine how someone might truly be attracted to her. She stared hard at him, trying to read his mind.

'What were you doing out on such a night?'

Falconer suddenly remembered the urgency of his task, and looked around. 'The prior – is he here?'

'No. He and Jack set out some time ago. They'll be across the Kent by now.'

The big man lurched to his feet, and gasped. He didn't know which hurt most – his side or his ankle. At least the pain in his head was only a dull throb.

'Just tell me one thing – does Jack know who his father is?'

Ellen frowned, and was about to tell Falconer it was none of his business when he stopped her.

'Please. It is important.'

She sighed, and nodded. 'I told him just the other day.'

Falconer looked grim. 'I feared so. We need to get to them. It's a matter of life or death. Jack overheard me saying something about the rivalry between the prior and de Langetoft. I fear what he might do.'

Ellen looked at him, her lips pressed tight. 'You know who killed them, don't you?'

Falconer nodded, the rain splashing off his tangled hair. She looked into his piercing blue eyes a moment more, then grabbed a piece of sacking from a hook by the door. She threw it over her shoulders, and picked up the lamp from the table.

'Come on, then. I'll guide you.'

Outside the rain still poured down, striking their faces like shards of ice. There was nothing for it but to bow their heads into the gale, and press on. The first part of the route out to the bay was through short tussocks of grass, whose stalks were like knife blades. But at least it afforded some grip. As they stepped on to the sand proper, Falconer nearly went over on the slippery mud. His left ankle was sore, and hardly supported his weight. He gritted his teeth, and grunted thanks for Ellen's steadying arm. She looked briefly at him and trudged on. He kept up close behind, afraid of losing her in the darkness. He would not be able to find his own way in these conditions.

As they moved further from the protection of the shoreline, the wind got stronger. It buffeted them, tearing at their clothes and nearly lifting them off their feet. Ellen glanced nervously out to sea. She could not see the incoming tide, but it was out there in the darkness. And when it came in, it came with the speed of a galloping horse. Unless they were over soon, they would be caught by it. There was still no sight of Jack or the prior, and Ellen doubted whether they could catch them up. Their only hope was that Henry Ussher was slowing Jack down, being unused to walking so far.

They reached the first watercourse, and held on to each other for safety as they waded across. The water was so cold, Falconer felt as though the very bones of his legs ached. They were both soaked from head to foot now, their clothes heavy and clinging. Having gained the opposite side of the river, Falconer stopped to get his breath, but Ellen grimly motioned him on with a wave of her arm. He followed her zigzag path across an endless vista of water. To Falconer there was now no difference between the sky and the land – it was all water. For all he knew, the tide could be in and he could be walking on the sea itself. So when Ellen spoke, he was glad of conversation in order to keep his mind straight.

As they talked, they plodded on grimly through the rain. Then suddenly Falconer heard something that resembled the cry of a gull wheeling in the sky. Except no bird would be so foolish as to be in the sky in these conditions. It was Ellen – she was shouting and pointing ahead of them. Falconer half expected to see a cloud-ship floating past, but at first saw nothing in the gloom. Then he thought he saw a flash of light. He blinked and shook the water from his eyes. There were two shapes huddled over a lamp, standing by the bank of a stream. It had to be the Keer, and they had to be Henry Ussher and Jack Shokburn. They were in time.

But even as they looked, the lamp tilted at a crazy angle, and the two figures melted into one, swaying first one way then the other. They were fighting. Ferociously.

Henry Ussher had doggedly followed Jack Shokburn across the vastness of the bay, the only view he had being the hunched shoulders of the youth. The rain was teeming down and the prior was wetter than he had ever been before. His waterlogged robes hung on him like heavy chain mail, and his legs felt leaden. He had never been so uncomfortable, and the journey appeared endless. Fording the Kent had been a nightmare – he had almost been swept away. But for the strong arm of the youth grabbing him as his legs gave way, he would have been gone. He prayed for deliverance from this watery hell.

He was suddenly aware that the youth had stopped in his tracks. He lifted his head into the howling gale, and squinted through half-closed eyes to see what was wrong. They stood on the lip of the Keer stream, and though it flowed fast it looked easily fordable.

'What's the matter?' he yelled, against the driving rain.

Jack Shokburn's eyes were bright and feverish. A wolfish grimace contorted his lips, and he hopped from one foot to the other, almost dancing round the prior. He yelled back at the shivering cleric.

'Recognize the spot?'

Ussher was puzzled. What did the lad mean? Shokburn pushed his angry face close to the prior's ear, and yelled again.

'Recognize the spot?'

'Why should I?' This was crazy — arguing about God knows what in the middle of a storm in Lancaster Bay. The youth, still jumping around as though he were on strings, answered his question.

'It's where you killed my father.'

'Killed? I've killed no one . . . Your father?'

'My father. John de Langetoft.'

The name hung in the air between them, and Henry Ussher's mind raced as he tried to understand what the boy was saying. *His father was John de Langetoft? And I am alone with his son in the middle of Lancaster Bay, accused of murdering him.* The full import struck him like a blow. *He means to kill me, and there is no help for miles. I could disappear here, and my body would never be found. Except as a bag of bones in fifteen years' time, just like de Langetoft's.*

He struggled to lift his feet from the clinging mud — to run to safety — but he was held fast. That was why the youth had been shifting from one foot to the other as he spoke. Shokburn had led him into quicksand. Ussher squealed and fell forwards, knocking the lamp from Shokburn's grasp. It fell to the sand, flickered, but remained alight. Ussher scrabbled at Shokburn's sleeves, refusing to let go. The youth, for his part, flailed his arms wildly to try to get them free. The cloth tore on his right sleeve, and he yanked his arm above his head. With the prior staring up at him, squealing like a stuck pig, he rained blows down on the man's face. This was not how he had planned it. He had intended to leave the man sinking in the quicksand, with the tide soon to rip in across the mud. But if he had to kill his father's murderer with his own hands, he would.

He grasped the terrified man by the throat, and squeezed. Though he was only a youth his labouring life had given him more strength than the soft-living prior possessed, and the monk's face turned a mottled red. Jack was aware of a bird-like cry carried on the wind. Then it became a voice — his mother's voice. Was he dreaming? No, he saw her splashing through the shallows towards him. The tide was running faster than he had gauged, and they were all in danger. Behind his mother stumbled another figure, large and powerful. The water splashed up from his heavy boots, which were cracked around the seam.

Ellen clawed at her son's arm, and begged him to stop.

'But he killed my father – he killed John. And now I'm going to kill him.'

The woman's face screwed up in anguish, and her voice carried on the gale. 'No he didn't. The prior didn't kill him. I did.'

Jack Shokburn looked with disbelief at his mother, his grip on Ussher's throat slackening for a moment.

'I killed him because he was going to abandon me . . . us. I was carrying you, and about to tell him so. All he could think about was his preferment. He wanted to be prior, and I stood in his way. I had become a sin of which he found it all too easy to repent.'

Jack released his grip on Ussher, and the prior fell to his knees, gasping and retching.

'But why did you kill him?'

Ellen's face set in hard lines. 'I killed him because he had used me and was ready to discard me like a worn-out tool, and that made me angry.'

Salt tears started on the boy's face, mingling with the salt spray that threatened to engulf them. Still he stood unmoving and disbelieving. It was a low moan from the prostrate Ussher that brought them all to their senses. The tide was rising around their legs, and there was still the Keer and yards of sand to cross before they were safe.

Falconer grabbed the prior's arms, and, with a sucking sound, drew him out of the quicksand. With Ellen and Falconer supporting him between them and the boy stumbling behind, they forded the Keer. The water now came up to their waists, and they were buffeted first one way and then the next as tide and wind ripped the waters back and forth. With a fearful eye,

Falconer looked out to sea. All he could see were the white caps of waves as the tide rose higher and higher. Even on the sandbank the salt water had reached their thighs, and it was becoming more and more difficult to take each step.

'We're nearly there.'

The cry came from Ellen Shokburn, and she pointed to the murky loom of a grassy bank. A few straggly trees tossed back and forth in the gale, but to Falconer it looked like sanctuary. Then Ellen gasped in dismay. They had been pushed off course by the onrushing tide, and instead of walking up a shelving beach they were faced with clambering up a steep and muddy bank.

'You climb up first, and I'll push the prior after you from here,' commanded Falconer. But Ellen shook her head.

'I'll never be able to pull him out. I haven't the strength. No, you go first.'

Reluctantly, Falconer had to agree, and grabbed hold of some slippery roots that stuck out from the bank. He heaved, and at first the roots gave way, scattering earth on his upturned face. Coughing, he wiped the muck from his lips and tried again. Finally he got one knee on the grassy top of the bank and hoisted himself to safety. He allowed himself a moment to get his breath then shouted for the prior to give him his hand. Ellen was standing behind the shocked Ussher, supporting him. As the monk numbly offered an arm to Falconer, Ellen looked anxiously over her shoulder. She couldn't see her son, and turned back into the heaving water. Falconer's concentration was on getting Ussher on to the bank, and it was a while before he realized what she was going to do. As he struggled with the sodden body of the prior, he cried out.

'Stay here. Jack can look after himself.'

But she was gone.

When he had the prior safely on the shore, he leaned his head close to the man's lips. Though they were a frightening shade of blue, Falconer could feel the warmth of a shallow breath on his cheek. He was alive, for the moment. Now he had to decide whether to re-enter the water himself in search of Ellen and her son. The idea chilled his soul, but he knew he had to try.

He sat on the bank and lowered his legs into the choppy tide. Just as he was about to launch himself, he spotted two heads bobbing in the waves. It had to be them, though his poor eyes could not be sure. They came closer, and he could see that Ellen was dragging her exhausted son. The water was so deep now, they were swimming rather than wading. They were above where Falconer sat on the bank, and momentarily he thought they would be swept past him. But he managed to lean forward and grab Jack's leather jerkin. His fist closed over the cracked and worn garment, and between them he and Ellen repeated the exercise of pushing and pulling an almost dead weight up to safety.

With the last of his reserves of energy, Falconer now stuck out his hand towards Ellen. She looked at it briefly, then her eyes rose to meet the Oxford master's. He knew what she was about to do, and could see the joy spark in those formerly hard, cold eyes.

'No,' he cried. 'Don't. There is no need to tell anyone it was you.'

She shook her head, knowing Falconer did not really mean what he had said, smiled and let her body go limp. His mouth formed words to cry out, but nothing came. Then her head slid under the waves, and it was too late.

VESPERS

Thou Lord dost make my lamp burn bright,
And my God will lighten my darkness.

Psalm 18

Chapter Seventeen

The fishermen found her the following morning in the middle of the bay. She had been captured by one of their fishing traps set to catch flukes, two long baulks of woven hazel pinned in a v-shape by ash stakes with a cage of netting set over it. The lower end remained just below water level, and the upper end was open to the sky. But it did not seem as though she had truly been snared. On the contrary, the fisherfolk who found her said it looked more as if she was in the act of flying the trap. Her arms were spread wide as though embracing the expanse of earth and sky that surrounded her. Her smiling face was as pale and unlined as a child's. Her empty eyes stared up at the sky, and the sun sparkled on the pool in which she lay.

They brought her to the hovel on Hest Bank, where the previous night Jack Shokburn, Henry Ussher and William Falconer had sought refuge. Henry Ussher's saddlebag full of finery had gone, and he looked no more than he really was – a tired, ageing priest with grey hair whom ambition had passed by. He intoned a prayer over the body, and slumped back on the straw mattress where he had lain all night. He was drained of all of his energy, and his chance of meeting the Papal Legate was gone. Jack Shokburn was dry-eyed, having shed all his tears for his mother during the night over William Falconer's revelations. With nothing else to do but talk, the Oxford master had retold to Jack what Ellen had told him while they had been giving chase the previous night.

Once she knew that Falconer had deduced she was the

murderer, the normally taciturn Ellen had filled in for him all the details that he could not have worked out for himself. It was as if he was hearing her confession, though he had no way of knowing then it was a dying confession.

'What finally convinced you I had killed John?' she had asked as they plodded over the mud, having crossed the first watercourse.

Falconer looked embarrassed. 'I have to confess that it was more a process of elimination. At first it seemed everyone had a reason to kill de Langetoft, except you. He knew something about every member of the community at Conishead, and all of them stood to lose if he gave up his secrets in return for preferment. And Henry Ussher would have lost most of all – the prior's position he so coveted. I suspected each in turn, especially when none could prove where he was when Adam Lutt was killed. But there was always one stumbling block.'

'What was that?' Ellen's eyes were strangely jaundiced in the yellow light cast by the lantern she carried. Falconer raised his voice against the growing buffeting of the wind.

'No one knew de Langetoft was abroad that night. No one knew he was in Lancaster Bay. Except whoever guided him across. And then I knew there was another secret hidden within the walls of Conishead Priory. A secret that no one but John de Langetoft knew, because it was his own.'

A steady drizzle had begun, and Ellen and Falconer bowed their heads against its attack.

'It was when I was standing in the camerarius's office that I realized. The office that had been both Adam Lutt's and John de Langetoft's. I saw you through the window arch working in the fishponds pretty much as John must have done. You reminded me of someone, and I knew then that John could not have resisted the temptation you represented. Next I saw your son go over to you, and you embraced him. Suddenly he looked younger than I had imagined he was. He is only fifteen, isn't he?'

Ellen nodded grimly. 'And about to make a terrible mistake, unless we catch them up.'

For a moment, Ellen fell silent, but Falconer was determined to draw the full story from her.

'You couldn't have planned to kill him.'

'Of course not. I knew I was carrying our child when he came to me that night to guide him over the bay. He wanted to cross in secret, and didn't want my father to be the guide, so I agreed to take him over. He was boasting about how he was going to ruin Henry Ussher. Showed me some books he said were blasphemous that he had taken from him. Henry was the only one who stood in the way of John's becoming prior. Except for me and the baby. Before I could tell him about little Jack, he was telling me how he would have to cease visiting me. How his preferment was more important. He was so matter-of-fact, I felt like a piece of dirt picked off the hem of his gilded robe, to be flung away. That made me almost angry enough to want to kill him. But then I thought of something much more important than my anger.

'Once he knew I was bearing a child, he might have thought the risk of disclosure was too great. That I might have blackmailed him for the sake of the infant. As I would have done. That was a chance he would not have taken. I reckoned my life, and the life of my baby, were both in danger. So I killed him.'

The hardness had returned to Ellen's voice, and Falconer felt a chill run down his spine.

'And Adam Lutt?'

'I feared that he knew my secret and was going to tell the prior. And that my son would lose his job as guide, if it came out he was de Langetoft's bastard. That job means everything to Jack — it's his life and his future. I carry messages for the priory, so it was easy to convince one of the lay brothers that the prior had asked me to pass on a message.'

'A message summoning Brother Adam to the ironworks?'

Ellen nodded, the wind whipping her hair across her face like a veil.

'So the prior really was just going to fetch his gloves that night,' muttered Falconer to himself.

'What? I can't hear you for the wind.'

He shook his head. 'Nothing. But . . . the trip-hammers?' Falconer shuddered at the thought of crossing this determined woman.

'I hit him with a log, but he was only stunned. So I dragged him over to the crushing bench and . . .'

Mercifully, she didn't finish the sentence. But, fingering the bruise on the back of his head, Falconer suddenly remembered the attack on himself that same night. It couldn't have been Ellen who attacked him, for she had been at the ironworks. So who else, other than the murderer, wanted him dead? And had the 'accident' with the molten iron been aimed at him also? Those puzzles remained unresolved because Ellen suddenly cried out and pointed.

'There they are – I see them.'

They buried Ellen Shokburn at Hest Bank, her grave overlooking the bay she so loved. A local priest performed the ceremony, as Henry Ussher had fallen sick after his soaking. No bells tolled at her departure, but the mournful calls of the sea-pie and the curlew seemed more fitting anyway. Only Jack and Falconer stood at her graveside, the Oxford master wondering wistfully about Grosseteste's books. Were they still lodged somewhere in the shifting sands of Lancaster Bay? Would they have survived all this time? Perhaps he would have to wait another fifteen years for another storm to reveal them.

At the next low tide, a silent Jack Shokburn fetched over Falconer's saddlebags from Conishead. There was nothing left at the priory for him, and suddenly he was anxious to see his friends back in Oxford. And one in particular, whom he was tutoring in the Aristotelian sciences. He hoped she had finished reading *Metaphysics*, because he planned a most searching examination for her.

Chapter Eighteen

The last rays of the dying sun traversed the wall of Falconer's room, high under the eaves of Aristotle's Hall. As darkness settled in the corners of the room, Balthazar opened his eyes and contemplated the night's hunting ahead. The blonde-haired woman glanced up at the owl's perch as he ruffled his feathers, then returned her gaze to Falconer.

Humphrey Segrim had come back from his travels no pleasanter than when he left. Indeed, he seemed even more surly. He had refused to tell his wife where he was going when he left, and was equally adamant on his return that there was nothing for her to know. Used to Humphrey's perpetually abortive plots and schemes, Ann had given it no more thought, and had arranged a visit to the market in Oxford. At the bottom of her basket hidden under a cloth lay Falconer's copy of *Metaphysics*.

Now she sat before its owner, bursting to reveal her own deductive abilities. Unfortunately, her polite enquiry about what she presumed had been his quiet sojourn in Conishead Priory had resulted in the lengthy tale of his own prowess. She listened with increasing impatience as he told the story in full. He had to admit that even he had been misled at the beginning, when he strove to fit the missing books into the picture. The thefts that had taken place over fifteen years or more had only led him to the unfortunate sacrist. And Grosseteste's lost books had eventually pointed at the prior, whose only sin had been that of scientific ignorance. Lutt was about to blackmail him about his meddling, but it was obvious Ussher didn't kill him because of that. After all, why would he have set up the faked embezzlement if he meant to do away with Lutt all along? No, the loss of Grosseteste's books had been due to de Langetoft's taking them with him as evidence when he crossed the bay. Their removal was probably the reason why Brother Thady had followed him, and had witnessed his murder.

'So I suppose in a way the missing books did contribute to my solving the killing. They led me to Brother Thady, who told me from the start that de Langetoft was a sinner. I should have taken him seriously, especially as on my first day he preached on the subject of celibacy. I think he never revealed that Ellen was the murderer because he saw the act as just retribution. My vision of Fridaye de Schipedham just brought all that to the fore of my mind finally. He reminded me of the temptations of the flesh, and I saw an image of de Langetoft and Ellen.'

Ann asked him if he believed that Fridaye de Schipedham had actually been present, or if it had been an apparition. He smiled.

'I shall never know. Did he project his body across the bay to put me on the right track? Or did I conjure him up in my own imagination from facts that were already hidden there? My vanity says the latter, but . . .' He shook his head. 'I am used to dealing with truths, and logic. Everyone up there seemed contaminated with a sense of the unreal. I mean, how could Ellen kill someone she loved so easily?'

Ann gritted her teeth, stared at her exasperating companion, and muttered that she would find it quite simple. If Falconer heard and understood, he feigned not to have done so. She began to raise the question of her own logical powers, but William cut her off again.

'I hear that Nicholas de Ewelme has been appointed chancellor of the university. I am not surprised that Henry de Cicestre did not last long – de Cantilupe ran rings round him over that business at Christmas.'

Falconer was referring to Thomas de Cantilupe's recent subterfuge in sending the then chancellor on a wild goose chase after a sick relative. A ruse which left the former chancellor de Cantilupe in a position to benefit personally from the arrival of the King in Oxford for the Christmas festivities. De Cantilupe had engineered his own advancement, despite being tangled up in a murder that had taken place before the very eyes of the King.

'I was fond of de Cantilupe – he was a worthy adversary. I wonder if de Ewelme can replace him?'

Ann's patience gave way at last. Subsiding under a deluge of tender blows from her fists, Falconer wondered what he had done wrong. Did not ladies prefer a diet of tittle-tattle? Rather than losing her temper anew, Ann decided to play up to William's view of women, and in a pretty, simpering tone pandered to his vanity.

'I have a little puzzle that you should find simple to solve.'

He raised a quizzical eyebrow. Was there any doubt that he could solve it easily, and he the Regent Master in Aristotelian Logic? So she told him of the murder in the locked nunnery of Godstow. How she had at first been led to believe it was the abbess in a fit of religious fervour who had killed Sister Eleanor. But then she had learned the gatekeeper was up to his old tricks of letting people into the nunnery for money. And that one of those visitors had been a sister Eleanor did not have. That had put a different complexion on things. Before she could finish, Falconer cut in.

'Ah, I see. The "sister" that visited her was really Eleanor's former lover, this Thomas . . .'

'Thubbs.'

'Thubbs. And he killed her because she had rejected him.'

Ann clapped her hands with glee. She had defeated the great William Falconer after all.

'No, no. Why should Thomas kill her? He had found her again, and had visited her several times in the guise of her sister. He was a slim and peach-faced boy, so it was easy for him to dissemble. Especially as the gatekeeper is as purblind as a regent master of my acquaintance.' Falconer winced. 'I know he had visited her often, because the same gatekeeper admitted so. Though he still thought it was a girl he was admitting, and no harm done.

'No, Eleanor did not reject him. It was Gilda who was rejected. The poor misguided child interpreted Eleanor's friendliness as more than what it was. When she caught Eleanor with Thomas, she was devastated, waited until he had gone, and accosted Eleanor in the cloister. I am told Eleanor could be quite haughty, and no doubt her response to Gilda's professions of affection drove Gilda to the same extreme action as Ellen Shokburn. She drowned her in a few inches of water.'

Falconer sadly shook his head. 'And what is to become of her?'

'I don't know. When I told the abbess what I believed had happened, she closed up as tight as the gates of the nunnery. I left as fast as I could or I might be there still, and Peter cannot now gain entry. The Church will resolve its own affairs in its own way, no doubt.'

There was a long silence as both pondered on the fate of the unhappy Sister Gilda. Ann was the first to break it.

'By the way. You never explained how the attacks on you fitted with Ellen's being the murderer. You said she could not have attacked you the night the hermit came to your rescue, because she was at the ironworks despatching the camerarius. But could she have loosened the stopper on the furnace?'

'She could have, but it must have been the same person both times – I don't have all that many enemies.'

He grinned at his feeble joke. But suddenly Ann thought of her husband's long absence, his sense of failure, and his refusal to talk of where he had been, and her face paled.

COMPLINE

Strike dumb the lying lips,
Which speak with contempt against the righteous,
In pride and arrogance.

Psalm 31

Epilogue

Henry Ussher, his ambition spent, resigned his post of prior of Conishead and eked out his last days in a solitary cell in Northumberland, far from the place he had so poorly run. John Whitehed also revoked his position as sacrist, and did penance for his misdeed by labouring beside the lay brothers in the fields. Ralph Westerdale was unanimously elected prior, and under his governance the priory prospered. There were no more visitors to the rather depleted library.

Thady Lamport garnered a reputation as a seer due to his wild pronouncements. His sustenance was provided by grateful, if perhaps gullible, pilgrims to his cave. One day, someone visited his cave to find him gone. Locally, it is said that a cloud-ship took him up into the sky.

John Shokburn continued his work as guide across Lancaster Bay – a tradition that continues to this day.

In Oxford, nothing is recorded of Ann Segrim's life. She no doubt lived many years in happy obscurity. Godstow Nunnery was again the subject of a severe revision of its conduct by Bishop Gary in 1434, and did not survive the Dissolution of the Monasteries.

Peter Bullock died a warrior's death as he might have wished. His soldier's instinct deserted him for once, and he stepped in the way of a rusty sword wielded by a student in the midst of a pitched battle between northern and Welsh clerks. But not before he was involved in many more mysteries unravelled by his friend Regent Master William Falconer.

William Falconer was to have many further adventures, occasioned by his insatiable curiosity. He is said to have returned to travelling later in life, reaching as far as Cathay. He did finally make contact again with his lifelong friend and mentor, Friar Roger Bacon. He always regretted never recovering Bishop Grosseteste's texts, especially *De infinitate lucis*, of which there was no other mention in the records.

HERALDRY, ANCESTRY AND TITLES

QUESTIONS AND ANSWERS

HERALDRY, ANCESTRY and TITLES

Questions and Answers

BY

L. G. PINE

B.A. Lond. Barrister-at-Law, Inner Temple,
F.S.A. Scot., F.J.I., F.A.M.S.
Formerly Editor of Burke's Peerage,
and of Burke's Landed Gentry, etc., etc.

Gramercy Publishing Company
New York

Contents

Chapter 1. Heraldry

5

Contents

Contents

Contents

Contents

Chapter 3. Titles

Contents

Contents

11

Contents

List of Illustrations

Introduction

I have had thirty years' experience with these subjects which includes twenty-five years' connection with *Burke's Peerage, Burke's Landed Gentry*, and the other genealogical books associated with the name of Burke. During the greater part of that time I was the Editor of these publications and as such I received some very varied and remarkable questions and requests. When putting an epitaph on a peer's tombstone, should one put, in addition to his title, his surname, or his Christian names only? How does one get one's obituary into *The Times*? Was the name of William the Conqueror's mother Charlotte Skinner? Is the Queen styled Duchess of Normandy? Can anyone get a coat of arms? What is the Roll of Battle Abbey? How many people in England can prove Norman descent? Can the Queen deprive a peer of his title?

This is only a selection of questions which have been put to me, sometimes at lectures or over the telephone, or in letters. I continue to receive a huge correspondence from all over the world, which is addressed to me, about fifty per cent. to my home, the rest care of publishers, agents and newspapers, and at times simply to L. G. Pine, Author (or Genealogist), England.

This volume of correspondence and inquiry bears witness to a widespread interest in the subjects of heraldry, ancestry, titles and peerage. Yet in very many cases the inquirers have tried to find the answers elsewhere, in books or other sources, and have failed, largely, I think, because the official custodians of knowledge are not sufficiently aware of the outlook of the ordinary man or woman. I have had the great advantage of personal contact in over 600 lectures and through some thousands of letters, so that in writing on these subjects I am able to envisage real persons who have asked real questions.

The illustrations are by W. J. Hill.

1

Heraldry

1. In the first place what is heraldry?

It is a system of the use of hereditary symbols handed down in families or in institutions. It originated in western Europe about the middle of the twelfth century. The correct term should be armoury, for the real meaning of heraldry is the 'art or office of a herald'. In course of time heraldry has come to be the term used to cover the science and art of these hereditary symbols or coats of arms.

2. What is a crest?

A crest is part of a coat of arms. It was fixed on to the top of the helmet of the knight in armour. It is perfectly possible to have a genuine coat of arms without a crest, but not to have a crest without a coat of arms. (It is true that there is one case recorded at the College of Arms of a man for whom only a crest is recorded. It is improbable that many people will want to imitate this example for the man in question died when his crest was approved and before the rest of the coat of arms was passed.)

3. Why then is the term 'crest' used so frequently instead of the correct term 'coat of arms'?

Pure ignorance, as Dr. Johnson said of his definition of the word 'pastern'. On one occasion I was awakened at

1 a.m. by an unfortunate journalist who was forced in the still watches to wrestle with what he called the problem of Earl Mountbatten's 'crest'. Next morning I had the great satisfaction of reading for once the correct description of the arms as a coat of arms.

For reasons of space, crests have been used on small objects such as spoons or other silver ware, on motor-cars, rings, livery buttons, notepaper, etc., often in conjunction with the family motto, but without the full coat of arms which would have been more bulky to engrave. Hence the idea has arisen in popular speech of a crest as synonymous with a coat of arms.

There are, in fact, four terms which are correct usage, these being, coat of arms, armorial bearings, heraldic achievement or shield. The last named is somewhat poetic. It occurs (usually quite wrongly) in Tennyson's 'Idylls of the King'. Most of the notable English writers are at sea on the subject of heraldry, though William Shakespeare is a great exception. He was, however, an arrant snob and spent three years trying to get a coat of arms. He succeeded and so was able to be described as 'gent', on his funeral monument.

Suffice to add that no one who understands the rudiments of Heraldry refers to a crest other than in its proper usage as part of a coat of arms. 'Crest' in the wrong sense is paralleled by 'bar sinister' (see below) which again is frequently used in popular writing to denote bastardy.

4. Is there a coat of arms for every name?

No. This idea is much the same with the belief that every Scottish family is entitled to wear a tartan. There are a very large number of coats of arms in existence, about 100,000 being included in *Burke's General Armoury*, but these have all been either (1) granted to the bearers or (2) assumed by them. There is not, however, such a thing as a crest for every surname.

5. What is the bar sinister?

There is no such thing in heraldry. 'Bar sinister' is a popular phrase much used by novelists with whom it probably originated. By them it is used as an expression denoting illegitimacy. 'He started life with the bar sinister on his shield' is the common remark in novels, meaning that the man in question was a bastard. There is a term in French heraldry – *barre sinistre* – which is a translation of the English heraldic term, bend sinister. The French *'barre'* translates 'bend' but it is not the equivalent of the English 'bar'. 'Sinister' in heraldry has no unpleasant connotation but is simply a term of Latin origin which means 'left', and is the opposite of 'dexter' – right. What about the bend sinister? Has some mistake been made and is this the sign of bastardy which the popular writers have mistaken in their bar sinister? No, although a bend sinister has sometimes been used to denote illegitimacy, it is merely one of the marks or charges on a coat of arms, a band which runs from the top left corner of the shield down to the bottom right.

It should be added that a baton sinister is often used as a sign of bastardy. This is particularly the case with royal bastards, and anyone who looks at the arms of the Dukes of Buccleuch, of Grafton, or of St. Albans will see the baton sinister 'debruising' the royal arms of the original duke's father.* It may not be out of place here to mention the subject of royal bastards which may be placed under the form of the following question.

6. Are the bulk of the peers descended from royal bastards?

The answer is an emphatic no. Many English sovereigns did have by-blows, children born on the wrong side of the

* 'Debruising' sounds pretty bad, but has nothing to do with any bruising. It merely means a mark or baton set right across the royal arms.

blanket. Charles II is usually debited with twelve bastards, from whom have descended some of our modern peerage. The Earl of Munster is derived from William IV. The winner in the royal bastard stakes was Henry I. Nineteen of his illegitimate offspring are known. Robert Duke of Gloucester who is buried in St. James's Church, Bristol, is the most notable, but no particular mark has been left on the peerage by the exploits of Henry Beauclerk (Henry I's nickname).

The majority of our peers are descended from nothing more exciting than the less competent politicians of the eighteenth century or the more successful business magnates of the industrial revolution.

Strange as it may seem, there are many more legitimate than spurious descendants of our royalty. It has been said that every middle-class Englishman is descended from Edward III. This does not mean that in addition to his foreign conquests, Edward was prodigiously active at home. It is simply that his family survived the rigours of medieval upbringing and lived to have children of their own. The descendants of these were not married within their own royal circle, but gradually spread throughout the whole nation. Today there are known to be some 100,000 persons descended legitimately from Edward III.

It is a comforting thought too, that this king is a kind of genealogical Clapham Junction. Get to him and you are on to the main lines of most of the royalties of the Middle Ages.

7. What other way is there in heraldry of denoting bastardy?

Another way in which heraldic bastardy can be denoted is by the use of the device known as a bordure. This is described as 'an uniform border or edge to a shield, and occupying one fifth of the shield.' It occurs in the coats of arms of some eminent families, but it should not be taken universally as the sign of bastardy. So many Scottish families have it! As my first editor (a Scotsman) remarked, in some of the Highland clans marriage was an institution of late arrival. It appears that during the last two hundred years, the English heralds have got into the habit of using the bordure to signify illegitimacy.

8. Who can get a coat of arms?

It would be rash to exclude anyone from the charitable sweep of the heraldic authorities. Sometimes the question is put in another way; can anyone get a coat of arms? To this I am bound to answer, that I know of no one who has been refused. Of course, no one is likely to apply for a grant, unless he knows what is meant by arms, that is unless he is in a state of grace when arms are the most desirable thing in his mental horizon.

9. How does one obtain a grant?

By applying to the College of Arms (if one lives in England or Wales). The cost is between £140 and £200. It takes usually about a year for the application to be processed through the College. There is an elaborate system of checks and counter-checks. If you are a Scot, you come under the jurisdiction of the Lyon Office in Edinburgh. Heraldry in Scotland is part of the legal system which is distinct from that of England. There is a little difficulty here because people of Scottish descent are supposed to come under Lyon's administration wherever they may be, anywhere in the world; similarly people of English and Welsh descent should look to the English College. There are many variations of these rules. In practice it would be a good thing for each country to have its own heraldic jurisdiction, as it does in everything else. An example where this occurred was in Ireland, where the Republican Government did not like to continue under the heraldic jurisdiction of an official in Dublin whose title was Ulster King of Arms and who was appointed by the British Crown. So an amicable arrangement was reached whereby on the death of Sir Neville Wilkinson in 1940, his post was not filled again at Dublin. Mr. de Valera then appointed his own official with the title, Chief Herald of Ireland, who sits in the old Ulster Office with the Ulster records.

In the meantime the British Crown united the title and office of Ulster King of Arms with that of Norroy King of Arms in the English College, and in practice the Norroy and Ulster King of Arms exercises heraldic control in the province of Ulster, covering the six northern counties. The remaining twenty-six counties of Ireland are in the jurisdiction of the Chief Herald of Ireland. So in theory this means that people of English and Welsh descent wherever they may be should come under the rule of the College of Arms; Scots descended folk under the Lord Lyon; Ulstermen under Norroy and Ulster and republican Irish under the state official in Dublin.

10. You refer to the College of Arms, is this the same as the Heralds' College?

Yes, it is one and the same institution which is located in Queen Victoria Street, London, E.C.4. No one properly acquainted with heraldry refers to Heralds' College; the latter is a colloquialism. The correct term is College of Arms. The Scottish equivalent is: The Lord Lyon, at his Court, H.M. Registry Office, Edinburgh. The Irish office: The Chief Herald of Ireland, Dublin Castle, Dublin, Ireland.

11. When was the College of Arms founded?

In 1484 by King Richard III. There were royal heralds

long before that time, who were members of the royal household. They were formed or consolidated into a College or corporate institution by Richard III.

12. Who are the members of the College of Arms?

There is the head, the Duke of Norfolk, who is hereditary Earl Marshal (i.e. responsible for ceremonial functions such as a Coronation or a royal funeral or the state opening of Parliament). By virtue of his position as Earl Marshal, the Duke presides over the College of Arms.

Under him he has thirteen officers. These are three Kings of Arms: Garter, Clarenceux and Norroy (now combining Ulster). Six Heralds: Windsor, Somerset, York, Lancaster, Chester and Richmond. Four Pursuivants (i.e. followers or junior Heralds): Rouge Dragon, Rouge Croix, Bluemantle, and Portcullis.

The delightful medieval flavour of these names derive partly from the old archaic Norman French language of heraldry, and partly from titles which were connected with the royal family in the reign of Edward III (1327–77).

13. What exactly is the function of the College of Arms?

In a nutshell, it is to look after the use of arms in England and Wales. In past centuries it has had other duties, e.g. the Heralds used at one time to manage the funerals of the nobility, not as undertakers in the ordinary sense but as arrangers of the dead man's standards and of the order in which his mourners should follow him. Then also, because the character of the Herald was supposed to be inviolate, they were much employed as ambassadors and bearers of important messages to foreign rulers. While these tasks are no longer entrusted to them, they have acquired a fresh function in the last 300 years and that is the keeping of pedigree records. Their main duty, however, continues to relate to coats of arms, and they have to grant arms and to regulate arms when in use.

14. When you talk of the control of arms by the College of Arms, do you mean that the use of arms by anyone and everyone in England and Wales must be controlled by the heralds?

Strictly, yes, though in practice their control is so slight as to be unexercised in very many cases. I estimate that there are in this country not less than 50,000 persons (including some corporations) who are using arms to which they are not entitled.

15. How has this situation come about?

Because the regulation of arms in England was carried out by two methods both of which became obsolete over the past 300 years. These methods were (1) Visitations or tours of inspection by the heralds. These were conducted roughly once a generation and covered one county at a time. They began in 1529 and ended in 1686. In 1688 James II abandoned his throne. His four immediate successors were not too sure of their position, and three of them were foreigners. They did not issue any commissions to their officers of arms to conduct Visitations and the practice has never been resumed. (2) The Court of Chivalry sat under the authority of the Earl Marshal, but it aroused great opposition and was abolished by the Puritans under the Commonwealth. In 1660 it was revived but did not sit after 1735 until 1954.

16. Was there not a case before the Court of Chivalry some years ago?

Yes, in 1954 the Court was impressively revived with full splendour. A test case was brought; the Manchester City

Corporation sued the Manchester Palace of Varieties because the latter used the City Arms on its drop curtain and on its documents. Judgement was given for the Manchester Corporation. Thus the existence and the jurisdiction of the Court of Chivalry was affirmed.

17. What effect has this judgement had on heraldic law breaking?

Very little. The City of London put its arms right. For some centuries the City had been using a crest and supporters without being recorded with the College of Arms, although the shield of the City arms had been duly recorded. The rectification cost £200. Generally speaking, however, the sitting of the Court of Chivalry in 1954–5 (the judgement was pronounced in 1955) has had very little effect on heraldic law breaking. Why should it? Is it likely that the Court, so laboriously convened once in two and a quarter centuries, would sit to judge the case of someone who had granted the local golf club a badge? Moreover, Lord Goddard who acted as Surrogate or Deputy to the Earl Marshal, was careful to state in his judgement that if it were the intention of the conveners to make a frequent use of the Court, they should obtain statutory authority for its pains and penalties, in other words a Bill to regularize the modern position of the Court of Chivalry. This has not been done.

18. Can anyone design his own coat of arms?

Yes, if he can square his conscience, for penalties are unlikely to be visited upon him. I recall a conversation which I had with the Garter King of Arms in 1955. I asked him if the Court would be sitting frequently or with fair frequency in the future. He replied that he did not know.

Meanwhile I recall cases such as that of a friend of mine

with whom I was standing in a pub one day. He pointed out to me a man crossing the floor whose blazer bore an heraldic device on its pocket. 'I devised that,' said my friend. 'Then you may do penance in the dungeons of Arundel Castle,' I answered. In truth there is little likelihood of the artist being summoned before the Court.

19. You have referred to the Scottish organization of heraldry. What is it?

No one ever attempted to conduct a Visitation in Scotland, though strange to say, there were three Visitations in even more unruly Ireland. Can you imagine Rob Roy MacGregor being interrogated by a herald as to the validity of his arms? To avoid tiresome difficulties of this sort, the Scots passed a law in 1672, under which the registering of arms in Scotland became obligatory within three months. Since the expiration of this period of grace, all arms borne in Scotland must be registered with the Lord Lyon in his office. If not so registered or matriculated as the term goes, the arms are illegal. The Scottish position is thus delightfully simple. Moreover, the Lord Lyon being a judge of the Court of Session, contempt of his judgements is contempt of court, punishable by fine or imprisonment. I once talked with the present Lord Lyon about ways in which the English College of Arms could cope with heraldic law breaking within its boundaries. He favoured the revival of the Visitations in England. 'I've told them,' he said, referring to the English Heralds, 'that I am prepared to come and help them, give them the benefits of my experience!' They would rather face another Bannockburn!

The plain facts are that the Scottish system works, whereas the English heraldic arrangements are better than the Scottish. A grant of arms in England lasts for ever. Anyone who can prove descent from the original grantee is entitled to use the arms. Thus although the £200 paid for a grant sounds a lot of money, it is not really so, when one realizes that it lasts for ever. Under Scottish heraldic law a grant costs only about £50, but there is the necessity of rematriculating every generation, costing some £20.

20. But I thought that one had to pay a licence each year in order to use arms?

Yes, there was once, previous to 1945, a licence of two or three guineas per year, payable for the use of arms on such articles as carriages, silver, signet rings, and others. This charge was abolished with effect from 1 January 1945, mainly because of the difficulty of collecting it. An amusing comment on governmental views of heraldry is found in the fact that the law which ordered the paying of the licences, made it clear that they must be paid without any distinction made between arms recorded with the College of Arms or self-granted and home made.

21. Can someone who possesses arms grant them to someone else?

No, the arms are granted to a particular individual and to his legitimate descendants, or to a body. However, in the case of corporations they can and frequently do give permission for their arms to be reproduced on programmes and commemoratory leaflets. Such a usage is temporary. It ought to be noted that the reproduction in a book, by way of illustration of someone's coat of arms is perfectly permissible. Not even the Duke of Norfolk can object to his coat of arms being shown in a book on heraldry or history, provided of course that the drawing is accurate.

22. Is the motto part of the coat of arms?

No. In modern grants the motto is always included but it still does not form part of the grant. You may change your motto each day if you wish. If you have inherited as your motto, *Virtus sola nobilitat,* you may change it to *What's in it for No. 1?* as being more appropriate to modern times. One word of caution. Should the motto form part of a block of your coat of arms, a new motto means a new block, and editors are reluctant to incur what will appear to them an unnecessary expense.

23. What is the queer-looking language which heraldry uses?

Ultimately it is Norman French, because during the central Middle Ages French was the language of chivalry (itself a French word) and even as late as 1348 when there occurred the pestilence known as the Black Death, French was still the language of the Court and the monarchy. Half a century later English had taken its place, though it was an English which had itself been much influenced by the Norman French of 300 years past. About 1400 there was a movement in England to use English terms in place of foreign ones, as 'gold' for 'or' etc., but this did not succeed.

In fact it is not hard to learn heraldic language. The essential terms can be learned in a week; as to the rest they are very numerous and it is not worth while to burden your memory with them. Some of them occur perhaps half a dozen times at most in the life of an heraldic student. How much less frequently then in the life of the ordinary reader. 'Yale', for instance, is the name of a mythical monster which was one of the Queen's Beasts set up outside Westminster Abbey at the time of the Coronation, but the term is otherwise very rarely used.

24. What are the various parts of the coat of arms?

The shield, in the centre. On top of it should come a helmet, and on top of that a crest which is supposed to be bound on to the helmet by a wreath of the colours. This is

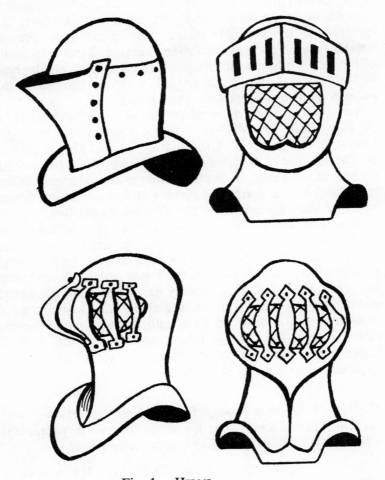

Fig. 1 – HELMS
(showing rank)

Upper left: Esquire or Gentleman.　　　Lower left. Peer.
Upper right: Knight or Baronet.　　　　Lower right. Sovereign.

shown in six partitions, one and one, being the two principal colours of the shield. From the helmet flow down the lambrequin or mantlet which, like everything else in heraldry had a strictly utilitarian function. Made originally of linen or cloth, the lambrequin helped to keep off the heat of the sun and also catch or deflect sword cuts. Over the main body armour was worn the surcoat.

Some persons are allowed figures on either side of their shields. These are called supporters. They are the prerogative of peers, Knights of the Garter, of the Thistle and of St. Patrick and of Knights Grand Cross of the other British Orders of Chivalry. In Scotland things are arranged differently, and in addition to the owners of supporters just listed, many of the untitled lairds are allowed supporters.

Again, in the case of a Knight of the Garter, he may have his shield surrounded by the ribbon of the Garter. Other knighthoods may be signalized in this way, and so may membership (without title) in the lesser orders. A man who has the C.V.O., O.B.E., etc., may hang them from his shield rather like inn signs. Finally, the shield and whole coat of arms may be represented on a compartment which hovers rather like Swift's Flying Island of Laputa. Still it is an improvement upon the old-fashioned Victorian gas bracket as groundwork for a coat of arms.

25. Does it not seem strange that all these essentially practical things should have survived and now be used by people who will never put on armour unless it be in fancy dress?

Yes, but heraldry managed to survive the disuse of armour, because it had become (*a*) ornamental and (*b*) a symbol of gentility. With the latter its fortune was made, for if arms were the sign of gentle blood, then no one was going to forgo them merely because their wording and symbolism was centuries out of date. Even England's greatest poet was not above armorial ambitions and pursued a coat of arms until he obtained it, and the right to have the description 'gentleman' on his burial register.

26. What is the meaning of the term esquire?

Although this is more properly dealt with in our last section we can consider it here, for anyone who obtains a grant of arms is automatically created an esquire, since this term occurs in the grant. As late as about 1870, Queen Victoria created her favourite servant, John Brown an esquire, without any question of arms. Originally an esquire was the follower of a knight, one who himself aspired to wear the gilded spurs. Gradually the term came to be applied to persons who were of gentle birth and who were of the class from which the knights were made. In course of time elaborate rules were framed to define the classes of persons who could be termed esquire. These rules still exist but have become almost obsolete owing to the well-nigh universal popular use of esquire on commercial communications.

27 What are the objects called which appear on a shield?

Legion would be a not unfair answer. First comes the groundwork of the shield. This must be a colour, a metal or a fur. Then on top of this ground come the charges as they are called. These fall into two classes, the honourable ordinaries, and the extraordinary charges. The former are charges or marks which are very common, such as the cross, or the bend or chief. As to the extraordinary, there is hardly any limit to them. Almost anything can have an heraldic significance.

28. What are the heraldic colours?

There are five principal colours which are here given with

that and the other in a coat of arms. Most of these stories can be discounted. The origin of arms which are at all old must in the majority of cases be lost in impenetrable darkness. As to modern arms, i.e. those granted in the last three or four centuries, in many cases their meaning can be discovered by research. Often the charge is a play on a name, a spear for Shakespeare, a fish weir for Wear, etc., in many other instances there is a reference to some circumstance in the life of the grantee. With the oldest arms, such as azure a bend or (blue with a gold bend) the coat may originally have been simply an easy design in someone's favourite colours.

33. How old is heraldry (or as a questioner put it to me at a recent lecture) – who invented heraldry?

Heraldry in western Europe appeared about the middle of the twelfth century (see answer to question 1). As to the inventor of it, we are completely in the dark as to whether it was in fact invented by one man or was a general movement, born of the need for distinguishing signs in battle. Owing to the fact that newsapers were not invented until some 300 years ago, we are often ignorant as to the time or manner of appearance of various changes. We can say of heraldry that it was not in existence before the Norman Conquest of England in 1066. The shields of the warriors on the Bayeux Tapestry do not show heraldic designs. When we move on a generation to the time of the First Crusade, 1095–9, we find a good account of the western knights in the writings of a learned lady, Anna Comnena, daughter of the Greek Emperor. She says nothing of any designs on the shields of the knights, though her description of their appearance and armour is exact. The first evidence we have of a coat of arms appears on an enamel of 1127 which shows Henry I of England arming his son-in-law, the Count of Anjou. Thereafter the evidences multiply rapidly, and during the rest of the twelfth century we have plenty of seals, and other monuments which show coats of arms.

We have only to reflect upon the history of the aeroplane in the last sixty or so years, and the large part which its story has taken in the newspapers, to realize that a modern innovation is at once chronicled in the Press; lacking this powerful aid in the Middle Ages we cannot do more than surmise as to the origin and growth of heraldry.

34. I would like more detail as to the cessation of the Visitations to which you refer in the answer to question 15

Yes, the position about the Visitations is that they were regularly conducted from 1529 (when Henry VIII issued the first commission to the heralds) until 1686. They were part of the movement, general in Europe, for the Crown in each country to control all matters of honours and titles; in England this movement obtained keener edge from the Tudor desire to control everything in the country after the near anarchy of the Wars of the Roses. So the sovereigns began to issue commissions to the officials of their College of Arms to visit one county at a time. The practice would be to go down to, e.g. Berkshire, and stay at the house of the principal nobleman, and thence to issue a proclamation requiring everyone to come in and register his arms. The heralds had the power to make the person disclaim his arms, that is declare that they were not his. Such disclaimers were often posted in the offender's home town, in the market-place, which must have been a frightful blow to the well-known English trait of snobbery and of 'keeping up with the Joneses'. However, many lists of such disclaimers exist, and in some cases the reasons are given. A man's only evidence for the use of arms by his family was an old red seal of his grandfather's. This was not considered sufficient, to justify the use of arms. Sometimes the arms were respited, as it was termed, for further proof. In one case of a family still current in the pedigree books, this respiting has lasted since the end of the Visitation period, so that for more than 250 years proof has been awaited. In another instance, the heralds when they visited one of the Midland shires, undertook to write up the pedigree of the nobleman with whom they had been staying. The notes they made were left behind at the country seat, and have never been written up, though 350 years have passed.

35. Do cases ever occur in which a grant of arms is made to a man, and then later it is discovered that his ancestors had lawful arms? If so, what happens in such cases?

Yes, cases of this can and do occur. I know of one instance in which a man who had become the High Sheriff of a county, and had as such to have a banner with his arms displayed, obtained a grant of arms, somewhat in a hurry. I should explain that if an inquiry is made of the College of Arms to find out if someone had arms, it can easily occur that the grant of arms some generations back could be overlooked, because the pedigree of the ensuing generations had not been recorded there, and so the connection with the grantee is not clear. This must have happened in the case cited, for the arms grant went through in order for the grantee to have arms to use on his banner; but later his son made further investigations into the matter and found that there had been an arms grant some generations earlier. Now the family use only the coat of arms of the earlier vintage. The more modern coat is retained and shown to the curious, only as a curiosity. In fact, the modern family have the right to use both coats of arms. This sort of anomaly used to occur more frequently in the past than at present, and it is the origin of the, at first sight, puzzling practice which one finds in accounts of eighteenth- and early nineteenth-century coats of arms, in which two coats of arms of the same family name are quartered together. Thus: 1 and 4 Smith

Heraldry

Ancient; 2 and 3 Smith Modern. It only means that there
have been two coats of arms granted or registered for the
same family. This habit of using both arms in the same coat
does not now prevail.

36. What do you mean by quartering?

Quartering is the showing of four coats of arms in the
same shield. The best-known example is that of the royal
family arms, in which we have the shield divided into four
quarters. In the top right hand (a shield must always be
thought of as held by someone and therefore the left of the
shield as it faces us, is really the right hand of it), appear
the arms of England. Then these will appear again in the
bottom left, which is No. 4. In the top left No. 2 come the
arms of Scotland, and in the bottom right No. 3 are the
arms of Ireland. This usage of quartering different shields
is used to denote, as in the royal arms, the union of the
crowns, and of the national arms. It is also used to denote
family alliances. Perhaps we had better come to this part of
the explanation through the answer to another but allied
question.

37. How are the arms of husband and wife shown?

In heraldry the man is supreme, unless he happens, as in
rare cases, to marry a queen who is sovereign in her own
right. So if a woman comes from a family which has arms
(i.e. is armigerous) and her husband does not possess arms,
then her arms cannot be shown. There is no shield on which
to display them. A very uncomfortable position, for the
husband that is, and one which has led many a man to
petition the College of Arms for a grant. But if the husband
has been sensible, and has arms, then the normal practice is
to divide his shield by a straight line down the middle, put
his coat of arms on the right and those of his wife's family

on the left. This method is known as impaling, or dimidiating (i.e. halving). Now, should the wife be what is known as an heraldic heiress (quite different by the way from being an heiress in the financial sense) then a different practice prevails. The man's arms fill the shield but with a small shield put on the middle of his shield. This small shield is called an escutcheon of pretence.

38. Can the children of a marriage where both parents are armigerous use the arms of both father and mother?

Only when the mother was an heiress or co-heiress as described above. In that case the children of the marriage can quarter the arms of mother and father. In other words, their shield is divided into four equal parts and the father's arms occur in 1 and 4, while those of the mother come in 2 and 3. It can easily be imagined how confusing the set up can be when, with the passage of a few generations, and marriages to heiresses in each generation, the shield gets cluttered up with quarterings. Resort has to be had to the practice known as grandquartering, and that I leave to the reader's imagination. There are instances of noble families, whose quarterings run into the hundred. One case had over 300 quarterings, while in the families of such great noblemen as the Duke of Atholl there are supposed to be as many as a thousand quarterings. To do justice to such an array, one would need a very large hall or castle window.

If the mother was not an heiress, then no suggestion of quartering arises, and the children of two armigerous parents can use only their father's coat of arms.

39. You referred to the arms of a prince consort? How are they shown?

Generally by shirking the issue. I have never seen a representation of the arms of Prince Philip in the same shield with those of the Queen. If they were to be shown together, then I would think that the arms of the Prince should appear on the left of the shield with those of the Queen on the right, just as though the Queen were the husband. The reason for this inversion of the normal arrangement is that the Queen though Philip's wife is also his sovereign, since sex does not enter into the conception of the monarchy in England. The sovereign of England is sovereign irrespective of sex. Moreover, the royal arms of England are those of the country, since they have been used by every dynasty – Tudor, Stuart, Hanoverian and Windsor – since they were first adopted by the Plantaganets, Richard I being the first sovereign to employ a recognized coat of arms.

If we look back to the last Prince Consort, then we find a recognition of the principle which I have set out above, albeit in a very peculiar form. For the arms of Prince Albert of Saxe-Coburg and Gotha, the husband of Queen Victoria, and the great-great-grandfather of both the Queen and Prince Philip, were represented with those of England, but in a quarterly form as though he had been Queen Victoria's son instead of her husband. This form did, however, show that the Prince was a subject of the Queen, like all other of her subjects, although he was her husband also.

In the Middle Ages, we sometimes find the example of a man of lower rank than his wife who has his arms on the left of the shield while hers are on the right. In some cases, too, a man of low degree will bear his wife's arms alone.

40. What about a woman who is not married, and who has arms, can she show them on a shield?

On a shield, no, unless she is a sovereign in her own right, like the Virgin Queen, Elizabeth I. A single woman can bear arms on a lozenge or diamond shaped compartment, and without a crest. Despite the occurrence occasionally in the Middle Ages of someone like Joan of Arc, it was the general view that ladies did not take part in war, and so could not have either shield or crest. The bearing of arms on a lozenge is the rule for a woman who is a maiden lady, or again for a widow, or a divorcee who has not remarried.

41. What is the position of heraldry today? Are many coats of arms granted?

Yes, many grants of arms are made each year, and these to private individuals. Indeed, I should be inclined to think that heraldry has never been more widespread or had a greater interest for so many people. Most of the officers of the College of Arms or of the Lyon Office are very busy, and much occupied. Not only do private individuals take out grants of arms, but many corporate bodies do so. Since the war there have been many grants of arms which take in the nationalized industries, some large modern corporations, such as the Atomic Energy Authority, and many cases of arms for countries which have been carved out of the old British Empire. Again, there have been many grants of arms to the big banks, insurance companies, and to other businesses. I found quite recently that of the five big banks ('the Big Five'), only one had had an arms grant as far back as 1928; of the others, one had had a grant in the 1930s and the remaining three since the last war. Then again, we must remember that many coats of arms have been taken out by people who before the war would have been very unlikely to have applied for arms. Now that the Labour Party has become so to speak acclimatized in England, the Labour peers have taken out arms, and many other comparatively 'new' folk have done the same. Then too there is the supply of arms to Americans.

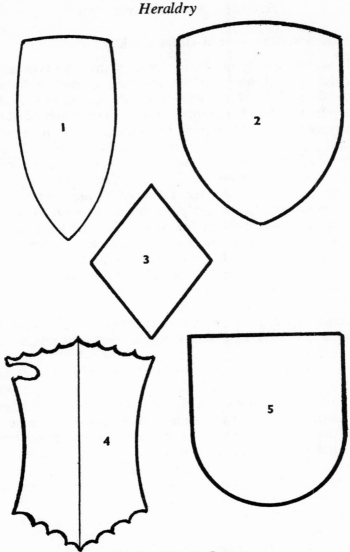

Fig. 3 – SHIELD SHAPES

1. Flat-iron (Norman) 13th Century
2. Modified form 14th Century onwards
3. Lozenge used by ladies
4. Florid form (series of concave curves) late 14th Century. Also showing 'Bouche' for resting lance.
5. Continental form of Shield with semicircular Base.

42. Do Americans care at all for heraldry?

It would be easy on the evidence of my own postbag to say that a great many do, but one must remember the vast population of the States. However, I think it fair to say that a large number of Americans are keen on titles and heraldry. Many of them come over or write to England, in order to obtain a grant of arms. Others who are of Scottish descent go to the Lyon Office. At one time so busy were the heralds in satisfying their transatlantic clients that a cartoon in one of the papers showed the tabarded figures getting the pedigrees down the assembly line for shipment to America. It was about this time (a few years after the war) that an American approached me and asked me to get him a coat of arms. I set out to do so, and almost before I had begun my work in contacting the College of Arms, the officer who was to deal with his case was astonished to receive sterling to the value of £105 (then the charge for a grant), from the American gentleman. For the next eleven months while his grant was being prepared, I received numerous letters asking me for 'the bearings'.

There are, however, more Americans who do not feel that they should approach the sovereign of a foreign state for a grant of arms. Or else they do not know enough about the matter to do so. At any rate, some scholarly Americans long ago formed themselves into a body which registers, and in some cases actually grants, arms. This is the Committee on Heraldry of the New England Historic Genealogical Society. It issues Rolls of Arms, an old English practice extinct in this country for some centuries. These Rolls of Arms are entirely authentic and worth while. It would be a good thing if more Americans had their names put on to them. I understand that a similar body exists in the southern states of the Union.

To these two classes in which authentic heraldry is flourishing, we have to add a much larger section of the

42

armigerous Americans, and that is composed of people whose thirst for gentility must be slaked at lower costs. An American correspondent of mine told me of a lady in the U.S.A. who showed him an illustration of her coat of arms. He asked where she got it, and she replied, 'From an old man who called at the door.' She added that 'he was a rather dirty old man'. I have myself seen advertisements of 'grants' of arms for so many dollars, pictures for more, and pedigrees for even larger sums. These initial charges may run for as little as five to ten dollars. The persons who run these businesses are well informed, for my correspondent went on to say that he had challenged them as to why they were using his (duly registered) coat of arms. He got the reply that they did not use his coat but the coat of the family in general to which he belonged. There is some shadow of justification for this reply. It need not be added, that despite such a principle, many American families are receiving arms to which they are not entitled. Their surnames are the same as those of armigerous English and Scottish families, but beyond that they have nothing to commend them to the bearing of these so-called ancestral arms.

43. What about heraldry in other parts of the world, outside the British Isles and the U.S.A.?

There is a considerable volume of heraldry; in countries such as Canada, Australia and New Zealand, it is largely controlled from England and Scotland. In South Africa, something of the same sort applies, but there recently an Act was passed for the setting up of a heraldic establishment, which would grant arms and register pedigrees as well as regulate the state ceremonies. In continental Europe, heraldry has had a chequered and often unhappy history in the present century. One of the great forces in maintaining heraldry is a monarchy, and so many of the great monarchies of the past have been driven out of their countries that the practice of heraldry has been difficult. When there is a monarchy, the sovereign will always want to control the heraldry of the country because coats of arms are just as much honours as titles are, and therefore must be controlled by the sovereign as he or she is the Fountain (or source) of Honour. Consequently when a monarchy is abolished, the means of controlling heraldry goes too. This is the case with Germany, Austria, Russia, and now Italy. France has no heraldic system of value. Spain owing to its adherence to the past, is better in heraldry and extensive studies of the subject come out each year. Portugal, too, has not neglected its heraldic wealth. It can be imagined what havoc the Communist régimes in eastern Europe have made of heraldry. Outside the countries mentioned, there are relics of heraldry in the Philippines, in India, in some other countries of Asia. In Japan there is an age-old system of the use of crests which is very close to the Western style. In fact Japan is the only country in the world outside the area of western Europe, in which we can be sure that an heraldic system has developed.

44. What are difference marks?

They are used to distinguish the different degrees of cadency in a family. These degrees arise from the position of the various sons. Thus the eldest son (in the lifetime of his father) bore on his shield a label; the second son bore a crescent; the third a mullet and the fourth a martlet (i.e. bird without feet, the fourth son being likely to have no land to alight on, as with John Lackland!) and so on. The use of these cadency marks has gone very much out of fashion in England, where one can see all sorts of cadets of a family using the full arms which are applicable only to the head. The royal family do use cadency marks, and these are labels which bear on them the distinguishing designs

Fig. 4 – CADENCY MARKS

(Indicating various sons on paternal arms).

1 Label	5 Annulet
2 Crescent	6 Fleur-de-lys
3 Mullet	7 Rose
4 Martlet	8 Cross Moline
	9 Octofoil, or double quatrefoil

approved by the sovereign. It is not always realized that the members of the royal, unlike other families, have no right to arms as such, but must await the pleasure of the sovereign. Thus, when a son of the sovereign is created a duke, he will receive a grant of the royal arms suitably differenced, and this will mean that a label is shown over the top of the arms with certain marks upon it, such as a crown, or a lion, or an anchor. In Scottish heraldry, however, the use of difference marks is imperative, owing to the system of matriculation, which requires special marks for each generation, as they matriculate their arms.

45. What are hatchments?

They are the display of arms over the door of a house when a person who was armigerous has died. The practice was once very common in England, and anyone who visits old country churches is likely to see several specimens of hatchments hanging in the church or the vestry. Very rarely is a hatchment used today, but a few years ago one was displayed at the death of Lady Catherine Ashburnham, the last of a very ancient family. The hatchment follows the rule of arms, by showing the arms of a man on a shield, or those of a lady, if single, on a lozenge.

46. What are the Seize Quartiers?

Here again is the sort of heraldic stuff which delights the historical novelist, or even the serious historian. To talk of sixteen quarterings is always somewhat dangerous. The term denotes the continental idea of tracing a man's ancestry through both sides, and showing that each family in turn was armigerous. The seize quartiers are the sixteen ancestors from whom a man descends. To render them complete, the table must show that each of the sixteen ancestors was armigerous. The idea is to get back to eight great-great-grandparents all of whom were entitled to arms. Sir Bernard Burke, who evidently did not like the idea, said 'according to our English notions, this test is rather, I think, one of curiosity than real value; for compare the continental nobility, which very generally still possess it, with our nobility, which very rarely does, and observe the difference between them. Our own aristocracy yields to none other in high breeding, honour, and brilliancy of ancestry; and yet, comparatively speaking, few even among that elevated class can trace their descent up to sixteen families on both sides entitled to armorial bearings.' To which I would add that the preoccupation of continental nobility with marrying only into their own class, has given them an exclusiveness which the English nobility has never possessed; but it is also very much responsible for the overthrow of the continental nobility, because they were viewed as a class apart from the mass of the people. The English nobility, however, are closely allied with every class, and so too is our royalty, this giving a stability to our institutions which the continent has lacked. (See answer to question 6, for royal connections with the bulk of the nation.)

47. What are the best books on heraldry for reading and instruction?

I shall include this question only because I am so frequently asked it. It would be invidious to do more than to mention my own books on the subject. I shall merely remark of them, that *Teach Yourself Heraldry*, is designed to help the student who knows nothing of heraldry and to lead him on to a fair knowledge of the subject; and that *The Story of Heraldry* is a more advanced book, which requires some heraldic knowledge to appreciate.

Coming to books by other authors, I should strongly recommend those by the late A. C. Fox-Davies. *Heraldry Explained* is out of print. It is a small work, and very useful in giving clear expositions of the subject. Copies can be obtained secondhand. Then there is the author's larger work, *Complete Guide to Heraldry*, which is in print, and which has been brought up to date. This is a very fine book, partly for reading, partly for browsing. The author produced other works on heraldry, including his *Armorial Families*, and his *Book of Public Arms*. All of them are well worth getting for reference. His main defect was his dogmatism as to the past of heraldry, for the rules governing modern heraldry were by Fox-Davies applied to the past where they did not always by any means apply.

The writings of Sir Bernard Burke abound in heraldry and in references to the same. His main work in this respect is his *General Armory*, without which no student of heraldry can hope to deal with the innumerable references which he will encounter. This work has been produced afresh in recent years and can be obtained for seven guineas. When it was out of print, it sometimes fetched as much as £28. It gives the reference to almost every coat of arms known in the British Isles up to the time when the text was last revised, in 1884. In addition it has a very useful glossary of heraldic terms, plus an introduction and notes.

2

Ancestors

48. What are ancestors?

The dictionary answer is, one from whom one has descended, a forefather. The word is derived from the French, *ancêstre*, itself coming from *antecessor*, Latin from *antecedere*, to go before. It may seem a very simple question to ask and answer, but if we say that Queen Elizabeth II is the descendant of Queen Elizabeth I, or to put it another way round, that Queen Elizabeth I was the ancestress of the present Queen, we shall at once be answered with an indignant exclamation: 'But Queen Elizabeth I didn't marry!' So at the very beginning we have to explain the difference between direct ancestry and collateral. The term 'direct ancestor' is rather misleading. There cannot be an indirect ancestor in the proper sense of the word. By 'direct ancestor' we must always mean someone from whom one has descended. The indirect ancestor is the collateral. While it is untrue that Her present Majesty has descended directly from the Tudor Queen Elizabeth, she is certainly a kinswoman of hers, since Queen Elizabeth of Tudor days was a niece of Queen Margaret of Scotland, the daughter of Henry VII, who married James IV of Scotland. Without going into these exalted and distant relationships, you need only think of some of your uncles and aunts, who are obviously connected with you by blood, but from whom you do not descend.

D   49

49. Why trace your ancestry?

A very pertinent question and one which many people would have been wise to ask themselves, as we shall see in the course of our questions and answers. The brief reply is – to find out where we came from. That should always be the right answer, and in the majority of cases of ancestry tracing it is the right one, but there are many examples of people who have embarked on pedigree research for unworthy motives, such as bolstering up their own vanity, and running after titles which they can never obtain, and which would be a great expense to them if they could get them. However, the aim to discover one's forebears and to find out as much as possible about them is as legitimate as most forms of human curiosity.

50. What is a pedigree?

A genealogical table, i.e. a drawn out account of how someone is descended. The word is said to come from the French *pied de grue* or crane's foot, taken from the marks used in showing descent on a pedigree table. Pedigrees or genealogical tables abound in the general run of history books, for one cannot properly understand such historical periods as the Wars of the Roses, or the War of the Spanish Succession, or the conflicting claims of the Stuarts and Hanoverians, unless a table is provided to show the relationship of the various cousins who had anything but cousinly love for each other.

51. Are pedigrees only for the 'nobs'?

No, they are the right way to set out anyone's line of descent. If you can show only your descent from your grandfather, then you ought to have a pedigree because without one it will not be easy to know the degrees of relationship of your cousins, uncles, aunts, etc. Many people think of pedigree as something which belongs only to very exalted folk, dukes, marquesses and the like. Well, it may come as a surprise to many such people to learn that in many so-called humble pedigrees, there are numerous cases of distinguished names turning up. A few years ago when Prince Andrew was born, a table was published to show his descent on father's and mother's side. On his mother's side, that of the Queen, there were plenty of plain misters, because the Queen Mother's forebears had intermarried with people who were not of grand family and who were untitled. This is a very common phenomenon in the pedigrees of a vast number of British people. The reason is very simple. In continental Europe the royal family circles kept very much to themselves, and formed a kind of marriage trade union. The same thing happened with the nobility, so that they were not contaminated with commoner folk. In England and Scotland, however, these rules were not observed, so that from royalty to peasant, there were degrees of relationship over several generations. The consequence is that many distinguished connections turn up in families of plain folk, who are very often quite surprised at their noble and even royal affiliations.

52. How far can you go back with a pedigree in this country?

Provided that, as far as you know, your family has lived in England for some centuries – and not come here from Europe within the last few decades – then with any reasonable luck you should be able to get back 200, 250 or 300 years. There is nothing unusual in a pedigree of tradesmen or yokels going back some 300 years. I have known many such, and they witness to a stability in British institutions which many Continental countries would envy. For stability means that records have a much better chance of being kept than where there is trouble, and civil commotion.

53. How do you do it?

This is really the biggest question of all in this subject and I think that before I answer it, I ought to consider another question I am often asked, namely – Are there people who will undertake research for one? Yes, and their charges vary enormously. I knew one research worker who never undertook a case at a fee less than 100 guineas. There are many cheaper labourers in the genealogical field, and they may begin your research at charges as low as five guineas though I doubt whether with all-round price increases anyone now would begin at less than ten guineas. If you do go to one of these workers, you will find that charges must increase with time and the work done, so that if one begins at, say, ten guineas, there will have to be further charges as one progresses. The essential thing to grasp, if you employ someone else to do your research is that you must pay for that person's time. Suppose that they search a parish register for two or three days, even without any successful result as far as your ancestry is concerned, they must still support themselves during that time. Therefore if you are employing them for the work, you must pay for their time. If on the other hand you do it yourself then, you are providing the time.

54. What then is the cost, if I do it myself?

There are various do-it-yourself kits, so to speak, and quite a large number of books exist which profess to give you information on the subject. Among these, perhaps I may mention modestly, are some of my own, but there are others, and most libraries will find you a book on the subject of tracing your ancestry. In addition, as I will show in process of question and answer there are many reference works which are useful to you in tracing your family history. For the cost, apart from the charges of an employed genealogist, the amount involved in obtaining certificates and official documents is small. Very rarely does the charge exceed £1, unless some will has to be copied, or some document at the Public Record Office translated from medieval script. Even then the official scale of charges is very moderate and reasonable.

55. Well then, where do I start and how do I set about it?

You begin with yourself, which is quite natural and right. You start off with your own birth certificate. Then you must determine whether you want to trace father's or mother's side. In other words you have to be either a normal person or a feminist. Perhaps it is not quite as bad as that alternative sounds. Seriously if you try to trace both sides of your family you will end in about two or three years with a pedigree of a truly formidable width but of very little depth, for each generation doubles, so that while we have two parents, we have four grandparents and so on. Tracing these is quite a task. I advise, then, that you decide to trace one parent's line, and not both. Choosing then, you must next have the marriage certificate of your parents. You know how old they are or were, but could you state exactly the date of their birth? The day of the month no doubt, but what about the year. I have known some of my hearers answer up without a falter, 1873, or whatever it happened to be, but answers such as, 'well he was in the first war, but he wasn't in the first batch, so I think he must have been out of the late teens in 1914' or that sort of thing will not do. Believe me, you would be surprised at the number of well-equipped folk whose answers as to parents' years of birth take some such form.

56. Where do I go for these certificates?

To Somerset House, in the Strand, London. There are a great many valuable documents here, apart from birth, marriage and death certificates, including much interesting material about the income tax affairs of thousands of citizens. However, for the moment we are concerned with Somerset House as the repository of certificates of birth, marriage and death. Owing to the activities of the Welfare State and the thirst for personal information which it has caused, many people now go into the galleries of Somerset House who would never have been seen there in days gone by. I cannot help recalling a conversation which I involuntarily overheard as I was leaving there one day. Two women had been inside the building to obtain the marriage certificate of one of them. Result, a negative search. The dialogue which followed was most amusing. It consisted of downright scepticism on the part of the one woman, and on the other side, a catalogue of dates, which were remembered chiefly because of the second woman's association at some time with various men. On another occasion, a man whose birth was not legitimate spent over two hours searching the books for his birth certificate. He then got someone better skilled than himself to visit the records, and they produced the necessary information very quickly, by the simple expedient of looking for his birth under his mother's and not under his (putative) father's name. Lastly, there can sometimes be seen in the Strand a sandwich-board man with a large notice, somewhat hard to decipher but the purport of which is that he has been deprived of his pension because the details of birth cannot be found at Somerset House.

All of which may serve to warn you that when you arrive there, you should seek the help of the courteous officials whose duty it is to assist you. In addition to much useful verbal assistance they will get you some leaflets which will explain much to you, as to how to look for the certificates. Charges amount to a few shillings, and the certificates will arrive within a day or two.

At Somerset House you cannot go back beyond 1837 when the registration of births, marriages and deaths began in England and Wales. Scotland was later, in 1855, and Ireland not until 1864. There are gaps in the records, a few here and there when someone's birth was not entered. This accounts for the difficulties met by some people who are trying to get a pension.

57. You say that Somerset House goes back to 1837, but what about the time before that?

In theory for 300 years before Somerset House recording began, the vital statistics on birth, marriage and death, were kept in the records of each parish. I say, in theory, because although the parish records are supposed to begin in 1538, in fact they do not start at that date in a great many cases. The celebrated historian of the parish registers, the late Mr. A. M. Burke, says that failure to comply with the order to keep the records was of constant occurrence. This was not unnatural for the order emanated from Thomas Cromwell, Henry VIII's tyrannical Vicar-General, and all sorts of sinister motives were attributed to him in making this order. It was even suggested that he had a mind to put taxes on births, marriages and deaths. However, as a budding genealogist you are concerned with the record of your ancestors. In practice most parish records begin in the seventeenth century, and you should find this a great help to you in tracing your ancestry before 1837.

58. This is all very well, but how am I to get from the state registers of 1837 on to the parish registers?

There are about 14,000 parishes in the Church of England in England and Wales, and if the last parish mentioned on a certificate at Somerset House does not give you the parish of your ancestor, then all you have got to do is to run through the remaining 13,999. This is facetious, but it is a serious problem or would be if we had not some fortunate help in the matter. Generally speaking anyone living today would be able to get back to the marriage of his or her great-grandparents through the records at Somerset House. In my case to take one instance, I am able to reach the marriage date of my great-grandparents at Somerset House about 1850. Fortunately a bridge does exist over which you can travel from these records to get into the parish records. This is the census return for 1851.

59. How can the census return help me?

Very much indeed. The first census return which was kept was that of 1841, and this also can be looked up at the Public Record Office in Chancery Lane (it was originally a home for converted Jews), but although it is often very useful it does not give the place of birth of the entrant. When the idea of a census was first broached in England, there was a great deal of opposition to the suggestion on the supposition that it would bring down divine vengeance upon England. However, with the progress of events, including the loss of the American colonies, the French Revolution, and the rise of Napoleon, the people felt no doubt that they could risk a little more, and so in 1801, ten years after the Americans had decided to hold a census, one was held in Britain. For the first time it was known how many people lived in the island, total some 12 millions. But once the return had been made, the detailed papers were destroyed. It took some genius in the civil service to suggest that it might be worth while to keep the papers, and that was not until 1841. Even then, from a genealogical point of view, the records are not all that they should be. When it came to asking the entrant his place of birth, the recorders could only think of saying, 'were you born in this parish?' i.e. the place where the entrant was living at that time. It took another ten years and another genius – someone of the same calibre as the man who first thought of using fire – to sub-

stitute the master inquiry, 'Where were you born?' This
first appeared in 1851. If you take the place where your
great-grandfather lived in or about 1850–2 – and as I have
explained you can get this as a rule from the records at
Somerset House – then you can look up the particular parish
in the 1851 census returns (this costs less than 2*s*.). Very
often you will find that he lived at the same place as that
mentioned on his marriage or other certificate. If not, you
will at least have the answer, and that turns you on to the
local parish where you can look up the parish records or
get the clergyman to do it for you. If you want to find his
name look in the details listed in Crockford's *Clerical
Directory of the Church of England,* where all C. of E.
clergymen are listed.

60. What if my ancestors were Nonconformists?

Here you may get some help because at Somerset House
there are preserved records older than those of 1837 and
which relate to the statistics of the Nonconformist bodies.

61. What about parishes in Scotland and in Ireland?

In Scotland, parish registers unlike those in England are
gathered under one roof. They do not usually go back to
the same date as their English counterparts, but being all
together, they are much easier to search. Conversely, this
togetherness could result in a sad loss if some catastrophe
were to descend upon H.M. Register House, Edinburgh.
This is what happened in Ireland, where in 1922 (please
note after the wicked British had left), the commotions
among the Irish led to the destruction of the Four Courts
and to large quantities of Irish family history records. It is
very unusual to find parish records available in Ireland, but
to make up for this Irish genealogists have laboured hard
to find other sources of information.

62. What of Quaker or Roman Catholic records, i.e. of bodies separated from the established churches in England or Scotland?

The Quakers have been very careful in keeping their records, both in England and in America, and I would suggest that you should contact the Secretary of the Religious Society of Friends, Friends House, Euston Road, London, N.W.1. Roman Catholic records can be found through the Catholic Record Society, St. Edward's, Sutton Park, Guildford, Surrey.

63. What about the Huguenots?

This is a very important subject, because a lot of people whose names are undoubtedly French are under the impression that they are of Norman descent, whereas in reality they come from the Huguenot influx in the seventeenth century. For particulars of this source apply to the Hon. Sec., The Huguenot Society, c/o Barclays Bank, 1 Pall Mall East, London, S.W.1., or the same source but c/o The Society of Genealogists, 37 Harrington Gardens, Kensington, London, S.W.7.

64. What other public sources are there?

An immense number, indeed it is hard to say where they begin and end. However, I expect you mean that there are some special sources in London, which are of more than ordinary value. Yes, there are the Public Record Office, which I have mentioned in my answer to question 59, and which holds a huge quantity of valuable documents; the British Museum Library, in Bloomsbury, where every printed book in the history of publishing in England is available; and the Society of Genealogists at 37 Harrington Gardens, Kensington, S.W.7. I should say that you would be well advised to consult these, but not to do so until you have a very firm grasp of the principles of ancestor research, although it is true that at the Society of Genealogists you would find a number of useful text books, and also the whole library there is arranged in such a way as to help the researcher, and to save him time. For wills, you must consult the Principal Probate Registry at Somerset House, where all wills have been stored since the passing of the Probate Act in 1858.

65. What about wills before that date?

Before 1858 wills were under the jurisdiction of the Church as they had been from the beginning in England, and they were dealt with in various ecclesiastical courts over the length and breadth of the country. If, however, a man happened to have property in more than one area, in more than one ecclesiastical jurisdiction, then the will could not be handled locally but had to go to the Prerogative Court of Canterbury, known as P.C.C. to researchers. These P.C.C. wills have been lodged at Somerset House. For the other wills which did not go to P.C.C., they are situated in many places in the country, and the best course is to consult a book especially devoted to them, namely *Wills and Their Whereabouts*, by A. J. Camp.

66. You said that most English or Scots or Welsh folk could go back some 200–300 years. What about tracing ancestry before that time?

It depends very much upon what social class your ancestors belonged to. If they were landed folk, in some way owners of land or even tenants, then there would probably have been a record of them. If they were substantial tradesmen or functionaries in a town, again there would be record. If they did not belong to these two classes, there would not be the same likelihood of finding out anything about them. This applies equally in England or Scotland, and even more in Ireland. In England some classes of the community who were not very exalted can be traced for some generations, notably in the case of the villeins, who were normally bought and sold with the land. As it was of great importance to them to establish their freedom, they used to struggle hard to show that their fathers or grand-fathers had been free. Hence sometimes four or five genera-tions of villein pedigree. But as a rule, unless your family belonged to the better classes you are not likely to trace it before 1500. As for the number of pedigrees which can be traced in the Middle Ages, these are much fewer than those after 1500 or 1600. They are the pedigrees of the county families as they used to be called in England, of the lairds in Scotland. Many of them have had to sell up their landed property in recent years owing to the pressure of taxation. As we go back we find that records have a tendency to decrease and to concern smaller and smaller groups of people.

67. How many people can claim Norman descent in England?

A very large proportion of the population, if we reckon that Norman blood over the nine centuries since the Con-quest has permeated the nation. But if you mean who are the people who can say truthfully that their ancestors were at Hastings, they can be numbered on the fingers of one hand. The families of the Giffards and the Malets in the *Landed Gentry* and the Gresleys of Drakelowe in the *Peerage*, with De Marris again in *Landed Gentry*, and we have filled up the number of persons whose ancestor was at Hastings. I refer here of course to descent in the male line. There are also a number – possibly 200 – of families which are Norman but whose ancestor was not at Hastings, or at least not known to be. Such families as Curzon are unquestionably Norman, but I think it most doubtful that the original ancestor was at Hastings. We simply have not the records to prove or disprove it, but generally those who profit most in upheavals are not the hardy fighters who first go over the top.

68. What of pre-Conquest descent?

This is even rarer than Norman and for an obvious reason. The conquered either fled to other countries, or went under cover. Consequently it is only when a lucky find shows a Norman name at the beginning of what is otherwise a Norman-looking pedigree that we realize the essential native quality of some of our great houses. The FitzWilliams and the Berkeleys are cases in point, for both of them are native English in origin.

69. Why are so many people keen to have Norman blood?

A good point because it is does seem strange to want to come from a set of hoodlums, whose only difference from Hitler's Nazis was that they were more successful. However, there it is, the worship of success is very strong, and most English people want to be with the best people, whether they are alive or dead. Hence the wish for Norman ancestry, though bless the hearts of most of the would-be twentieth-century Normans, they are innocent of any connection with them.

70. What is the longest pedigree known?

Possibly that of the Emperor of Ethiopia. His descent is said by tradition to come from the marriage of the Queen of Sheba and King Solomon. This must have occurred about 1000 B.C., but there is no documentary evidence for the matter. However, in the fourth century A.D. the tradition was alive, and that is older than the oldest of the European monarchies. In Japan the line of the Mikado is reputed to go back to ages far lost in time. Even if we accept only the historically ascertainable line of the Mikados, it will stretch into the early Middle Ages, but I think that the principle of adoption has been brought into the family of the Japanese emperors as with the Romans so that one cannot reckon their pedigree as a contender in the lists of ancientry. In China some families claim descent from Confucius, according to one account amounting to as many as 40,000 persons. Confucius lived 2,500 years ago, so that if these claims are well founded, these Chinese pedigrees should be the oldest in the world.

71. What of European pedigrees?

There are all sorts of stories about Italian princes whose ancestry remounts to the later period of the Roman Empire; it may be so, but I do not think it can be proved. I well recall an occasion at one of the international congresses on genealogy which I attended, and at which an Italian expert put forward a motion that no pedigree should be accepted which went back earlier than the twelfth century. The only exceptions to this would be in the case of some of the royal families. The pedigree of Earl Mountbatten begins traditionally with an Earl Ydulf in the sixth century. A connected line is traced from Gislebert, ruler over what is now Belgium in the year 841. This corresponds very much to the line of ancestry of Her Majesty the Queen. The latter is traced back through Egbert of Wessex (who died in 839), and beyond him to Cerdic, King of Wessex, who like most of the Saxon royal lines traced his ancestry back to Wotan. The last-named apparently lived in the third century A.D.

However, once we have passed over these royal lines we can readily admit that the noble houses of Europe are as much bounded by the darkness of the early Middle Ages, as are our own distinguished families.

72. What do you think of the stories about Irish families going back into a very far time?

I take what I know is a reasonable standpoint with regard to Irish pedigrees. If you look them up in some books, such as the well-known O'Hart's *Irish Pedigrees*, you will find the lines of the various royal houses of Ireland traced back to Noah. For this reason what are called Milesian pedigrees (so named from a man named Milesius, King of Ireland about 1000 B.C.), have been laughed at for a long time. However, the considered judgement of scholars is that the two or three generations in a pedigree immediately before St. Patrick landed in Ireland (A.D. 432), can be taken as genuine. In any event they are strings of names which could easily be handed down by oral tradition. If this is the case a pedigree for an Irishman of the old royal lines could be correct back to approximately A.D. 400. After the time of St. Patrick, writing and Latin letters spread across Ireland, and the traditions began to be written down with the inevitable result that they were corrupted. The record of the generations nearest to St. Patrick's time would be the least corrupted. Such is the modern theory, and I can see no reason to doubt it. Ireland never had a kingship in the sense of Scotland's or England's central monarchy. There were four Irish provinces with kings of their own, and among these a high king or Ard Righ would be elected, in other words he proved the strongest. The pedigrees of these kings from about A.D. 400 are not doubtful. Before that date it is quite probable that they are genuine but we do not know and cannot prove or disprove. For the ascription of the Irish royal lines to the Biblical patriarchs we must remember that such was the practice in most western European countries after they became Christian. The line of the local kings was traced from the gods, and this line, gods and all was tacked on to the genealogies in the Old Testament.

73. What about the long Welsh pedigrees?

Here again we have a traditional element of some importance. Until the time of Henry VIII (himself half a Welshman) in 1542 English law did not apply to Wales. From 1542 England and Wales have been one entity with the same laws applicable to both. Before that date, Welsh law prevailed and under Welsh law the property of the father had to be divided equally among his sons. This meant a great deal of economic misery but it did promote genealogy. A man had to be ready to carry half a dozen generations of his family names in his mouth. He had to show who he was and that readily, so that he used the word 'ap' meaning 'son of'. He was, e.g. Rhys ap Tudor ap Morgan ap Griffith, ap Sais, ap Morgan, with 150 years of pedigree available at a moment's notice. This sort of thing promoted long memories of family history and many Welshmen could recite perfectly genuine pedigrees far longer than the half-dozen generations I have postulated here. In fact, as among the Highland Scots, there were officials whose duty it was to memorize the genealogies of the great men, the princes and kings. Consequently when one understands the nature of Welsh pedigrees one ceases to doubt their authenticity, for who would want to invent long lists of names merely for the sake of doing so.

74. You seem to place some value on tradition, do you think it is of use?

Yes and no. It depends entirely upon the place and the time. In some places such as old Ireland, or in Wales, the value of tradition is great. But in countries where a great store has been set on documentary history, or where there is a long tradition of learning, the value of tradition is greatly lessened. This applies to England. I think that before the Norman Conquest (1066) there were many traditional pedigrees which were recited by bards or handed down in tradition in families and that if the Normans had not over-thrown so much of the English tradition, these pedigrees could have been handed down very much as in Wales or Ireland. As it happened the Normans broke the tradition and after some while a quite new standard arose. For many centuries England has had a literate class among her nobles, and where there are documents there is much less reliance upon tradition and oral remembrance, so that a tradition which appears in England in the fifteenth, sixteenth, or seventeenth centuries has very much less value than among more primitive peoples.

75. When you were the editor of *Burke's Peerage* you had the reputation of being a great wrecker of pedigrees; is this cor-rect?

Not by any means, though as soon as it is announced that you have drastically revised some pedigrees, you will get the fame of being a pedigree breaker. In actual fact by my work at Burke's I was able to build up many pedigrees which otherwise would have continued to appear in the volume with an abbreviated account for the particular family. I did remove a large quantity of legends and myths, for which no adequate foundation could be provided.

76. What is the oldest pedigree in England?

The longest documented pedigree now known in England is that of the Arden family. This is a pedigree blessed by the great scholar J. H. Round – himself always accounted a great iconoclast – and who says of the Arden family tree: 'It had not only a clear descent from Aelfwine, Sheriff of War-wickshire in days before the Conquest, but even held, of the great possessions of which Domesday shows us its ancestor as lord, some manors which had been his before the Normans landed, at least as late as the days of Queen Elizabeth.' This is high praise from so great a genealogist, and it enables the Arden family to rank as the only English pedigree with a certainty of going back before the Conquest. There are others which are almost equally certain but where no absolute documentary proof can be found. These include the Berkeleys (in Scotland Barclays) whose descent from Eadnoth the Staller is almost beyond cavil. Eadnoth was killed in some fighting near Bristol in 1068. He was called the Staller as being a chamberlain to Edward the Confessor and evidently he transferred his allegiance to the Conqueror. Then there is the great Scottish family of Swinton whose ancestor is considered to have been the Edulfing or ruler of the district between the Tyne and the Forth in the days of Alfred the Great. Like many English families who did not care for the rule of William the Conqueror they migrated northward and were welcomed by the Scottish kings. In addition to these we can add the name of Wilberforce, famous in connection with one of its members, William Wilberforce who led the anti-slavery movement in Great Britain. This family claims a descent from a hardy soldier who had the distinction of fighting both at Stamford Bridge and at Hastings. When we have gone over this short list of four we have run over the families of England whose ancestry is pre-Conquest. The Ardens have a distinction of even greater fame. They produced Mary Arden, the mother of William Shakespeare. It seems peculiarly appropriate that the greatest of English poets should have been born of a family of undoubted English pre-Conquest stock.

77. What is the oldest pedigree in Scotland?

I should plump for the pedigree of the Earls of Mar. No date can be given for the origin of this earldom, and some of the greatest authorities describe the Earls of Mar as having been earls *ab initio*. The reason for this is that the original earls were known as the Mormaers or rulers of Mar, and after the Scottish kings extended their rule over the country, these Mormaers submitted to the crown and were known as Earls of Mar. The charter in which they are described as Earls of Mar is dated as early as 1114, and it was long before this that they had exercised power and authority in the mormaership. The family name is Erskine; the present holder of the title appears in peerage books as the 29th earl.

Scotland's history supplies many names of great families and it would be a difficult task to assign pre-eminence among them on the score of ancestry. The original people are generally called Celts, and among these we must place the Highland clans, a different race entirely from the lowlanders. There are many traditions of interest among the Highland clans, but in actual pedigree we do not get instances which correspond in length to those of their Celtic kinsmen in Wales and Ireland. For the great lowland families which often go back to the twelfth century in their authentic pedigrees, their origin is diverse. Some like the Haigs are probably Norman. Some are of English origin as Swinton is thought to be. There are even instances from farther afield. A very ancient tradition in the family of Drummond derives their origin from Hungary. Maurice who is reckoned as their progenitor came to Scotland with Edgar Atheling who had been born in Hungary and whose sister Margaret married King Malcolm Canmore in 1068. Hence the Dukes of Perth. In the earlier days of the Scottish kingdom, Scotland provided a good field of enterprise for ambitious men who found their own country for one reason or another unsuitable for them. In this way both dispossessed Englishmen and their Norman counterparts became Scots, and settled down in their new country; the Barclays for one thing are only the Berkeleys gone north. So too the Montgomeries were originally a great Norman family, a

branch of which went north to found the earldom o
Eglinton and Winton.

78. What is the longest pedigree in Wales?

There are about half a dozen Welsh pedigrees which hav
a millennium of family history behind them. One of th
most interesting is that of Lord St. Davids. This used t
appear in *Burke's Peerage* showing a descent from on
Maximus, who had made himself Emperor of Britain in th
4th century, he being a Roman governor of Britain wh
had rebelled against his Emperor at Rome. Also brough
into the pedigree account was Vortigern, the unlucky Britis
king who was responsible for bringing the Saxons int
Britain. This would have given Viscount St. Davids
pedigree as long, if not longer than, that of Her Majesty th
Queen. In modern versions the family history begin
modestly enough with a mere 900 years of ancestry. How
ever, it is fact that as far back as the tenth century there ha
been a tradition in the family of descent from Maximus o
Vortigern; so that at least a family capable of having suc
a tradition must have been anciently recorded as far back a
a millennium ago.

Others of interest in Wales, and about the same age a
the Philipps family (the surname of Viscount St. Davids
are Williams-Wynn; Lloyd-Davies; and Vaughan o
Nannau. None of these families show a descent of less tha
some 900 years, and in all probability if traditional pedi
grees are accepted, they could be taken much farther back

79. What about the longest Irish pedigrees?

In my reply to question 72 I indicated my outlook wit
regard to Irish pedigrees, and my belief that many of th
princely lines could be retraced to about A.D. 400. Amon
these one would certainly reckon the O'Conor Don; Mc

Loughlin (Maelseachlainn); MacCarthy (Kings of Munster); O'Kelly of Gallagh; O'Briens and O'Neills. Full details of these very interesting pedigrees are to be found in books such as *Burke's Landed Gentry of Ireland*. Indeed it was through my occupation in bringing out a new edition of this work in 1958 (the last issue had been in 1912) that I was able to study many Irish pedigrees.

80. You referred to the Highlanders; what is the position with regard to the clan system, is there really a blood relationship in the main clan lines?

I should say very definitely, No, to the question, but such an answer requires some elaboration and explanation. If you look in books dealing with the Scottish clan system, such as the present Lord Lyon's revision of Frank Adams's *Clans, Septs and Regiments of the Scottish Highlands*, you will find between the lines quite a distinction between the family of the chief, such as the Mackintosh, or the McNab, and those who bear his name. If you search farther and look up the pedigrees of the chiefs in the *Peerage* or the *Landed Gentry*, you will see that the chief's pedigree is given there in detail, but there are no signs of connections of descent for all bearing his name. In the parlance of the genealogists, the chief is the eponymous, the name founder of the clan. I do not question the descent of the various chiefs, more than I would query the descent of any other notable family; but I do question very greatly the idea that, for instance, all Macphersons are connected by blood with the chief of Cluny Macpherson. I think it much more likely that in the early days of the clan, there were besides the family of the chief, branches of his line which occupied a more and more lowly position; in addition to these truly blood members, there were many persons who wanted protection and who joined themselves to the clan and took the name of the chief, as being his men. In fact we can find plenty of instances where such things did occur, and where broken men, i.e. persons whose own clan had suffered disaster, joined up with a more successful clan and took its name. This will account for the enormous number of Macs in the world, whose connection with the chief of their name is not even tenuous; it does not exist.

I would, however, make one exception to this observation, and that would be with the MacGregors. This clan, as is well known, was subjected to severe persecution during the seventeenth and eighteenth centuries; indeed during the years 1603–61 and 1693–1774 they were not allowed to use their own surname. For instance, the famous Rob Roy lived all his life as an outlaw in the eyes of the law. Yet when the ban on the MacGregors was lifted, 826 persons came forward to name their chief and to acknowledge themselves as MacGregors.

Another point is, that if the idea of all members of the clan being blood relations is untrue, it yet serves a marvellous purpose. It helps the ordinary Scotsman who perhaps cannot trace beyond his great-grandfather, to feel that he descends from men of fame, whose exploits are recorded in the annals of the clan, i.e. in the annals of the chief's family. Had such an idea of clanship occurred to the Smiths, Jones, Browns, and Robinsons, how much stronger would English social life and feeling be.

81. How do the Heralds' Visitations help with genealogy?

I referred to the Visitations in England and Wales in the answers to questions 15 and 34, but I will now be more specific about the genealogical side of these visits. The prime purpose was not to compile family history information. This resulted from the Heralds' Visitations as a side-line which became very important. For their own purposes, the visiting heralds would draw up rudimentary pedigrees; these were enlarged as generations passed, and copies were kept in the

College of Arms. Gradually it became a function of the heralds to maintain pedigrees, and this is one of the main features of their work today. As to the value of the Visitation pedigrees themselves, they are almost beyond calculation. If you can hitch yourself on to one of these pedigrees, you are genealogically home and dry.

82. What about entries in family Bibles, have they any value?

Yes, they often contain a considerable amount of information and should be scrutinized most carefully. They were used to record names of members of the family with their vital statistics, of birth, marriage and death, and sometimes other incidents in their lives.

I should also strongly suggest or urge would-be seekers after family history to ask any aged relatives they have for details about the family. I have known an old member of a family keep something to himself for a long time, and then suddenly burst out with it, to the great surprise of a younger person. 'Why didn't you tell me of this before?' is a very natural inquiry, and it is usually answered with, 'Well, I never thought that you would be interested in it.' In such a way, I for one, learned of the existence of a relationship with some Sayer cousins, whose names in connection with my own genealogy had puzzled me for some time. Therefore if you have older members of the family, pump them for information. Remember that the day will come when you will be able to learn nothing more from their lips.

83. What exactly is cousinship?

It is much more difficult for us to use the word 'cousin' or 'kinsman' than it was for our ancestors. If anyone reads Shakespeare's plays or other documents of the sixteenth–seventeenth centuries, he will find the use of the word 'cousin' very frequent. It is a very simple and useful word, for once one has passed from the immediate family circle, or outside the range of aunts, uncles, grandparents, etc., what else is a man or woman to be called, but cousin or kinsman or kinswoman. With the latter words, too, our ancestors were much more liberal and sensible than we are. They recognized kinship and did not try to work out exact details where this was not too easy. The formal definition of 'cousin' is of course that of the son or daughter of an uncle or aunt. Cousin-german means simply first cousin; those who like can work out all the grades of first cousin twice removed, second cousin and the rest of it. Simply to refer to a person as 'kinsman' is simpler. Often with pedigrees in days gone by we know that a relationship existed between two men, but we cannot define it exactly. Those who lived at the time knew quite well that they were related, and did not bother about exact places in the family tree. The use of the same arms would not be tolerated between persons who were not of the same blood, and hence heraldry greatly aided genealogy.

84. What is the truth about the millions of money lying in Chancery?

The truth is often very unpalatable to people who are hoping to get large fortunes out of Chancery. As a general rule there are no large sums lying in Chancery. A leaflet is issued by the Supreme Court Pay Office of the Royal Courts of Justice in London, which gives some very illuminating details about funds held in Chancery. It states that the majority of the funds are of small amounts, and it tells inquirers where they can get the information about such accounts as are held there. It also very significantly adds a warning against syndicates and agents professing to deal with millions of money held in Chancery for various families. It even gives the names of some of these alleged benefactors, such as Drake, Hyde, Page, Everingham and Bailey.

It is a tragic fact that there have been many people who have deluded themselves into thinking that huge sums of money are awaiting them in the Court of Chancery. I had one instance brought to my notice, in which a woman (in America) was under the impression that the city of London had belonged to her forebears, and that she had only to put in her claim to receive untold sums of money from the English courts. Anyone who thinks that there is something waiting for him or her in the Chancery Court should write to the Supreme Court Pay Office at the address given above.

85. Are there sums of money going with titles. e.g. of peers?

This is another delusion similar to the one dealt with in the answer to question 84. There are a few cases in which estates are entailed, i.e. settled on a series of heirs, so that the present owner is more like a tenant. In fact in the case of an entail, the owner in being is referred to as the tenant for life, and he has definite bounds set on his powers of dealing with the estate. Only in such a case where an estate is entailed and where the owner is a peer can there be said to be any money accompanying the peerage. These cases grow fewer every decade. In the vast majority of peerages, no money of any sort goes with the inheritance of the title as such. I have known many peers who have inherited a title only to find that they are not thereby relieved from the necessity of earning a living. They have the peerage but they have nothing beyond the honour of it. If this fact could be grasped by most people, there would not be so much seeking after peerages which are dormant, or in abeyance.

86. What are peerages dormant or in abeyance?

A dormant peerage is where it is known, or at least thought that an heir exists, but where the heir has not come forward to prove his title. An abeyant peerage is one in which the succession to the title cannot be proved until a male heir emerges from among the female heirs to a title. E.g. a peer dies, and the peerage is said to lie in abeyance between his daughters, until one of them produces a male heir, or rather until from their lines emerges a single male heir. An abeyancy can be terminated by the sovereign if he or she feels so inclined.

87. How should one start to trace Welsh ancestry?

Your best beginning is to go to the Honourable Society of Cymmrodorion, 20 Bedford Square, London, W.C.1. If you join this society you will find many persons whose interests are in common with yours and who would help you. You will realize that from 1542 Wales and England are administratively one, and that what applies to English records from that time will apply to Welsh records also. Only if you think that you can get back behind 1542 will the wealth of Welsh genealogical material help you.

88. How should one trace Irish ancestry?

Get in touch with the Chief Herald of Ireland, Dublin Castle, Ireland. He will help you from the store of records under his keeping, but will also direct you to places where you can consult genealogical records in Ireland. Remember, however, as I have mentioned before that much of the most valuable of the Irish family history went up in smoke in 1922.

89. What about Northern Ireland?

Yes, unfortunately genealogy must take account of political differences. It would be so much easier if we could ignore them and get on with the sensible task of tracing a man's ancestry whether he belonged to the Republic or the

North. However, there it is, and if you want ancestry in Northern Ireland, you had better get in touch with the Registrar-General, the General Register Office, Fermanagh House, Ormean Avenue, Belfast. There is a Public Record Office, too, and this is in May Street, Belfast; you would contact the Deputy Keeper. For those of Presbyterian backgrounds, write to the Secretary, Church House, Belfast.

90. One last question on genealogy, do you think it is of any real value?

St. Paul warned his spiritual sons, Timothy and Titus against it, and he was used to it. Yet there have been times recently when genealogical knowledge could be a matter of life and death, in Hitler's Germany where the possession of a great-grandmother of Jewish blood spelt imprisonment, perhaps death. Between these two extremes comes the quiet study of one's predecessors, who they were, what they did; perhaps the recovery of some precious letter or a will from the centuries dust in which it has lain, and from those faded pages a man or woman steps forth, without whom we ourselves should never have been.

3

Titles

91. Is a retiring premier made an earl?

This is only a custom, but custom does acquire great force. The practice for some time past has been to offer a premier when he retires the choice of an earldom. Since the war two of our six prime ministers have accepted an earldom, Sir Anthony Eden as Earl of Avon, and Mr. Attlee as Earl Attlee. Mr. Macmillan has declined the offer, and so it is believed did Sir Winston Churchill.

92. What could happen in the case of Sir Alec Douglas-Home who gave up his earldom in order to become premier?

Many people think that when Sir Alec retires from political life he would simply be offered an earldom, and thus perhaps get his old earldom of Home back again. This is the popular impression which one gathers from conversations on trains and in shops, etc. In fact it is quite wrong, because under the Peerage Act of 1963, there is a definite statement [sec. 3 (2)] that a person who has disclaimed a peerage under the Act shall not receive any other hereditary peerage. It is true that this does not bar out the conferring of a life peerage, but a life earldom is something quite out of the ordinary and I doubt if this would be created. It looks therefore as if Sir Alec would have to be remaining as a commoner, after he leaves the Commons, whenever that may be.

93. What is meant by the Peerage Act 1963?

This Act is popularly known as the Wedgwood Benn enabling Act, because it was principally brought about by the exertions of Mr. Wedgwood Benn who inherited the peerage of Stansgate but who did not want to take it, as it meant him giving up his career in the House of Commons where he was sitting as an M.P. The Act, however, does much more than this, for it removes several strange anomalies which have lasted for a long time. It allows Scottish peers to sit in the House, whereas previously only those Scottish peers who were elected as representative peers, or had a United Kingdom peerage in addition to their Scots peerage, were allowed to do so. It also allows peeresses in their own right to sit in the Lords. It did not touch the position of Irish peers. Formerly the Irish peers were allowed to elect 28 of their number to sit in the House of Lords for life, and those peers who were not so elected were able to stand for seats in the Commons. Since 1921 when the Irish Free State was formed no elections of Irish peers have taken place, and there are since 1961 (when the Earl of Kilmorey died) no more representative peers for Ireland.

94. What is the Life Peerage Act?

This Act was passed in 1958 to allow for the creation of life peers, both men and women, the object being to alter the balance in the House of Lords so that a more democratic element should enter into the Upper House. This has not really been effective, because since 1958 just as many hereditary peerages have been created as life peerages. Consequently although there are more life peers in the House than there were – previous to 1958 the only life peers were the Law Lords – the proportion of life peers to hereditary who do attend the debates remains fairly constant. By allowing the creation of women life peers the objection to the peeresses in their own right was removed and this has now been put in order by the 1963 Peerage Act. Other changes have taken place in the House of Lords over the last few years; pay in the form of three guineas a day was introduced for those peers who attended at the House, for each day of attendance; and peers who do not want to take part in the business of the Lords are now allowed to apply to be excused from receiving the writ of summons.

95. Would the creation of life peerages only, be sufficient to reform the House of Lords?

This subject of reform of the Lords has been canvassed on and off ever since the passing of the Parliament Act 1911, when in the preamble to the Act it was stated that House of Lords 'reform brooked no delay.' In fact the substitution of life peers for hereditary would have one good effect, it would prevent the creation for the future of pauper peers. It does not need much reflection to realize that with our present system of heavy taxation, the handing on of money in large investments becomes increasingly difficult, and therefore within a generation or so, the heirs of a wealthy peer are often very hard up. Nor is it hard to think of instances within the last decade in which some very unbecoming behaviour, on the part of peers, occasioned by poverty, has been brought to light. But apart from a socially good result, the life peerage idea does not really reform the House of Lords; indeed paradoxically it is to hereditary peerages that we must look for the appearance of bright young men of ability. Most life peers are men and women of 60 years of age or thereabouts, and they have usually settled down to an established mode of life. Conversely the young heir to an old peerage may be full of ideas for progress. Consequently I think – it is purely my idea – that the House of Lords can only be reformed by taking it right out of the legislature, and by substituting for it a body similar to the American or Australian senate, which would be elective. I do not, however, advocate the abolition of titles, which do no harm to anyone, except sometimes their possessor.

96. Can you give up a title in favour of someone else?

No. My postbag has often contained letters from people who state that some forebear of theirs gave up his baronetcy or peerage in favour of someone else. This is all nonsense, and there is no truth in it. It may be noted, too, that under the 1963 Peerage Act, the fact that a peer has renounced his peerage does not accelerate the succession of his heir.

97. How do you put in a claim to a peerage or baronetcy?

By applying to the Home Secretary, the Home Office, Whitehall, London. You will be required to put in some extensive information in order to prove a claim, unless of course it is purely formal, as when a son claims to succeed to his father's peerage or baronetcy.

98. Why do so many titles in England become extinct?

I can only conclude that there must be an excessive failure in peers as opposed to other men to produce male heirs. Certain it is that the wastage in the peerage is very great, though it is much more than made good, as anyone can see if they study the Rolls of the Lords produced each autumn by the Stationery Office. These Rolls always show an increase in numbers. However, it is a strange fact that while peerages often become extinct, baronetcies do not, but an heir to a baronetcy turns up in some out of the way part of

the world. It could also be added that the following
illustrious names are no longer represented in the male line:
Shakespeare, Milton, Marlborough (Churchill), Nelson, Sir
Walter Scott, Chatham (Pitt), Edmund Burke, Fox, Can-
ning, Macaulay, Palmerston, or Disraeli.

99. Can a foreigner who becomes a British subject retain his title or coat of arms?

Strictly speaking, no. In fact there are quite a number of
people who are British subjects and who still use their
countships or other foreign titles; certainly there are many
foreign coats of arms in use in England. The principle is
that the sovereign of the country is the source or Fountain
of Honours, and she or he can grant or withhold whatever
honours it may please them. There has also been from the
time of Queen Elizabeth I a strong disinclination, to put it
no higher, on the part of our kings and queens to permit the
use of foreign titles by their subjects. Papal titles are right
outside, and the regulation of those which are of secular
origin, comes under a Royal Warrant issued by King
George V in 1932. This Warrant lays down the principle
that in due course the use of foreign titles shall cease in
England and permits only a relatively few to British
subjects.

100. What is the position of Canadians, Australians and so on who are offered British titles?

The subject is a sore one, for nowadays the fine old
principle that one was a British subject anywhere in the
Queen's dominions does not apply. People are Canadians,
New Zealanders, Australians, Trinadadians, etc., and only
those who are subjects of the United Kingdom can properly
be classed as British. Moreover, many if not all of the old
Dominions have decided against the acceptance of heredit-

ary titles by their nationals. The acceptance of a peerage
for instance by Mr. Roy Thomson, now Lord Thomson of
Fleet, is said to be likely to involve him in difficulties with
the Canadian legal position if and when he returns to
Canada. For some thirty years now Canada has set itself
against the acceptance by its nationals of honours, of the
titled variety at least. One has only to look through the lists
in the New Year's or Birthday Honours to see that very
few parts of the old Empire are now represented. In the
last Birthday Honours List there are sections for the
colonies which are still ruled from Whitehall or still fairly
closely connected with this country; there are sections also
for Australia and New Zealand, but even in the latter cases
they are only for non-hereditary honours.

Gradually then or perhaps one could say swiftly the scope
of the Lists is being restricted to the United Kingdom.

101. Is it correct to style a British peer a Baron, e.g. Baron Beaverbrook?

Baron is a designation of the lowest order in the peerage,
but it should not be used in English except in very formal
documents. It is certainly wrong to refer to anyone as Baron
Robens if he holds a British title. It is correct to refer to
Baron de Reuter, since his is a foreign title which he is permitted by Royal Warrant to use. All the other grades of the
peerage – viscount, earl, marquess and duke – are correctly
so-called. However, it is common form to refer to all peers
under the rank of Duke as Lord.

102. Is the form correct – namely the Lord X?

Yes, in formal documents, or even on letters if you want
to be very correct, but nothing could be more out of place
than to refer to The Lord Rank for example in an account
of some sporting event in which he had taken part. The

form The Lord X should be used, if at all apart from formal letters, only on envelopes addressed by strangers.

103. Is it right to put Rt. Hon. before the names of peers?

Yes, this matter was thrashed out some years ago. The usage of putting Right Honourable before the names of peers spread from the days – about 400 years ago – when the few peers who then existed were all members of the Privy Council. From this the habit spread on to the whole of the peerage below the rank of marquess. There was a controversy about it some years back, but it was settled by a ruling from Garter King of Arms that Right Hon. was right.

104. How is a lady to be addressed who has been married to a titled man, then divorced and married to an untitled man?

A woman's title derives from her husband or father as does her surname. Consequently a woman who has married a titled person takes the corresponding title due to his wife. Thus Miss X becomes the countess of Y on marriage to the Earl of Y. But on divorce from the Earl, the relationship has ended, and so the title can only be used as long as the former wife does not marry again. When she does, she takes the title of her new husband. If he is a plain mister, then her title is Mrs. It frequently happens that a woman having had a divorce, and married again, feels that she wants to keep her former title and does so. This is wrong and should definitely be discouraged by all concerned.

105. When a man has been knighted, may he be addressed as 'Sir'?

Only after he has received the accolade, that is had the sword-tip laid on his shoulder. Until then he is correctly

1. EARL

2. MARQUESS

Fig. 5 – CORONETS OF RANK

referred to as 'Mr.' Letters of congratulation should be so addressed. The same principle holds with a peer, except that his period of waiting, between acceptance of a peerage and actual peerage style, is ended by the official entry in the *London Gazette*. The new peer's style cannot be known until it has been officially settled by entry in the *Gazette*, so it would be a serious solecism to address him as Lord X before we can know how he is to be entitled. In the case of a baronet, it is possible to address him as Sir William X as soon as it has been announced that he is to be made a baronet. The reason is that he is not likely to ask to change his surname when he has got his baronetcy, and so we can call him Sir William X, since the only addition which the *Gazette* will add to that will be 'of Tower Green Hamlets, etc.' or whatever territorial designation he is going to take.

106. What position does a foreign duke have in this country?

This is purely a matter of politeness, and the same thing applies to other foreign titles. As a general rule a foreign duke would take precedence behind the British dukes. Obviously his position in his own country must be a recognized one.

107. How can one check on a foreign title?

This is difficult. In a great many continental countries the monarchy has gone, and this means that the official check on the nobility has gone too. As a result it has become very hard to check a foreign title. There are some books which might be useful to a searcher, such as the *Libro d'Oro* of Italy, which gives particulars of noble families. There is not likely, however, to be in any, except a few continental countries, any official check list such as we possess in the House of Lords, the Home Office and the College of Arms. The best thing to do if the matter is one of importance, is to consult the embassy of the country concerned.

1. DUKE

2. ROYAL DUKE
(e.g. Sovereign's Grandchildren, or sons of Sovereign's brothers)

Fig. 6 – CORONETS OF RANK

108. What are courtesy titles?

These are the secondary titles of peers which are used by their sons out of courtesy. No subject seems to exercise more difficulty than this one. Yet if one thinks about it, it is quite simple. Consider the titles borne by the Duke of Marlborough. He is beside his dukedom, Marquess of Blandford, Earl of Sunderland, Earl of Marlborough, Baron Spencer and Baron Churchill. Clearly the Duke cannot use all these titles at once. It therefore seems quite in order for his eldest son to be styled by his father's best secondary title. Thus the Duke's son is called out of courtesy, the Marquess of Blandford. He is not a peer, and being a commoner, can stand for and sit in the House of Commons. Courtesy titles are found in each rank of the peerage, but they are only recognizable as peerage titles when they belong to earldoms, marquessates or dukedoms. A Viscount may be also a baron, but even so his eldest son will be called the Hon. The latter is also a courtesy title, but is not a peerage dignity. With earls, it is very unlikely that they will not possess a secondary or even tertiary peerage; the theory is that a man was advanced through various grades until he reached the dignity of an earl. Thus today anyone created an earl, is likely or almost certain to have a viscounty conferred on him also.

109. Which is correct – "marquess" or "marquis"?

The latter is a foreign form, and the former is the English variant. The former should therefore be used.

110. What should be the style of the grandson of a duke or marquess?

Plain mister is enough, but nowadays the custom is to give one of the courtesy titles to the grandson. A case in

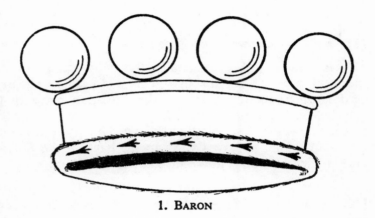

1. Baron

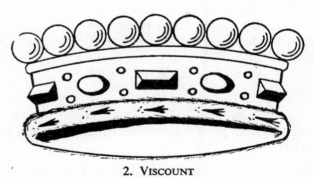

2. Viscount
Fig. 7 – Coronets of Rank

point is that of the Earl of Sunderland, the son of the Marquess of Blandford, himself the son of the Duke of Marlborough. It is purely a matter of custom, nothing more.

111. Is the term dowager ever used now?

It is still found occasionally but very rarely does a widowed peeress describe herself as a dowager. The style used most frequently is to put the Christian name of the lady before her rank. Thus, Mary, Lady Petworth, instead of the Dowager Lady Petworth. This habit of using the Christian name, apparently began far back in the reign of Queen Victoria and is now well established.

112. What is the difference between a diocesan bishop and a suffragan bishop?

A diocesan bishop holds sway over a see in which he is the sole responsible bishop. He is styled correctly the Lord Bishop of London. A suffragan bishop holds his position under the rule of a diocesan bishop whom he is appointed to assist. He is of course a bishop, but he should never be styled Lord Bishop; his correct style is Right Rev. A.Y.Z., Bishop of X. Suffragans have no official place or precedence.

113. You refer to precedence, what exactly is it and how is it regulated?

Precedence is governed by an Act of Parliament, the title of which – for the placing of the lords – explains what it is about. This Act still governs the rules of ordering those persons who are to be present on official occasions. As may be imagined it has had to be altered or amended many times, for it was passed in the reign of Henry VIII (in 1539).

It did not include the Prime Minister, since at that time no
such office existed. Indeed until 1905 there was no official
place for the Prime Minister in the Table of Precedence; he
found a place as First Lord of the Treasury. To this day
such notable office holders as the Lord Mayor of London,
or the Cardinal Archbishop of Westminster may be sought
in vain in the list of V.I.P.s, though the Table does find
place for Esquires and Gentlemen. Since the last war the
High Commissioners of the great Dominions such as
Canada, or Australia have been given the precedence and
place accorded to Ambassadors of sovereign States. This
Table is used on high State occasions, but it has often
proved unhelpful to harassed secretaries of organizations
when some great dinner is being staged. For once one is
outside the circle of the truly great of the land, there is some
remarkable difficulty in finding out exactly how to place
one's guests without giving offence.

114. What is the precedence among foreign sovereigns?

This means the precedence of sovereigns who are visiting
the court of St. James's. The answer is very short, all
sovereigns are viewed as being equal in rank, as sovereigns,
and their precedence is determined by their dates of
accession. This situation could formerly have been very
serious, when many monarchies existed in Europe. It is not
of great importance now.

115. What do the letters C.D. mean on a car?

Corps Diplomatique. They have an almost magical power,
and can ensure the rightful user of them of a vast range of
immunity. As he represents a foreign sovereign power, he
cannot be made subject to the usual procedure of the courts
of this realm. If he commits some crime or falls into some
civil legal difficulty, he cannot be sued or prosecuted, and

Fig. 8. BADGE OF BARONET (United Kingdom)

the only redress is to request the government which he represents to withdraw him from Britain. This immunity applies not only to the ambassador or to the first or second secretary but also to many members of the staff of an embassy if not to all. It springs in England, from a commotion in the reign of Queen Anne, when an ambassador was illtreated by a mob. It is, whatever its abuse on occasion, a valuable privilege of civilized life.

116. What is the surname of the royal family?

Windsor. In 1917 King George V issued a proclamation declaring that the name of Windsor is to be borne by his royal house and family and relinquishing the use of all German titles and dignities. This continued until the death of George VI in 1952 and the accession of Her Majesty the Queen. At the time of her accession the Queen bore the surname of Mountbatten, this being her husband's name. On 9th April, 1952, the Queen signified her pleasure that from henceforth she and her children should be styled as the House and Family of Windsor, and that her descendants other than female descendants who marry, and their descendants, should bear the name of Windsor. By a later warrant the Queen went so far as to allow the use of Mountbatten–Windsor for certain descendants in the distant future, three or more generations away (by declaration of 8 February, 1960, 'descendants who will enjoy neither the style, title or attribute of Royal Highness, nor the titular dignity of Prince and for whom therefore a surname will be necessary,' i.e. a younger grandchild of Prince Charles). This is the first time that a hyphenated surname has been used in our royal family. However, if we go back before 1917 it was the considered opinion of that great genealogical scholar Sir Bernard Burke that the royal family had no surname. Writing of Queen Victoria he said: 'I feel persuaded that the Royal House of Saxe-Coburg has no surname. When the adoption of surnames became general, the ancestors of that illustrious race were Kings, and needed no other designation than the Christian name added to the Royal title.' Some have contended for Guelph, or Welf, but in 1917 when George V asked the College of Arms for his royal surname there was no considered opinion opposed to that of Sir Bernard Burke.

117. Is there any means of checking foreign decorations and orders?

The only way is to approach the embassy of the particular country and to inquire there. Often the embassy has not

the specialized information. The members of the staff cannot be experts on everything, though one would expect them
to understand their country's orders and decorations.
Mostly they depend upon official statements. To be quite
fair to the embassy staffs, in many countries there has been
a change of régime, and orders which were formerly held
in high esteem, are now out of fashion, and in fact sometimes dangerous to the owner, as marking him as a member
of a bad government. There are few books on the subject of
orders, and hardly anything which gives a full view of the
whole field. How could this be, considering the vastness of
the subject. As more and more states appear on the scene,
as empires break up and independent countries come into
being, the number of decorations continually increases.
There are many completely 'phoney' orders which circulate,
usually being bestowed for money. Anyone who is approached on this subject should at once ask for the name
of the country concerned and consult its embassy. Whatever
the extent of the embassy's knowledge on genuine orders,
it will nearly always have the necessary information on false
orders, since they do seriously lessen a country's prestige.

118. What is a morganatic marriage?

The popular idea is that it means a marriage in which a
man of exalted rank gives his 'left' hand to a second wife, in
other words a means whereby a man is able to have two
wives at once. This is bunkum. The term morganatic marriage arose in Germany where a very high idea of rank has
always prevailed, causing the usual amount of human suffer-
ing as a result. Among the exalted Teutonic conceptions of
high breeding there came the idea that a man of royal
position who wanted to get married to someone of lower
social status, should indeed marry her, but that his wife
should be excluded from his family name, his arms and
title. The marriage is genuine and the children legitimate,

out they too are excluded from inheriting their father's
titles or the entailed property of the family. Their only
inheritance is what may be settled on them by contract, and
hence the term morganatic, since it is derived from the
German *morgen-gave* meaning the gift from the bride-
groom to the bride on the morning after the marriage. Many
will recall the mention of this idea of a morganatic marriage
in the case of the Duke of Windsor as a possible solution of
his difficulties when as Edward VIII he wished to marry
Mrs. Simpson. The idea was at once scouted as not being
within the terms known to English law.

119. What is the Red Hand of Ulster?

This is the hand which appears on the badge of the
baronets (except those of Nova Scotia, who have the royal
arms of Scotland on the cross of St. Andrew). The Red
Hand of Ulster has become familiar to many people from its
appearance on the sign of a well-known brewery. The Red
Hand was the badge of the old O'Neills, the ancient Kings
of Ulster, who were driven out by the plantation of Ulster
under King James I in 1611, when the order of baronets
was instituted in order to pay for the settlement of Ulster.
The hand as used by the baronets is not however the O'Neill
badge, which was the right hand as the baronets use the left
hand; the brewery does use the right hand.

120. What are the flags which are often seen flying over private houses in England, and which are not readily identifiable?

These are the flags of the owners of the houses, and
which are their owners' arms. Cases in point which I have
seen are those of Viscount Scarsdale over Kedleston House,
of the Marquess of Bath over Longleat, and of Lord
Montagu over Beaulieu. It is a picturesque and attractive
sight and one which I hope will not die out in this country.

121. Can a baronet claim a knighthood for his eldest son?

He could until 1827, for on 19th December in that year King George IV gave orders that in future a baronet' patent should not contain the clause which permitted hi eldest son on attaining the age of 21 to be knighted Previous to that a baronet whose patent of creation con tained this clause could request the honour of knighthood for his eldest son when the latter became 21. This seems to have been a very curious habit, for why should a youth o 21 be made a knight just because his father was a baronet whose title the young man would in the ordinary course o nature inherit? In addition when father and son bore the same Christian name there must have been a great con fusion.

122. Who is the Deemster?

There are in the Isle of Man two judges or justices who are called Deemsters. The style used is His Honour the Deemster X (the latter being of course his surname). For over 150 years the Deemster has been socially and officially designated 'His Honour'. I am informed that in 1925 the question was raised as to the designation of a Deemster or his retirement. The Governor of the Isle of Man was noti fied by the Home Office that the title of His Honour may be retained by a Deemster after his retirement from office.

123. Who are the Bailiffs in the Channel Islands?

There are two in the Channel Islands, one in Jersey, and the other in Guernsey and its Dependencies. They are supreme civil officers in each case, and they preside at the royal court, also over the states parliament, and represent the Crown in all civil matters. The Bailiff of Guernsey is so styled and is addressed as Mr. Bailiff. The Bailiff of Jersey

styled as such and is written to as 'Dear Mr. Bailiff',
while in address he is Mr. Bailiff. (Presumably the Bailiff of
Guernsey would be addressed in writing as 'Dear Mr.
Bailiff'.)

24. What is the style of a county court judge in England after retirement?

His style after retirement is, as during tenure, 'His
Honour'; he is referred to as Judge X, though I am informed that this is by courtesy only, and that strictly he
should be referred to as Mr. X.

25. What is the Clan Chattan?

Right at the beginning we may say that it is pronounced
as Clan Hattan. It is an association or group of clans which
comprehends the Macphersons, MacGillivrays, Farquhar-
sons, MacQueens, Macfaills, Macbeans, and others. An
account of it occurs in Sir Walter Scott's romance, *The Fair
Maid of Perth*, though it must be admitted that Sir Walter
in his quotations from old Scottish historians shows that the
earlier authorities gave Clanwhewyl, and Clachinya, or
Clanquhele and Clankay as the names of the two groups
with whose fortunes his story is concerned. In other
chronicles they became Clanquhele and Clankay, but
Hector Boece, so Scott tells us, wrote of them as Clan-
hattan and Clankay. These two groups of clans had kept
the Highlands in turmoil and disorder greater than usual
until at last the authorities in Scotland had decided to
arrange for them a combat to the death. This was to consist in thirty picked men on either side led by their chiefs
fighting to death at Perth and this combat actually took
place in 1396. It resulted in the victory of Clan Chattan,
while the defeated Clan Kay broke up into minor groups.

However, this may have been embroidered in the hands

Fig. 9. – BADGE OF BARONET (Nova Scotia)

of the great romancer of the north, certain it is that Clan
Chattan as a group of tribes held a dominant position in the
Highlands in the time of Robert III of Scotland at the end
of the fourteenth century. A Declaration of Lyon Court
on 10th September, 1672, from the Lord Lyon gave the
necessary details regarding the composition and headship
of Clan Chattan. The Laird of Mackintosh is the only undoubted chief of the name of Mackintosh and the chief of
Clan Chattan. None of the families of the other names
mentioned will be given arms by the Lord Lyon except as
cadets of the Laird of Mackintosh's family, because his
predecessor married the heiress of the Clan Chattan in
1291. The chief of the clan has the name in Gaelic of Gillie-
chattan Mor, which means the Great Servant of St. Catan

96

This is thought to mean that originally the founder of the Clan was the bailie of the Abbey of Kilchattan, in Bute. No less than seventeen tribes are given as members of the Clan Chattan by the present Lord Lyon, Sir Thomas Innes of Learney in his revision of Frank Adams's book, *The Clans, Septs and Regiments of the Scottish Highlands*.

126. Is it correct to style a Scottish chief, The Mackintosh? etc.

Yes, it has been done since the fifteenth century, when there was a custom of styling some of the Lowland chiefs with 'Le' before their surname or title. Today the practice prevails of styling the chief of the whole name or clan as it is called, 'The'. Thus we have 'The Mackintosh', one of the most famous of all. This form is used in official records such as the Register of the Lord Lyon. As was noted in the answer to question 125, the chief of a great clan like Mackintosh can also be correctly styled Laird of Mackintosh, although it has been pointed out by Sir Thomas Innes that in this case the reference is not to a landed estate but to the clan or family of Mackintosh. A very common form of reference to these highland chiefs is in the style, MacGregor of MacGregor, where the reduplication is meant to give greater distinction to the fact that it is to the chief that reference is made. In Scotland, both highland and lowland, the territorial designation is frequent, and so we get Urquhart of Cromarty, Cameron of Lochiel, etc. When the name of the property is the same as that of the family (a fairly frequent occurrence with very old recorded families), the words 'of that ilk' are often used, so that Udny of Udny could be rightly called Udny of that ilk.

Before passing on from the subject of chiefly designation, I cannot forbear to mention the case of the Chisholm chief, whose clan is not perhaps one of the most numerous. What it lacked in numbers it appeared to make up in importance, for of old, it was held by the clan that there were in the world only three persons of consequence, The Pope, The King and The Chisholm.

Readers of Scottish romances may be puzzled by the title Baron of –, as in the case of Sir Walter Scott's *Waverley* where he refers to the Baron of Bradwardine, though the latter is not a lord in our sense. According to Sir Thomas Innes, Lord Lyon, the title of Baron X etc. is a highland custom in place of the more usual Laird of X employed in the lowlands. He points out too that on the European continent the words laird (or baronet for that matter) are not understood, but Baron like Knight or Chevalier is.

127. What is the meaning of the Scottish expression 'of that ilk'?

It is a term used to designate the laird or possessor of an estate when the name of the estate and the surname of the family are identical. In the current *Landed Gentry*, of 1952, on page 2,459 there is a reference to Swinton of that ilk. On looking into the pedigree we see that the laird of Swinton is described as 33rd of that ilk, and the family history states that 'the family of Swinton takes its name from the lands of Swinton, which it has held for more than eight and a half centuries.'

See also answer to question 126.

128. What does the term 'younger' mean when applied to the name of a Scottish gentleman?

It denotes the heir apparent to a Scottish lairdship. Thus, my editor when first I became connected with *Burke's Landed Gentry* was Harry Pirie-Gordon the Younger, of Buthlaw, so styled because at that time his father was still alive. Today he is Pirie Gordon, 13th of Buthlaw. The numbering used here and in the answer to question 127 in the case of lairds is to denote that their territory is really an old feudal barony, that they are in short, Barons of X.Y.Z., etc. but not peers of course in the sense of being Lords of Parliament.

129. When then, is a Baron not a Baron?

As pointed out in the answer to question 101, a British Baron, i.e. a peer in the lowest order of the peerage is not styled Baron except in very official documents, but is addressed in speech and in normal writing as Lord X. A foreign Baron is correctly referred to as Baron X. The holder of a foreign barony whose right to use the title in England has not been granted by the Crown, i.e. a British subject who owns a foreign barony is in a very awkward position. If he styles himself Baron X, he is not likely to incur any penalties greater than those of being excluded from official gatherings at St. James's or Buckingham Palace. But if he allows newspaper reporters to refer to him as Lord X, he is in the position of appearing to be a peer of the realm which he is not. The life of such a person is fraught with difficult moments.

In the instance of Scottish Barons to which I have referred in questions 126 and 128, we deal with the idea of old feudal baronies, which went with the land. These baronies, might, but did not always, carry with them the right to a seat in Parliament. If they did, the owner of the feudal barony was also a lord of Parliament, and today the feudal barons of Scotland are only a relic, sentimental and interesting be it agreed, of the time before the passing of the Heritable Jurisdiction Act, 1746. For that matter no country can be more interesting to the student of history than Scotland, for it contains numerous relics of practices from feudal and heraldic times which have long since disappeared in England and elsewhere.

130. Is it true that anyone who buys Arundel Castle would become Duke of Norfolk?

No. In England in centuries now long past there were many cases, no doubt, of titles which went with the land, peerages by the tenure of certain properties, as they are termed in English law. They have no existence now. As long ago as 1819–22 the Redesdale Committee in their Reports upon peerage concluded that there were no peerages by the tenure existing at that time (1819), and that none had existed since the time of Henry III or Edward I (the latter sovereign reigned from 1272 to 1307). The conception of the feudal barony to which reference has been made in the case of Scotland (see above) does not exist in England.

131. What is the correct mode of address for the wife of a laird in Scotland?

In this respect I cannot do better than give you the view of the highest Scottish authority. The Lord Lyon in his *Scots Heraldry*, page 209 (1956 edition) says: 'Feudal rank is legally communicated to the wife, and a Laird's wife is legally "the Lady Lour". In rural Scotland, at any rate, this correct address (invariably used in the old Scottish Law Reports) is still in use.' Consequently the lady would be correctly addressed in writing as Madam, and referred to in speech as Lady X. In formal invitations in Scotland in recent years I have had notes from the Baron of Y and Madame Y. It is, however, much more frequent to refer to the wife of a laird as 'Mrs. X of Y' the Y being the name of the husband's estate.

132. Can the Order of the Garter be conferred upon a lady?

Yes, there are usually one or two Ladies of the Garter. At present there is the Queen Mother, who was made a

Fig. 10 – ARMORIAL COAT
showing—
Shield in "Cauché" position (slantwise)
Lambrequin, or mantling
Chapeau, or cap of estate

Lady of the Garter on 14th December, 1936, when she was the Queen Consort of King George VI. So, too, had the late Queen Mary been a Lady of the Garter from 3rd June, 1910, until her death. In addition among the list of additional knights, which is usually composed of foreign sovereigns, is the name of Princess Wilhelmina of the Netherlands. She was admitted a Lady of the Garter because she was a sovereign. Similarly the Sovereign of this country, whether King or Queen is always Sovereign of the Order of the Garter and of the other orders of chivalry of the United Kingdom. The Queen was admitted a Lady of the Order in 1948 at a solemn ceremonial which marked the 600th anniversary of the founding of the Order and at which her husband, the Duke of Edinburgh was also installed as a Knight.

Thus the number of ladies of the Order is much restricted to those who are of the highest royal rank. It was pointed out by Sir Bernard Burke that in the early days of the Order it was the custom for the wives and widows of the Knights of the Garter to wear the habit of the Order on the feast-days of St. George, and to be in fact Ladies of the Order. The habit died out in Tudor days, and was only revived in the present century, though the Garter is now of course much restricted in its bestowal on women as compared with medieval times.

133. Who and what is the Knight of Glin?

He is the holder of one of what can only be called three hereditary knighthoods which have existed in Ireland since the fourteenth century. Although the knighthoods are hereditary they do not carry the title of 'Sir' which seems very fitting in the case of this certainly curious Irish title. The present holder of the Knighthood of Glin is Mr. Desmond John Villiers Fitz-Gerald, 29th Knight of Glin, of Glin Castle, co. Limerick. In addition to the Glin knighthood there is that of the Knight of Kerry, held by the Baronet, Sir Arthur Henry Brinsley Fitz-Gerald who is the 22nd Knight of Kerry. There was also the White Knight, the first of whom was Sir Gilbert Fitzjohn Fitz-Gerald, but his line died out in the seventeenth century in the male line.

No really satisfactory explanation of this curious title exists. Sir Bernard Burke stated that the three hereditary knighthoods were created by John FitzThomas Fitz-Gerald Lord of Decies and Desmond, by virtue of his royal seigniory as Count Palatine. But other authorities, Betham and Russell state that the knights were so created by King Edward III at the battle of Hallidon Hill, 19th July, 1333. There is no definite conclusion to the controversy on this subject, but the Knights have been styled as such in Acts of Parliament, in patents under the Great Seal, and in legal proceedings. The full ancestry of this family will be found under the title of the Duke of Leinster, in *Burke's Peerage*, together with that of the line of the Knights of Kerry (Baronets) and in *Burke's Landed Gentry of Ireland*, under Fitz-Gerald, the Knight of Glin.

134. What is a Count Palatine?

In England there are no native counts, the title count never having been able to supersede that of earl, but the influence of count is shown in the term county, which exists alongside the old English shire. Now a count palatine was a great earl who had within the area over which he ruled the same powers as those of the sovereign, these being of course granted or conceded to him by the latter. Earldoms of this type did exist in England before the Norman Conquest, and indeed the great earls who ruled over vast tracts in England were often in a position of strength *vis-à-vis* the king which enabled them to dominate him. William the Conqueror was determined that such mighty subjects should not exist under his règime, but even he had to grant considerable powers to two of his nobles. One of these was the Earl of Chester and the other was the Prince Bishop of Durham. It must be clearly understood that the term Count Palatine or Bishop Palatine was not used or known in England before 1066, and that such terms, like those of duke, or marquess, viscount or baron, are importations from the continent. The Earl of Chester had the task of watching and guarding what was in effect the western frontier of England against the incursions of the Welsh who despite all efforts of either Saxon or Norman kings remained independent until the conquest of Wales under Edward I in 1284. The ruler of the dangerous area of Durham had likewise the task of facing the Scots, but here the title of Palatine was given to a churchman. On the continent there were many prince bishops in the Middle Ages, and as churchmen they could not have legitimate heirs, hence they were not so likely to try to build up a semi-dynastic position as against the king. John Selden, the greatest writer in English on titles, and whose grave can now be seen in the rebuilt Temple Church in London, writes of the Bishop of Durham that the seals of the Bishops showed on one side 'a Bishop sitting in his chair, and on the other an armed man on horseback, his sword drawn, and the Bishop's arms sometimes of his family, sometimes of his bishoprick on the shield circumscribed with the like words (i.e. *Dei gratia Episcopus Dunelmensis*, by the grace of God, Bishop of Durham), which shape on the reverse is expressed, *tanquam Comitis Palatini*, as of a count Palatine'. Selden, *Titles of Honour* (Second Part, Chapter V, s.8). Selden also refers to the ancient Earls of Pembroke as being Earls or Counts Palatine, from the fact that they dealt with the sometime dangerous country of South Wales. In Ireland it would be quite natural for a great Anglo-Norman nobleman to have palatine jurisdiction, but all such jurisdictions lapsed with the progress of government throughout England, Wales and Ireland.

135. What other Irish titles are there?

While the title of the three hereditary Knights mentioned in answer to question 133 is of English origin, there are quite a number of titles in Ireland which correspond to those of the Scottish Highlands. Among them may be reckoned such famous titles as those of O'Conor Don, MacGillicuddy of the Reeks, O'Donoghue of the Glens, O'Grady of Killyballowen, O'Donovan of Clan Cathal, MacDermot of Coolavin, and many others. Most of these are descended from the ancient kings of the Irish provinces, and sometimes from the High Kings of Ireland. The style of 'The' is used before their names in most references to them, and their wives are usually styled Madame. In Thom's *Directory of Ireland*, there will be found a list of chieftaincies whose titles have been investigated by the Chief Herald of Ireland, though out of a potential seventy, only some twenty have been cleared. This is only a matter of time, however, since most of these ancient chieftaincies require only a careful genealogical examination in order to ascertain the date from which they may approximately be reckoned.

136. What are Jacobite titles?

These are titles of nobility created by the princes of the House of Stuart after their exile to the continent in the reign of James II. The latter was held by the British Parliament to have abdicated in 1688, when he left England and went to France. He created a number of honours in Ireland during his time there, 1689–90. Among these were the titles of Marquess and Duke of Tyrconnel conferred on the Earl of Tyrconnel; that of Lord Fitton of Gawsworth on Sir

Alexander Fitton; of Baron of Bophin on Col. John Burke and several others. In addition to this there were patents of nobility made out afterwards by James II, and by his son the Old Pretender (known to many sentimental persons even now as James III, and even so styled by Prof. Trevelyan), and his grandson, the Young Pretender, Bonnie Prince Charlie. There is a large work on this interesting subject, by the late Marquis de Ruvigny, *The Jacobite Peerage*, 1904. None of these titles was recognized by the Government or Court of Great Britain.

137. Is it true that the legitimate heir to the British throne exists in the line of the Kings of Bavaria?

No, the legitimate and lawful heir to the British throne is Her Majesty, Queen Elizabeth II. It is amazing to me that there should be people, even officers who have served in the armed forces and who have presumably taken an oath of loyalty to Her Majesty or her predecessors, who can still talk about the Stuarts as being the legitimate heirs of the kingdom. The Stuart family had proved themselves to be an enormous nuisance to the country and were sent off in favour of a sovereign, descended from James I of England, but who would agree to uphold the law and religion of the country as established by Parliament. I have known men who have written about ancestors or connections of theirs as having served in 'the Hanoverian army' meaning the British army in the eighteenth century. This is of course rubbish, and not even sentimental rubbish at that.

For those who like to trace genealogies, it can be said that the present representative of the Stuarts in the female line is Albert, Duke of Bavaria, son of Crown Prince Rupert, the eldest son of Maria Theresa of Modena and of Ludwig III, formerly King of Bavaria. This line of descent comes from the fifth daughter of Charles I, Henrietta, who married the Duke of Orleans and who lived from 1644 to

1670. The line is traced through the Kings of Sardinia into the family of the Kings of Bavaria. It must have been a little awkward for those who still cherished some vague Jacobitism to realize that in the war of 1914–18 they were opposed by Prince Rupert (Rupprecht) of Bavaria, their 'rightful' king.

The male line of the Stuarts became extinct with Henry Stuart, Cardinal York, who died in 1807. He sent his royal jewels to the British sovereign, George III, and in the view of some Scottish Jacobites this constituted George III as the tanistair of Henry, in other words, the heir to the royal line appointed by the last of the male line. By this means it has become possible for Scottish Jacobites to write offensively about George I and George II, but to accept subsequent Hanoverian sovereigns as legitimate.

The Houses of Stuart and Hanover were of course cousins, since both descended from James I. Hence too the term Jacobite, from Jacobus, James.

138. What is the proper title of Queen Elizabeth – I or II?

I include this question, although it ought not to require an answer, in deference to Scots, some of whom put this question to me when I was lecturing at Inverness in 1953. The correct title is of course, Elizabeth II. The matter was discussed in Parliament at the time of Her Majesty's accession, and follows on the principle which prevailed in 1901 when Edward VII became king. In neither his case nor that of the present Queen has there been a sovereign of Scotland with the name respectively of Edward or Elizabeth, but since the union of the two countries, in 1707, as Great Britain, the numerals employed in England have given the principle of numbering the sovereigns of the United Kingdom. Numerous instances can be cited from the history of Europe that show the practice has often prevailed in foreign countries of following the numeration of one country after a union of two lands rather than starting a new series of numbers. Thus with the union of France and Navarre, in 1589, the line of succeeding kings followed the numeration already used in France. The Kings of Prussia when they became Emperors of Germany carried on with the same numeration which they had already used.

Objection to the title of Queen Elizabeth II is an example of nationalist feeling. No doubt objection to it will continue in Scottish sentiment, and occasional instances be seen of the II being crossed out on the Queen's portraits and photographs, and substituted by I.

139. Who is Black Rod?

His full title is Gentleman Usher of the Black Rod, and he ranks high among the officials of the Court, coming under the Lord Chamberlain. His name or title comes from the ebony stick which he carries as his badge of office and which is surmounted by a gold lion. His office dates from the foundation of the Order of the Garter in 1348, and he is the usher of that Order. He attends for the most part upon Parliament, and one of his chief duties is to bear messages from the House of Lords to the House of Commons. When he goes ceremonially to the House of Commons, the door is always slammed in his face, and he must then knock and announce his errand. The reason for this is that once King Charles I went down to the House of Commons to arrest five members whom he regarded as obnoxious to him, and from that time no sovereign has entered the Commons.

140. Why cannot the sovereign enter the House of Commons?

For the reason given at the end of the answer to question 139. I may add, however, that it would hardly ever have been likely that the sovereign would want to be present in the Commons. The two houses began to be spoken of as separate bodies from the end of the fourteenth century, and it seems that earlier than that they had begun to sit in separate chambers. Thus arose the practice of the sovereign summoning the Commons to the bar of the House of Lords to hear the Gracious Speech from the Throne. As I have pointed out elsewhere (in my book, *Ramshackledom*), the whole procedure of the Queen's opening of Parliament is an elaborate play, anachronistically staged, to take the on-lookers back to the days when monarchy ruled as well as reigned in this country. The Prime Minister stands at the bar of the Lords listening to the sovereign reading the speech which he has written for her. It looks just as though the situation of 500 or more years back were still true, and that the sovereign ruled, while the Lords occupy a very much more important place than the Commons. In fact of course all the roles in actuality are reversed.

It is true that when the House of Commons was rebuilt, the late King George VI went over the building to look at it, before any sitting took place. It is also true that the members of the royal house can sit in the special gallery listening to speeches in the Commons, and it is a fact that as late as Queen Anne, the sovereign would sit incognito in the gallery of the Lords listening to debates which often touched closely upon her views and policies.

141. What is the difference between the office of Lord Great Chamberlain and that of Lord Chamberlain?

The Lord Great Chamberlain is one of the Great Officers of State. He holds a position of some considerable respon-sibility, in that he is concerned with the management of the Houses of Parliament, and especially on great ceremonial occasions such as the state opening of Parliament. The Houses of Parliament meet by the sovereign's permission in the Palace of Westminster, and therefore it is fitting that an officer of the sovereign should administer the Palace. The office of Lord Great Chamberlain became hereditary in the family of De Vere who were Earls of Oxford. On the failure of this family in the male line, the office passed to the representatives in the female line, so that the office alternates between the Earls of Ancaster and the Marquesses of Cholmondeley. Thus the Earl of Ancaster held the office in the reign of George VI, and the Marquess of Cholmondeley in the reign of Edward VIII and at present in the reign of Elizabeth II. The Lord Chamberlain has many more duties than those of the Lord Great Chamberlain. The latter has been superseded in many important duties by the Lord Chamberlain. The duties of Lord Chamberlain are many and varied. He deals with the applications of all those who wish to attend Court, and although Courts in the sense that debutantes are presented at them no longer exist, there is still a great deal for the Lord Chamberlain to do in connection with the Palace Garden Parties, and the Royal Enclosure at Ascot. Then there is the matter of the Diplomatic Corps. Although the Lord Chamberlain works through the Marshal of the Diplomatic Corps, he still has to be ultimately responsible for the ceremonial which is observed at the reception of ambassadors at the Court of St. James. For just as we observe the form of opening of Parliament by the sovereign which prevailed centuries ago, so all ambassadors must present their credentials to the Queen at her Court of St. James's. This applies although the actual reception takes place at Buckingham Palace whither the state landau conducts the new ambassador.

In addition the duties of the Lord Chamberlain include the appointment of the royal warrant holders, one of the most closely hedged about of all royal privileges. It is hard to obtain the royal warrant, but easy to lose it by some flaw in conduct, or by the death of the holder for the warrant is always a personal matter. The Lord Chamberlain also appoints the Poet Laureate, and the Master of the Queen's Music. He is responsible for the licensing of plays. This comes within his scope because there was an old office known as that of Master of the Revels which was transferred to the Lord Chamberlain. It therefore happens that every play must be licensed by the Lord Chamberlain.

142. What is the difference between *Burke* and *Debrett*?

I have often been asked this question, and although my service with peerage works has been exclusively with *Burke*, I think that I can answer it without undue bias. Both books deal with the peerage, but while *Debrett* is concerned largely with biography, of the living, *Burke* is equally concerned with the dead, and their biographies. In other words *Debrett* is biographical, *Burke* is genealogical or concerned with family history. Both works are essential to a proper comprehension of our titled system and for reference to our notables, but no one who is primarily concerned with genealogy is likely to use *Debrett* in preference to *Burke*.

143. Why do some princes have the title of Serene Highness?

The answer to this question goes very far back into the Middle Ages, in fact right to the later period of the Roman Empire. Serene derives from *serenitas*, and there were other titles of a similar nature such as Excellentissimus, Illustrissimus and Celsitudo (the last could be literally 'Highness'). In the course of time as medieval Europe climbed out of the dark ages, these forms of title became applicable to great personages who were yet not of the ranks of kings. The most august ruler who bore the title of Serene was the Doge of Venice, known always as The Most Serene. In our time, the Prince of Monaco is His Serene Highness.

144. What was the practice known as 'touching for the King's Evil'?

This practice arose from the habits of life of St. Edward the Confessor. The latter as anyone can see who takes the trouble to read Shakespeare's *Macbeth*, was believed to possess the power to work miracles. There seems to have been great evidence for this, from the early lives of the saint. It was further thought that he would bequeath this power to his successors. At least the practice developed from this and it was not until the time of William of Orange that there was a break in the continuity of the practice. Queen Anne resumed it, and one of the last to be touched by her was the famous Dr. Samuel Johnson, when a small child. The 'King's Evil' was particularly skin disease or nervous disorder.

145. Who is the High Constable of Scotland?

This is the holder of the earldom of Erroll, which can pass through the female as well as the male line. At present the hereditary Lord High Constable of Scotland is the Countess of Erroll, the 23rd holder of the title. She is the 27th hereditary High Constable of Scotland, and in virtue of her position she has the right of precedence over all other hereditary honours and next to the royal family. This position has been acknowledged during the state visits of George IV, Edward VII, George V and Elizabeth II. The Constable has the right of presiding over the Court of the Verge, with jurisdiction of all matters of assault and riot within four miles of the sovereign's person when the latter is in Scotland. These rights were preserved in the Treaty of Union in 1707 between England and Scotland, and also in the Act of 1747 for the abolition of Hereditable Jurisdictions. In addition the Earl or Countess of Erroll together with the Earl of Angus (the Duke of Hamilton) are the hereditary Lords Assessors in the Court of the Lord Lyon. A sitting of this Court was held during the time of the 6th International Congress of Heraldry and Genealogy in 1962 in Edinburgh, when the two assessors sat with the Lord Lyon to hear a case.

146. Is there an office of Lord High Constable in England?

Yes, but the appointment is made only for a particular time, this being for the Coronation, *pro hac vice*. In 1953 the holder of the office was Viscount Alanbrooke, who died in 1963. Until the time of Henry VIII the office was hereditary and held for life, then passing to the next heir. It came into the family of Stafford, Dukes of Buckingham, but the 3rd Duke of Buckingham fell a victim to the jealousy of Henry VIII, egged on by the machinations of Cardinal Wolsey. With his execution, the appointment of Lord High Constable ceased to be a permanency, it being alleged that it was dangerous for one man to have the command of the whole of the forces of the kingdom, and to be able to pass this on to his son. For the duty of the Constable was to command the royal army. Henceforth, the post would only be temporary and would in fact last only for the coronation period, being also only ceremonial in its function.

147. Who is the Earl Marshal?

The Duke of Norfolk, who is hereditary Earl Marshal. This position he holds from a patent of 1672 which gave to his ancestor the 6th Duke of Norfolk, the office of Earl Marshal with remainder to numerous branches of his family. Thus although the present Duke of Norfolk has no son this does not mean that the title of Duke of Norfolk will become extinct or that the Earl Marshalship will revert to the Crown, as the Duke has plenty of relatives in the male line, one of whom will inherit both the dukedom and the Earl Marshalship. The duties of Earl Marshal are partly concerned with ceremonial, at times such as a royal wedding, or a coronation; and for the rest with the management of the College of Arms.

148. Who is the hereditary Grand Falconer of England?

The Duke of St. Albans. He descends from Charles II and Nell Gwynn. It was to the first Duke, his bastard son, that Charles II granted the position of Master Falconer, and also Registrar of the Court of Chancery. Neither of these offices is now exercised by the holder. Falconry has ceased to be a royal pastime though still pursued by a small number of enthusiasts, in England and Wales.

149. Who was the Lord Keeper?

He was the Lord Keeper of the Great Seal and was appointed by letters patent. He was the equal of the Lord High Chancellor, but the last Lord Keeper was Sir Robert Henley who became Lord Chancellor in 1760.

150. What is the office of the Lord High Chancellor?

He is the head of the legal system of England and Wales, and in addition is the Speaker of the House of Lords. He is the keeper of the Great Seal. He was originally the secretary of the sovereign, and his office can be traced to the reign of Edward the Confessor (1042–1066). Through the office of the Chancellor there developed the peculiar English legal device of equity, whereby cases which could not be satisfactorily solved by common law, were cleared by recourse to the sovereign, access being through the court of the Chancellor. As late as 1876 there were still the two systems of law, one of equity, the other of common law. They were then merged, with proviso that in case of conflict the rules of equity were to prevail. Until that time there had been two Lords Chief Justice, one of the Common Pleas, the other of the King's (or Queen's) Bench. The latter was known as the Lord Chief Justice of England; the former post was abolished at the merger of equity and law. The

Lord Chancellor advises the Crown in the appointment of judges, except in the case of the Lord Chief Justice.

151. What is the Board of Green Cloth?

This picturesquely named body is a relic of the past which formerly had powers somewhat on the lines of the Court of the Verge (see question 145 and answer). There were also other courts within the jurisdiction of the Lord Steward who presides over the Board of Green Cloth. Nowadays the Board is concerned with the examination of the accounts of the royal household. The name of the Board is derived from the green covered table at which its business was formerly transacted.

152. Who is the Lord Steward of the Household?

The Duke of Hamilton is the Lord Steward. His symbol of office is a white staff which he receives from the sovereign personally. His appointment is not political but in the peculiar manner in which everything is conducted in England, his name like that of the Lord Chamberlain is submitted by the Premier to the sovereign.

153. Who is Master of the Horse?

The Duke of Beaufort. His duties consist in the management of the royal stables, hounds, kennels, and mews, etc. The actual detailed work is carried out by the Crown Equerry.

154. What is the office of Lord High Steward?

This is not to be confused with that of the Lord Steward. Until the passing into law of the Criminal Justice Act of 1948, it was the privilege of peers when charged with felony to be tried by their peers. At such a trial a Lord High Steward was appointed by a royal commission to preside, and he would be in fact the Lord Chancellor. The ceremonial of trying a peer by his peers was impressive but somewhat long drawn out and expensive.

155. Who is the Queen's Champion?

This is John Lindley Marmion Dymoke, whose title is The Honourable the Queen's Champion and Standard Bearer of England. This office is hereditary in the family of Dymoke which appear to have inherited the right and privilege from their predecessors, the Marmions. Previously it was the custom for the Champion to ride into Westminster Hall at the Coronation Banquet and to challenge anyone who denied the sovereign's right to the throne to single combat. There is an account of this ceremony in Sir Walter Scott's *Redgauntlet*, though there is no record in history, as there is in the romance, of anyone taking up the Champion's glove. Since the time of George IV (1820) no Coronation Banquet has been held, and hence no appearance of a Champion, but in lieu the Champion has borne the Standard of England at the Coronation.

156. Who is the Standard Bearer for Scotland?

The Earl of Dundee, better known perhaps as Mr. Scrymgeour-Wedderburn, who proved his claim to be 11th Earl of Dundee on the 18th May, 1953. As far back as 1298 Sir Alexander Scrymgeour received from Sir William Wallace the right to bear the standard of Scotland. This had previously been the privilege of the Bannerman family. At Bannockburn, Sir Alexander's son, Nicholas Scrymgeour bore the royal standard. The circumstances in which the earldom of Dundee was regained by the present earl are among the most romantic in the annals of the peerage, the title having been 'out' of his family for over 250 years.

157. Who is Lord President of the Council?

This office consists in the management of the Privy Council. The latter body antedates Parliament, or at least the House of Commons. It was the original organ of government under the early sovereigns after the Norman Conquest, and indeed a Great Council functioned for centuries before the Conquest, though under the name of the Witan. Today the appointment is a political one, and the holder is a Cabinet Minister. The Privy Council's work has been largely taken over by various ministries, but it still has work to do in the issuing of Orders in Council, and through its judicial committee, which hears appeals from certain lower courts, though with the granting of independence to the former colonial empire, the volume of appeals to the Privy Council from abroad has greatly lessened.

158. Who is the Lord Privy Seal?

This office dates from the fourteenth century when it was created in order to provide a greater safeguard to the use of public money by the sovereign. The Privy Seal had to be given in order for the Lord Chancellor to be able to affix the Great Seal to documents, and to allow the expenditure of money from the treasury. The Lord Privy Seal is quite often a Minister without portfolio or departmental duties, but usually with extra duties of a very onerous nature. It was the late J. H. Thomas who, during his tenure of the office, was asked what were his duties, and who replied that he did not know the meaning of the term, but that it did mean a lot of damned hard work.

159. Is the position of the Prince of Wales to be properly described as an office?

No. There is no office of Prince of Wales. If there had been such an office, it would hardly have been possible for Queen Victoria to have kept her heir, later King Edward VII in ignorance of state papers and state business for the bulk of his life until his accession to the throne. The Prince of Wales is a title and nothing more. It is conferrable only when the sovereign decides that his or her eldest son shall have the title, and be created Prince of Wales.

160. How many Orders of Chivalry are there now in the United Kingdom and Commonwealth?

There are four Orders which are obsolescent. They are, the Order of St. Patrick, to which no appointment has been made since 1922; and three Orders connected with the former Indian Empire, namely, the Order of the Star of India, the Order of the Indian Empire, and the Order of the Crown of India. To none of these three has any appointment been made since 1947.

Leaving these four on one side, we have six Orders which confer a title and two which do not. The six are: The Order of the Garter; the Order of the Thistle; the Order of the Bath; the Order of St. Michael and St. George; the Royal Victorian Order; and the Order of the British Empire. The recipients of these honours, if made Knights of the Orders are given the prefix 'Sir' before their names.

In addition we have the Order of Merit and the Order of the Companions of Honour. These confer no title, but holders are able to add the letters, O.M., or C.H. after their names.

161. Are titles ever bought today?

I would say, no. I would also add that not very long ago

there was a traffic in honours. Those who are curious on the subject may care to read the book about the life of Maundy Gregory, entitled *Honours for Sale, the Strange Story of Maundy Gregory*. This is by Gerald MacMillan, It details as much as is ever likely to be known of the operations between 1922 and 1932 of the late Maundy Gregory, who was reputed to possess an income of some £30,000 per year from his ability to introduce into the right quarters the names of those who wished to receive honours.

It should be added that the history of the sale of honours begins in the reign of James I, who hit upon the expedient of getting money by selling peerages and baronetcies, sometimes upon a sort of commission basis; on one occasion he gave a blank patent of nobility to his favourite Buckingham, who then proceeded to fill in the name of the person to be 'honoured' after of course having extracted from the latter a large sum of money for his services.

Owing to the trial and sentencing of Maundy Gregory for his much lesser efforts in the field of honour begetting, the sale of honours was brought to an abrupt end. 'Sale' in the sense of large donations to charities or to party funds may continue but can hardly be classed with the activities of honour mongers.

Index

121